DOWN RIVER

Out in the turbulence, a man was weakly trying to scramble out of the surf and onto the shore.

He was face-down in the rising tide. He was wearing a thick blue serge jacket, a fisherman's jacket, and the weight of it sodden was holding him down. As the spent waves lifted him he'd make an ineffectual grab to stop himself being pulled back in the undertow, but there was no strength in him at all. He was lifted and dragged back, lifted and dragged back, and his hands clawed at the sand and the sand simply ran through his fingers. He was an anonymous hulk, swollen by the sea, and the mammoth effort that must have brought him to the shore had drained him of the energy to complete his salvation.

Harry didn't even hesitate at the water's edge. He splashed straight in, oblivious to the soaking and the sudden and penetrating cold, and as he came close the fisherman raised a hand from the water as if in supplication to a saint.

Harry took the man's hand. Gripped it.

And the hand broke up in his own.

The flesh seemed to dissolve at his touch. The hand slid out as if from a glove, bone-white and slender, leaving

**Also by the same author,
and available from NEL:**

VALLEY OF LIGHTS
OKTOBER

About the author

Stephen Gallagher lives with his wife and their daughter in North Lancashire's Ribble Valley. He is the author of four novels, CHIMERA, FOLLOWER, OKTOBER and the bestselling VALLEY OF LIGHTS, which is currently being filmed.

OKTOBER

'His prose is clear and diamond-sharp, his imagination dark and vivid . . . a terrifying walk along the edge of nightmare – a beautifully crafted novel of paranoia and shadowy horror'

Starburst magazine

'Ranks among the best thriller/horror novels of not just this year, but of any year . . . style, insight and a riveting sense of suspense'

Mystery Scene magazine

'Its climax is horrifying . . . this is a fast-paced thriller'

Fear magazine

'Gripping, part thriller, part something darker'
Neil Gaiman, Time Out

'Gripping combination of thriller, horror story and romance'

Bookworld

STEPHEN GALLAGHER

DOWN RIVER

NEW ENGLISH LIBRARY
Hodder and Stoughton

For A.,
with thanks

Copyright © 1989 by Stephen
Gallagher

First published in Great Britain in
1989 by New English Library
hardbacks

First New English Library Open
Market edition 1990

First NEL edition 1990

Printed and bound in Great Britain for
Hodder and Stoughton paperbacks, a
division of Hodder and Stoughton
Ltd., Mill Road, Dunton Green,
Sevenoaks, Kent TN13 2YA (Editorial
Office: 47 Bedford Square, London,
WC1B 3DP) by Richard Clay Ltd.,
Bungay, Suffolk. Typeset by Hewer
Text Composition Services,
Edinburgh.

British Library C.I.P.

Gallagher, Steve
    Down river.
    I. Title
    823'.914[F]

    ISBN 0-450-51112-X

September 27th, 1963

If you really want to know how and where it all started, here's probably as good a point as any; by a small piece of deserted beach on a stretch of the east coast one afternoon in late September.

It was a wild-looking kind of a place, with dunes backed by marshes and topped by reeds against a grey sky with a wide grey sea beyond, and the odd rusted coil of barbed wire, a leftover of wartime defences. When the wind came in from across the water it would start to bury the coast road in a blanket of drifting sand, and when this got bad enough they'd have to send out an ex-army caterpillar truck to scrape it all down to the tarmac for a distance of two miles or more. After that the road swung inland for a way, and the sandplough would raise its blade and turn around to head for home; the curving scars of its tracks over successive years could be read on the road surface like dinosaur prints, always turning in the same place and always taking out a chunk of the banking because the beast was tough to handle and the man in the saddle could hardly care less. To a small boy watching from the dunes, it all had the air of a ritual of some deep significance.

But then, at around nine years old, doesn't everything?

In a car on the cleared road heading south, a travelling sales rep named Harry Waterson was wondering what he could do to catch up on the half-day that he'd dropped behind on his schedule. Just outside his thoughts, like a patient stranger waiting to be recognised, stood the fact that he was thirty-three years old and didn't much like what he'd become. His suit jacket was on a hanger in the back of the car, his knuckles were on the wheel, and when he looked in the mirror all that he could see was a thin slice of the world behind him receding beyond a horizon of Toffee Button cartons. Toting those same cartons across the pavement at eleven o'clock in the morning while some shopkeeper watched from the doorway, it was all too easy to feel the world's eyes upon him and about seven inches tall. He could think about all the good things that he had going for him, but it didn't pay to think too hard. He had a free car. He got commission. He had a council-owned house and two children that he loved but rarely saw in their waking hours, and a wife who never said it out loud but who still managed to make plain her feeling that he was grabbing all of the good things of life's buffet and bringing none of them home.

What he'd actually wanted had been to become a fighter pilot, but that had been back at school in the last years of the war. Even if they'd managed to spin the conflict out until he was old enough, he'd have run into the twin problems of poor maths and even worse eyesight. The other kids used to say that since Harry could just about see as far as his own dick without his glasses, he ought at least to be able to add up to eleven. And as for being any kind of a fighter, you could push him and push him and all he'd do would be to avoid your eyes and look panicky until you hit him, if you could bring yourself to do it after such a performance. Admitting to wanting to fly Spitfires was the first and the last time that he'd let one of his dreams out into daylight; two years after that, he'd gone to work for his uncle.

Harry had never seen a dead body before. He'd seen spilled blood after a road accident one time and it had surprised him because it hadn't been red at all, just dark

2

and wet like a flood of black coffee. And then another time before that, when he'd been a child, his mother had sent him down on an errand to a dusty second-hand shop in a back street near to home; nobody had answered the bell and so he'd waited for a while, and when still nobody appeared he'd made his way through the stacks of old, grim furniture and hearse-like baby carriages to see if he could find anybody in the back room. There, in cramped living quarters no lighter and no better furnished than the junkstore out front, he'd come upon an unattended coffin on trestles. It was deeply polished and the handles were bright silver and there was a wreath of black crêpe and lilies on its lid. Run? For a couple of minutes there, back through the shop and out down the street, he'd been convinced that he was flying after all. That, and the accident, were the closest he'd ever been to looking death straight in the dulled and drying eye.

Until today.

In fact it almost happened sooner than was planned, because he was thinking about other things and was late hitting the brakes when he saw the kid with the bicycle. The boy was standing right out in the middle of the road and looking straight at him, the bike turned sideways like a shield, and as the brakes locked on Harry felt with a deep and blossoming horror that he was going to slide all the way and the kid was going to die. The boy was frowning at him, a pained and distant kind of look that had nothing to do with the fear of being run down; he was just a child, and what did he know about trying to get a couple more thousand miles out of tyres that were nearly bald, or the dry sand that could make a road surface as slick as any oil patch? He lived in a world where the ground might speak and statues might move, but if you stepped out in front of a car with an adult behind the wheel then it had to stop. Harry knew that there were things that an ace driver could do, but he couldn't for the life of him remember what any of them were. All that he could manage was to stand harder on the brakes, and then harder still as if willpower alone would draw him back from the edge.

The rear end of the car started to go. The stock on the back seat shifted. Harry could already hear the sound, first the bike and then a thud like a fist into a side of meat.

But maybe willpower was enough. The car slid to a graceful halt about a yard short of the boy, and the boy rolled his bicycle forward and then lifted and leaned it neatly against the radiator grille as if the Ford had been put on this earth for no other purpose. Harry was wondering whether a couple of strong men with crowbars might have a fighting chance of getting his fingers unclenched from around the steering wheel, and whether he himself might ever have the strength to walk unaided again, when the boy beckoned to him and then turned around and set out for the dunes.

Harry took his hands from the wheel. He was actually trembling. He took a deep breath, and felt better.

The boy obviously expected him to follow, and hadn't even looked back yet. He couldn't drive on because there was a sodding *bicycle* stuck on the front of his car, for God's sake. He opened the door and started to get out, thinking that at the very least he could throw the thing out of the way at the side of the road for the kid to find when he came back, but then as he did the saddle and the handlebars abruptly dropped out of view and there was a crash as the bike slid down and hit the tarmac.

The boy was almost at the crest of the first line of dunes when the sound reached him. He looked back at Harry, and then beckoned again. And then he went on.

Harry didn't know what to do. He was out in the middle of nowhere and there was all of his stock in the back of the car. Besides all the usual stuff he had two gross of chocolate Santas and snowmen that he was supposed to try talking his regulars into taking early this year, as well as promotional packs and window stickers for a couple of lines that hadn't been moving too well throughout the summer. A few less fat kids with bad teeth on Harry's piece of ground, and Harry was in trouble.

Poor Harry. Poor, short-sighted, seven-inch-tall Harry.

And then he thought, *To hell with it*, and with a terrific sense of release he slammed the door and set out toward the dunes to follow the boy.

There was a wide path of sorts, of railway sleepers buried under the sand. Most of them were submerged but every now and again one would be tilted slightly so that its edges showed through and made an abrupt step. To either side of him was gorse so dense that a stick thrust in would have stayed exactly where it was when released. Harry came up onto that first, low line of dunes, and paused to look for the boy; he'd left the wider track and was now following the edge of the brush along the higher ridge ahead.

This path was softer and well-trodden, and harder work. Harry had to stop after a minute to get his breath. He'd left his jacket in the car and was in his shirtsleeves, and the sea-wind cut right through the cotton. About two miles out stood the nearest of the big freight ships, one of an endless procession that waited for pilotage around the head and into the bay, faded by light and distance until it and the others beyond seemed to exist in some other zone of reality. Closer in, the incoming tide was beginning to cover the stained light and dark bands of the shoreline.

The boy had stopped, too, and was watching him.

Harry raised a hand to signal that he was ready to go on, and the boy turned.

They came down between two shallow ridges that were actually buried runs of picket fencing, with just the picket-points showing like the tips of animal bones. Litter and scraps of old newspaper had been caught here as if in the teeth of a rake, and they fluttered in the wind. The boy had slowed. He didn't look tired, but he seemed to be giving Harry a chance to catch up. Harry was beginning to feel uneasy about how this would look, and wondering whether he wasn't making a big mistake. Even after all this time he was still uncomfortable about buying dolls for the girls if they weren't along with him; a man of his age, and alone, could so easily be taken for a child molester shopping for bait. The further behind they left the road, the less sure of himself he felt. There was nothing out here but sand and rabbit shit and grasses that stung like whips as he pushed through them.

The boy had stopped again, on another rise in the path. They'd almost reached the edge of the incoming sea by now, and this time he seemed to be waiting for Harry to reach him.

"What's the matter?" Harry said as he laboured his way up the final slope, and his voice sounded thin and stripped of authority in the wide open air. "Is somebody hurt?"

"I don't know," the boy said, and he turned to look down over the crest of the dune as Harry came up level.

Harry found himself looking down into a shallow creek where a freshwater stream, cut so deep into the dunes that it wasn't even visible until you stood right over it, ran out into the sea. Its sides had been shored-up with bales of rocks and stones, and some of those bales had been levered open by driftwood so that a spreading fan of pebbles marked the place on the beach where river and ocean met. Harry recognised the nature of the location straight away. It was a kid's secret place. Something in him responded to it, like hearing a forgotten language after so many years. It had the isolation and the diversity and that essential hint of mystery, like the aura that hangs around shut-down machinery.

Out in the turbulence, a man was weakly trying to scramble out of the surf and onto the shore.

He was face-down in the rising tide. He was wearing

a thick blue serge jacket, a fisherman's jacket, and the weight of it sodden was holding him down. As the spent waves lifted him he'd make an ineffectual grab to stop himself being pulled back in the undertow, but there was no strength in him at all. He was lifted and dragged back, lifted and dragged back, and his hands clawed at the sand and the sand simply ran through his fingers. He was an anonymous hulk, swollen by the sea, and the mammoth effort that must have brought him to the shore had drained him of the energy to complete his salvation.

Harry didn't even hesitate at the water's edge. He splashed straight in, oblivious to the soaking and the sudden and penetrating cold, and as he came close the fisherman raised a hand from the water as if in supplication to a saint.

Harry took the man's hand. Gripped it.

And the hand broke up in his own.

The flesh seemed to dissolve at his touch. The hand slid out as if from a glove, bone-white and slender, leaving Harry with a grasp on . . . what?

He stopped, knee-deep in the freezing water. He looked in his own hand and saw the mass of shrimps that had been stripped from their human feast, curling and writhing and breaking up and flaking away. The man in the surf was being drawn out again, sucked by the undertow, and his half-consumed hand dropped back into the water. Harry was screaming. He felt as if he'd grabbed a fistful of live maggots. He was shaking them away as he staggered back, and as he stumbled out he saw the drowned man's body making another bid for the beach, a puppet moving with the action of the sea. It briefly lifted its face as if to grab a breath, and presented a black slit-eyed mask that Harry would never forget even though he would try his best over the years to come.

The boy on the dune had been watching it all. Harry made an effort to get a grip on himself. The boy was pale-faced and serious, shocked and wary but hardly panicking, and Harry was suddenly intensely aware of how he must look. If every encounter was a snapshot handed to someone else, then this had to be one of those where Harry wanted to be at his best. Inside, he felt about the same age as the boy. But for the record, he'd have to see how much better than that he could do.

The boy said, "Is he dead?"

"You bet he is," Harry said. "Come on, let's tell somebody."

"Aren't you going to pull him out?"

Harry looked back, even though a part of him didn't want to. The dead man must have been washed in alongshore to this place of cross-currents, and here he was being held and played around with like unwanted food. Until the tide turned, he'd probably stay here.

Harry said, "I've been about as close as I care to get. Come on. What's your name?"

"Nicky," the boy said.

They trooped back over the dunes. Harry asked the boy how he'd come to find the body, and then didn't pay much attention to the story he got in reply; he was breathing harder and harder, and knew that he was only kidding himself if he thought that he wasn't going to have to stop and throw up any moment now. He was also wiping his hand repeatedly on the side of his pants, although he hadn't yet noticed that.

Suddenly he stepped off the path, and dumped his breakfast into the gorse.

The boy waited patiently, without expression or comment.

Someday, Nicky, Harry thought as he stepped back onto the path; he was feeling cold and wrecked and miserable and his wet clothes were making him shiver, and he knew that he was cutting something rather less than a dash here. *Someday, when you're older, perhaps you'll understand*. And they started on again, coming down where the sand thinned out over the buried railway sleepers, and the boy reached up and took his hand as they covered the last quarter-mile back to the car.

Nothing had changed. Harry could see the great length of his skid drawn clearly on the road surface but this was only a detail that he hadn't noticed before, not something that had been added. The boy picked up his bike and set it upright, and Harry got his jacket out and put it on. It had taken some creases when the stock had fallen over against it.

The boy said, "I'm coming with you."

"There's no room in the car."

The boy's sudden eruption of feeling startled him. "I found him!" the boy objected, and his expression was one of outrage rather than any common form of anger. "He's mine! I didn't stop you just to let you take him away from me!"

For Harry, it was as if he'd unexpectedly touched something hot. He watched the boy for a moment.

And then he said, "There's a Shell garage with a cafeteria. About a mile inland on the right-hand side. Do you know it?"

The boy nodded.

"Well, that's where I'm going. You can follow the car and meet me there."

———

After he'd made the call, Harry went out onto the forecourt to wait. He could never understand how places like this stayed in business, and he saw plenty of them; this one had the pumps out front and a repair shop with an oil-stained pit around the back, while the main building had been painted white and turned into a country-kitchen kind of a place. There were curtains at the windows, checkered plastic cloths on the tables, new oilcloth on the floor, and only one paying customer behind a newspaper at a corner table. From out in the open, Harry

could look in any direction and not see one other building. And the land was flat and mostly drained around
here, so that one look covered quite a lot of distance.

The boy came freewheeling in a couple of minutes
later, half-out of the saddle and running the bike down
to a halt over the last few yards. He'd made pretty
decent time. Harry had been forced to stop once, racked
with uncontrollable sobs as the drowned man had come
surging up in his imagination once again, his face
blackened like inner-tube rubber and blown up tight
with something gassy and green; but after what had
seemed like an hour (and was actually less than a couple
of minutes) he'd been able to take out a handkerchief to
dry his eyes and blow his nose. He felt strangely purged,
and able to go on; it was as if he'd sucked on a wound
and spat out poison.

And – could he be mistaken in this? But he didn't feel
anything like as bad as he might have expected.

The boy was flushed from pedalling hard, his eyes
bright and his hair in unruly spikes. "Who's coming?"
he said.

"I called the police," Harry told him, and he resisted
the urge to put out a hand and flatten down the boy's
hair as he'd have done with one of his own. "The local
man's coming out. We'll have to show him where to
look."

"Is he coming in a police car?"

"I should think he will."

The boy was fumbling in his saddlebag. "I'm going to
show him this," he said, and after a moment he brought
out an Airfix model car from amongst the lead soldiers
and the golfballs and the bubblegum cards. It was a Ford,
the same model as Harry's own, but it had been painted
in the livery of a police vehicle.

"Who made that?" Harry said. "You?"

"My dad," the boy said, and he held it up to the light
to check on the interior. "It's got all the seats in, and
everything."

Something definitely seemed to be happening here. As that first flush of awfulness receded, Harry was beginning to feel . . . well, it was something like the feeling he'd get when things were going his way. There was pity for the poor soul whose bloated corpse was struggling around out there and fattening up the seafood, but also a strange sense of vigour that had crept into his day. His lousy little schedule counted for nothing, now. He couldn't help thinking of the more interesting times that lay ahead, the stories to be told afterwards, the awe and, yes, the *envy* of others . . . and as his eyes met the boy's over the model car, he realised that the two of them were thinking in more or less the same way.

"Don't forget," the boy warned. "It was me who found him."

"I won't forget," Harry said.

And then he walked over to his own car, which he'd left alongside a row of half a dozen museum-pieces with rust around their sills and sale tickets in their windscreens. Each screen was a near-perfect mirror of clouds and sky.

When he came back a minute later he said, "Here you go, Nicky," and he tossed the boy a couple of bags of Toffee Buttons.

"Thanks," Nicky said as he caught them.

And then the two of them sat together on the garage's low roadside wall to wait for the police car, and all that would follow with it, to arrive.

PART ONE

The Fall of Johnny Mays

1

They'd tossed a coin to see whose car they'd use today. This was how they came to be riding in Nick Frazier's old Granada.

"What do you think of that one, then?" Johnny Mays said, and Nick had to turn and look across the top of the car to see what he meant. Nick was gassing up the Granada, and Johnny had stepped out to loiter against its side on the filling station forecourt. His tie was loosened and his arms were folded. Johnny wore good clothes, but he always looked as if he'd slept in them; he had the air of a lounge lizard perpetually in transit between lounges, rumpled and faintly surprised to find that the world carried on turning through the daylight hours.

Nick followed his look over to the next aisle along, where a woman was unhooking the four-star pump to feed a waiting Porsche. Nick wondered for a moment which Johnny was talking about, the woman or the car. Knowing Johnny, it could have been either.

"Too classy for you," Nick said, which would cover it both ways.

"You reckon?"

"I reckon."

Johnny considered it further. Now Nick could see that he was contemplating the meat on the hoof, rather than the hardware. Nick's guess was that the woman was somewhere in her mid-thirties and fighting it too hard, a bleached-blonde with a deep suntan, white trouser suit and white shoes and a little too much gold around her hands. She'd turned to face away from them, perhaps

15

deliberately, but as far as Johnny was concerned this had only improved on the view.

He said, "Good lines, but that isn't class. That's just town money."

"Whatever," Nick said. "You still wouldn't get your nose past the door."

Johnny thought it over a little while longer.

And then he said, "Watch me."

Oh, shit, Nick thought, and cut off the pump. He didn't want to stay around for this. Johnny was, quote, a mad bastard and Nick could imagine him ambling over to a bomb and giving it a kick, just to see what would happen. He always seemed to get away with it somehow, but it didn't always pay to be a bystander when Johnny Mays was on the roll. As Johnny was sticking his hands into his pockets and sauntering over to the next aisle, Nick was making for the forecourt office to settle the bill and pick up a receipt. If anything was going to happen he'd see it from a distance, and in safety.

What he actually saw, watching through the teller's window on the far side of the counter, was nothing much. The woman's hair was whipped across her face by the wind when she looked up to speak to Johnny. She brushed it away with her free hand. She didn't smile. He gestured out toward the skyline of tower blocks and dark clouds crowding low; he either had to be saying something about the threat of thundery weather, or else he was asking how she came to be passing through this blighted side of town.

Whatever he was saying, it didn't seem to be working.

Johnny was sitting in the car when Nick got back to it, seat reclined a few degrees and his head tilted back on the rest.

Nick said, "How'd you get on?"

"She's a really sad case," Johnny said. "Frigid as polar bear crap, no hope for her at all."

"What did she say to you?"

"Just drive. Pull out onto the street and wait."

"For what?"

"I'll tell you as we go."

So Nick started the Granada, and did as Johnny had said.

Technically, they were equal partners. But Johnny knew the ground whereas Nick had only been working it for a couple of months, and so Johnny tended to make the running. As they emerged from under the shadow of the filling station's metal awning, the small radio that Johnny had left propped on the dash did a sudden fade-in and came to life. Johnny always boosted a radio from the station sergeant, even for a plainclothes detail when it wasn't considered necessary. Johnny seemed to have grown jumpy, these days. Nick was starting to see him as a spider, in need of some sense of the web to feel secure.

"What now?" Nick said as they pulled in by what had once been a row of shops. Now it was just unpromising-looking wasteland with an Enterprise Zone billboard set back from the road, where stuff thrown from cars couldn't reach it so easily.

"Now we wait," Johnny said.

The Porsche came out about a minute later.

Johnny said, "Warp factor six, Mister Sulu," and Nick said, "You want me to follow her?" And Johnny turned to him, and gave him an infinitely pained look.

"Yes," he said, "I want you to follow her. Preferably today. Get right up close, so she'll see us in the mirror."

It was a four-lane highway cutting straight through the badlands out of the heart of town, and it wasn't hard for Nick to find a space in the traffic flow and slide in behind the Porsche. There wasn't much of any rear window in the sports job, but Nick could see the woman as she glanced at her mirror and then glanced again, quickly, when she realised that the car behind her was something more than just another late-afternoon

17

commuter making an early run for home. Now she was obviously beginning to wonder what they might have in mind.

Nick was kind of curious to know, as well.

The road dropped into a concrete underpass, yellow lights zipping over their heads like tracer bullets, and as the Porsche started to pick up speed Nick matched it and stayed on her tail. This wasn't a part of town where anyone would care to be stopped and in trouble; extensively bulldozed and worked-over in the 'sixties building boom, it now had the atmosphere of a long-abandoned landing field for airships that had never arrived. After about a quarter-mile they came up into a daylight that somehow seemed darker than the tunnel that they'd just left; it was grim enough to have triggered the photo-cells in some of the high overhead floods so that they burned like new stars against an iron-grey sky.

The woman was starting to get worried, now. She was looking for a way out.

Radio reception had ghosted away again as they'd gone below ground, but now as it returned Johnny picked up the radio and called in. There was about a ten-second lag before the dispatcher responded.

"Need some car licence details," he said. "Name, address and anything outstanding." And then, holding the radio in plain sight and leaning forward to get a look at the Porsche's plate, he read off the registration. Nick couldn't tell for sure whether the woman was getting all of this, but he could sense some of the pressure that she was probably feeling.

"You're too much," he said.

Johnny grinned, happily. "I am, aren't I?" he said, and as he waited for the details to come through he fumbled around in his jacket and brought out the Little Black Book.

It was as Johnny was adding the woman's address to whatever current list he was keeping in the book's pages that Nick saw the Porsche suddenly swing over into an exit lane at the last possible moment, no signal or anything. Nick could have stayed with her, but a quick check told him that Johnny's eyes were off the road. He let the woman go, and Johnny didn't look up until it was too late for him to object.

He'd achieved what he wanted by now, anyway. Nick's Granada stayed on the level and the Porsche ran parallel for a way, before starting to rise and move out on an elevated ramp that wouldn't take her home but which would put some distance between herself and the two menacing weirdos in the battered old saloon. Johnny finished his notebook entry with a flourish, closed it, and then clicked the little ballpoint pen that came with it.

Nick said, "What's the idea?"

"Just for the record," Johnny said, and as he stowed the book he smiled pleasantly across the increasing gap between the two vehicles. Nick saw the blonde giving him a brief, cold stare. She looked as if she might have been a beauty contest winner, once. Nick always thought that such women didn't age well, they tried to go on being Queen of the May all the way through summer and into December. She still had her looks, but she also had all of the signs.

But then the ramp took her up and beyond their eyeline.

Nick said, "You push it sometimes, Johnny."

And Johnny said, "Nobody walks away from Johnny Mays until Johnny Mays says it's okay."

Nick didn't bother trying to argue. He knew a lost cause when he saw one. Johnny had worked hard on his 'mad bastard' status in the Division, raising it almost to the level of mythology, and Nick had come along too late in the day to think about putting any kind of a dent into it. And while there was no approval for the abuse of licence data, most of the officers that he knew had done it at some time or another. Back when he'd been in uniform, one of the oil companies had been running a promotional campaign involving car numbers displayed

on petrol station forecourts. There was a cash payout
for any driver who spotted his own number anywhere
in the list; some of the boys had done pretty well out
of tracking down owners and doing a deal for half of
the prize money in return for telling them where to
claim, until somebody decided to put in a complaint.
Everything had tightened up for a while after that, but
there was no way of sealing the system completely.

Johnny was looking at his watch.

"Wouldn't have wanted her to make us late, anyway,"
he said.

They parked the Granada on an asphalt lot at the foot
of a tower block. The lot was neglected although many
of the cars on it were pretty new; there were rental
garages somewhere around, but most people seemed
to prefer to keep their vehicles out in the open. Garages were no more than a convenience for the gangs of
small children who could get in and strip a car down to
nothing with awesome professionalism, bringing along
their own tools for the job. This wasn't the roughest part
of town, but it won hands-down as one of the bleakest;
the fourteen-storey towers, seven of them arranged in a
prehistoric formation that dominated the skyline without adding to it, had all of the charm and some of the
function of vertical prison stacks. The square mile sur-
rounding them was an architect's sketch of access roads
and empty plazas, and pointless grass embankments
crossed by unofficial footpaths that had been made with
the dogged obstinacy of water refusing to flow uphill.
Ground-floor windows were covered by plywood boarding, the boarding was covered by graffiti. Where there
were trees, they were young and mostly dead.

"Beverly Hills looks a lot like this," Johnny Mays said.

Nick gave a quick check to make sure that their summons documents were in order before they got out of the
car. As Nick was locking up after them, Johnny stood by

the Granada and stretched and took a deep breath of the air. Whatever might be in his mind, Johnny Mays gave the impression of a man who felt himself to be pretty much on top of it.

He glanced back at the car as they walked away. "You couldn't find anything older?"

"Couldn't find anything cheaper," Nick said.

"That, I can believe."

They came around by the side of the nearest building, one where the street-level units had been designed to house shops and a doctor's surgery but had never been anything more than howling spaces of darkness, litter and the stink of urine. There was a white van in the turnaround by the entrance to the block, and although it carried no markings Johnny immediately said, "Hang about, that's one of ours."

They went over instead of going straight into the lobby, and Johnny made a brief gesture for silence before leaning close to listen at the van's windowless loading doors. Nick stuck his hands into his pockets and stamped around as he waited a few yards back. He wasn't exactly cold, but this wasn't the kind of place that would ever seem warm. From here he could look out across the estate and see the skyline of the town's centre way off in the distance, looking like some other and better country and about as reachable.

Johnny was grinning at something he'd heard. He raised a hand, then listened and waited a moment longer to be sure of getting his timing right.

Then he hammered on the doors so hard that the van shook as if in a storm.

A few seconds of this, and then he flung the doors open. The tableau inside was one of utter shock and incomprehension. Half a dozen men sat crammed together, three to either side, their jaws hanging wide and half-loaded revolvers open on their knees. Johnny turned to Nick in the manner of an eager naturalist who'd just lifted a rock to uncover a clutch of blinking specimens underneath, and said, "Look at this bunch. Alert to every danger." And then he gestured at the guns. "And more tooled-up than Rudolf Nureyev."

"Fucking Johnny Mays," came a voice from the far end of the van and the man nearest the door, whom Nick immediately took to be the squad's leader, said, "You trying to get yourself shot?"

"Do me a favour," Johnny said. "This is the CID. The people who'll hit anything as long as it isn't the target."

The squad leader seemed unruffled by this. He snapped the loaded revolver shut, and stowed it away inside his military-style bomber jacket. He was in his forties, his hair prematurely silvered, and he'd have looked like some ordinary middle-aged, middle-management man but for his broken nose. He said, "And what do the Woodentops want?"

"Got a piece of paper for old friend Winston up on floor nine. Non-payment of child support."

"Well," the squad leader said, climbing out of the van, "you can get in line for him. We're all turned out on a section twenty-one."

Section twenty-one, the Firearms Act; possession of firearms by persons previously convicted of crime. Nick said, "What did he do?"

"He was seen standing in front of a mirror in his Y-fronts practising fast draws with a revolver."

"Knowing our Winston," one of the others said as he emerged – he was a shorter, thickset man with dark hair that he was beginning to lose, and was the one who'd recognised Johnny – "I should think that nine times out of ten he probably pulled out the wrong weapon."

Nick said, "Seen how?"

"By a little old lady on the same floor in the next block."

Nick looked up at the buildings. They towered like cliff faces, and from here seemed impossibly high; the spaces between them were cold and vast and desolate. "What's her name?" he said. "Hawkeye?"

"Nah," the squad leader said as the last man came out of the van. "She uses binoculars. You in on this, or do you want to wait in the car while the big boys do their stuff?"

"We're in," Johnny said without any hesitation.

The squad leader looked at him and said, "What are you like with a sledge?"

"Poetry in motion," Johnny said.

So Johnny was handed the sledgehammer to break down the door, and all of them went into the block together.

There were two lifts, one of them out of order. The foyer was a squalid no-man's-land and reminded Nick of some neglected launderette. The working lift took an age to arrive and as they were waiting, the youngest-looking of the CID men said, "Nick Frazier, isn't it?"

"That's me," Nick said, and searched his memory for some light to follow the spark of recognition. It came a moment later; the main practice range, at his last qualifying shoot some eighteen months before.

"Still on the marksman list?"

"No. I reckoned three years as an AFO was enough for anybody."

"Oh, I dunno," the young man said, not without irony. "Look at what you're missing."

When the lift doors parted it was to catch three giggling urchins in the act of punching every button for every floor to take them back up again; at the sight of eight grim-looking coppers and a sledgehammer they abruptly froze up into silence and walked out stiffly, breaking into a run before they got to the exit doors. Everybody squeezed in except for one officer, who stayed below to watch the stairwell. There was no way of over-riding the lift controls and so they lurched upward one floor at a time, each stop a flash-photograph of a different vinyl-floored hallway with its dash-rendered walls.

Nick was right in front of Johnny, the sledge handle poking him in the back like an inconvenient hard-on.

Around the third floor, Johnny leaned forward and said, "You didn't tell me you were a firearms officer."

"I'm not," Nick said. "I dropped out."

By the time that they reached the ninth, it was as if the car was rising entirely on a crest of tension and energy from those within. Nobody spoke as they came out, and there was almost no sound at all as the team slipped into position with Smith & Wessons drawn. Nick had heard some talk down below of sending in a dog, but the squad leader had obviously decided against waiting around until a handler became available.

After a quick nod from each man, the leader spoke.

"Let's take him," he said quietly.

Johnny's first swing splintered the veneer on a door that looked solid but patently wasn't; on his second the door burst inward with pieces of the lock and the frame flying everywhere. They went in one at a time, diving through the opening with the speed of a parachute team; Nick, unarmed, was next to the last, and Johnny followed him with the hammer.

The entire storming took a little under twenty seconds.

Internal doors slammed open, and rooms were quickly covered with a barked-out warning of *Armed police!* The flat was bigger than Nick had expected, and nothing like as rough as the public spaces in the block. A young woman appeared screaming in a doorway and was quickly hustled out; a fast search of the room beyond her revealed only a crying child of around three years old. The carpets were remnants, the furniture was rock-bottom cheap, and there wasn't enough of it to make the place look much like a home; the only bright colour anywhere was in a stack of Fisher-Price toys in the middle of the floor. The young officer who'd recognised Nick bent to lift the child, and the child screamed so hard in surprise and fear that Nick was half-expecting it to be sick over him.

They'd swept through every room like an incoming wave, and their target was nowhere.

"I wouldn't put it past the stupid sod to have nipped out the window," the squad leader said to nobody in particular, briefly covering a living room that was dominated by one of the biggest colour TV sets that Nick had ever seen. It was fairly new, probably rented, and Nick didn't have to see it switched on to know that the picture would be badly-tuned and unbearably lousy. By contrast, the view from the big panoramic windows on two sides of the lounge – it was a corner flat – was nothing less than spectacular.

Two of the team had moved into the kitchen and were checking the cupboards for hiding-places when there was a splintering crash from somewhere back along the hall. It had come from the main bedroom, just off the hallway by the entrance. And the racket didn't stop there; it got worse. Everybody dived for it like seals after a herring.

Most of the noise was coming from a black male down on the floor of the bedroom; the rest of it was coming from Johnny Mays, standing over him with the sledge-hammer raised and roaring, *"Come on. You devious fucking spade, just give me an excuse!"* The man on the floor was screaming and squirming in an energetic fit of terror, obviously convinced that Johnny Mays was the original Wild Thing and that his head was about to lose a lot of its depth for a big increase in hat size. The wall behind them had been half-destroyed, torn edges puckered out as if it had burst to spit forth some oversized seed.

The entire CID team went for Winston, shunting the bed aside to give themselves room to work; they each dropped onto a piece of him and turned him face-down while the squad leader fumbled with his handcuffs. Winston didn't appear to be armed in any way. As Johnny lowered the sledge and moved back, Nick stepped over and around them to take a closer look at the wall.

In fact it wasn't actually a wall; it was a false front made out of plasterboard, and it had been pulled into an alcove by a couple of makeshift handles from behind.

The board had been papered to match the surface around it – not too successfully, judging by the way that Johnny had spotted and split it with a single blow – and, added as a final touch, there was a Michael Jackson poster that now hung in tatters.

"You can't do this," the man was saying, mostly into the carpet. "I'll sue."

"Save it, Winston," the squad leader said, trying to get in with the cuffs through the scrum of his own men.

"I done nothing wrong this time."

From somewhere in the scrum came, "How'd you spot him, Johnny?"

"I didn't," Johnny said. "But I was damned sure I'd never heard a poster fart, before."

Nick was now looking into the space behind the ruined board. It made a hiding place around two and a half feet deep by three wide, just about enough room to stand or sit and not much else. A few haphazard supplies had been laid in as if for a siege, including a bucket and a toilet roll; all the signs were of somebody with a little imagination, but not enough. Winston's record was all juvenile offences and petty theft, nothing that could warrant such a desperado type of a scheme. Nick saw some canned fish, a flashlight, some old holiday brochures and back-copies of *Knave*; and in the corner behind the magazines, something bundled-up that clanked like tyre irons when he lifted it out.

He threw the bundle onto the bed. The cloth was an old shirt, the contents an unstrung and dismantled crossbow with about half a dozen bolts. Winston, his hands now shackled behind his back, was hauled up onto his feet to face the evidence.

"Nothing illegal in that," he said, but Nick wasn't finished yet. The crossbow components had spilled across the cover leaving something heavy in the last fold of the shirt; Nick delicately tugged the material free and laid it back as if undressing a recent wound.

"And I suppose this is for the kid to play with," he

said, and there was a silence as the uncovered handgun seemed to suck in all of the sound and the attention in the room.

Then Winston said, lamely, "That isn't mine," but it was pretty obvious, even to him, that this was one of those days where he'd found himself on yet another of life's losing streaks.

A quick search of the rest of the flat turned up nothing else. To the sound of slamming drawers and falling clothes, the squad's leader held up the discovered handgun for a closer look before dropping it into an evidence bag. Nick watched over his shoulder. It was an old .38 Webley, probably wartime issue, and it hadn't been particularly well cared for. In fact it didn't appear to have been cared for at all, because when the squad leader broke it open and spun the cylinder he said, "There's dust in here that's got to be ten years old. And God only knows what it's been oiled with."

And Johnny Mays, who was over on the far side of the room thumbing through one of the hideaway magazines, said, "Since there isn't even a single round of ammo in the place, it all seems pretty pointless."

"Same point as those dirty books," the squad leader said. "Everybody likes a trip to Fantasy Island now and again."

When they took him out, Nick was half-expecting a big crowd to have gathered; but this obviously wasn't a block where community spirit ruled, because the man's common-law wife had stacked up no more than half a dozen supporters to back her as she waited out on the landing. The continued squalling of the child on her hip echoed around the space like feeding time in a dolphinarium; the woman was white and the child, Nick could see now, was of mixed race, and he was screaming and screaming inconsolably. Nick wouldn't have believed that he could have got any louder, but he managed this at the sight of his daddy being hustled away in the midst of a gang of strangers with his wrists pinned behind him. Someone had jammed the lift on one of the other floors – nobody on the team doubted that it was for their benefit – and so they had to go down by the stairs. The cries of the child, along with some further choice abuse thrown in, followed them all the way to ground level.

The squad leader checked his wristwatch as their prisoner was being helped into the back of the van. Winston was looking so abject that it had taken some of the kick out of the pinch, and the squarely-built officer with the thinning hair was trying to talk about football, basketball, anything that might lighten him up a little.

"I know you mean well," Nick heard Winston saying to the man, "but I'm *really* not in the mood."

"This won't help, then," Nick said, and stuffed the summons down the front of Winston's shirt before stepping back. As the van doors slammed, he was looking down at the end of the paper as if it was something curious that was crawling up his chest.

The squad leader said, "We'll get this sorted, then we're going to eat. You two fancy an Indian?"

"That depends on whether her father finds out," Johnny Mays replied promptly.

It was early in the evening, and the Indian restaurant was empty but for the police party around the big table. The atmosphere and décor weren't so much ethnic as faded Empire; red, and gold, and lots of shadow, and the waiters in black tie and waistcoats as formal as royal footmen at a tiger shoot. They moved around the table setting out dishes in silence, deaf to all the petfood and Gunga Din jokes that passed below them. For the CID men, it was the end of their relief and time to unwind; for Nick and Johnny on plainclothes, this was only a midway break in their shift.

Johnny was milking the sledgehammer incident for all

that it was worth. Fortunately, his currency seemed to be high in this company; everybody around the table seemed to know him by reputation if nothing more, and they gave him any encouragement that he seemed to need. Nick found himself staying out of it, a little. He smiled at Johnny's story about the time when he'd been in uniform and a bunch of them had scared the daylights out of a new policewoman in a faked call to the top deck of a darkened bus, but he sensed something that he didn't much like under the general enthusiasm. Johnny Mays as a circus act, that was fine; but take away the outrageous conduct, and Nick suspected that plain old unremarkable Johnny would have to start getting by without his regular fix of limelight.

And like all withdrawals, the real pain wouldn't come from the loss of the narcotic; it would be from those drowned shapes that the drug had concealed for so long, surging back up into daylight as the waters receded.

Nick wondered what he'd see, if ever it happened. He'd now spent two months in Johnny's company, and it had been long enough for him to glimpse some awesome-looking shadows down below.

He stopped one of the waiters as he was passing.

"Sir?" the waiter said, and Nick pointed to the dish closest to his plate.

"Can you tell me what's in this one?"

"That's a house special, sir."

"But what's in it?"

"Seafood."

"Does that mean like in shrimps and stuff?"

"Shrimps and prawns," the waiter said. "They're fresh in from the coast every morning. Is anything wrong?"

"Nothing wrong, thanks," Nick said, and with the long-suppressed thought of a dead sailor's hand reaching up from the sea, suddenly decided that for him the meal had better be over.

One of the CID men, name of Frank, asked them what the rest of their shift was likely to hold; this was as they were pulling on their coats and ascending the basement steps into an evening that no longer had a scrap of daylight in it. The commonest misconception about the plainclothes squad, mostly held by those who'd never served in it and who were unlikely to get the chance, was that its officers spent all of their time either getting free drinks or getting laid.

Nick said, "The sergeant wants us down at the swimming baths for the evening session, see if we can warn off a body who can't hide the bulge in his trunks every time the little girls swim by. Then we get to cruise the fleshpots for kerb-crawling bishops. Then we get the gay clubs. Then we've got a couple of late-drinking licence checks and then, if we're lucky, we might get to go home."

Home was a location that Nick reached sometime around two the next morning, after a long night that had run about as close to the plan as any of them ever did.

He let himself into a dark and empty flat. There was a scent of perfumed steam as he walked past the bathroom, and it told him that he'd missed her by maybe an hour. He switched on the lights in the kitchen to check the cork noticeboard. She'd left him a note.

It read

> Dear Nicky . . .
> Just used the last of the hot water,
> please ring plumber tomorrow unless you
> can work some kind of magic on the tank.
> See you on turnaround; shopping on
> Thursday!
> Love,
> Jen

Yawning, he ambled back down the hallway to the airing cupboard and opened the door. The copper tank almost filled the space from side to side, buried in lagging like a fat man on a football terrace in winter. He took a look at the timer box on the wall and saw that the switch had stopped working about five hours before. He gave the plug a whack, blue sparks flew, and the timer started to tick; after that he closed the door, walked into the bedroom opposite and dropped onto his own side of the empty double bed. His eyes were shut before he hit.

In the silence of the flat, the tick of the timer could faintly be heard.

"Magic," Nick murmured.

2

The first time that Nick had heard Johnny's name on the Division had been in the operations room, not too long after Nick had transferred in. There was some confusion over the airwaves about organising the pursuit of a stolen car, and an exasperated mobile officer had cut in to say, "Look, is this an actual chase, or is it another Johnny Mays affair?"

And Nick had thought, Johnny Mays? Could he mean the *same* Johnny Mays? He'd found out the answer when he'd walked into the squadroom on his first day of plainclothes assignment.

The rest of the officer's meaning had filtered through a little more slowly.

Today was their anniversary as a team, according to Johnny; Nick made it seven weeks and three days, and wondered what Johnny could be talking about. He was a strange companion. They'd be getting along fine and then suddenly he'd come out with something like this, which made no sense at all. Sometimes Nick wondered if Johnny had simply developed a weird sense of humour over the years since he'd first known him. As far as Nick was concerned, he could have done without this extra dimension to their partnership.

They were visiting some badly run-down deck-access flats about half a mile out of the centre of town, looking for a teenaged kid called Dean. The kid's main claim to fame before he'd skipped probation had been the efficient trashing of a red Lancia in the supervised parking lot next to the town's biggest nightspot. He hadn't done it alone, but he was the only one who'd been caught; he hadn't been able to run with his trousers around his knees, on account of what he'd been dumping on the driver's seat when the parking attendant had shone a torch in through the windscreen. He was nine years old at the time, and beyond prosecution. Since then he'd progressed, mostly to theft and joyriding, and also to more ingenious methods of damage; he'd last been caught in the act of dropping home-made grenades from a motorway bridge onto speeding cars, the grenades consisting of knotted contraceptives filled almost to bursting-point with paintstripper. They hit like stones, they exploded like impacted birds, and they left their targets needing nothing less than a complete new spray job. And yet, Johnny had said, you'd look at him and credit him with the imagination of a slug.

This place was about as bad as they got, Nick thought. Four storeys high, a great bullring of a development like some low-rise Babel. They came into the amphitheatre through one of the brick arches that corresponded more or less to the points of the compass, and Johnny parked his Capri well away from the overhang of the open-sided balconies that ran all the way around each level. The central area had been planned as a garden, but now it was no better than a dustbowl. Nick had known estates like it when he'd been back in uniform. They were pretty well impossible to police – the approaches were too visible, and there were too many ways in and out – and they had a distinctly front-line atmosphere about them. He always remembered the story about how rats would spontaneously begin to eat their young when placed under the same kind of conditions. This one was more desolate than crowded – the plan was to get everybody cleared out and resettled by the end of the decade, and then either to bulldoze or sell to a private developer – but the feeling of oppression was exactly the same.

Johnny had been right to be cautious with his car. As they were ascending an open stairwell, Nick glanced out at exactly the same moment that a TV set, power lead trailing behind it like the tail of a kite, was falling past on its way down from one of the upper decks. Johnny said, "What the fuck was that?"

And Nick said, "It could have been a Sony. It went by too fast to be sure."

The TV tube imploded when it hit the ground three floors below, and after only a moment's lag it seemed to be answered by the first far-off echoes of thunder from somewhere out toward the coast. They went over to the rail, and looked down to where the busted set lay in amongst the split bags of garbage and the rest of the crap that regularly seemed to get tossed out into space around here. Nick could see that already about half a dozen dirty-faced kids had come swarming in to see what was new.

"Mad dog weather," Johnny commented, and they moved on.

Many of the flats on the third level were empty, wooden Xs covering their doors and windows. The one that they were heading for looked hardly better; half of the glass was missing from its entrance door, replaced by a sheet of cardboard pinned on the inside. They knocked and there was no reply, but Johnny moved along to the window and looked in.

"He's there," he said after a moment. "Looks like he's on his own."

"What do you want to do?"

"Well, we didn't come all this way just for the scenery."

So then Johnny moved back to the door. He punched out the cardboard and reached through to open it.

They went inside.

Technically they were way out of line – the summons that they carried didn't give them any of the powers of a warrant – but somewhere like this, it didn't always pay to let the line seem too clear. Johnny, who'd been here before, led the way through. Nick's first impression was that of stepping into a dimly-lit timewarp; the place had been recently decorated and the furniture wasn't old, but the taste from the wallpaper down reflected everything that had made him wince from about the age of seven.

Dean was in the kitchen.

He was looking nervous and unsure, but not entirely surprised. Nick thought that he seemed a delicate-looking kid. It was nearly four o'clock in the afternoon but he was wearing jeans and a pullover over pyjamas, and a pair of threadbare Pirelli slippers without any socks. In his hand was a chipped mug containing some kind of luridly-coloured orange squash.

"Come on, Dean," Johnny said. "Don't pretend you weren't expecting us. Where's your mother?"

"Out," Dean said.

"Let's go for a talk in the car."

Dean looked around him, uncertain, seemingly in a haze; Johnny took the mug from him and set it down gently by the draining board.

"You won't need shoes," he said. "We're not going far."

They went in line back to the car, with the boy in the middle. Johnny didn't say anything to him and Dean didn't say anything at all, simply tagged along in complete submission. Some of the small children at ground level saw them go, but nobody else as far as Nick was aware.

"You drive," Johnny said to Nick, throwing him the keys as they came around by the car. "Dean and I have a few things to talk about."

The back seat of a Capri had to be the most cramped interview space that Nick had ever seen put to use, but the move had its purpose. Dean was now on Johnny's ground and under his control, and he knew it. He couldn't turn away, he couldn't look for help. He could only listen, and do as he was told.

When Nick was behind the wheel and adjusting the rearview mirror, Johnny leaned forward to speak quietly to him.

"Just drive us around slow," he said. "You know the docks, at all?"

"I've been by there a couple of times."

"Start by heading out that way. I'll call the turns as we go."

It was a two-mile drive, mostly through the part of the town that had already died on its feet; much of it along a road where the tall, gloomy Victorian corner pubs were the only original buildings standing and still in use. Even these seemed to be doing little more than waiting out their time, dreaming stone dreams of the days when merchant seamen would pack the bars and no evening was complete until a fight had spilled out into the open somewhere. Nick took it slowly, glancing in the mirror every now and again as Johnny talked to the boy.

Johnny knew what he was doing. Nick only wished he didn't have to listen.

Johnny kept his tone low, his voice reasonable. He silenced Dean every time he tried to speak, even in response to a question. Johnny stripped him down to nothing. The whole thrust of what he was saying was that the boy was a creature without value, beneath notice, beneath even contempt, that his entire life was an open book with nothing of any worth written there. "I suppose what I'm saying, Dean," he explained, "is that you're snot on my shoe just asking to be stepped on. A freak like you should have been drowned at birth. You understanding what I'm getting at, Dean?"

At first Nick assumed that the kid was shucking it off, as insensitive as a side of meat under a beating; but a glance in the mirror as they came out into daylight from under a wide iron bridge showed the boy's stone face to be streaked with reluctant tears. His expression didn't vary.

Johnny leaned forward for a moment. "Turn left through the gates," he said to Nick, "and take us down to the end."

The dock entrance consisted of a derelict gatehouse and pinned-back iron gates with weeds growing up through their bars. The car bounced as it went over a patched-in part of the road where the dock railway had once run. They were driving along the wharf road now, disused cranes standing tall over the water; no ships had visited here in years, and the land between the road and the quayside now sported a row of modern workshop units in brick and pressed steel that had been thrown up quickly and rented out cheap. They passed a sunroof installer, a truck components store, a small business for overhauling refrigerator motors. The workshops were numbered and the numbers ran out quickly; Nick drove on past empty buildings and acres of rubble all the way out to the long stretch where the wharf ended, and here he swung the car around in the shadow of a great old grain warehouse.

They stopped. The only sign of recent attention that Nick could see was yet another of the Enterprise Zone hoardings, facing out across the wide, slow-moving river where no living soul would ever see it other than the gulls that hung in the air like crucified thieves.

Johnny reached over the seat, and opened the Capri's passenger door. "Got your bus fare on you, Dean?" he said pleasantly.

Dean shook his head.

"Pity," Johnny said. "Better start walking, then. It'll be dark before long."

Clutching his summons papers, Dean scrambled out onto the weed-infested cobbles. Nick thought that he'd probably have stepped out wet and naked into an Arctic wind rather than sit next to Johnny Mays for one minute longer.

Johnny said, "Let's go."

Nick hesitated. This was going too far. They were at least three, maybe four miles from the boy's home, and Johnny was proposing to leave him out in the middle of nowhere half-dressed, no shoes, no money. A lesson was a lesson, but somebody was going to have to draw the line, here.

"Speed it up, Nicky-boy," Johnny said.

Nick hesitated.

Then he did as Johnny had told him.

And as Nick let out the clutch to set them rolling again, Johnny leaned forward with his arms folded on the back of the passenger seat.

"The biggest mistake we could make," he said softly, "is to start assuming they're human."

Nick looked in the mirror as they headed back along the quay. Dean was a remote and solitary figure at the end of the dock, a boy-shaped silhouette against grey water and an even deeper iron sky beyond. He was watching them, and hadn't moved.

It was starting to rain.

Johnny said, "Where do you want to eat tonight?"

The rain had stopped by the time that they finally got to pull in across from the place that Johnny had in mind. It was also well into the evening now, and the washed-down streets had an electric glitter reflecting from all the neon in the centre of town. Johnny, back behind the wheel again, bumped the Capri half-onto the wide pavement alongside an intersection where four lanes of traffic were lined up and revving as they waited for the lights to change. There were a couple of big cinemas around here, and it was these that drew in the business and gave some kind of a focus to the area; everything else seemed to be a restaurant or a disco or a junkfood counter, and it was the kind of bright-lights and fast buck territory that Nick had been getting to know pretty well in Johnny's company.

Johnny crossed the road alone, and went into a fried chicken place that appeared to owe everything except its name to Colonel Sanders. Nick stayed in the car, and played with the volume control on Johnny's police radio. The uniformed branch – or the Woodentops, as the CID squad leader had so respectfully called them the day before – seemed to be having a quiet night of it so far. Nick's status was that he was one of them, and could be recalled into uniform if it ever became necessary; but otherwise, he was experiencing a kind of operational freedom that he'd never known before. People kept taking him for a detective, which wasn't the case, but that was a minor irritation and nothing to get worked up about. The CID tended to work office hours and to see more of the back end of a desk than anything else, whereas the plainclothes section moved mostly at night, and at street level, and got to see all of the weird and fascinating stuff that most people wouldn't even believe. And since there wasn't a dress code, he didn't even have to wear a jacket and tie; most of what he was wearing now wouldn't have looked out of place at a public bonfire.

Or on it, even.

Johnny was returning now, carrying two boxes and a handful of paper napkins. He dodged through the traffic that was currently backed-up from the lights, hardly even glancing at the cars around him. One that had been creeping forward had to brake sharply as he crossed before it, and the driver sounded his horn; Johnny gave him a pained look like a schoolteacher's, and didn't alter his course or his stride. The driver, a red-haired, red-faced youth with a skin problem, wound down his window and shouted something unintelligible after Johnny. But Johnny had now reached the Capri, and ignored him.

"Anything to pay?" Nick said as Johnny got settled and passed one of the boxes across.

"Not on my little acre. You been watching the arcade over there?"

Nick hadn't, but he looked now. The lights changed, the traffic jerked forward a few yards, and then the lights changed back again as if the whole thing had been a cruel joke. The arcade to which Johnny had referred was ahead and across from them, sandwiched between a very cheaply painted-up nightclub and a darkened transport café. From here it looked like a long, low-ceilinged cavern packed with gaming machines and of apparently unlimited depth; in the daytime it would have the effect of a pocket of night, but right now it had the effect of a doorway through into daylight. Somewhere deep inside, Nick could see a flashing red light that said CHANGE.

"How'd you rate the clientele?"

"Nothing special," Nick said. "Just the usual little-boy Lolitas and dirty old men."

"Not them. Her."

It took Nick a moment to zero in on where Johnny was looking; at first he thought that he was referring to a woman of terrific girth who was standing near to the entrance with a stack of carrier bags at her feet, playing one of the bigger and louder machines. But then another woman stepped out and around her, and Nick was corrected. This one was younger, in tight jeans and a checked shirt and with a huge bunch of keys on her belt. The big woman was saying something to her, and she was stepping forward with her hip tilted so that she could reach the machine with one of the keys on the ring; there must have been a payout stuck in the works which was now triggered, because the bells and the *chug-chug-chug* of falling money could be heard all the way across the street.

There couldn't be any doubt about it. She fitted the type; there was something about certain women that Nick couldn't put his finger on, something that they all shared that he couldn't define, but he'd begun to anticipate the click as Johnny Mays locked his sights onto them and wouldn't look away. The woman in the Porsche had fitted the pattern; so had the sixteen-year-old kid on the DIY store's checkout when they'd called by so that Nick could pick up a new timer switch for the flat; and so, now, did this ordinary-looking attendant in a sleazy corner full of noise that sounded like an army of Disney characters engaged in all-out Kung Fu slaughter.

Johnny said, "You reckon she's a tom?"

"No," Nick said, opening up the box on his knee and peering in at what appeared to be all bones and batter. "She works there."

"Yeah, but I'll bet you she's selling more than just loose change. Want to walk over and ask the price, see if we can get an arrest out of it?"

"Not tonight, Josephine." He pulled out a piece that, in the light available, looked like a deep-fried dead sparrow. "This stuff's terrible."

"I know," Johnny said. "I've had words with the chef."

Nick was about to suggest that they should dump it on the tramps in the park and go find something better, but then he glanced at Johnny. Johnny hadn't even opened his box yet. He'd taken out his little black notebook, and he was resting it on the boxlid while jotting down the number of the car that was now at the head of the line, waiting for the lights to change again. It had moved up about five spaces, but there was no mistaking that it was the car with the red-haired, red-faced young driver.

All of a sudden, Nick wasn't too hungry.

"You wouldn't believe it," Nick told Jennifer. "He keeps a grudge book."

And Jennifer said from the next room, "Doesn't everybody?"

"I mean a real one. And he uses it, too."

"For what?"

"Anything and everything. Once he gets a licence number, he can get a name and an address. I'm not even sure I want to know what he does after that."

He'd almost had a chance to sneak a look at Johnny's

notebook at the end of the relief, which for once they'd finished more or less on time. Johnny had gone off somewhere for a couple of minutes, leaving his locker door wide open and the notebook in plain sight on the top shelf. It was well-used and battered, and had scraps of torn paper added in amongst its pages. But Nick had hesitated and then Johnny had reappeared, wanting to know if Nick was interested in calling by an after-hours club which had a back room in the bar where late relief officers were welcome to unwind. Nick had checked his watch, realised that he could still get home and see Jennifer before she went out, and made an excuse for some other time.

Jennifer said, "How do you know he does anything at all?"

"I don't, for sure," Nick said. He was sitting at the kitchen table as Jennifer moved from bedroom to bathroom and back again in varying states of undress. It was like a sequence of semi-erotic snapshots that would lead him to nowhere, because Jen was going to be out of the flat in ten minutes' time and, as usual, she'd left all of her preparation until the last moment. Nick could see that she'd been studying for much of the evening, mainly because her books and her ring-binders were still taking up most of the table's surface; he picked up her copy of *A Level English Law* and riffled the pages so that they fanned his face. No, he didn't know for sure that Johnny Mays acted on the information that he collected . . . but it wasn't something that he'd care to place a bet against.

He said, "He tries to get something on any woman that he likes the look of, whether they're interested or not. Does that sound harmless to you?"

"That sounds creepy."

Jen dipped across the hallway again. She was tall and long-legged and twenty-five years old, and when she let down her dark hair – which she didn't do often – it would fall to her shoulders in a way that made Nick feel as if something had just turned over inside his chest.

She was great to live with, even though they hadn't been together much in the last couple of months. She was also probably the most serious-minded and ambitious woman he'd ever known; under the girl-next-door looks and the sense of fun, there was iron.

She said, "If it's worrying you so much, you'd better report him."

"I don't know. I've got nothing solid, and life's too short. Nobody loves a sneak. And it's not only that . . ."

"How long have you known each other?"

She was standing in the doorway now; even from down the hallway she'd been able to read him, and had spotted the true source of his inner conflict. She was ready to go, wearing the uniform that she called her second-best because a terrified five-year-old in an abuse case had peed down her newest one as she'd carried the child out to her patrol car the previous morning. Nick dropped the law book, almost guiltily. How long was it that he and Johnny had known each other?

"Since we were kids," he said. "And it wasn't around here. My family moved west when I was about fourteen, so I didn't see him again until I walked into the squadroom and found him waiting there for me. Biggest shock I'd had in years. He'd heard about me transferring in from the other end of the division and he'd pulled a few strings to get us teamed up together. He's pretty good at getting what he wants. He always has been. His family had money."

"You mean he's rich?" Jen said, with a half-smile to let him know that she didn't mean it. "Maybe he doesn't sound so bad after all."

But that half-smile was enough to drive thoughts of Johnny Mays right out of Nick's mind. He said, "What is it that's so sexy about a woman in a uniform?"

"This woman's in a uniform and a hurry."

"Damn. If I try hoisting an eye open around sunrise, you think I might get lucky?"

"Even if some drunk's been sick over me?"

"That's no way to talk about a fellow-officer."

Jen raised an eyebrow. "What's this?" she said. "You're telling me you're feeling frustrated?"

"No," Nick said, "don't worry about me. I'll just go back to stealing women's underwear from washing lines and I'll be perfectly happy."

There was a brief, almost awkward silence. And then Jennifer said, with some tenderness, "I'm sorry, Nick. It's just the way it's been going, these last few weeks."

"I know," Nick said.

She briefly touched his shoulder, and he briefly touched her hand. It was supposed to be a comfort, so why did it hurt him a little? Because of her tone, he supposed. It was like that which a parent would use with a young child, trying to explain how the kind of Christmas presents that his friends were asking for and getting couldn't exactly be managed on the family's budget.

Which brought him back around to Johnny, again.

Jen must have seen the kitchen clock. "Is that the time?" she said. "I have to go."

"I'll walk down to the car with you."

"Fine," she said, "but don't forget your key again. Listen, I hate to raise it, Nick, but can I chase you for the rent? I've got a mortgage payment due on the fifth."

"It's in an envelope on the cork board," Nick said. "You walked straight past it."

She turned and looked. The cork noticeboard by the kitchen door was such a jumble of notes, memos and money-off vouchers that they'd clipped and would probably never remember to use, that Nick's envelope had more or less blended in with the background. "So I did," she said. "Thanks."

"No need to mention it," he said.

They walked out to the parking area together. Jennifer's flat was on the second floor of a housing association block, nothing too expensive but about as far removed from the towers and the bullring as it was possible to get. It had the plain wood fittings and white interior walls of an office building, and in daylight had the look of a residential hall in some newly-built college, all pale brick and glass with a flat roof and intermittently-tended gardens. Within a week of arriving in the area, Nick had put up a card on the station's board advertising for a flat-share; he'd originally been put into lodgings where the rooms were full of hideous china and the 'guests' – all of them middle-aged, single men – took their meals around one big table. When he'd come out on the first morning and found three of the others in a patient queue for the bathroom, wearing dressing-gowns and with their towels over their arms like waiters, he'd known that he'd already had enough. Jennifer had answered the ad, and Nick had moved his stuff over into her spare bedroom; their combined rental allowances were almost enough to cover her repayments. Over the weeks that had followed, the spare bedroom had gradually been returned to its former disuse.

Now, as they walked down the path in darkness, Nick was telling her some more about Johnny Mays.

"I wouldn't exactly say that his people were rich," he said. "They had more than we did, but that wouldn't have been difficult. My dad was in and out of work like a brewer's dipstick. Johnny's dad had a transport yard with a couple of coaches, half a dozen lorries, a couple of vans, you name it. They didn't have much time for Johnny, so they'd buy him anything he asked for just to keep him quiet. Anything I ever had, he'd turn up the next day with one bigger and flashier and needing twice as many batteries. I don't think it's a coincidence he joined the force. He followed me in just about everything else."

They were approaching Jennifer's Renault hatchback, which was in the space alongside where Nick had left his Granada. The parking area never got crowded.

Jen said, "Has he changed much?"

And the answer was so simple, so obvious, that Nick couldn't understand why it hadn't hit him before.

"That's the trouble," he said. "I'm not sure that he's changed at all."

3

It was about a week later and nothing much out of the ordinary had happened, and Nick had been beginning to forget his darker thoughts about Johnny. The weekend had helped; Friday night with Jennifer had left him drained and happy, so that on Saturday he was even ready to trail around town as she searched for some second-hand textbooks. Nick wasn't much of a reader. He liked good stuff, but the good stuff was so hard to find. Of the paperbacks on Jennifer's bedside shelf, most seemed to feature glamorous, capable women doing little other than dropping expensive brand names and getting laid by younger men in all kinds of kinky ways.

Too much like real life, if the rest of the day and the evening were anything to go by.

Johnny was driving, today.

He wasn't in the best of moods because he hadn't been able to get hold of a spare radio, and that made for a bad start. Nick had made the point that they didn't need one and could probably even be disciplined for taking out equipment without proper authorisation, but this line of argument had cut no ice.

"I just like to know what's going on around me," Johnny said. "Knowledge is power, haven't you heard that?"

Nick had heard it. He just wasn't paranoid enough to want to put it into practice every minute of his working day, that was all. Although this was what went through his mind, he said nothing. Johnny had been this way before, and he'd settled after a while. Nick wondered if he was maybe getting too sensitive on the subject.

He was soon to find out that he wasn't.

They were in an area of big old Victorian houses, sooty buildings in the shadow of the railway, and the Capri was purring along at about fifteen miles an hour. Johnny had said that he'd given the car a tune-up over the weekend. As far as Nick could make out he lived alone, and didn't appear to be seeing anybody; presumably that left only his wheels to soak up all of the loving and lubrication. They used their own cars on the job because the section didn't have any vehicles to assign, and they claimed back expenses at public transport rates. For Johnny, this would be chickenfeed. With Nick's old wreck, it just about covered his outlay.

"Do we have business around here," Nick said, "or what?"

"Just something I like to keep an eye on," Johnny said.

They made a turn into a side-street, a short connecting road that was still surfaced in its original stone cobbles. Most of the householders around here were either Indian families or students in bedsits; reported crimes were few, mainly petty thefts with the occasional burning newspaper shoved through some Bengali's letterbox. Nick couldn't see any reason for a plainclothes detail to come prowling around the area at all. A tom on the lookout for kerbcrawlers would stand out like a singing telegram.

He said, "Anything you want to tell me?"

But Johnny was giving a closer-than-usual inspection to one of the bigger, seedier houses that stood on a corner with the high brick arches of the railway behind it. Their speed fell even lower as they rolled by, but then Johnny picked it up again as soon as the house had dropped away behind them.

He said, "Don't trouble your head, Nicky-boy. I've got all kinds of battles that you don't need to know about."

And as he said this, he turned back and pulled in by a red phonebox that stood almost opposite the house. "Give me a couple of minutes," he said, and as he hopped out of the car he was reaching into his jacket.

And then as Johnny walked over to the phone, Nick saw that the black notebook was now in his hand.

Even though the engine was running, the car was still close enough to the house for Nick to be able to hear a ringing from the hallway. The front door was the original Victorian design, a couple of hundredweight of painted timber with stained glass panels, and through these Nick saw a blurry outline as it moved to answer. He looked from the house, to Johnny, and then back again. What did he think he was doing?

The person in the hallway picked up the phone.

Johnny hung up.

As he walked back to the Capri he was giving the house a level stare, and his message was obvious; a little touch of menace for you, courtesy of Johnny Mays. Nick looked back, and saw the dowdy net curtains in one of the ground-floor windows move a little. Johnny broke it off at the last possible moment as he slid into the Capri. The grudge book was back in its hiding place, inside his jacket and close to his heart.

Johnny smiled over the wheel, not even looking at Nick.

Then they drove on.

———

The stop at the old house seemed to have lifted Johnny's mood by a notch or two. For Nick it had been like something overheard, an incident that made no sense but which set up a low resonance suggesting an episode in a long and untold story. And how many more of them were there, buried in the dog-eared pages of Johnny's notebook? Just for a while, Nick had almost managed to convince himself that he was looking at nothing more serious than a means of blowing off steam. But now it was taking on the aspect of a sinister Thousand and One Nights.

And it brought him back to the question that Jennifer had raised. What was he going to *do* about it?

From the cobbled streets they followed the line out to where the old railyards had once been, and pulled into a darkened archway where they could wait unseen. Most of the businesses around the yards and arches seemed to deal in trash of one kind or another – waste chemicals, scrap metal, rags, old newspapers – and the premises ranged from the derelict-looking to the downright squalid. And yet in amongst the squalor, as much a fixture as the decaying fencework and the razor wire, the owners' Jags and Mercedes stood out like silver in the dirt.

One of those owners, according to information they'd received from the local Customs Office, had cleared some space in one of his units and turned it over to imported stocks of *Paedo Alert News* and *Beach Boy*. A raid had been arranged with the uniforms, timed to catch the Big Man on the premises in about twenty minutes or so. He wouldn't sweat too much about it – he'd have all the legal protection and the cutouts already in place, and as usual only the footsoldiers would go to the wall – but with any luck they'd be able to pressure him into coughing his mailing list and his Amsterdam contacts.

Johnny killed the engine, and sat back to wait. Above them was a yellow streetlight, permanently on, and perversely it seemed to give the brick tunnel a more cavernous atmosphere. Like the cellars under the Ghost Train, Nick thought. The most memorable Ghost Train he'd ever been on as a child, at the big fair that had seemed to take over his home town every October, had featured all of the usual crap like rubber bats and water sprays and trailing gauze; but what he hadn't been prepared for had been the roustabout in a skeleton suit who waited at a bend to throw out his arms and roar over every car as it turned. For maybe a quarter of a second, Nick had experienced genuine fear; this wasn't the lurching dummy that he'd tuned himself to expect. It was as if all of the rules had suddenly been broken and the ground had dropped away from under him, but then he'd realised that what he was looking at was nothing more than a guy in tights and a mask with beer on his breath and an unconventional way of making a living.

Johnny had been with him in the car on that occasion, too.

Now Johnny was gently drumming his fingers on the hide steering-wheel cover, beating soft time to some piece that was playing only in his head.

He said, "Do you suppose Frank Zappa's his real name?"

And Nick said, "Whose?" Which killed the conversation for a while, as Johnny carried on drumming and Nick struggled to think of a way to guide the talk around to what was troubling him most.

Then Johnny said, "Tell me something interesting."

"Ernest Hemingway never wore underpants."

"Something else."

"Penguins can't tell the sex of other penguins."

"So how do they manage?"

"They fight a lot. Now you tell me something."

"Okay."

"What battles, Johnny?"

There was silence for a while. Johnny had stopped beating time. He looked at Nick, his expression unreadable. But it was as if something of the spirit of the Ghost Train had suddenly slipped into the car along with them.

Nick said, "It won't go any further than this. But I have to know."

Johnny watched him a while longer. Then he said, "Do you like policework, Nick?"

"That isn't an answer."

"It's the start of one. Well?"

"It suits me okay."

Johnny started to smile, slowly, and he nodded as if in dawning understanding. "You don't like it at all," he said.

"We're not talking about me," Nick said, with some discomfort at a barb that had sunk in deeper than he might have expected. "We're supposed to be talking about you."

"Me?" Johnny said, and he turned his gaze out front again. "I think it's the best thing in the world. I never got to do anything better than what I'm doing now. You know what I like the most? I like not being one of the herd." He nodded toward the arched rectangle of daylight ahead of them, beyond which the world went about its business. "I'd hate to be out there. I'd hate to be one of them, just another nobody. Don't tell me you never feel that way."

"I know," Nick said, "but all this – where does it lead?"

"You think too much, Nicky. That's always been your problem. Who gives a fuck where it leads? Who says it leads anywhere? Things just are. Understand that, and you'll understand everything you need to know. What's the worst thing you ever saw?"

"You mean, in the job?"

"It doesn't even have to be the worst thing. Just the first one that comes into your mind."

The worst thing? Nick didn't have to spend any time on the question; keeping the scene *out* of his mind was something that he'd been working on for nearly seven years and hadn't quite yet mastered. He'd seen floaters and he'd seen autopsies and he'd seen the long-undiscovered bodies of old people half-devoured by their starving pets, but he'd never seen anything that lingered in the mind quite so much as when he'd been called out to some cheap cabin homes late one Friday night in August. It had been unusually hot, and most people had their windows open, and a neighbour had called in with a report of a child's screaming. Nick, just a probationer at the time, had managed to look into the place through a gap down one side of the drawn curtains, and what he'd seen had sent him and his tutor constable straight through the front door like a couple of rams. A nineteen-year-old was sitting on the threadbare sofa, his seven-month old son on his lap. The boy was being sodomised. Across on the other side of the room, the child's mother was watching. By now the baby was insensible with pain, and the violent uncoupling that followed had almost killed it. The nineteen-year-old had been handled with the delicacy of expensive glass throughout his police custody; but within an hour of entering the remand centre he'd lost an eye in a wound from a home-made knife that had slashed down by his ear and then across to the opposite shoulder. *First of many*, his prisoner assailant had whispered in his ear as the warders came running.

Nick didn't say a word. He didn't have to; Johnny wouldn't need details, he'd know.

Johnny said, "And what did you feel like, afterwards?"

Nick looked at him, uncomprehending.

"Put it another way. What did the world look like?"

"Tainted," Nick said. "Fallen."

"And that's what sets us apart from the rest of them, Nick. They don't see what we see, they don't know what we know. They're just civilians, the second fucking division and that's God's own truth."

"And what about all this stuff with the car numbers?"

"That's just playing around. It's nothing to what I'd really like to do. I'd take a scythe to them if I could. I'd paint the walls with blood and take no prisoners. I'd really clean things up."

Suddenly, the spirit of the Ghost Train seemed like nothing more than the kid's fantasy that it really was. This was something else. For Nick, it was as if the rubber mask had been pulled away to reveal not a face, but an airshaft boring all the way straight down into Hell.

"Jesus, Johnny," he said, his voice barely more than a whisper.

And Johnny seemed to realise that he'd gone too far.

He cracked a nervous smile. "Yeah, I know," he said. "I get carried away, sometimes."

"You don't mean it?"

"Of course I don't mean it. I get carried away, that's all. Don't tell me it never happens to you."

"I suppose that it can," Nick said. But he was watching Johnny like a man who'd just handed a decent watch to a bad magician. Johnny was looking out towards daylight again, almost as if he were gazing at some distant land where he had no right of entry.

"And the bad dreams," he said. "Don't you ever get bad dreams?"

"I get my share."

"I get *really* bad ones. I reckon it's part of the price." He looked at Nick again. "I never told this to anyone else, you know."

Yeah, Nick thought, I can believe that. He said, "Have you ever considered looking for help?"

"I don't need that kind of help," Johnny said dismissively. "But I'll tell you what. You keep me on the rails, just like the old days. You'll do that, won't you, Nick? The old team again, the way it used to be?"

"Give or take a couple of decades, Johnny."

But Johnny didn't pick up on the irony in Nick's voice. "Remember when I said it was our anniversary?" he said. "I could tell you didn't know what I was talking about. But I'd worked it out – it was twenty-five years to the day since we started kicking around together."

Nick couldn't believe it. "You actually kept track?"

"It was just something I remembered. It wasn't an obsession, or anything. But I miss those days, Nicky. I miss the way things were." He looked across the car.

"I've never been able to count on anybody the way I used to be able to count on you."

And Nick thought, *Oh, great*.

The fact of it was that Nick probably hadn't thought about Johnny more than twice, at the most, in all of those long intervening years. But then Johnny didn't have too many friends, even in those early days. Other kids would stick around him for a while, but then they'd back off. Nick didn't really know why the two of them had hung around together for so long, but he was fairly sure of one thing; in the end, their friendship would probably have gone the same way as all those others. It was his leaving the area that had broken the pattern. There was a lot that was likeable in Johnny Mays, some of it right up-front and some of it buried deep; but maybe it was the flame of his ego, and the ferocity with which it could burn sometimes, that made it difficult to stand too close for too long.

There was a patrol van passing the end of the tunnel, bouncing hard on the ruts of a track that hadn't seen repair since the days of horse-drawn traffic. Nick checked his watch. It was time. Johnny was already starting to get out of the car.

"Let's go to work!" he said, his voice echoing in the brick confines of the archway, and Nick climbed out over on the other side of the Capri. Johnny watched him with a kind of amused disapproval. It was as if the conversation of the last quarter-hour had never even taken place.

Nick slammed the door.

"Try to perk up a little," Johnny suggested. "You look like you're on an outing from some home."

And then he set off to join the rest of the gathering team, and Nick followed.

But more slowly.

4

Jennifer said, "I'm not concentrating too well today, am I?"

"Anyone can confuse a bread roll and a toilet roll. Happens to me all the time."

"I've had something on my mind."

"I can tell."

They were unloading the morning's haul from a shopping trolley into the open hatchback of Jennifer's car. Nick loved to shop about as much as he liked to have teeth pulled, but this was about the only point in the week when the two of them were certain of being able to get together. Jennifer had changed out of uniform only a couple of hours before, and Nick's relief wouldn't begin until some hours later in the day. They'd met at the breakfast table like a couple of passing comets. Now they were in a crowded car park by an edge-of-town superstore, and as usual Nick was looking with dismay at the stack of cans and jars that constituted an essential support system for two people. There were a couple of bag ladies in town who pulled their entire stock of worldly goods around in old shopping carts, and neither of them toted a fraction of this.

"Maybe we eat too much," Nick said.

"Speak for yourself. I eat like a bird."

"So does a vulture."

They'd grabbed a couple of useful-looking empty boxes from by the checkouts, and now Jennifer was loading one of these with tuna cans and coffee jars and Mister Sheen. She said, "I got a memo last night. They're going to give me an interview. If I get through it, I'll get a CID tryout."

"You already did an attachment?"

"For three months, last year. I put in the application as soon as it was over. Now I get twelve months as a probationer and if that works out, they'll send me on the detectives' course. I've been pushing for it, but I really didn't think I had a chance."

"Why didn't you say something?"

"I didn't want to make a big thing out of it and then see it all go pop. You know what it's like. There's nothing worse than having a disappointment and then having to put up with sympathy as well. Makes you wish you'd never bothered in the first place."

"When is it?"

"Next week. Wish me luck?"

"Yeah. Who knows, we might even get back onto something like a regular timetable."

Nick returned the trolley as Jennifer was getting in behind the wheel of the car. He was pleased for her – of course he was – but what was that little round stone of something lying hard and heavy at the bottom of his feelings? It surely couldn't be jealousy of her success, because he'd once been on a CID attachment of his own and had never been tempted to push it any further. Maybe he'd have made it or maybe he wouldn't, the question never arose; so what exactly was happening here?

Admit it, he told himself as he walked back to the car. We're not just talking about a job. We're talking about a rival, and one who's been around for longer than you.

Something of his mood must have leaked across to her as they were heading for home. But he was lucky, because she misread him. She said, "So how are you making out with Mister Weird?"

Johnny, he thought after a moment's confusion. *She means Johnny.*

"You should hear him," he said. And then he told

her about their conversation from the previous day, the one that had taken place in the darkness of the railway arch.

"He sounds mad," Jennifer said. "Seriously."

"No," Nick said. "He's not mad. But he's wrong."

"And this is all in his black book?"

"We haven't even *touched* on the little black book yet. I don't know what I'm going to do."

"Dump him," Jennifer said without any hesitation.

Nick stared out of the car. Houses, cars, people, street names. A decent area. Johnny might be wrong, but Nick's problem was that he couldn't say for certain that he was one hundred per cent in error. How could he – how could *any* serving officer – say as much, after some of the things that he'd seen? A tough shell, an emotional wall of defence, was one of the essentials of the job . . . but as with any wall, it was easy to lose any clear sense of what lay on the other side. Johnny needed help, but what Jennifer was suggesting sounded too much like betrayal.

Dump Johnny?

"I wouldn't know how," Nick said.

"I really am serious, Nick. Drop him, or he'll take you down with him. Don't be soft just because you were friends once."

"I wish it was so simple."

"It is. You're just too close to see it, that's all."

He didn't answer straight away. For a moment he was confused, alerted by something and he didn't know what; but then the connection fell into place, and he said, "What's the name of this road?"

She glanced at him, puzzled at this sudden switch. "Ashness Lane," she said.

"Does that mean there's an Ashness Close somewhere around here?"

"We just passed it."

He asked her if they could turn around and take a look, and she shrugged and said okay. "No need to go right in," he said. "Just a quick fly-past will be enough. I'm wondering if it's the same place that I'm thinking of."

It was.

In a small cul-de-sac of expensive, modern and boxy-looking apartment buildings, stood a Porsche that wasn't exactly difficult to recognise. Over on the other side of the Close, in the shade of some long-established trees, stood Johnny Mays' Capri. Nick could see that Johnny was sitting in it, alone, and as the Renault turned around in the wide opening of the Close Nick ducked down in his seat in case Johnny should look their way. Now he knew for certain where he'd heard the street name before; it had been on Johnny's radio, in response to his call for the Porsche's licence details.

When they were safely away, Nick pulled himself up again. Jennifer said, "What's the matter?"

"Nothing," he said. "Just someone I didn't much want to see around here."

———

Later.

They tossed a coin again, and this time the Capri got it. So Nick went out to move his Granada from a meter onto the long term car park – nothing more than a patch of unused building land around the rear of the station with some nasty old fart in a booth taking money – and walked back around to the yard.

The station building was adored by the town's conservation society and generally loathed by anyone who had to spend time inside it; this applied as much to those who worked there as to those who came in through the windowless vestibule marked *Prisoners Only*. It had an imposing frontage with a big sandstone arch leading onto a cobbled yard where stables had become garages, and an interior that reminded Nick of an old public swimming baths. Most of this effect came from the bare corridor floors and the ornate municipal half-tiling in frog-green and cream, and from the antiquated cast-iron radiators under windows set high in the walls. It was a big, draughty, echoing Victorian structure, and the departmental signs on its doors all tended to look a little forlorn. Where there were computers in use, the high-tech screens and keyboards made for a jarring mismatch of time and culture as, only a few feet away, pipes clanked with hit-or-miss steam heat.

Nick was thinking hard as he re-entered through the buzzer-controlled door by the Enquiries desk. He barely responded to the duty sergeant's nod. Right now his thoughts were furiously concentrated because down in the locker room, just before the flip of the coin, he'd managed to get a look inside Johnny's Little Black Book.

Johnny had hung his jacket on the hook inside his locker door, and gone through into the washroom. Nick knew he'd never have a better chance than this. A brief touch found the shape of the notebook through the material; seconds later, he was leafing through it.

He could feel his heart beginning to sink as he turned the pages.

There wasn't an inch of blank space anywhere in it. The book was packed with details written over faded details, strings of exclamation points and question marks, weird notes, spiral doodles, unreadable personal codes; perhaps there was something in what Jen had said because it read like a madman's diary, and as he slipped it back into Johnny's jacket with only seconds to spare it left his fingers tingling as if he'd handled something hot.

Johnny came swinging back around the end of the row of lockers, whistling as he walked. Nick had an absurd feeling that he was now wearing guilt like a halo, and to distract Johnny's attention from it he said, "Been getting up to anything interesting?"

"Nothing much," Johnny said breezily, reaching for his jacket and pulling it on. "Spent the day at home with a book. We going out in your car tonight, or a real one?''

This time, Nick didn't go straight back to the locker room. Johnny would probably be trying to hunt out a spare radio as usual, at least for the next few minutes. Nick went on up to the third floor instead.

On this level were found the CID's rooms and most of the officers of Superintendent rank, including that of his own department's supervisor. Doors onto the corridor were mostly left open, all of the time. As much as he tried to fight it, whenever Nick came along here he couldn't shake off the feeling of being a kid at school again and walking down the staff room corridor.

His supervisor wasn't there.

Nick stood in the empty office, wondering if it was worth waiting around. Johnny might ask where he'd been, and that was one question that he didn't want to have to answer. Sorry, Johnny boy, I've just been upstairs to dump you in the *Scheisse*. Better duck, because here it comes. I did it for your own good, kid. But mostly I did it because . . .

Because . . .

Nick hesitated where he was, close to the door. It was an oddly silent room. There was a big, pleasant window looking out onto greenery, but the window obviously leaked and there was an old water stain in a widening fan on the carpet. To his right, a glass-fronted bookcase containing bound copies of *The Criminal Law Review*. Framed photographs on the wall; police college, presentation dinners, the divisional shooting team 1974. Over on the desk, memos that he was tempted to read even though he knew they'd contain nothing of interest or relevance to him.

The phone began to ring, its buzz muted.

Nick turned, and walked out.

He didn't know whether to count it as a failure of nerve because he didn't stay, or a failure of nerve that he'd come up here in the first place. However he looked at it, the situation seemed all wrong. There were correct solutions and there were solutions that could be lived with, and this didn't feel like either. If anything, it felt more like he'd be running away.

A man stepped out of one of the offices before him.

"Hello, Nick," he said easily. "Settling in?"

For a moment Nick experienced a brief stab of panic as if he'd been caught at something, but it quickly faded.

"It's about as good as it's going to get," he said.

Ralph Bruneau – Bruno, to just about everybody – was one of those rumpled, easygoing men who seemed to know and be known by everyone. The shirt hadn't yet been designed that could stay in the waistband of his trousers for long. He also had the most distinguished arrest record on the Division. Now he stood with his shirt-tail out and his arms folded, leaning in the doorway of his office.

He said, "That sounds less than wonderful."

Loosen up, Nick told himself. "Sorry. That isn't how I meant it."

"And how are you getting along with Johnny Mays?"

Nick wasn't fooled. The question sounded casual, but Bruno was watching him hard. Nick said, "We're doing fine."

"Really?"

"We don't always agree on methods, that's all."

There was an awkward silence for a moment. Now Bruno's phone had also started to ring, but he ignored it.

He said, "You want to talk to somebody, Nick?"

"Me?" Nick said. "About what?"

"Anything that's worrying you. The people up here don't always listen as hard as they might. Nobody wants to look like a bad manager."

"I've got no worries," Nick said.

Bruno watched him a moment longer. Then he shrugged.

"Well," he said, straightening to go back in. "It's not my place to say it. But maybe you should have."

And with these encouraging words in mind, Nick went down to the locker room to rejoin his partner.

———————

Johnny had picked up on Nick's mood by the time they'd reached the Capri. Girl trouble, he seemed to reckon, and set himself the job of snapping Nick out of it. While Nick was desperately trying to think of some way to lay his concerns on the line that would let Johnny know they were both on the same side, Johnny was running through his good-times repertoire for some favourite distractions. He loved to roust a gay bar, so they did a couple of the clubs even though it was late in the afternoon and there was almost no-one around. Then they drove over to a sex shop in one of the side streets near the cathedral, and went into the back to shine flashlights onto the kids who waited in the darkness by the video booths. Then they went to a flat over a grocer's shop, and Johnny rang the bell so that Nick could get a look at the Oldest Working Whore In Town. Johnny had told Nick that he wouldn't believe his eyes, and he didn't. Dinner was a couple of uncollected takeaway orders from a Chinese restaurant, courtesy of the management, with the Capri parked in the warehouse loading bay alongside the kitchens.

"And the night is still young, Nicky-boy," Johnny said. "We're going to haul you out of the pits, or die in the effort."

By around eight, it was even starting to work. Johnny's singing clinched it.

Johnny was, without a doubt, the worst singer that Nick had ever heard. He had a tin ear, and only the sketchiest idea of a lyric. He beat time on the wheel and used the brakes like a wah-wah pedal, and it was as they cruised around by the park that Nick finally cracked.

"Looking out as lonely as a *what*?" he said.

Johnny broke off the chorus. "What's the matter?"

"Are you listening to what you're singing?"

"Why?"

"Every night I sit here by my window, looking out as lonely as a gnu? What the fuck's a gnu got to do with anything?"

"Those are the words," Johnny said confidently.

"My *arse*," Nick said. "It's avenue. Lonely avenue."

Johnny thought it over for a moment.

Then he said, "Nah," and started over again from the top. Nick covered his ears and howled like a dog until Johnny was laughing too much to sing any more. Somehow it was all going to work out, Nick thought. Catch him in this kind of a mood and there had to be a good chance of pulling him around. In fact, he thought as they left the park behind and passed under a railway bridge, now might be as good a chance as he'd get.

Nick was about to speak, when he realised where they were.

The big house stood completely dark as they pulled in by the same phonebox as before. Nick was sitting there with all of the short-lived good spirits draining out of him as Johnny, still grinning, hopped out of the car and went over to the phone.

A minute went by. Nick could hear the phone ringing out in the empty house, a faint sound like a final summoning of the dead. Johnny looked around at him. He seemed pale and unreal in the booth's overhead lighting. He made an *okay* sign to Nick, and then hung up.

He stepped out of the booth and made straight for the house, slapping the roof of the Capri as he passed. "Come on, Nicky boy," he said, "we're in business," and by the time that Nick was out of the car he'd already disappeared around the side of the building.

When Nick caught up with him, Johnny was in the rear yard of the house and had just popped open the door into the kitchen with the leverage of a short wrecking bar. The bar was disappearing back into Johnny's pocket as Nick arrived, and before he could question or protest Johnny was inside the kitchen and switching on the lights.

"Fucking students," Johnny said, looking at the half-washed crockery piled up in the sink and what looked like days-old breakfast debris on the table. None of the mugs or plates matched. Against the back wall, in place of cupboards, stood plywood food lockers with a different name and style of padlock on each. There were a couple of unhappy-looking plants by the drainer, and somebody was growing cress in a line of margarine tubs along the windowsill. "Talk about a dump."

He went on through, switching on more lights. Nick gave a nervous glance around, and followed.

There couldn't be any doubt that this was a student house. As far as he could see, all of the other rooms on the ground floor had been converted into single study bedrooms. As the light from the hall fell through half-open doors he could see books and wall-posters and cheap veneered desks under anglepoise lamps. The carpet underfoot was like tough coir matting and ahead of him there was a pay phone – the one that he'd heard ringing – on the wall behind the main door. Beside this, a noticeboard carried faculty memos and fire drill instructions and a colour-coded housework rota in rounded, almost childish handwriting. There had to be, what . . . eight people living here? And none of them home.

Johnny had gone through into the bedsitter at the front of the house, and almost as if in answer to Nick's unspoken question he called back, "We're somewhere into the last couple of weeks of the summer break, that's why the place is so empty. Makes a lot of sense, wouldn't you say? Ten weeks of listening to rock bands and screwing your brains out and you'd need a long rest, too."

There was a crash from the room, as of a shelf-load of books being hurled to the floor. Nick moved to the doorway in time to see Johnny getting his arm behind the second shelf, and then raking its contents off to thunder down onto those of the first. Books spun and papers scattered, and Johnny looked up at Nick and said, "I don't suppose you'd know what a thesis actually looks like, would you?"

Nick stared at him. Johnny kicked around in the pile like a man searching through the ashes of a bonfire, and then he turned his attention to the desk drawers. This room wasn't quite like the others. The differences were small – no posters, a few earth-colour ceramic pieces over the old blocked-in fireplace, a crocheted spread on the divan – but they told another story. It wasn't the bedroom of a kid away from home; it was a young woman's room and Nick could almost see her, serious-minded, perhaps a little drab . . .

And probably with that hint of an indefinable something that Nick was beginning to think of as the Johnny Mays Factor.

"I'll wait for you in the car," he said.

Johnny was down on his hands and knees, rummaging through the contents of some cardboard files that he'd uncovered; he didn't even look up as Nick withdrew.

Nick had been in plenty of other people's houses. Sometimes it was with an invitation, often it was without. The worst that he'd ever felt was uneasy, but this was the first time in more than twenty years that he'd walked through strange premises in the certain knowledge that he was in the wrong. Even though the house was just a tall, empty space and Johnny was making enough racket to send echoes all the way through it, Nick moved back down the hallway and into the kitchen in a selfconscious silence. A board creaked in the kitchen floor as he stepped around the paraffin heater, and Nick hunched at the sound as if half-expecting a blow from behind.

He wanted nothing more right now than to be out of here, away from the taint of the guilty air. Johnny had gone way out over the edge, and Nick had followed along just one step too far. And the toughest part wasn't so much the glimpse of the terrifying void below, as the knowledge that the same abyss had become Johnny's natural territory.

He wanted to be out of the house, but he paused for a moment.

The paraffin heater moved on castors, and one of them squealed. Nick looked up quickly, but Johnny didn't seem to have heard. The kitchen floor's covering was a plain raffia square, and when Nick lifted it he saw the pattern of the weave printed in dust on the boards underneath. The creaking board was loose, its edge slightly raised. Nick hooked it up with his fingernails and looked down into the space below.

The cavity was about a foot deep. Grey plastic cabling, some of it fairly new, ran through the gap like uncovered sinews. Below the wires and sealed into transparent polythene, there was a typescript of some kind. Nick couldn't tell from here whether it was an original, or a xerox, or what it was. He hadn't noticed a typewriter back in the room, but if the tenant had moved out and taken it with her then perhaps this meant that Johnny's calls and silence had scared her away.

As Johnny had intended, probably.

Nick replaced the board, dropped the matting over it, and moved the heater back into its place. Then he wiped the heater where he'd touched it. Then he went out through the damaged door.

Johnny got back to the Capri about five minutes later. He hadn't found the thesis, but he'd brought along some of the cardboard files and he tossed these over into the back seat before he got in. He showed about as much sense of impropriety as if he'd just stepped out to pick up a newspaper.

Nick said, "Do you have to be anywhere tonight?"

"Why, got something in mind?"

"I thought we might go somewhere quiet. There are a few things we ought to be talking about."

"Suits me," Johnny said, missing Nick's point entirely as he started the Capri. "Until you came along, I hadn't thought about the old days in ages."

"That isn't what I mean."

"Remember the winter when we busted into that beach cottage and mixed up all the jigsaws in the cupboards?"

Nick remembered – and he'd been stiff with anticipatory fear on that occasion, too. Johnny always seemed to have been adept at landing him in such situations; like another time, when the two of them had wound up hammering on a lighthouse-keeper's door for sanctuary in the belief that a group of bigger boys were out to turn them into burger meat with a cricket bat. What had been the reason? Almost certainly it would have been Johnny's chronic inability to keep his mouth shut at those times when a tactful silence would have served him better.

Nick said, "You're talking about when we were ten years old."

"I know," Johnny said as they pulled out. "Nothing's changed much, has it?"

They put some distance between themselves and the house.

And that, Nick was thinking with regard to Johnny's last remark, was exactly the problem.

5

They'd have ended the relief earlier if it hadn't been for Johnny wanting to get a look at a BMW that had been found abandoned in a demolition area along by the old gasworks. He'd picked up the call on the radio, and when they reached it a couple of uniforms from Traffic were looking it over and making an inventory of damage. Nick stayed in the car while Johnny got out to take a look around the BMW and exchange a few words with the Traffic men. The vehicle had a shattered rear screen, some bad scrapes along its side, and was nose-in to the pavement with its tail about a yard out into the road. There would probably be a raw-edged hole in the dash where the radio had been levered out, but unless the engine was totally screwed-over there was nothing that a competent body shop couldn't hide.

Johnny came back, shaking his head. "Fleet car," he said, and they swung out and around the two-car tableau and headed back into the town centre.

Car theft could be like burglary, it carried an emotional charge unrelated to the value of the goods. Some owners would take a low cash offer rather than sit behind the wheel again; then all it would take would be a weekend with a spraygun and a classified ad in the newspaper, and let the good times roll. But with a fleet car, it was a waste of time. Fleet operators got about as emotional over their vehicles as Easter Island statues over the tennis season.

They signed off the relief, and Johnny went up to the squadroom while Nick went around to collect his car.

They'd arranged to meet at a late-licensed place called the Theatre Club; police personnel tended to avoid it even though it was only a couple of streets away from the station, mainly because it always seemed to be full of solicitors and their secretaries.

Johnny's Capri was already parked half-on the pavement when he got there, and Nick pulled in behind. The bouncer on the door didn't know him, but he knew a warrant card when he saw one. "Oh," he said, "life membership," and moved aside.

Johnny had bagged them a quiet corner table and had lined up a couple of drinks. There was no music, and the air was hazy with smoke; about a hundred people were crowded into the club, and a fair sprinkling of them were probably major-league local villains. Nick hadn't been on the division for long enough to recognise many of them, but he nodded to a couple and got a greeting in return.

As he sat, he said to Johnny, "All square on the paperwork?"

"Fuck the paperwork," Johnny said pleasantly. "What's been bothering you?"

Nick met his gaze. "You want it in a word?" he said. "You."

"How's that?"

"Your attitude, Johnny. It bothers me. No, it more than bothers me, it scares the shit out of me. What do you think you're doing?"

"I haven't got the faintest idea of what you're talking about."

"I'm talking about working the system. I'm talking about treating the rest of the world like it's a river of sewage and you're walking through it on a golden ticket. I'm talking about abuse of the registration procedure, breaking and entering, stitching up anybody who happens to cross you, you name it."

Johnny stared at him for a moment. "You going to tell on me?"

"I don't know what I'm going to do."

And after watching him for a moment longer, Johnny said, "No. You won't tell. I was right about you. Out of all of them, you're the only one that I know I can trust."

"Don't push it, Johnny."

"Who's pushing?"

"And don't try to take me for a fool, either."

Johnny wasn't angry, he wasn't desperate. If anything, he seemed like the reasonable one here.

"Listen," he said. "I'm not saying I haven't bent the rules every now and again. Who hasn't? And I'm not saying that I haven't cut a few corners to get things done, and that I don't get a bit of fun out of the job sometimes. But that's as far as it goes."

"I wish I could believe that."

"Come on. What do I have to say to convince you?"

"You could consider seeing somebody."

It didn't sink in straight away. "Like who?" Johnny said, but then he understood. "You talking about a shrink? Me?"

And Nick, not wanting to be pinned down to anything that would bring the argument down to specifics so soon, said, "Not necessarily."

But Johnny was shaking his head. "Oh, Nicky," he said. "I think you've been seriously misled."

"All I know, is what I've seen."

"What you've seen is just housekeeping. Don't assume it's typical."

But Nick was thinking about other words, on another occasion; *I'd take a scythe to them if I could. I'd really clean things up.*

He said, "Woman in the Porsche?"

Johnny missed a beat, but his face betrayed no reaction. "What about her?"

"I saw you hanging around her place this morning."

"Not me."

"It looked like your car."

"Couldn't have been. I was playing squash."

"You told me you'd spent the day with a book."

Nothing happened for a moment. Nick could almost hear wheels turning and circuits buzzing as Johnny sorted and checked and recompiled in a rush effort to rewrite this recent history so that he could come out ahead.

But all that he could say was, "Look, Nicky. Why are you so intent on giving me a hard time?"

"You wanted me to keep you on the rails, right? Well, that's what I'm doing. If that's your idea of a hard time, then I'm sorry. Every time I kid myself into thinking I'm over-reacting, you pull something else out of the bag. That's what has to stop."

"Okay," Johnny said.

Nick waited, but there was no more. "That's all? Just okay?"

"What do you want," Johnny said, "something signed in blood? I'll tone it down."

"I think I'll live longer, if you do."

"Then it's settled," Johnny said with the faintest trace of what might have been bitterness. "Wouldn't you say?"

They went out into the night. Nick wasn't sure how he felt. There was relief, but there was also an indefinable unease . . . as if he'd taken a step toward a solution, only to begin to doubt his grasp of the problem as he drew closer.

If only Johnny hadn't been so reasonable.

Nick didn't think he could trust him.

But at least it was a start.

They parted with an unenthusiastic *See you later*, and each went to his own vehicle. The side-street was narrow and its lighting was perfunctory, just a yellow lamp at either end and deepening darkness in between, and by this feeble illumination Nick could see that someone had stuck a handbill under the Granada's windshield wiper. He pulled it out, opened the driver's door to check it under the interior light, and when he saw that it was nothing more than an amateurish stencil-cut advertising a local band he screwed it up and tossed it into the gutter under the car. And then he froze, because he'd realised that he'd somehow managed to open the door without unlocking it.

He opened the door wider, and looked inside.

"Oh, Christ," he said.

There was a turd on the seat.

6

It was a few moments before Nick became aware of Johnny. He'd come around from his own car, and he was looking over Nick's shoulder into the Granada's weakly-lit interior.

Johnny said, "Young Dean isn't even bright enough to vary his methods much, is he?" He sounded pretty grim.

"I can't drive it like this," Nick said hollowly. He'd attended after break-ins where burglars had done something similar into drawers or onto bedding, but he'd never quite been able to understand the disproportionate shock of the householders' reactions. Until now. He felt helpless – what was he going to do, unbolt the seat and throw the whole thing out, covers and crap together? And he couldn't even think of anything so simple as cleaning up and then getting behind the wheel because when he did, his mind turned away from the idea like a horse at a high fence.

It had never been much of a car but for him, it was ruined. For now, and forever.

"I can't drive it," he said again.

"Why should you?" Johnny said. "Come on."

"Wait a minute," Nick said. He was struggling to get his mind back into some kind of order. "I've got to think what to do."

"I know what to do. Come on."

Johnny's firm hand on his shoulder clinched it. Nick turned and let himself be guided back towards Johnny's Capri, not even bothering to lock the Granada before walking away. What could be the point, after this? And as he waited for Johnny to unlock his own doors and switch off the contact alarm that had probably protected the Capri's interior, Nick saw the great blistering scar that lay in the shadows across the car's bonnet like a lava burn. Wherever the paintstripper had flowed, the Capri's skin had bubbled and turned white.

After a couple of minutes on the road, Nick's dead-inside feeling was beginning to turn to anger.

"I'm just going to get it towed away and scrapped," he said. "It isn't worth anything. And I'm damned if I'm going to set foot in it again after this."

"It's the personal touch that gets to you."

"Damn right."

Nick was in no doubt about it. Dean alone, or Dean with friends, had to be responsible for what had happened. They'd probably been hanging around all night, watching the police yard from one of the unlit alleyways across the street. It might sound like risky business, but none of that would have worried them; they might look like ordinary kids but Nick had met their type before, and they seemed to have no nerves at all. Johnny's car would have been recognised as it emerged, and there were enough sets of lights in the short drive from the station yard to the club to have slowed down the journey and made it possible for them to have followed on foot. Nick's arrival a couple of minutes later must have seemed like some kind of a bonus.

They drove around the centre of town for a while, checking the obvious places like the all-night snack wagon on the bridge by the railway or the boomy open spaces of the concrete shopping mall. They saw two or three groups of kids, but nobody looked like Dean and none of them ran at the sight of the disfigured Capri. Most were boys, sallow and underfed and looking more like rejected pressings than real human beings, and the few girls were shockingly child-like under their makeup. They'd fall silent as the car drew level, and shift uncomfortably under Johnny's hard stare as the Capri rolled by in low gear before abruptly picking up speed and moving on.

"We're wasting our time," Johnny said after about their fourth circuit. "He's probably heading for home by now."

"Little bastard," Nick said. "Let's catch him there."

Johnny glanced across at him, and grinned. "That's the trouble with the milk of human kindness," he said. "One turd in your car, and suddenly it all turns into yoghurt."

Then Johnny made a U-turn on the main boulevard and, with a burst of speed, they headed out past dead shops and through empty streets toward the fringe of town. There was almost nothing to get in their way at this hour. Nick felt himself being pressed back into his seat as the needle climbed, and he took hold of the grab-handle above the passenger door and hung on. He did it unconsciously, not with any sense of concern; speed was a drug that seemed to help with the burning ache that he was feeling inside.

Against a kid, a small and doubting voice said at the back of his mind. But for now, he didn't even hear it.

Johnny was slowing, and Nick glanced back over his shoulder on the assumption that one of the night relief cars had picked them up. But nothing was following, and when Nick turned to face front again it was to see that they were now pulling in by the side of the road. As far as Nick could tell, there was nothing around here; just a low brick wall on the far side of the pavement, the cut-down remains of what had once been a sizable factory or mill. Beyond the wall there would be an acre or so of broken glass and rubble and, on a fairly secure assumption, yet another dented billboard announcing an Enterprise Zone.

Johnny was getting out of the car.

He said, "You take it from here. Meet me at the flats in ten minutes."

"How will you get there?"

"In style, Nicky boy. In style."

He didn't explain any further, and he was walking away without waiting for questions. This was the middle of nowhere, but he seemed to know where he was going. Nick crawled across into the driver's seat and when he adjusted the mirror, he was just in time to catch sight of Johnny disappearing around the last corner into yet another street of fallen workplaces.

It was about half a mile or more before Nick got his bearings, thrown by the fact that Johnny seemed to have taken them way off their route before handing over the car. This was the wrong side of the old gasworks, a fact that suddenly gained in significance about a minute later when Johnny overtook him, accelerator down to the floor and lights flashing, in the stolen BMW that they'd seen just over an hour before.

Nick went cold. He felt as if he'd suddenly been drained.

Johnny had spent most of his childhood around a transport yard. By the age of fourteen he'd been able to enter any locked car and start it without keys – which put him pretty much on a par with the likes of Dean – and it appeared that the skill hadn't deserted him. By now the BMW would no longer be computer-listed as a missing vehicle, and the fact that the owner probably wouldn't be informed until the morning gave it a kind of in-limbo status; but exactly what this said about Johnny's plans or anything else that he might have in mind, Nick had no idea.

By the time that he'd reached the bullring of deck-access flats, the BMW was already standing out in the best-lit area of the courtyard. Johnny was waiting by it, scanning four levels of decks that overlooked the arena like the balconies of an empty theatre. Nick came to a halt alongside him, and as Johnny came around the Capri he indicated for Nick to leave the engine running.

"I don't get this," Nick said.

"You will," Johnny said. "Move over."

Subtlety obviously wasn't a part of the design. Johnny backed the car off about a hundred yards or so with screaming tyres, and then with a touch more care he guided the rear of the vehicle a couple of dozen yards further into one of the brick access tunnels. It closed over them like a second, more intimate night. Johnny sat with the engine purring low, bringing it up to a beefy growl every now and again with a light pressure on the pedal. Confined here like a big cat in a cave, they could watch the BMW and a part of the bullring beyond it.

"I'll give you ten to one that the little bastards have been waiting for us to show," Johnny said. "They think we're going to walk up there and get nineteen different kinds of shit thrown down on us. I've seen an engine block go through the roof of a Metro before now. Well, this time it's going to be on our terms."

"And then what?"

"Then we plug a few gaps in young Dean's education."

Nick looked up at the third of the gallery levels, the one that they'd visited. It was against the lighter colour of the plywood boards that he caught a moving shadow-shape, a sign that some definite interest was being taken in their arrival.

He said, "I'm not so sure that this is a good idea," and Johnny looked at him across the darkened car.

"Give it a chance," he said. "It'll grow on you."

Four of the shadows materialised into substance at the edge of the ring of light, only yards from the BMW. There was something eerie about the way that they'd moved down from the building, almost as if they'd simply faded out from one place to reappear in another, but Nick knew that this was only a trick of the light and the hour. They spread out and surrounded the car. Nick recognised Dean. Two of the others were also teenagers, but washed-out and ageless under the sodium glare; the fourth, Nick would have sworn, had to be no more than eight years old, but apart from his size he moved and acted exactly like the others.

Johnny revved a couple of times, and as one the four of them looked toward the Capri. Nobody nodded or gave any kind of a sign, but all the same Nick knew that a challenge had been offered and taken.

They piled into the BMW.

Barely more than ten seconds later, they had its engine running.

"Not too shabby," Johnny said. "For scum."

And as the BMW started to jerk forward, Johnny put the Capri into gear in readiness to follow.

"Hey, now," Nick said. "Wait a minute."

"You already put your side of it once this evening," Johnny said, "and I listened. Now you're going to get it from my point of view."

"We're way out of line already."

"Let me put it this way," Johnny suggested reasonably, and Nick was briefly aware of the blur of Johnny's knuckles snapping up in front of his face before a bomb seemed to explode inside his head. He wasn't knocked unconscious, but he was certainly taken out of it for a while; he didn't know for how long, but by the time that he'd started to see around the edges of the glare they were out and rolling again.

He was twisted, somehow. He tried to straighten. He couldn't.

His head ached, he felt sick. Johnny had caught him right across the bridge of his nose. He was blinded as if by flashguns, but that was now improving. He wondered if his nose was broken but Johnny had caught it high, which was why the effect had been so devastating. Nick moved to touch it, but his right arm met a tug of resistance when he tried.

He screwed his eyes shut for a few seconds, and then opened them again. The inside of the car finally came into focus, as slowly as the picture on an old valve TV.

Now he could see why he was twisted. His right wrist

had been taken across his body and handcuffed to the grab-handle over the passenger door. About the most significant act of rebellion that he could manage would be to wind down the window left-handed. What did Johnny think he was playing at? Nick jerked on the cuff, but the grab-handle didn't give.

"Don't waste your time, Nick," Johnny said.

Nick jerked again, fighting a rising sense of panic at being tethered. "I hate this," he said.

"I know. I'm sorry."

The BMW was ahead of them on the road.

The skill shown by the kids in starting the vehicle wasn't immediately evident in the way that they drove; Johnny was staying well back, giving them a chance to get the feel of the strange car. They were almost half a mile away from the flats before they found out how to turn the lights on. They were slow and their progress was ragged, weaving from side to side and clipping the paving when they rounded a corner; whenever they passed under a streetlight Nick would see them in shadowplay on the milky rear window, arguing and gesturing in what was obviously a team effort.

They seemed to be heading out of town, in the direction of the motorway.

"A lot of use that's going to be," Johnny said, "if they can't even find their way out of second gear."

Nick could hear the whining protest of the BMW's engine above their own, even though Johnny was keeping a distance of a hundred yards or more. This way, should a uniformed patrol cut into the chase, the Capri could simply fade away. Johnny had obviously concluded that it wouldn't look good to be seen chugging along behind a carload of offenders at the speed of a milk float, waiting for them to get their act together so that he could start a decent hot pursuit.

But then the kids managed to shift up, this time without crashing the gears, and where the BMW had been was suddenly just smoke.

"That's more like it," Johnny said, and they took off so hard that Nick felt as if the floor had been pulled out from under him.

The kid at the wheel, presumably Dean, seemed to find it easier to steer straight at speed; not that it was easy for Nick to tell, because the BMW had grabbed such a lead on them that he could only see their tail-lights in the distance. But this was a distance that Johnny was working quickly to close.

The road that the kids had chosen was long and straight and, as far as Nick could remember, led to nowhere other than a big motorway intersection and the new trading estates that had clustered around it on the very edge of town. At this time of night the estates were dark, their big parking lots empty, and the deep cut of the motorway passing beneath glowed with the allure of a firefly. The kids had two choices, the coast or the mountains.

They went for the mountains.

Before the motorway there had been only two routes which allowed a driver to travel over into the next county without having to swing all the way to the south, and these were narrow little passes that could be guaranteed to get snowed-up every winter. The new road had changed all of that, six lanes slamming up through some wild terrain where there had previously been nothing but sheep and stones and open moorland, and the occasional farm in those few places where there was enough shelter. Most of the farms were now in ruins. Once over the top, a traveller would cross the border and come down along the side of a valley that had been dammed in stages to make it into a series of descending shelves of water, stored-up life for those mill towns whose lights would seem to merge across the open country ahead.

But that would be a good fifteen or sixteen miles ahead of them. Right now the two cars were climbing steadily in the long haul up the lower slopes, passing an almost solid line of lorries and night-freight wagons that were rumbling along nose-to-tail like circus elephants in the slow lane. Johnny had lost a little more ground to the BMW in finding a gap to get onto the motorway, but now the Capri was eating up the distance.

"I was wrong about you," Nick said. "You're not just on the edge. You're fucking certifiable."

But then Johnny looked at Nick, and not at the road at all, for a terrifyingly long time; Nick glanced at the speedo and they were coming up to ninety.

"I wouldn't piss around with the driver's concentration if I were you," he said seriously. "Somebody's liable to get hurt."

And only then did he return his gaze to the road, just in time to take them out and around a milk truck that was out in the second lane and straining hard to move up the line. Nick had only ever once seen anything like that stare before, and it had been in the eyes of a man in a straitjacket. They'd pulled him on suspicion of attempted rape, and doctors had found more than forty pins, nails and spikes that he'd pushed into the various tender parts of his own anatomy over the past twenty years.

They were the eyes of a man who, wherever he looked, saw demons.

Johnny eased up behind the kids in the BMW and stayed there for a while, pacing them.

In a straight bet on flat-out speed Nick would have put money on the BMW, but these were kids whose driving skills were based on word-of-mouth and scant practice in stolen cars. They'd probably know as much about sex, and be about as good at it. It also didn't help that the BMW's engine had taken a serious battering at the hands of another set of joyriders already. Johnny swung into the outside lane and moved up alongside, slick and smooth and with no more than a couple of feet of space between the cars.

Nick looked across. Nobody looked back or met his eyes. Dean was gripping the wheel hard with both hands, while in the passenger seat alongside him a younger boy sat ready with his hand on the gearshift. In the motorway lighting their faces were lined like those of old, old men.

"This ought to make them notice us," Johnny said, and without warning he twitched the wheel and made a feint as if to ram the other car sideways. Even though he was already chained to it, Nick made a reflex grab at the handle overhead. Out of the corner of his eye he saw the BMW slide away as the teenager over-reacted. Their car seemed to be dropping into the immense maw of a big articulated rig only a few yards back from the Capri, but then an earth-shuddering blast from the rig's horn sent them bouncing out again like a silver ball on a pin table. For a few seconds Nick could see them swinging wildly from side to side, but then they'd slipped back out of his line of sight and he'd lost them.

Johnny was watching his mirror. Their speed began to fall. Nick turned a little in his seat and saw the BMW close behind and getting closer, and then without any warning Johnny briefly stabbed at the brakes so that the gap between the two cars snapped down from yards almost to inches. Nick's seatbelt pulled tight and his insides threatened to flip, and the driver behind them over-reacted again and slammed on all of the anchors so hard that his tyres seemed to scream with the agony of it.

Johnny moved out a lane, dropped down, and slid back alongside them again.

"That's better," he said.

Three of them looked back at Nick in terror now, one spark of emotion in each pair of dead little eyes in each of their death-camp faces; only the youngest seemed not to have grasped what they were getting down to here, and he was grinning wildly to show teeth so rotten that they didn't look real.

Then *bang*, they were away.

"Thank God for that," Johnny said, speeding up in pursuit again. "They finally found top gear."

The convoy in the slow lane had begun to thin out as they came up onto open moorland through a man-made gorge of sheer rock, the gaps between the trucks and the sixteen-wheelers increasing as the road levelled. This was about as bleak and bitter as it would get. The way Nick had heard it, the angles on the road surfaces for this stretch had been calculated so that winter blizzards would scour away their own snow to keep it clear. That wouldn't happen for some weeks yet, but even now as they came out of the gorge Nick could feel the Capri rocking in the crosswinds. He glanced at the speedometer, and in the glow of the dash illumination he could see that the needle was hovering somewhere around the hundred. Then Johnny's hand moved, and the dash went dark.

Johnny had killed all the lights.

They could see with no problem but they couldn't be seen; they were just a fast-moving shadow that came up behind the BMW and then suddenly exploded in light and noise as Johnny put the beams on full and leaned on the horn. Nick would have sworn that the car in front of them lifted six inches off the road in shock. He reckoned that if he'd been inside the BMW, by now he'd have needed a pacemaker and a new pair of pants.

Johnny said, "They should've gone for the back roads. This is getting boring." But then, just as he spoke, they both spotted a little black hole that had appeared off-centre in the BMW's shattered rear screen. They watched with an odd fascination as the hole grew bigger, much as one would watch something hatching its way out of an egg; except that the ugly duckling which emerged was the eight-year-old, chipping the edges of the glass away with what looked like a screwdriver.

"What are they doing?" Johnny said, but Nick couldn't see anything more than he could. He was wondering if he'd be able to reach his right-hand pants pocket with his free left hand, and whether he had any chance that Johnny might not notice the manoeuvre. His key-ring was in there, and his own handcuff key was on it. There weren't so many lock configurations on the standard-issue cuffs, and there was a chance that his own key might fit. But say it did, and say that he managed to reach it. What exactly did he think he was going to do then?

Ahead of them, the boy continued to enlarge the hole. Two of the others were moving around inside with a definite sense of purpose, but that was about all Nick knew until the BMW's spare wheel was abruptly manhandled up through the rough opening and then released to slide down the boot lid. Nick could only assume that they must have torn the rear seat apart to get through to it; and Johnny must have been as taken aback as he was, because he reacted almost too late as it hit the road edge-on and came bouncing up with terrific energy straight toward them. Johnny swerved and Nick heard a glancing bump on the side of the car, about as loud as he'd expect with a blow from a well-wrapped fist, and the Capri rocked so hard with the manoeuvre that for a moment Nick was sure that they were going to turn over.

It had to be luck, because Nick didn't believe that their timing could have been as good as it seemed; but as Johnny was fighting to keep all four wheels on the tarmac and the rogue spare was bouncing off to become a hazard for someone else, the BMW was taking the first exit to come along in the past five miles.

The Capri overshot.

For a moment Nick was certain that Johnny was simply going to slam into reverse and head back into the oncoming traffic. But he got them over onto the hard shoulder first . . . and then he did exactly as Nick had feared. Several of the big trucks rocked the car in their slipstream and blasted off their horns as they thundered by only feet away; Nick couldn't bear to watch but he couldn't bear to close his eyes, either. He looked down the grass banking to the lights of the sliproad, where the BMW was slowing to a halt.

What were they planning to do, abandon the car? That was the usual procedure with in-town joyriders. As soon as they'd been run down they'd stop and fling the doors open and disperse like fleas out of a rug. But this was the middle of nowhere, and it hardly seemed like an option.

Johnny lost patience with reversing. Instead he turned the Capri forward to lurch down the grass embankment, cutting straight across the rough in darkness and giving the vehicle a terrible hammering in the descent. Nick didn't get the BMW in his sights again until they skidded out onto the asphalt of the sliproad, and then it was to see that only one of the doors was open and one of the figures was out; the youngest, he could see now that the shaking had ended, and he was putting up a fierce fight against his expulsion. A hard shove sent him sprawling back, the door slammed, and the BMW was gone before he could bounce up again. He was dancing with rage as the Capri came through only seconds behind, more a strange little monkey-man than a child, and he showered them with dirt and turf grubbed up in handfuls from the roadside.

Johnny didn't even glance back. All of his attention was for the car ahead.

Nick could only keep on thinking; one of them had pushed his little brother out.

And he said, "Call it quits, Johnny."

"I don't call it quits with shite," Johnny said, changing down fast as the road began to climb again. "Tonight they finally get to learn what life's really about." And Nick looked at him and he would have sworn, without the green reflecting up onto his face from the dash his eyes would have been burning with a light all of their own.

They were going on up, this time on a narrow lane between dry-stone walls which had crumbled in places. The gaps had been patched with wire, and when Nick glanced back it was through one of these that he could see the lit ribbon of the motorway dropping out of sight in the distance below them. Now it was just two cars heading on into a darkness relieved only by the occasional dart of lightning from the distant storm that had been building since the afternoon, revealing endless moor to either side.

They were right on the kids' tail again as the road crested out and began to drop. Johnny's lights blazed into the stark interior of the BMW and picked out the three remaining boys in sharp detail. The one who was now alone in the ruined back seat turned to look at them, his face twisted in terror and with tears streaking clean lines down the grime on his cheeks as he screamed something at Johnny which the wind carried away.

And Nick heard Johnny say, softly, "Yeah, that'll do nicely."

Now he began to pressure them harder. They were all over the place while Johnny was keeping such tight control that the Capri might have been on rails. The BMW wobbled, sparks flew from the stonework to one side, its brakelights came on and Johnny had to stamp down hard to avoid a pileup; but then the BMW's lights cut completely and the car disappeared from view.

It was like some conjuring trick. It took several seconds to dawn on Nick that it had even happened, and by then the car was slowing to a stop.

He'd just about managed to work his key-ring half-out of his pocket in the darkness of the backroads. It was at an awkward angle and he didn't want Johnny to get any idea of what he was doing, so he held off for a while as Johnny put his head out of the window and guided the Capri back along the track. After about fifty yards Johnny stopped the car again, and this time he got out. He took the flashlight with him.

Now or never, Nick thought . . .

And thirty seconds later he was scrambling out of the Capri and squeezing some life back into his deadened right shoulder, leaving the opened cuffs swinging like an abandoned stage property in the second major illusion of the evening.

Johnny turned a moment after hearing the engine being switched off. He'd been working out how the disappearing stunt had been managed; in the flashlight beam from where he was now standing Nick could see a single-track road going off to the right of them, a sharp turn descending at such a steep angle that the BMW had simply dropped out of sight too fast for the move to be seen. In the silence after the Capri's engine died, some stray breeze brought them a noisy gear-change from a racing engine about a mile down and away across the moor.

Johnny, looking puzzled, said, "What's the idea?"

Nick had taken Johnny's keys from the ignition, and now he was going to make sure that the car stayed between the two of them. He said, "I'm keeping you on the rails, Johnny. Remember?"

"But – "

"No arguments. I'll drive us back. You need help."

Johnny sighed. Closed his eyes. Shook his head like a disappointed man.

He said, "You haven't understood a damn thing, have you?"

"More than I'd care to."

"You just won't open your eyes," Johnny said bitterly, and as he spoke he moved toward the car. Nick moved along as well, ready to dodge around if he had to. If necessary, he might have to go back without Johnny. In fact the more he thought about it, the more he wished he'd simply slid across into the driving seat and left him behind.

"I did my best for you, Nick," Johnny said. "Nobody could have done more. Well, I've had it with you."

And as he was speaking, Johnny reached down into the forward wheel arch of the Capri and came out with a small magnetised key box. Nick could only watch with a sick kind of fascination as Johnny took out a spare set of keys and tossed the empty box away into darkness.

"I'm going to remember this," he said. "When I've finished with them, I'm coming back for you."

There was a dark fire in his eyes.

"As of now, you're in the book."

And as he slid back into the car, right up until the very last moment, those eyes held onto Nick's like the eyes of a snake to its prey.

So there it was, Nick's best shot, and he'd effected nothing more than a hiccup in the rhythm of Johnny's madness. He ran to the wall to watch Johnny's descent, but the Capri's rear lights could only be glimpsed intermittently. As he strained to see, lightning briefly illuminated moorland falling away and a sheen of dammed water some way further down. When thunder rolled a few seconds later, it seemed shockingly close after having been a part of the background for so many hours; and for some inexplicable reason Nick thought of that falling TV set, and of the way that the thud of its implosion had seemed to be answered from far away as if some cub had called to its mother.

He listened for the sound of the Capri's engine as the thunder rolled away and faded.

But there was nothing, nothing at all.

So then, as the mad dog weather started to turn to rain, he picked up the flashlight at the roadside where Johnny had left it, still switched on and with its beam spilling out across the asphalt. He shone it downward and found that he was looking at little more than a dirt road with the parallel scars of the night's use showing fresh.

He followed them down. He passed an open gate and a couple of Water Authority signs, but there was nothing else to indicate that the track was ever much used. At the bottom was the reservoir, black water puckering in the rain; here the track swung left to cross the dam.

The dirt scars didn't. They went straight out to the edge, and ended there.

For more than a minute Nick stood on the dam and stared out into nothing, the skies above him trembling so hard that the ground itself seemed to be shaking in unison. The rain was increasing steadily, a dense shower of silver darts through the flashlight's beam; this showed a bank so steep that he wouldn't have cared to tackle it without a rope even if conditions were ideal. Beyond that the light just wasted itself out in nowhere, almost as if he were shining it into a bottomless pit.

He heard only the thunder.

He saw only the rain.

7

Nobody even asked.

At least not straight out, although some senior officer that he didn't know rang him just after eleven and asked him when had he last seen Johnny Mays. Nick replied that it had been when they'd separated after the previous night's relief, which was true enough. He didn't plan to let out any more information than was necessary, at least until he knew how he stood. Being a witness to Johnny's demise was one thing; to be seen as his partner in terror would be something else again. The senior man rang off without telling him any more, other than to see his sergeant as soon as he'd reported in.

Nick had walked to the nearest main road and picked up a lift back into town with a couple in a Bedford van. By that time, he was so sodden that even the most hardhearted of drivers couldn't have passed him by. At the flat he stripped off and sat hunched on the tiles in the corner of the shower stall until the water that beat on him no longer ran hot. He knew that he'd slept afterwards, although he felt as if he hadn't.

And how did Johnny Mays sleep now, he wondered?

With the dead, of that much Nick was sure. He felt an awful, empty ache, the kind that made him want to run back the tape and erase the last few hours so that he could record over them and this time, he'd make certain it came out the way that he'd meant it to be.

Like the man had said. Everybody needed a trip to Fantasy Island, now and again. Today Nick just happened to need one more than most.

"Sorry, Johnny," he said to the grey sky outside the living-room window.

And then he got out the Yellow Pages and called a breakers' yard, and told them where to find his car.

They hauled up the empty Capri at about two in the afternoon. Three plastic body bags and the even more damaged shell of the BMW were already on the grass by the side of the reservoir, broken pieces from a dangerous game. Now it was Bruno's job to work out the plays with little more than the scorecard to go on; that, and just a few witnessed fragments from the early hours of the morning.

The first couple of calls to come in had been second-hand, relayed CB messages from night-freight drivers out on the motorway. They'd told of a fierce pursuit at dangerous speeds and one of them, who was now proving difficult to track down, had referred to a Capri without any lights. By the time that regular phone reports had started to come in, a motorway patrol had already been out and found nothing on the stretch apart from an abandoned car wheel on the shoulder and, in an irrelevant aside, some ladies' underwear hanging from a bush. When licence numbers given in one of the calls had been tracked down, interest had intensified at the discovery that one of them was listed as stolen (since the paperwork for its removal from the register was still lying in an *Out* tray in a second-floor office), while the other was the personal vehicle of a plainclothes officer.

And if anybody raised an eyebrow at the thought of the officer in question being a certain Johnny Mays, nobody actually went public in their thinking.

There had been nothing to add until twenty minutes after nine, when a Water Board worker had climbed out of his Land Rover to look first at the two sets of tyre tracks angled out into nowhere – a night's rain had blurred them, but they were still unmistakably fresh – and then at the youth floating face-down in the reservoir some distance below. He'd reached the rapid conclusion that all was not quite as it ought to be·in the world of flood levels and filtration, and he'd called his supervisor. The village man from the next valley was the first police presence on the scene, and in heading out to gaff the body with a boathook he'd felt a bump as the inflatable had passed over some shallow-lying obstacle. The obstacle had proved to be the roof of the BMW, and the village man decided that life in the sticks might have something to offer after all.

Now the scene was quite different. The first run of emergency traffic had turned the dirt track into an impassable mire, and part of a stone wall had been taken down to provide an alternative access. There were cars and vans and police divers and police divers' support vehicles, and in the midst of it all the big crane that was now lifting Johnny Mays' Capri from one of the deeper and darker stretches of water. The car spun slowly on its cable as the giant hydraulic arm brought it in, three of the divers wading up out of the shallows behind it, and Bruno was reminded of some absurd fairground apparatus. What did his kids call them? White-knuckle rides.

He glanced at the kids on the ground, anonymous and cold in the solitude of their plastic shrouds. Pale as the whitest of knuckles, all three of them. The mortuary people had wanted to know how many of their re-usable steel coffins they should bring.

"Bring whatever you've got," he'd told them. "We're not finished yet."

The Capri came down to earth with a bump, spewing water at every seam. Scenes of Crime moved in immediately, and the divers' team leader dragged off his mask as he squelched over to Bruno.

"What's the score?" Bruno said.

"It's bloody freezing, I can tell you that."

"And?"

"No sign of him, just the empty car. There's a lot of area to cover, and there can be some strong currents when the sluices are open. We'll find him, but I wouldn't like to say when."

"Thanks."

"You could always sit on the bank and wait it out. Give him a few days for the gases to get going and then he'll come up like a cork."

"Wonderful."

"You want to save manpower, just leave a couple of cadets with an inflatable and a boathook."

"And a good supply of sickbags. This is city drinking water, George."

The team leader shook his head. "Never touch the stuff myself," he said. "I've heard what fish do in it."

Bruno watched the activity around the Capri for a while. From here, his men resembled a bunch of cargo cultists re-enacting open heart surgery with garden tools. One unusual detail that stuck in his mind; from this angle he could see right through the car to the man-made lake beyond, and in clear silhouette he could see the regulation handcuffs that hung, open-ended, from the grab bar over on the passenger side. But then somebody moved into the way, and Bruno let the thought go.

He looked up, trying to judge the distance that both cars had fallen. The turfed face of the upper dam was almost as sheer as a cliff, and neither vehicle had managed even so much as a touch-and-bounce on the way down. They'd simply sailed straight out and then, long seconds later, lost all grace in one shattering instant. Now they were side by side, beaten and seeping and no longer driveable.

Bruno called over his sergeant. "George says it's empty," he said.

"George isn't wrong," the sergeant agreed. His name was Bob Glover, and he was an ex-Navy man with five years in the Hong Kong Police before he'd moved home and onto the Division. "The driver's side-window was open and the seatbelt wasn't engaged. He could've been sucked out as the car settled."

"Any chance he might have survived?"

"If we find him and he's something other than ground-bait, I'll say yes. Otherwise I'll just say forget it. I mean, look at the drop."

Looking at the drop was easy. It was thinking about it that made Bruno's sphincter pucker up. He said, "Let's set up an area search, just in case. Make it a one-mile radius with whoever we can spare. And check on any likely-looking farmhouses or cottages."

"For what? Johnny Mays knocking on the door at midnight? He was a mad bastard, but there's a limit."

"I know. But let's do it anyway. I'll bet you a gold brick to a dog biscuit that we'll have an enquiry to worry about on top of everything else."

Bob Glover looked thoughtful. "Do the lads know?" he said.

"The lads are already in action," Bruno assured him. "It'll be all that I can do to tone their efforts down a bit."

So then the sergeant glanced over to the lone figure who'd been watching from the banking for most of the past hour. "And what does he know about it?" he said.

"That's what I'm hoping to find out," Bruno said.

Nick had to sit in the back of Bruno's car as they came away, because the passenger seat was almost buried under files and file boxes. It was all the same to Nick. He wasn't feeling at his most communicative, anyway.

He'd never actually been into Johnny's place before, although they'd stopped by there during working hours one time so that Johnny could pick up his cashcard. He had a lease on the upper storey of a house, a four-flat conversion with a caretaker/landlord in the basement who, according to Johnny, emerged like a Morlock every now and again to fix pipes or replace lightbulbs, or to tack nasty notes about bicycles to the door of the school-teacher on the second floor. They picked up Johnny's key from under the teacher's mat – a trade arrangement intended to confuse any housebreaker who made it into the communal stairway – and climbed the stairs to the top.

Bruno opened the door, Nick followed him into the short hallway.

And froze, as Johnny Mays emerged from the room at its end to demand what the fuck was going on.

Except that it wasn't Johnny, didn't even look much like him, and the expression on his face was one of wary apprehension rather than outrage; he was obviously a stranger in the place himself and when he recognised Bruno, he seemed to relax a little.

Bruno said, "What are *you* playing at?"

"Just a spot of housekeeping, boss," the man said, and from the room behind him came the sound of drawers being opened and cupboard doors thrown back. Nick glanced through the door to his left, into the apartment's single bedroom. The bed was unmade, and there was a damp smell in the air as if a dog had peed somewhere around.

"Well, I haven't seen you," Bruno said in a tone that didn't allow for any argument, and then he indicated for Nick to precede him into what turned out to be the kitchen. There were plates and dishes stacked high in the sink, and opened cans on the side. Over on the blue formica-topped table, a breakfast cereal packet stood with a small handful of its contents scattered around it. In amongst the flakes, the faint glitter of sugar that had been spilled and then forgotten. Signs of life, Nick would have called these at almost any other time . . . but not today.

Bruno closed the door behind them, and the message was clear.

Time for some straight talk.

Nick said, "How are you reading it?"

"Off-duty policeman in pursuit of a stolen car. Or have you got anything else in mind?"

"What about witnesses?"

"Enough of them, along the way. It must have been like the Circus Maximus up there, for a while."

Nick half-smiled. "Johnny wasn't the safest driver I ever saw."

Bruno's expression didn't change, but his stillness lasted too long for comfort.

"You've got a fucking nerve," he said at last, and he said it quietly.

Nick felt something inside him drawing tight. "Oh?"

"You watched him going right down the tubes. It was plain enough that Johnny Mays was falling apart, and you didn't lift a finger to help him."

There was a *thump* from the next room, as of something being dropped. Nick said, "Sure. It's all down to me. And where were you while all this was going on?"

"I was around."

"Offering a shoulder to cry on, but you sure as hell weren't offering to take any of the weight. How many people around here knew how it was going with him? Let him walk through his appraisal once a year with his happy-face on as if there wasn't a thing wrong in his world?" Nick looked down at the floor, which didn't appear to have been wiped-over since the day the tiles had been laid. What was the matter, here? One moment of intense anger, and now it was all running out of him like dry sand.

He said, "Johnny Mays should have been out of it long before I ever got here. I wish he had been."

"Nobody else was that close to him."

"I wasn't close to him. He just kept telling me I was. It's not the same thing."

"Yeah, well . . ." Bruno said. He seemed less certain now, glancing around as if he'd only just woken up to find himself somewhere strange; or perhaps he was simply thinking that he'd misjudged the situation with Nick and Johnny, like a man punching at a shape through a curtain and hearing a small child cry out. He said, "What's done is done. At least this way, Johnny gets to be a hero."

"And it's the wrong time to rock the boat."

"You said it. Making him look bad after the event could lose you a lot of friends around here."

"Come on, Bruno. Basically, I'm screwed whatever I do. I could have been the shit who turned him in, but now I'm the shit who didn't. Try to set things straight, and I'm dancing on a good man's grave."

"Let it rest, then," Bruno suggested quietly.

"And how long do you reckon I've got?"

"Until when?"

"Until the whispering starts."

"Now you're just being paranoid."

"Easy for you to say. I've been here before. Why do you think I had to make a move to this town in the first place?"

"I didn't know you'd *had* to do anything."

Nick moved to the window and looked out. The window was . . . oh, what the hell, there was no point in cataloguing all the details; Johnny kept house like a cockroach. Through the smeary glass Nick could see a vista of roofs and fenced-in gardens down below, everything from the basic dog-dirt and chickweed variety right up to the obsessive.

Nick said, "One time, I saw something I wasn't supposed to and I didn't like it, so I did my canary number. I got a pat on the head, and forever after it was like living below zero. There are limits, Bruno. You can only stick that kind of treatment for so long."

The truth of it; Nick had been on the squad cars, night duty, when he'd seen two fellow-officers take hold of a drunk by an arm each and boost him headfirst into a concrete post. The drunk was a man of about twenty-four, hair cut so close that his head was almost shaved, an elaborate tattoo on his skull above the hairline. He'd spat upon the uniform of one of the officers. He bounced off the post and then sat down heavily, legs giving way beneath him. He was booked, slung in a cell, and checked every fifteen minutes until the police surgeon stopped by. Then he got a transfer to hospital where it was discovered that he could no longer speak, read, or feed himself. The family sued. Nick had gone to his chief and told what he'd seen. That same night, he got the first of the phonecalls. Three days later, when he came into the building and opened his locker, it was to find a slashed-open bag of used hospital swabs, leftovers – he was later to learn – from a cancer exploratory at the local Infirmary.

It wasn't just the two men on suspension, it was everybody. He was made to feel worse than a leper. More unwelcome around his own station than even a social worker. So he'd invented some excuse for a transfer on compassionate grounds, determined never to risk pulling the sky down onto himself like that again . . .

And with the wit of the gods, they'd given him Johnny Mays.

Bruno said, "Have you ever thought of finding some other line of business?"

"Strange you should say that," Nick said. "I think about it more and more."

When they went out from the kitchen, the two men who'd gone in before them were closing doors and getting ready to leave.

Bruno said, "Anything I ought to know about?"

"Just some rubbish for the shredder," one of them said. "Nothing to make the earth move. And we found these."

From out of a plastic carrier bag, his colleague produced two police radios. The damn things cost two hundred apiece, easily, and they were supposed to be tracked around more closely than spy satellites. How Johnny had managed to get away with them was anybody's guess.

And Johnny wouldn't be telling. Not unless somebody wanted to fix up a seance.

The radios went back into the bag, and the first man said, "We're done, now. Place is all yours."

"Nah." Bruno glanced at Nick. "I think we've covered what's necessary. Isn't that right?"

"I should think it is," Nick said.

———

He'd been told to go home, but he didn't. He went back to the station and up to the squadroom; all of the plainclothes people were out but there were a few uniforms around, chatting and killing time and checking their watches for wherever they had to be next. Nick had always liked squadroom atmosphere, because it was a time-out from the endless and sometimes brutal game that was being played on the streets. The fact that it was mostly endless and only infrequently brutal didn't seem to matter so much, here; the powderkeg theory of local civilisation was essential to all of the better stories and, as Nick himself had once said, where was the point in having a tin star without a Dodge City in which to wear it?

Perhaps it was his imagination. A couple of people said hello. But within five minutes of his arriving, the squadroom had all but emptied.

He went through into the writing-room next door. The tables in here were like old school desks and the typewriters – well, whenever Nick had to use one of these old manual heavyweights, the sight of the hammers slamming down onto the ribbon always reminded him of the slave beating two-handed time on the galley in *Ben Hur*. There was no-one else around, although over by the sink a dented Russell Hobbs kettle was just coming up to the boil.

The kettle switch clicked out, the empty mugs on the tray waited, but nobody came in.

Nick seated himself at one of the tables. Picked up a sheet of paper, and rolled it into the machine.

"Ramming speed!" he said, and started to type.

8

The inquest on the boys was opened in the coroner's courtroom in the dowdy building that stood next to the police station. Nick was there, but he wasn't called. Bruno was, but only to say that police enquiries were still continuing. The coroner took identification evidence and then adjourned the hearing to await the outcome of the police investigation.

No date had yet been set for the inquest on Johnny Mays. The divers were still looking for his body.

Nick was beginning to wonder what kind of a state Johnny would be in when he finally surfaced, and who was going to be asked to make the formal ID; he had an uneasy feeling that it was going to be him, and he wondered if it would be worth taking some leave and putting himself at an inconvenient distance for a while. He'd seen his share of the dead, and he'd come to recognise them for what he believed them to be – discarded husks, nothing more than the empty mansions of the living – but a floater was something else. After a few days a floater became a gross caricature of a human being, hard enough to bear in a stranger but the stuff of nightmares when it was someone cl

(*But we weren't close*, he had to remind himself)

when it was someone closer to home.

The courthouse and the police station were linked by one set of double doors on the second floor, where prisoners could be taken through from the Bridewell cells for their moment in the spotlight. To get to this, Nick and Bruno had to walk through the custody area where

Bruno stopped to ask the Bridewell sergeant about his daughter, who'd apparently undergone an eye operation a couple of weeks before. Nick could have walked on alone, but he waited.

"I suppose that makes it official," he said to Bruno as the two of them went through the doors and back onto home territory.

"As good as," Bruno said. "Why, you think they missed anything?"

A WPC stepped aside for Bruno as they turned into the stairwell; and for Nick, since she didn't know him or his rank. Nick said, "I kind of got the feeling we were detailing the effects and glossing over the causes. Nobody's asked me anything, here. The biggest risk I seem to be running is of getting deafened by the silence."

They stopped at the stairs. Bruno said, "And what, exactly, did you want to add?"

Nick glanced over his shoulder, but the WPC had gone.

"That I was with him until about two minutes before he went over," he said in a lowered voice, not wanting it to carry to every floor in the building.

Bruno was stony.

"You're kidding me," he said.

"I was in the car, I saw it all. Had to hitch back afterwards. Everybody's been avoiding me, nobody even asked how I got the black eye, and there hasn't been one accurate conclusion in the investigation so far. Says a lot for our methods, don't you think?"

"I don't think I want to hear this," Bruno said.

"Your choice, Bruno. Here."

Bruno looked at the envelope without taking it. "What's this?"

"The full story."

Bruno was on the spot, and he didn't like it. Nick didn't much like putting him there, either, but he also didn't feel that he could carry on like this alone.

Bruno said, "What good's it going to do now?"

"You don't want to read it, then stick it in a drawer somewhere. But that's your decision, Bruno, not mine. I've had it with listening to everyone's problems and then turning around to tell mine and finding that I'm looking at the wall."

"And if nobody believes it? Because I can tell you now, nobody's going to want to."

"There's stuff in there you can check. Start with the handcuffs, nobody's even mentioned them yet. But once you've started, there won't be any going back."

"Thanks a bunch," Bruno said bleakly.

And then, hesitantly, he took the envelope. It felt heavy, and not only with the weight of the typescript pages inside. Nick was watching him, and he knew that Bruno had just turned a corner into a new country under the light of a different sun. The landscape wasn't so welcoming here . . . but at least Nick would no longer be the only surviving figure in it.

Bruno said, "What are you going to do now?"

"That's what I have to decide," Nick said.

———

Bruno entered his office. He only usually closed the door for disciplinary interviews, and never when he was alone; but he closed it now.

He dropped Nick's envelope on his desk.

And as he walked around to his chair he found that he couldn't take his eyes off it, as if the envelope were some dangerous device that he would soon have the job of defusing.

Bruno reckoned that he was as straight as anyone could ask, but he was also a realist. There probably wasn't a single sworn officer on the division who didn't harbour some unspoken suspicion about the fatal chase involving Johnny Mays, particularly when Johnny's past character was taken into consideration. Bruno had spotted him early, and had noted him as someone to be watched; Johnny's problems had seemed to be those generated by a dangerous combination of high self-regard and a mediocre level of ability, the kind of flaw that distilled aggression out of bitterness and disguised the cocktail with a dash of low cunning.

But he hadn't seen any great virtue in raising the matter now. Maybe Johnny had pushed the kids, but that was the worst reading he'd been able to give it so far. All three of the boys had previous form for the same kind of offence, they'd probably been looking forward to lives of petty crime or worse, and the only people who were weeping for them now were the people who'd failed them the most when they'd been alive. Johnny may have pressured them out there on the road, but surely that was as far as it went. And who would be helped by having it said aloud, apart from those critics of the police who selected their examples so carefully that even the Chunky Bears could be made to look like stormtroopers?

It was so quiet in the office, with the door closed.

Not something he'd care to have to get used to.

Bruno sighed, and pulled open one of his desk drawers. There was nothing inside other than the usual bits and pieces of office junk and a fat Nelson De Mille paperback that he'd started once but never had the time to finish. He hesitated for a moment, and then he reached across for Nick's envelope.

He dropped the envelope into the drawer, where it lay amongst the half-used Biros and form pads and a tangle of elastic bands resembling a nest of snakes. He was contemplating it there when someone tapped at the door; he closed the drawer quickly, almost like a scoutmaster panicking over a spanking magazine.

"Come in," he called out, and the door opened just far enough for the civilian secretary from the pool at the end of the corridor to look in.

"Everything all right?" she said. She had some typed

letters for his signature, but this apparent change in routine had thrown her.

"Everything's fine," Bruno said. "Come on in."

She came into the office.

And he added, "You can leave the door open."

That evening, after Nick had explained everything to Jennifer over a can of Breaker from the fridge, some pizza from the freezer, and the usual stack of law books and police manuals on the kitchen table, she said, "Why couldn't you at least have told me?"

"I did," he said.

"I don't just mean about Johnny Mays. I mean about you being there with the cars and the kids."

"When? All we ever seem to do is pass in the doorway. I couldn't exactly leave a note with the rent on the cork board, could I?"

They were sitting by the warm light of a shaded table lamp, and the rest of the kitchen was just a sketch in the darkness around them. What he really wanted her to do was maybe come around to stand beside him and touch his shoulder and say *Sorry, Nick*, saying it gently as she had once before, and then he could put his hand over hers and say *It's all right*, and somehow it would be. But that would have to be some other Jennifer, the one that didn't seem to be around so often these days. He was still getting a recurrent vision where he'd take her by the hand and lead her down to the sea; but that was in dreams, and nowhere else.

This was all wrong. How was he supposed to make her understand how it was for him, when she could seem more of a stranger now than she ever had been in the beginning?

She said, "What's going to happen now?"

And in his mind, after the briefest contact, her hand slid away and left him holding nothing.

"I don't know," he said. "It's really down to Bruno."

"You're finished if it comes out. You know that."

"It's one possibility."

"I don't see any other. How can you stand it, just waiting for the axe to fall?"

Nick shrugged. Outside, rain dashed against the kitchen window like a handful of beads. As if in response Jennifer pushed back her chair and stood, rising out of the light.

He said, "I can't explain it. Part of me thinks of how I let Johnny down and that it's okay, I deserve whatever I get. And another part of me thinks fuck it, what did I owe him anyway. But mostly," he said, "I just feel dead, right here." And he tapped his chest, right in the middle. "You know I spoke to Johnny's parents last night?"

"I didn't even know they were around," Jennifer said from over by the window. She was looking out through the jewelled glass and into the rain, which had been threatening its arrival like an unpaid creditor since the late afternoon.

"I called them. They were all set to come out when they heard, had the car loaded up and everything, but then his mother wouldn't leave the house. Couldn't face it. Said it would be like killing him, making it all final, and she couldn't bring herself to do it. Can you understand that?"

"People get strange under pressure."

"I knew what she meant. They asked me if I'd see that Johnny's personal stuff got sent back to them, and I said that I would. But I've been thinking about it. I reckon I ought to take it myself."

He could see her turn her head to look at him, but that was all he could see. He was in the light and she was in the shadows, and there seemed to be something more than distance that was separating them now. And the light was artificial whereas the shadows were real, and this sense of inversion only helped to confirm the feeling that Nick had somehow lost his grip o₁ the certainties of his life.

She said, "You're going away?"

"For a while. For all kinds of reasons. I need to get out of it, and I don't want to see Johnny when they bring him up. I've got a lot of thinking to do and I haven't had much practice."

"I think it's the right thing for you. Going home, I mean."

"I don't call it home. I don't think I call *anywhere* home. And as for roots, I don't know that I've got any. Maybe I'm just trying to find the point where it all started to go wrong."

"You can't change anything now."

"I know."

Jennifer shifted in the darkness. "Nick," she began, but then her voice tailed away uncomfortably.

And Nick, making a guess at what might be coming next, said, "Don't worry about the money for the call. I left it by the phone."

"The money doesn't matter. It's something I've been wanting to ask you."

"Oh?"

"I wanted to ask if you'd consider moving out. Permanently, I mean."

Nick sat in silence as he took this in, the only sound in the kitchen the intermittent drumming of the rain against the glass.

"Find somewhere else?" he said at last, aware of how stupid it sounded – what else could she have meant, get himself a cardboard box under a bridge somewhere? But unable, for the moment, to think of any more coherent response.

"It isn't anything personal," she said with a tad too much eagerness, and Nick realised that with this on her mind she'd probably only been half-listening to him at best. "But I mean, you and me, we're known about . . . and I'm being dead honest with you, Nick, I don't want to lose the chance of this transfer for *anything*."

"I can see that," Nick said.

"And I mean, it's not as if we were really serious, is it?"

He knew she could see him, so he managed a smile. "Doesn't look that way."

"We can still be friends. And when it's all straightened out . . . oh shit, I had it all worked out what I was going to say, and now I hate the way I'm sounding."

"It's all right," Nick said. "I understand."

"You do?"

"It's something important to you, and you don't want it put at risk."

"And you're not angry?"

"I'm not angry."

But he wished that their positions could have been switched, so that he wouldn't have to worry about the brightness of the stage lights showing up the flaws in his performance. Not that it would have mattered. He was only telling Jennifer what he knew she wanted to hear, which made her an easy house to play to.

She said, "I might have known that you'd take it this way. Thanks, Nick."

"Pleasure," he said.

"I'm not asking you to clear out straight away, or anything like that. And you're welcome to leave your stuff here until you've decided what you're going to do." And as she was saying this, she moved around behind him.

He felt her hand touch his shoulder, gently.

"I do like you a lot, you know," she said.

And Nick thought sadly, *Too late.*

Too late.

And he said, "I suppose I'd better rent a car."

9

The key was gone from under the schoolteacher's mat, but the landlord allowed Nick into Johnny's flat with ill-disguised bad grace. Once inside, he followed Nick from room to room. No taller than Nick's shoulder, he was overweight and seedy-looking and appeared to be wearing two of everything – two shirts, two equally worn-out pullovers and, for all Nick could tell, two sets of grimy pre-war underwear. Nick was obviously supposed to feel guilty for all the trouble he was causing and he thought Yeah, like keeping you out of the singles bars or away from disco-dancing practice.

The man said, "How many times are you people going to want to turn the place over?"

"Why?" Nick said. "Do we leave a mess?"

They were in Johnny's bedroom, and mess was hardly the word for it. No police search, covert or official, had created this; there was too much method in the disorder, too much indication that the find-it-where-it-fell philosophy was the key to Johnny's domestic habits. The last time he'd been here Nick had progressed no further than the kitchen, but now he saw nothing to surprise him or change his mind. The duvet on the bed was like some animal's nest, and scattered with toast crumbs. A portable TV set stood at the foot of the bed, on two old suitcases which served as a table. The reading lamp had no shade; but no matter, it had no lightbulb either. On top of the bedside unit next to the lamp was a stack of second-hand paperbacks, and it was impossible to tell whether these were discards or waiting to be read. Only one of them, a dog-eared copy of *Tarzan and the Leopard Men*, had any kind of a page marker in it.

No, when it came to mess, Johnny could obviously handle the whole show without need of support.

"All this coming and going, it lowers the tone," the landlord said. "What are people going to be thinking?"

"If I knew that, I wouldn't be here. I'd be out getting rich."

"Me too, pal. Me too." Then the landlord eyed the Tarzan book that Nick was riffling through. "Intellectual, was he?"

"He was an old friend of mine," Nick said, and the landlord at least had the wits to shut up for a while. Nick moved the TV set from the empty suitcases and laid these open on the bed, ready to take any minor bits and pieces that would fall within his brief of 'personal stuff'. They wouldn't be interested in what things were worth, Johnny's father had told him over the phone. Just the little things that said 'Johnny Mays' and nobody else. They'd worry about the rest of it later.

The flat was a place of odd contrasts. The carpets hadn't been vacuumed since Day One and the toilet handle must have broken sometime soon after that, because the cistern lid had been laid to one side so that anybody using it could reach in and pull up the hook to make it flush. Out in the lounge, Johnny obviously had a favourite chair and used the others as storage for his records and old magazines. A top-of-the-range compact disc player stood on a broken table. On the floor amidst a mess of wires were two video recorders, looking as if he'd just taken them out of the boxes and was trying them out with the intention of finding a permanent spot for them later . . . except that they'd stayed where they were and gathered dust, like abandoned artifacts in the shadow of some distant volcano. A second TV stood in here, a big one with stereo speakers and a stack of pre-recorded tapes up on top.

Toys and squalor, Nick thought. Toys and squalor.

And wherever he went, the landlord followed him like an old pet dog.

"I'm sorry?" Nick said suddenly and for no apparent reason as they looked into the boxroom, which it had to be because there were so many empty boxes lying around.

The landlord was puzzled. "I didn't say anything."

"Oh," Nick said. "I must be hearing those voices again."

"What voices?"

"The ones that tell me what to do. They say they're angels, but I'm not so sure."

The landlord stared at Nick for a moment.

Then he decided that he had some traps to lay down in the basement, and left Nick to it.

The task was a short-lived and dispiriting one. Almost anybody could have lived here; the most personal thing that Nick could find was Johnny's passport. Most of what he threw into the suitcases was junk that may or may not have had some significance for the owner, but it was really too late for a stranger to know. But what did it matter? Johnny's mother would look over them and see Johnny's favourite paperweight, his second-best wristwatch, the electric razor that he used every day (when he remembered). And if the effect was actually fakery . . . well, that was magic for you.

He hesitated only once, and that was over the book. For the second time, he opened it up at the place that Johnny had marked.

It wasn't the novel itself, but the marker that interested him. It was a photograph, a narrow sliver cut from a bigger print, and it showed a skinny teenaged girl leaning on a radiator with a big window behind. It was pretty old. Time had leached the colours into pastel shades of white.

Nick studied it for a while.

Then he put it back into the book, and slipped the book into his jacket pocket.

Half an hour later, he brought down the two cases and a box. On his second trip down the stairs, he found the landlord waiting for him just outside the main door. He followed Nick to the estate car (rented) that was standing in Johnny's old space on the asphalt patch that had once been the front garden. He didn't make any move to help as Nick steadied the box against the chromework so that he could open up the tailgate, but stood with hands in pockets while watching and sucking at his teeth.

He said, "How much are you going to be taking?"

"Just the personal stuff," Nick said, and after making sure that the box and the cases were secure he slammed the tailgate down. It took him a couple of tries to make it stay. "I don't know what's going to happen to the rest of it."

"Nobody seems to be able to give me a straight answer. Is he dead, or isn't he?"

Nick walked around to the driver's door.

"Well," he said, "I wouldn't count on him coming back."

And at about the time that Nick was driving away from his former home, Johnny Mays was waking up in heaven.

10

It had to be heaven, because hell could never be this cold.

Johnny lay hunched under the mouldy-smelling covers, staring up at the ceiling and trying to find some point of access into his memory. It was like running through a deck of empty cards. He didn't know where he was or how he came to be here, and he didn't know why he'd come around with such a headache and such a desperate thirst. Had he been ill? Johnny hated to be ill. Sick people made him angry, sucking up all the attention from everyone around them, because when Johnny felt bad he always had to crawl off like a dog and suffer alone.

Nothing.

What if it was a brain tumour? The idea of a brain tumour had always fascinated and terrified him, even more than the thought of a stroke. The thought of a stroke just terrified him, period. He closed his eyes and tried to get his mind back up to speed, but his mind didn't want to respond. He felt as if he was wandering around in a strange house, bumping into sheeted furniture. What he needed was something, any one thing, that he could pick out and hold onto, some notion that was safe and unambiguous, and then he could take it from there.

He thought he had it.

I'm Johnny Mays, he whispered, and began to feel better.

Maybe he'd taken a hammering. Some of those fairies

in the gay clubs lifted weights, and it showed. And they might just about have had the nerve, in some unlit back alley with bags over their heads, and Johnny getting out of his car alone and without looking around him first . . .

But no. Such a scene had no place in Johnny's self-image, which was widescreen and in full colour and played to a continuous John Barry soundtrack. If Johnny Mays was going to suffer then he'd be Spartacus on the cross, and nothing so pitiful as a victim.

Johnny hated victims.

There, now, he thought. Isn't that something to hang onto?

And then he opened his eyes again.

The ceiling above him was angled, and decorated in a woodchip paper that had become waterstained and dotted with black spores. Cheap and old, he thought. I'm somewhere cheap and old. Holding up the ceiling was a thick beam dotted with woodworm holes, and on the beam hung a silver-painted horseshoe – not just some ornament but the real thing, coarse and heavy and beaten out on an anvil.

And if he wanted to know anything more, he was at least going to have to move his head.

Ten minutes later he was sitting on the edge of the mattress and fighting the almost overpowering urge to let himself fall back into the outspread arms of something that, as he now half-appreciated with a sense of unspoken awe, might actually prove to be a state darker and more permanent than sleep. Physically he was at his limits, and that was no exaggeration. He was starved and he was dehydrated, and even his kidneys hurt.

His clothes were gone and he was wearing stale pyjamas that hung on him like a tent. He'd been lying on an unmade bed and covered by a heap of old overcoats. On the floor by the bed were an empty soup-bowl and spoon. The only heat in the room was from a single-bar electric fire that seemed to be having no effect at all;

Johnny was racked by uncontrollable shivers, and so he reached for one of the overcoats with the idea of pulling it on.

There wasn't much else to see. It was a room from deep in his past, the kind of grim bedchamber that as a child he'd always associated with elderly relatives and the smell of embrocation. A cast-iron fireplace and a threadbare carpet, a wardrobe like an oak sarcophagus, a squat and ugly chest of drawers in matching timber . . . even the daylight in here seemed strained and enfeebled, and to speak of times long gone and best forgotten.

With his arms finally into the sleeves and the sleeves hanging down over his knuckles, Johnny tried to stand.

The room was dim but the landing outside was darker, and when he tried to call out he could manage no louder sound than the whisper in which he'd spoken his own name – how long ago, now? It was impossible to tell. Johnny had no illusions about the seriousness of his situation, here. Something vital hung in the balance, and although he didn't know its name he knew that his opportunities to influence the outcome were diminishing by the minute.

But he was Johnny Mays. Johnny Mays didn't let go so easily.

Creaking like a scarecrow, he made his unsteady way downstairs.

From the living-room window he could see one end of a stone-walled yard with open country beyond. There were hills in the near distance, bleached of detail by a fine mist that wasn't quite rain. The yard stones were a deep, slaty green, as probably was the house itself. Somewhere outside a solitary cow or calf was lowing in distress, but Johnny ignored it. He had problems enough of his own.

It was even colder down here than it had been upstairs. There had been a fire in the living-room grate, but it had burned out and its ashes weren't even warm. By the hearth, in the room's only armchair, sat the tenant of the cottage. He was at least sixty years old, thin and weatherbeaten and not too strong-looking, and like the fire he was several days dead. His fingers were locked like claws onto the arms of the chair, as if in reaction to a spasm of agony that had hit and killed him with the speed and surprise of an unscheduled train.

Johnny studied the slack face, but not for long. Death didn't look so remarkable on old people, he always thought. He went looking for something to eat.

He found his clothes in the kitchen. They'd been hung out on a clotheshorse to dry, but they looked pretty well ruined. He couldn't remember how. On the well-worn plastic cloth that covered the table, the contents of his pockets had been spread out.

His black book was there.

It was swollen and impossible to open, but he felt a strange excitement as if he now held the key to everything – who and what he'd been, where he was heading, the strange rite of passage that he was undergoing now. It didn't matter that he couldn't actually read the pages. He'd never known his mother to open a copy of the Bible, although she'd always claimed it to be on her side when she was laying down the law and he'd grown up with the name of the book ringing in his ears like a doorbell.

No, this was all that he'd need. This for the spirit, and some fuel for the guttering flames way down in the Johnny Mays boiler room.

It was an old man's kitchen, plain painted cupboards meagrely stocked, but one of the cupboards was filled with Heinz soup cans in cardboard boxes. Johnny took two and then, as an afterthought, took another. He moved back through the living-room and past the fireside tableau of death without a second look.

He stopped at the turning of the stair, where a framed mirror hung. He'd gone by without seeing it on the way down. Most of its silvering had peeled, but enough remained to catch his reflection like a passing fugitive.

He started to feel panic. He didn't recognise the haunted, unshaven wreck who looked back at him.

But then, after a moment, it was as if some cutout kicked over. It didn't matter. Nothing mattered. Stop thinking, Johnny, you just aren't ready for it. Concentrate on the job in hand.

Concentrate on your comeback.

In the bedroom, he crouched before the electric fire. He hacked open the first of the cans with the end of the dirty spoon from the bedside bowl.

And then, with utter concentration, he began to eat the soup cold from the can.

PART TWO

The Devil Behind the Glass

11

The next day, in his rented car, Nick headed for home.

He left by the motorway through the mountains, retracing the first stages of the night chase that had led to the long fall of Johnny Mays. He turned the radio up loud and did his best to think of nothing; not Johnny, not Jennifer, not anybody.

And when that didn't seem to be working he found another, even louder station, and tried even harder.

When he hit the top of the road he could see brighter day ahead through a cleft in the hills, like the promise of a better country. At its highest level it bellied out across flat moorland, and the rental car seemed to be racing in a narrow slice of brightness between the land and the dark sky; Nick felt as if he was running for the light under a door that was slowly falling shut just some way beyond his reach, but then the descent began and the countryside opened out and the road itself seemed to widen and empty, and as Nick put his foot down the engine also opened up and ran at a pitch that was almost ecstasy. It was at this point that he began to get a sense of the trip as some kind of a homecoming; he'd thought of it before, but this was the first time that he'd really begun to feel it.

There hadn't been much in the way of goodbyes. Jennifer was still embarrassed and Nick, recognising a no-win situation when he saw one, just wanted to be out of it. He'd left her a note about the rest of his stuff which had ended *See you, Nick*. He couldn't really say how he felt. Not exactly wronged; more like a man who'd become too accustomed to losing, left holding a lottery ticket that was one digit short of being a winner.

He was into the low country now, and passing under power lines every few miles caused the radio to fizzle out so often that Nick finally gave in and turned it off. This was a landscape of coalfields and power stations, still mostly green and open but here and there rising in a high plateau of grassed-over slag, scars in the land that were slow to heal. When, in the shadow of one of these, a police patrol Sierra zipped by Nick in the fast lane, he felt a brief moment of something that he belatedly recognised as nostalgia. It shocked him a little. This was supposed to be a break, not some kind of a farewell; but he realised now that perhaps he was taking the first steps towards letting go of the life that he'd put together for himself over the past decade. When a design didn't work out, what else could one do but go back to the beginnings?

Jen had seen it, more than him. If Bruno were to open the envelope and read his account, then Jennifer would probably be the one standing nearest to the fan when the ordure hit. No question of disguising it – all officer accommodation had to be cleared and approval given, and even though her record might stay untainted there would always be a lingering suspicion in the hearts and minds of the high and mighty. Only now did he begin to see what his own motives must have been in offering his actions – or rather, an account of his silence – for the record; wasn't it that he simply couldn't raise the nerve to pull the plugs and walk away on his own?

Maybe. What did it matter for now? He was going home.

His first view of the bay was through the arch of the suspension bridge, tension apparent across its estuary-wide span like that of a cat in the act of stretching. There had been no bridge at all when he was a child, it had been fought against, and now it appeared on T-shirts and souvenirs. Progress, he thought, and switched on the radio again to hunt for the local station.

He didn't go straight into town. He carried on by, past canneries and food freezeries and maritime company offices, past the great gutted hulk of the Fish Meal Company building and the smaller warehouses beside it, past docked ships towering above redbrick houses with pantiled roofs the colour of pale sand, and he didn't stop until, at last, he reached the sea.

There, he pulled the car in by the side of the road and got out.

Remembering, now, he climbed to the top of the dunes. This wasn't any specific place, but then he'd been away for so long that the coastline might have altered significantly anyway; nothing major, just a slow and steady shifting of the sands, but enough to be noticeable over the decades and to invalidate maps and charts as the centuries passed. Entire villages had been lost along here, leaving only their names and the legends of offshore steeples and church bells ringing when the tide was low. Nick and Johnny had gone looking for them, often enough, but they'd never even seen so much as a ghost light.

This had been their territory, once; the estuary town, and the broad curving headland to the east of the town, and the Bay villages and shoreline of the headland. As a playground it was vast, a whole day's cycling from the northernmost beaches down to the delicate hook of land at its southernmost tip, and the image that Nick had always carried in his mind was of seemingly endless roads between hedgerows that were packed with tall summer-growth weeds. He mostly remembered wide, undulating fields beyond the rows, with the occasional dense stand of woodland stopping the gaze from wandering all the way out to the edge of the world; and every few miles there would be the tall white spire of a village church, with dense cloud stacked low overhead.

Now, *there* was something that he'd forgotten; the way

that, over the flat open land, the sky made up about eighty per cent of any vista so that changes in the light and the weather were signalled long before they arrived. It was rather like watching the future shaping up on the distant horizon, inevitable and beyond influence or control. At one time, before he'd left, he'd begun to find the idea oppressive; but now, after the unpredictability of the past few weeks, he was almost ready to embrace it like some well-loved old dog.

He walked down to the beach.

Beyond the immediate whiteness of the dunes, the shoreline was stained in alternating dark and light bands by the retreating tide. By Christ, the stuff that they'd found washed-up along here . . . but then the beaches had always been more Nick's home territory than Johnny's, somewhere that he would come alone when he was upset or when the company of even the young Johnny Mays had become a little too much for him to bear. When that happened, he'd hide in the dunes and then, when Johnny came calling his name, Nick wouldn't answer.

He stopped. On the sand just before him, a child's shell collection that had been carefully gathered up and stacked and then abandoned. When the tide returned, it would scatter the shells; but Nick stepped around the arrangement, leaving it undisturbed for now. The wind stirred the coarse grass of the dunes, the retreating sea beat at the sand. There was no-one else in sight.

He had a promise to keep and here he was, putting it off.

It was time to deliver.

Johnny's parents no longer lived in the big house by the transport yard; Johnny's father ("Call me Frank, Nick, call me Frank,") had retired about seven years before and sold the business to someone who'd failed to make a go of it. Now the yard was disused and back on the market, and the Mays household had moved out of town to a more modest bungalow on the outskirts of one of the larger of the Bay villages. Nick found it easily; white-painted, with an overcrowded but well-tended rockery at the front, and the distinctive feature of two cast-iron cannon and an anchor arranged by the roadside.

He'd prepared himself for the inevitable shock of change when he saw Johnny's parents again, but the sense of dislocation was very short-lived. Frank Mays' hair was almost completely white and he seemed much smaller than Nick remembered, but the present moment and the memory quickly merged. Veronica Mays, who was taller than her husband and had always been vain about her appearance, had become stocky and slow in middle age. As she said hello and gave him a weak smile, Nick guessed that she'd perhaps had a minor stroke at some time in the past. The impairment was slight, but it was there.

The interior of the bungalow was quite extensive, and done out with a kind of chintzy affluence and not much taste. They sat and made small talk for a while – they asked after the health of Nick's own parents almost straight away – and Johnny's name had yet to be raised in the conversation when Veronica Mays, obviously upset, abruptly stood up and left the room.

Frank Mays went over to the door that she'd left slightly ajar because she'd rushed out in too much of a hurry even to notice, and he gently closed it after her. Then he returned to the sofa.

"You have to excuse her, Nick," he said. "She's taken this very hard. Both of us have."

"You don't have to tell me," Nick said.

"Johnny wasn't much of a one for writing or keeping in touch. How was he, Nick? How did he seem to you?"

"He was fine."

"Was he happy?"

Nick didn't have to be a psychic to see that Frank Mays was looking for good news, *any* kind of good news that he could take through as a gift to the sad and shattered woman at the other end of the house.

Stepping carefully, he said, "As far as I could tell. We were only together again for a few weeks."

"No big worries? No girl trouble, or anything like that?"

"I don't think so."

"What about money?"

"He did okay."

Frank Mays nodded, obviously hearing what he wanted to hear. This was probably how saints were made, Nick was thinking. Frank Mays said, "I'm sorry if it sounds like I'm going on, Nick. It's just that . . ."

"You feel as if there's something you ought to have done," Nick suggested, "and now it's too late."

"That's it. That's it exactly. There's no worse feeling in the world, you know?"

"I know," Nick said.

There was an awkward pause, and Frank Mays stood up and went over to the window. It was an aimless move, and when he looked out he obviously saw nothing of the rockery or the old cannons or the road beyond.

"We still keep thinking that the phone's going to ring, and it'll be him," he said. "I don't know why, because he'd never call us when he was . . ." here he hesitated, delicately, and then amended, "he never used to phone us at all. Veronica sometimes said she thought he'd forgotten how. Did he ever talk about us at all?"

And Nick, who'd heard Johnny mention the old days lots of times but his parents never once, said, "As a matter of fact, he did. Just the day before it happened. He was saying how much he missed being at home. The yard, and everything."

"Just goes to show," Frank Mays said, shaking his head at the wonder of it. "When he left, he said how much he hated it around here."

"Well," Nick said uncomfortably. "There you go."

Mays looked back from the window, forcing a smile

124

now. And in that expression, Nick could read all of the hidden insecurities of a generation who'd handed the reins over to their children and now had to watch the consequences of their lives being played out beyond their control. Where some minor kindness, long forgotten, could be a basis for humanity, and a harsh word on the stairs an acorn of great destruction. "I bet it was just like the old days with you two, wasn't it?" he said. "The old team? You and Johnny against the rest of them?"

"That's how it was beginning to feel, all right," Nick said.

Frank Mays saw no irony there. He said, "Can you do something for me, Nick?"

"Just say what."

"Come around again tomorrow, if you can. Could you manage that?"

And Nick, his heart sinking fast, said, "Of course."

"I'd like Veronica to hear some of the things you've been saying. Especially since it'll be coming from you. Johnny always looked up to you, you know."

"He did?"

"It was mostly because of you that he wanted to be a policeman. But I suppose you'll know all about that."

"I wondered," Nick admitted, and got to his feet. He sensed the prospect of being able to get back to air that wasn't stale with grief, and he didn't want to let it slip by. He could only take so much of this, like standing under a cold shower; he could force himself to do it, but he couldn't force himself to like it.

"Joining the police was the first thing Johnny ever did that gave us something to be proud of," Frank Mays said as he walked Nick to the car a couple of minutes later. "So we can thank you for that, anyway."

Don't mention it, Nick thought dully as he drove away.

———

He booked into the Railway Hotel, right in the middle of town; much bigger and grander inside than its name or exterior suggested, it belonged more to the days of steam trains and steam heat than to the more modern era of residential sports facilities and the jacuzzi. Queen Victoria had once stayed here, and they'd never forgotten the fact. The main entrance looked out onto a busy square with a war memorial; a second, smaller set of doors across the lobby gave direct access into the vast emptiness of the railway station concourse. The concourse had always been a popular spot for teenagers on Saturday nights; there were three big cinemas close by, and it was one of the few public spaces offering shelter when it rained.

His room was small, and looked out onto a car park. There was a washbasin and a colour TV with a pay-movie channel, three desperately dull-looking films that he'd never even heard of. Nick stretched out on the bed but then, after about an hour, had to concede that being tired didn't inevitably lead to relaxation. So then he splashed his face with cold water and went downstairs to look for some life.

The lobby between the two entrances was huge and high-ceilinged and was mostly given over to an open and well-lit coffee lounge. The chairs were low and looked comfortable, and there were flowers on each of the tables.

A staff member in a bright tan uniform and dressed-to-kill makeup asked him if he needed anything. Nick glanced around the lounge. It was now early in the evening, and all of the tables were as yet empty.

"Thanks," he said, "but I don't think you could squeeze me in."

"It *is* quiet tonight," she admitted. According to her lapel badge, her name was Shirley. "Are you in town on business?"

"Not exactly. I lived around here once, but it was a long time ago."

"Don't tell me. You came back for the fair."

"The fair still happens?"

"Every year, same time. Are you sure I can't get you anything?"

"I'll have a beer if you'll join me."

"I'm sorry," she said with a regretful smile that looked just a touch over-rehearsed. "They don't allow it."

"Didn't think they would, somehow," Nick said.

And as he walked out to the car he thought that Yep, the old knock-'em-dead charm seemed to be working about the same as always.

The fair.

How could he have forgotten? But the truth was that he hadn't forgotten, he simply hadn't stopped and thought for long enough to remember. Most years when the evenings turned cold and the first scents of woodsmoke touched the air, he'd think of dangerous rides and shitty hamburgers and all that kind of stuff. Recently he'd had too much on his mind, that was all. Mostly he'd just button up and carry on. But tonight he wouldn't have to.

This wasn't some tired old travelling show that would set up for a couple of nights on a tiny wet croft somewhere and then move on; it was a major event in the life of the town and one of the big dates in the showmen's calendar. It covered acres over on the western side where, for most of the year, a lorry park stood. Nick hadn't missed a year – hadn't missed a single night, when he thought about it – from the age of about three until when his family had left the area. Forget the fair? He could about as easily forget to breathe.

He parked the car and walked through the approaching streets, nose-to-tail with vehicles. Already the bright lights of the big rides could be seen above the rooftops and reflected in bedroom windows over the shops. He remembered how it was, first as a small child with his scarf knotted over his duffel coat and his face wide open with wonder as he hung onto his father's hand; and then later, in those last two or three years when a dozen of them had come along in a gang like dogs chasing heat but with their innocence touchingly intact under the loud talk and the bragging.

The fair had hardly changed at all.

But he had.

Maybe it was just his mood. After the events of the past week, life seemed like a long book that he'd paid good money for and which had him wishing that he'd picked up something better. Now he was beginning to wonder whether there was actually anything resembling magic left to be found, or whether it was simply a matter of penetrating layers of illusion until you hit this dull bedrock with nowhere else left to go.

To begin with, he couldn't forget that he was the law. It was there in the way that he studied the kids' faces, the young rough-looking girls with their hair plastered down in spikes and their black roots showing, and the young men in bomber jackets with their hands stuck into their pants pockets as they shivered and tried to look hard. He moved through them, battered by pop music and the loud throb of generators underneath, and found himself wondering about the provenance of rows and rows of some of the ugliest and most mis-shapen soft toys in the world. He studied the showmen in their day-glo slickers, their rides dripping and gleaming under the electric lights, and he wondered if any of them had form.

And he looked, without success, for the old Ghost Train with its patient skeleton waiting in the shadows.

The Wall of Death had gone, he noticed. And the freak show, and the knife-throwing act where a greaseball in a fringed suede jacket had tossed cutlery at a G-stringed assistant who'd looked like somebody's grandmother. Nick moved under cover for a while, and all of the background sounds merged and became like a distant thunder felt all the way through his body. He took a deep breath. Blew it out again. From where he stood, in the shadow of the Hellblazer, he watched a couple of teenaged girls in high heels tottering unsteadily through the mire. They looked breathtakingly pretty, and unsalvageably tough.

He turned away.

No place for you even here, Nicky boy, he thought to himself, and he walked around through the dark shadows on the wrong side of the ride. It was the innocence that had gone, he'd decided; and you could no more hope to regain it than you could study to become a virgin.

He wished that he could be five years old again. He wished that his father could be here, with a hand that could close over his own. He wished that he could sleep at nights, safe in the knowledge that the silhouette peeking in at the door was a benign one and would return if he called.

He could wish.

Rain was collecting and spilling over the edges of the sideshow awnings, and every now and again a stallholder would push up the canvas with a stick and shower the ground in front of the business. Some of the stalls had obviously been around for a while and were lovingly painted in reds and golds, leftovers of the showmanship of another age, but others were just battered to hell. Money was being raked in, change was being counted out at lightning speed. Nick made his way around by the Dodgems, pickup rods flashing like lightning and the deck rumbling as if in an earthquake, and he came out into a long avenue of fortune tellers' caravans and novelty stalls. Barely visible on the far side of the booths was an open field with allotments and greenhouses, their glass dully reflecting the hyperactive cartoon of life across the way. Nick eased on through the crowds, and instinctively watched for pickpockets.

The old Britannia stood where it always had.

He went in.

The pub was like an overlit barn, the fairground spilling in and the boundaries marked by the loud thirteen-year-olds who were hanging around just outside the doorway. Nick found it hard to believe that he'd ever been one of them. There was an average crowd inside, most of them looking like farmers at some low-rent country auction. There was rubber sheet protecting the carpet, and sentimental Country and Western playing on a jukebox that almost nobody could hear. Any changes in the fabric of the place were too minor for Nick to notice. But then, he thought, this kind of austerity probably never dates.

For most of the time, then and probably now, the Britannia was a lorry-drivers' pub. At weekends the median age of the clientele would plummet as the town's youth, some a shade under age and others blatantly so, would come in from all over the area for the Britannia's disco nights. Lorry drivers were quiet and sociable and would drift off at closing time to sleep in their cabs; the weekenders were loud and rude and, in some cases, unfathomably stupid, and most Saturday nights there would be a rush for the side door around ten as police cars slid to a halt outside the front entrance. Nick had almost been caught in the toilet, once. He'd never have made it out if Johnny hadn't pulled him through the tiny window.

There was some empty space at the bar, and he moved in. Somebody was feeding money into the jukebox now; there was enough noise to ensure that they probably wouldn't get to hear the sounds that they were buying, but then Nick knew that nobody ever wasted time listening to pub music. The act was more a declaration of taste that almost amounted to a challenge, and he'd seen enough of the resulting fights to know it.

The track came up. It was *Tie a Yellow Ribbon Round the Old Oak Tree.*

Then, feeling a touch on his shoulder, Nick turned. And because he'd been in lots of such places and because of some of the situations that he'd walked into, he turned so fast that the barman flinched back as if he'd touched something live.

"Nick?" he said uncertainly. "Nick Frazier? Remember me? Brian Burton?"

Nick's mind raced for a moment. Before him was a shirtsleeved, moon-faced, pleasant-looking man of his own age. He searched his memory for a card to match and then, when he found one, he relaxed a little.

"Yes," he said. "I remember. How are you doing, Brian?"

"I've known it worse," Brian said.

Brian Burton. His parents had worked the markets, and none of his clothes had ever had labels. The face of the boy and the face of the man before him seemed to merge before Nick's eyes, like something rapidly healing. They hadn't known each other terrifically well, so perhaps that was why it wasn't so much of a shock to see him again now; or perhaps it was that the process wasn't as inherently shocking as he'd thought that it might be.

Nick said, "Are you working here, now?"

"Only part-time." Brian Burton shook his head, and he folded his arms and leaned on the bar. Somebody further down was calling to be served, but he didn't seem to hear. "Jesus," he said. "This I can't believe."

"What do you mean?"

"Seeing you like this. I've seen others come back, but I never expected you. I was reading about you, only last week."

"Where?"

"Piece about you and Johnny Mays in the local rag. Has he turned up, at all?"

"No," Nick said. A harassed-looking woman was coming around behind the bar from the other lounge, and she grabbed up some empty glasses and stuck them under the beer taps with pressured haste. "But he will."

"He drowned, didn't he? I wouldn't like to be around when they *do* find him."

"Me neither."

"You remember Janice at all?" Brian said suddenly, and he called to the woman at the other end of the bar. "Over here," he said. "Look who I've found."

She finished serving, and came over. Nick didn't remember her and she didn't look as if she remembered him, but they both made a polite pretence. Hers lasted for exactly four seconds and then she said, pointedly, to Brian, "The lager's just about to go down."

"I'll see to it," Brian said, and he straightened without any hurry. "Listen, Nick," he said, "we're a bit tied up tonight, but are you around for a while?"

"A few days. I don't know for sure."

"We'll have to get together and do something. Okay?"

Nick agreed, although the two of them knew that absolutely nothing was going to come of it; and then, in an afterthought and taking what he assumed would be an impossibly long shot, he said, "You ever hear anything of Alice Craig these days?"

Brian was moving away.

He paused for about two seconds' thought.

"Alice?" he said. "Try the other bar."

And then he'd gone.

12

Nick went looking. He had his reasons. This ought to mean nothing to him but, strangely enough, it did. The other bar was called the Empire Lounge, and some attempt had been made to give it a hint of class; the hint went largely untaken, and the same downmarket crowd filled it with a buzz about second-hand cars and the previous night's game shows on TV. *"Hey,"* he heard a woman squawk to a young man just behind him, *"gerroff me bum!"*

Nick pushed forward.

In a crowd like this, Alice Craig wasn't difficult to spot. She was alone at a table, and Nick didn't for one minute think that the Britannia was a place where she'd spend much time out of choice. Not these days, anyway. Even as he saw her, she was fending off an attempted pickup.

Buy you a drink?

Fuck off.

Well, maybe not in those exact words . . . but that was the message, all right.

"Please," she said to him coldly as he stood by her table. "I'm waiting for somebody."

"You don't know me?"

She looked up and met his eyes, then. This time he had no problem in relating the woman before him to the teenaged girl he'd once known; maybe it was the practice he'd been getting, or perhaps she hadn't changed as much as some. He reflected that she was damned close to plain but that whatever she had, it came from inside.

She was slim and pale and, even with a touch of makeup, she looked as if a strong breeze might blow her away.

"Yes, I know you," she said. "It's . . .?"

"Nick," he said. "The name's Nick."

"You make it sound like I'd forgotten."

"I wouldn't blame you if you had."

"Give me some credit," Alice said. He saw her glance once, and quickly, at the clock behind the bar; so she *was* waiting for somebody, after all.

"The clock's wrong," Nick said. "Credit you for what?"

"For knowing the people I grew up with. Try this. We were twelve years old and you wouldn't join in the barndancing."

He managed to inject a suitable note of horror. "You remember *that*?"

"What's the matter?"

"I've spent the last twenty years trying to forget it."

"What's the big deal about a kid who didn't want to dance?"

"I was wearing khaki pants. I'd got a pee stain on the front of them. You know that kind of material, you touch it with anything wet and it goes dark. I was terrified of standing up because everyone was bound to see."

"A pee stain," Alice said, in what looked like a thoughtful and serious effort to understand.

"I had nightmares afterwards."

She nodded, trying to look sympathetic. But somehow, the expression wouldn't stick; and she snorted, like there was laughter that she couldn't hold in. And Nick grinned, because there was nothing that brought people closer than sharing a secret, and so much the better if that secret happened to be the most embarrassing thing that had ever happened to one of them.

She hitched along the bench to make room for him, and he sat down beside her.

He said, "I thought you were waiting for someone."

"Yes," she said dispiritedly. "But I don't know where he is."

"Want another drink?"

"No, thanks. I'll give him another ten minutes and then I'd better go."

"Do you have to?"

"It's business," she said, almost apologetically. "He's a friend, supposed to be helping me out. But I can manage without him if I need to."

Nick was looking at her and thinking that, from the way she'd picked her clothes and turned herself out, there was probably something more than friendship involved here; and there was the faintest edge in her voice when she referred to her no-show companion that suggested the annoyance of being stood up rather than the irritation of being let down.

Nick said, "What line of business are you in?"

"Nothing exciting," she said. "I just work in an office. What about you?"

"I thought you'd know about that. Wasn't it plastered all over the local papers about me and Johnny Mays?"

"Where does Johnny Mays come into this?"

"You didn't hear? He died."

She hadn't heard.

She sat there, looking as if she'd been socked with a bag of lead shot. Stunned wasn't even the word for it.

She said, "How?"

"He drowned. A bad accident. I'm sorry, I thought you'd know."

She shook her head, slowly. She was recovering fast, but the shock had obviously been a big one. "I don't get the papers," she said. "I'm living out of town." She looked at him. "Johnny Mays? You're absolutely sure?"

"I was there."

She shook her head again, and then she pushed the table back and started to get to her feet. "Look, Nick," she said, "this is . . . I mean, I'm sorry. It's getting late. I have to go."

"I seem to have been a lousy messenger," Nick said.

"I don't mean it like that. Really, I do have to go."

"I just didn't realise that you knew him so well."

"Know him well? I hardly knew him at all."

She knocked an empty glass from the table as she moved out. Nick caught it before it fell.

He said, "My mistake, then. Sorry."

"There's really nothing for you to be sorry about."

"Any chance that we might meet up again? I could be around for a while."

"No," she said as she backed off, and then she said, "I mean, yes . . . I don't know. Possibly." And then, before she could get herself any more confused, she turned and walked away.

Nick sat for a while, unaware of much around him. It didn't matter that he'd never barndanced in his life, nor even been close, and that the pee stain on the khaki was another incident from some other time.

But Johnny had cut out her picture, and kept it for years.

That had to be worth at least a couple of white lies, didn't it?

———

He caught sight of her again after walking the fair for a while, only this time it was at a distance and she didn't see him. The white picket barrier around the Ghostbuster ride was between them, and by the time he could make his way around it she'd probably be gone. She was talking to the owner of one of the smaller coin-in-the-slot arcades, an open-sided pavilion right next door to an old-time carousel. She was having a hard time making herself heard, but she appeared to be talking business. The rain seemed to fizz under the bright lights. Nick saw the owner shaking his head, and then gesturing towards his machines. Alice smiled – a touch nervously, Nick thought, although it was difficult to be sure over the distance – and nodded. It had the look of a concession of no hope, the kind that came along with being turned down for a job, although Nick didn't for one minute believe that employment was the issue here.

"Excuse me," he said as he pushed by a couple of young men who had their sleeves rolled up, comparing their tattoos. He was wondering if he might just reach her as she walked away.

He'd have managed it, but then the Ghostbuster ride ended and he was slowed by the crowd who came down its steps like a flash-flood. Bad weather didn't seem to have diminished the numbers around the fair; most of them hadn't even bothered to dress for it. Coloured lights and neon were like dying suns in the pooled rainwater underfoot. By the time that Nick had made it to the pavilion, Alice was nowhere to be seen.

The big carousel was slowing as Nick sought out the owner, a middle-aged man in a black leather trilby and a sheepskin car coat that couldn't have looked much more the worse for wear if it had stayed on the dead sheep. Nick had no problem in drawing him aside, because he could see in the man's eyes that he'd been spotted instantly for what he was. Didn't need to show his brief, or anything. Nick didn't really understand how this worked – he'd studied himself in the mirror and he couldn't see any giveaway signs – but what the hell, it could be handy.

As the carousel horses coasted to a halt, Nick said, "That woman. What did she want?"

The arcade owner shrugged. "Fuck knows," he said, and he hauled on a loop that showed at the neck of his buttoned-up coat. After about seven or eight inches of wire, the pickup box of a hearing aid came up like a fish on a line. The man shrugged again.

Nick started to ask him something else, but then the Ghostbuster ride began to thump out its theme and he knew that it was hopeless.

With a resigned wave, he walked away.

He started to check some of the other, similar arcades, in the hope that he'd find her there. He'd let her get away without even finding out how to contact her again, which if it was nothing else was less than professional. And besides . . .

Besides.

He hadn't seen her in a long while, but in the immortal words of Marlon Brando in some barely-remembered movie, she'd turned out okay.

Bright islands of noise. Take-down sheds with creaky plywood floors, crammed with video games and one-armed bandits and gambling machines so old they were almost museum pieces. Prize shelves full of bilious yellow teddy bears. An Alsatian with mud-splashed legs, slinking around the aisles with ears down and in no mood to see the boss having trouble. The backs of big lorries seen through the gaps between sideshows, generator engines running hard to provide the power and giving them an aura of dark gods of control standing out beyond the limelight.

Nick stood in a doorway and watched the passing crowds for a while. Pulsing light from one of the midway rides beat on his face like a physical blow. It was beginning to look like he'd lost her.

But there was one last place that he'd yet to cover.

It was a building set back from the street on the very edge of the fairground. The old terraced houses had gone and been replaced by neat brick boxes that stood with their curtains drawn and their windows dark, as if to turn their faces away from the centuries-old ritual that threatened to invade and engulf them. This place, a ramshackle warehouse enclosing an area roughly the size of a couple of buses, was one of the few remaining originals. It had been rented out and its doors had been thrown open, and because it was one of the few places on-site to offer shelter from the rain it was crammed shoulder-to-shoulder. Nick stood in the wide doorway and scanned the crowd, but the slot and video aisles ran all the way to the back and he could only see so far. The densest crush was around a bingo stall just inside the entrance, and the shed echoed all the way up to the roof with the amplified voice of the caller above the usual push and hustle. Nick could see him; raised over the heads of the players, he wore a stained white jacket and held a microphone too close for hygiene. He looked about fifteen years old, but he had the slick and nasal tones of a middle-aged man.

Nick went in.

He could see that there was some degree of organisation here, because about half a dozen young and not-so-young men were patrolling in uniform jackets with embroidered security badges. The uniforms had a home-made look about them and the men all looked like brothers and cousins, and Nick managed to catch up with one of them to ask where he'd find the boss. He was pointed towards a couple of small tourer caravans that stood, partly screened, right at the back of the shed. And has anybody else been asking? he added, but the response was a shrug.

He had his answer within a couple of minutes anyway, because that was when he saw Alice again.

The situation was impossible.

With only about twenty yards between them, he was bobbing helplessly like a spent swimmer in a rough sea. He was half-tempted to crack a couple of heads to speed his way through, but he fought it down. Crowds were the pits. He could see Alice talking to the showman in charge over by the tourers, but there was no point in Nick calling to her because she wouldn't hear. The man was small and stocky and slightly mis-shapen, almost a dwarf, and he wore a blue waterproof. Alice appeared to be giving him the same pitch as before only now she seemed to be getting a more positive response, one that seemed to say Yeah, maybe . . . so then she took out a notelet pad and started to scribble something down.

Nick forced a path around the back of a bank of

machines, almost getting into about three fights along the way. He came out closer to where he needed to be, just in time to see the showman reading Alice's note. Of Alice herself there was no sign, but there was a strong indication of where she'd gone when the man glanced toward a side-exit by the tourers before screwing up her paper and tossing it to the ground and walking off.

The floor had been covered with sheet cardboard, mostly cereal boxes opened-out, as an attempt to soak up the mud and the water tracked in by the clientele; that same clientele had trampled the cardboard to a mush, and it was from this that Nick had to rescue Alice's note. For one panic-stricken moment he thought that the pressure of bodies wouldn't allow him to straighten up again . . . but then he made it, and unscrewed the paper.

The ink had run. It might have been an address, but now it was illegible.

It was a relief to break free of the crush and make for the exit by the caravans. Both vans were lit and there was a TV set running in one of them, a glimpse of home in the middle of madness. He stepped over cable runs and around gas bottles and empty boxes, and eased out into the night.

There he stopped for a moment, and took a breath.

He was in the shelter of the side of the building, some way behind the vans and wagons on the main boulevard. This was empty land, a darker and different world to that of the fairground only yards away.

"Why are you following me?" Alice said.

She stepped out of the shadows where, it appeared, she'd been waiting for him. She was a silhouette against the bright lights, her hands thrust into her pockets and her face unreadable.

"I'm not," Nick said.

"Try again."

She'd caught him well off-balance. "I wanted to apologise," he said. "I didn't know I was going to upset you."

"Upset me?" she said. "You didn't." And then she turned to walk away. "Goodbye, Nick," she said, and there was a pointed finality in the way that she said it.

"How will I get in touch with you?" he called after her.

She barely glanced back.

"Don't," she said, and walked on.

13

Nothing much had been happening at the hotel when he got back. Through a half-open door he could see that there was a private wedding party in one of the ground-floor suites, a strobe-lit disco with a fair provision of gorgeous women and more heart-stopping jailbait than a convent school. But he wasn't in the mood for gatecrashing, and he was in even less of a mood for being thrown out; all of the men around his own age were in naval uniform, and nobody was so drunk that they'd need radar to spot a stranger. Instead he'd gone up to his own room, watched TV until all the stations had gone off the air, and then read a couple of dozen pages of *Tarzan and the Leopard Men*. During this he could hear the people next door come stumbling in, turn the bedside radio up too loud, hurriedly turn it down, argue in whispers, and then finally go quiet. Then he shut the book and switched off the light and turned over.

And for the first time in years, he dreamed a small boy's dream of the jungle.

Now, after sleeping in late and only just making it down to breakfast, he turned his car onto the gravel drive before the Mays' bungalow for the second time in as many days. It was a clear, if breezy, morning, but Nick felt a certain dread – nothing overpowering, more a sense that he'd done the penance that he considered necessary and this was an extension that he hadn't intended. What if they asked him to come back yet again? And again, and again? He knew that he wouldn't know how to say no, and it was a dismaying prospect. Seen from here it was rather like facing beans for every meal, forever.

Frank Mays' elderly but well-preserved Jaguar was out of the garage, and the garage doors were open; Nick heard his name being called as he walked past, and he looked in.

"Having a sort-through?" he said, stepping through the open doorway into the comparative twilight of the garage.

Frank Mays was inside and alone, with a couple of crates and tea-chests heaved out into the middle of the floor. The two suitcases that Nick had brought along were there as well, standing on scrubbed concrete where the ghosts of old oilstains lay. As Nick's eyes adjusted to the light he could see that the garage was obsessively neat and well arranged, a sure sign of a man with time on his hands and nothing better to do with it.

Jesus, Nick thought. He's wearing an *apron*.

Johnny's father was kneeling by one of the tea-chests and taking stuff out; Johnny Mays memorabilia, as far as Nick could see. Mays said, "The longer I leave it, the harder it's going to get." He looked up. "We appreciate what you did, Nick."

"I didn't do anything," Nick said, and wasn't *that* the truth.

He squatted down by the chest. Frank Mays said, "If you want a confession, I've been here all morning and I've done nothing but move stuff from one box to another."

"Can't bring yourself to throw anything away?"

"I know that most of it's only junk to other people. I mean, that's all it *is*, really . . . but it's memories as well. You know what I'm getting at?"

"I think so," Nick said.

"But if you see anything here that you want to take away with you, feel free."

"Tell me when you get to his money, then," Nick said, and both of them grinned although it wasn't anything terrifically funny, and some of the awkwardness that stood between their generations disappeared.

Nick took a look through the half-sorted pile on the garage floor. There were school exercise books and certificates, broken plastic models, some boxed games and jigsaws. Scores of model soldiers, some of them looking as if they'd been chewed. There were a few records, none of them in sleeves. The things we leave behind, Nick thought, and he picked up a copy of the *Valiant* annual from sometime in the mid-sixties and flicked through its pages.

Frank Mays said, "You'll have seen some sights, I suppose. In your line of work."

Nick recognised the wariness, almost a hesitancy, in his tone. Lowering the book he said, "Bad ones, you mean?"

"Accidents, and that kind of thing. Johnny would never talk about that side of it."

"It's something you have to get used to."

"I suppose you get hardened."

"Some do."

With a sideways glance at Nick, Frank Mays said, "Did Johnny?"

There was a pause, and then Nick said, "No, I don't think he did."

Mays nodded, and seemed to be relieved. "I'm glad about that," he said.

Whatever Nick might be feeling guilty about, he felt no guilt about hiding the truth now. How could he explain that Johnny's idea of a Christmas joke one year had been to sneak into the morgue and dress an elderly bearded male cadaver in a Santa Claus suit for the morning shift to find? Or how, after being called out to the tragic suicide of a quadriplegic in a swimming pool, he'd suggested that until they got an identification they should give the victim the provisional name of 'Bob'? Some of the reality might come out at the enquiry, if ever there was one . . . but until then, who would it help?

Fortunately, Frank Mays didn't press the matter. Nick didn't even have to change the subject, because Mays then said, "Did you bump into any old friends last night?"

"One or two," Nick admitted.

"I thought you might," Mays said. "Did you go to the fair?"

"I met Alice Craig. She didn't seem to know about Johnny. Seemed to take the news pretty hard. Did they know each other well?"

"I really wouldn't know," Frank Mays said.

But Nick could see that he was suddenly taking a more intense interest than before in the box before him; or perhaps it was just that he was avoiding meeting Nick's eyes.

"Must have been after I moved away, if they did," Nick added, but Frank Mays offered nothing further. Instead he dived into the tea-chest like a small child into a bran tub, and came out with one of Johnny's old toys.

"Well, will you look at this," he said. "I can remember how he pestered us for it. And look at it now . . ."

It was a big, once-flashy American police car made out of tinplate, almost certainly battery-powered and Japanese. It was terrifically gaudy, and more imaginative than accurate. Two of its wheels were missing, the paint was scratched, the roof was dented as if it had been carelessly stepped upon at some time.

Holding the big toy in his two hands and turning it over, Frank Mays said with some affection, "He never took care of anything, that boy. I think he only wanted it because you had one like it." He glanced up at Nick. "Didn't you have one like it?"

"I had one that my dad made," Nick said.

It was shortly after this that Veronica Mays appeared in the open garage doorway, and the two of them looked up at her as she spoke. Nick suddenly felt caught-out and guilty, although he'd have had a hard time saying why.

"Hello, Nicholas," she said, not loudly. "If you'd like to come into the house, I've set out some sandwiches."

And as he followed her in, leaving Frank Mays to hang up his workshop apron and close the garage doors behind them, Nick experienced a curious sensation. It wasn't déjà-vu, although it was something close to it. The feeling was more of duality, as if his adult self was little more than a dissolving shadow around the core of the child; almost, he thought, as if the child was the reality, and the adult self an act that we learn to perfect as time goes by.

"Don't forget to wipe your feet," Veronica Mays called back to him as they entered the house.

And Nick did as he'd been told.

I'm Johnny Mays, he whispered to the mirror, as he had done every morning since the day he'd been reborn.

Not that Johnny was losing his grip. He knew who he was and he had a vague idea about where he was; the hows and the whys seemed to elude him for the moment, but he was sure that they'd come. The whys, especially. Even through his weakness he could feel a driving sense of purpose, but he was damned if he could make out what it was. Everything from before the fall was like a shadow on the other side of the glass – vaguely familiar, half-forgotten, an inexplicable ritual of a life that might easily have been happening to somebody else. The new Johnny Mays was cleaned-out, pure, diamond bright; a laser, fine-tuned and focussed and itching to burn.

He'd already managed to shave himself. Maybe today he'd be able to take a few steps outside.

Most of the time he'd spent by the fire in the living

room, keeping it burning with anything that he could find. He'd tried to put on his old clothes, but mostly they were ruined. He'd found some acceptable stuff upstairs in one of the wardrobes – none of it the old man's, as far as he could see, but all of it bagged-up and then stored as if he hadn't quite been able to bring himself to throw it out – and he was wearing some of this along with two of the overcoats for extra warmth. Johnny had more or less forgotten the dead man in the chair. He was still there, fingers hooked and his face in shadow, but he had no relevance to the task in hand.

Whatever that might be.

The hearth was a litter of empty cans and boxes. Johnny had cleared a space before it and, as soon as he'd had enough strength, he'd dragged down the mattress from upstairs so that he'd be able to sleep somewhere warmer than the bedroom. Even with the heater burning, it was an icebox.

He'd looked out of every window and in every direction, and he was truly isolated; at night there wasn't a single light to be seen anywhere, and the only sound had been the agonised lowing that still continued in one of the nearer outbuildings. The house itself was a dump. Johnny had known some – made a contribution to the deterioration of most of them – but this place beat everything. There was woodworm all over, and mites had eaten the paste out from behind the old wallpaper. It was damp, it was gloomy, and in most of the rooms it stank like wet rope. Johnny had checked the place out once, and then left it alone; it hardly mattered anyway because this was only a way station, a short-term stop-over in a journey of much greater significance, and all that he needed to do was to stay tough and get stronger and wait for his destiny to build up its shape like an impending storm somewhere out over the sea.

He looked for omens wherever he could. In cloud formations, in the patterns of rain on the window, in the pictures in the fire. He listened to the wind and, when the wind dropped, he listened to his own heartbeat. Although he couldn't yet grasp the details he had a profound sense of the world as one vast, inter-related and co-ordinated machine, and he knew for sure that there was a Johnny Mays-sized hole in the works with an urgent need to be filled. He only wished that he could have seen it this way before; life then had been a shambling dream compared to this, now that his fall and renewal had cleared away the debris and made it possible for him to concentrate on the essentials.

Which he'd be able to do, if only that irritating beast would stop its racket.

He went into the kitchen. There was a key, but the door wasn't locked. After buttoning his outer overcoat and turning up its collar, Johnny opened the door and went into the outside air for the first time in a number of days.

He felt hesitant, almost as if he were taking first steps again. Everything seemed sharper than real. He was in the yard, and the yard was flagged with uneven stone, and the solid, unpretentious bulk of the moorland farmhouse stood behind him. It looked as if its walls would stand forever, even though its roof was beginning to sag and its windows were threatening to fall out. At one end of the yard was a gateway with a dropped gate, leading to a dirt track which was apparently the only access to the house. The gate was open and there was a scraped arc worn into the paving to show where it had been dragged before being pinned back with a boulder; the track went on and down the hill, disappearing over a rise. At the other end of the yard were two dilapidated sheds, low-roofed and patched with corrugated iron that had become streaked with rust. It was from here that the bellowing came, and had been coming on and off since he'd first opened his eyes. Even though he was now closer to the source, it was noticeably weaker than it had been.

He looked into the first of the sheds. Nothing lived

in here apart from an old Morris 1000 Traveller with L-plates that had curled up with age and no tax disc. But the tyres were good and there were keys inside, and when he reached in and turned the engine over it chugged along with a sluggish whine, not quite catching but holding out the promise that it might. Leaving the keys where they were, he stepped back and looked over its lines and winced. The question wasn't so much whether it would run, but whether he could bring himself to drive a half-timbered van that, in Johnny's view of an image car, best suited vicars, cripples, and old ladies. In the dark and with a bag over his head, maybe . . . but then, what were his choices?

Leaving the car, he moved through into the adjacent shed.

This one stank like a zoo. The penned bullock that had been making all the row suddenly reared and turned in surprise at Johnny's entrance, slamming into the wooden sides of its confined area and scrambling for balance as if on a greasy slope. Its eyes were showing mad white all around their rims, and its sides were daubed with the ordure that it had sprayed all over the slats. Johnny walked on straw around to the gate of the pen, one of three similar enclosures that took up most of the floorspace in here. One of the others stood empty, the last contained two weak-looking goats that were leaning against one another in the corner and didn't seem to have the strength to do much more than stare back at him.

There was no lock on the pen, just a bolt, but when he tried to undo it he found it stiff and unyielding. Perhaps there was some trick to it, he wondered, but he couldn't guess what it might be. He tried again and his hand slipped and he skinned his knuckles, and as he stepped back and sucked at his hand the bullock was threshing around and bellowing as if in a fit. So then Johnny looked around the back where there was a bench and some tools and a cupboard full of tablets and mineral supplements, and there he found a shovel which he brought around and swung a couple of times in sledgehammer fashion at the bolt.

Poetry in motion, he thought, and when he swung for a third time he hit the bolt square-on and tore it out of the wood to go flying across the shed like a stone out of a slingshot. It hit the wall with a bang and then bounced off somewhere out of sight, and Johnny dragged open the door one-handed and gestured the now-uncertain bullock toward the outside.

"Go on," he said. "Get lost. I can't feed you."

The bullock hesitated. It was unsteady and terribly dehydrated, and it seemed to be afraid of Johnny. But then he went around and banged on the side of the pen with what was left of the blade of the shovel, and the creature suddenly bolted; out of the pen, out of the shed, out into the yard and through the open gateway without stopping, its hooves spattering up mud and its flanks heaving in terror.

There was a welcome silence in the shed, at last.

Johnny now looked around at the goats, and the goats looked back at Johnny. They hadn't moved from their corner. This pen opened without too much problem, just a little lift to get the latch open because its hinges had sagged, but even with a way out to freedom before them the two animals didn't stir. So he went around the back and banged on the boards with his shovel until the blade and the handle parted company, and still they didn't move.

Unfinished business.

Johnny hated unfinished business.

He tossed the broken handle down into the straw, and looked around for something else. There was nothing useful under the bench, apart from a dented tin bucket. Nothing on the bench itself, nothing on the shelf above it apart from some unlabelled bottles and an old transistor radio. But there were a couple more useful-looking tools hanging from pegs alongside where the shovel had been, and one of these in particular seemed to suit the job exactly.

He took down the hand-scythe, and went around and into the pen.

The animals flinched once and made a weak attempt to bolt when they saw what was coming, but Johnny said, "You've had that chance already," and hacked right into them. It was all over in less than a minute, by which time there was blood running out from under the walls of the pen and a fair amount of it splattered all over Johnny's borrowed overcoat.

But what the hell, there were plenty more coats on the bedroom floor. Johnny shrugged out of the coat and threw it on top of the carcases, and then he went around and hung the scythe back where he'd found it. He wiped his hands on an old towel by the bench and then, when he walked back to the house, he took the transistor radio with him.

By the fire, with another of his dead host's hoarded cans standing ready on the hearth, he switched on the radio and fiddled around with the dial. Music stations came and went in bursts too quick to be identified, but none of these was of any interest to Johnny. He tracked the needle all the way through the wavebands, heading for the extreme.

Johnny sat on his carpet, the dead man sat on his throne. The dead man's chair wasn't close enough to the fire to get much of its heat, so he'd keep a while longer. Johnny had no curiosity about him; he belonged to the past, stiffly and emphatically so, and Johnny's interest now was only in the future.

In other business, perhaps, that remained unfinished.

The dial stuck, and wouldn't turn any further. From the radio's speaker came a formless hiss of white noise. Johnny turned the volume up as loud as it would go and set the radio down on the floor beside him.

"Knowledge is power," he said to the radio, whispering it like a catechism.

And then, content with these raw sounds of the ether and the sense of purpose that was beginning to grow within him, he picked up the swollen remains of what had once been his little black book.

————

Around the time that the two goats were falling under the sickle, Nick was getting out of his car at a sandy crossroads in the middle of nowhere.

At least that was how it appeared, although Nick knew exactly where he was. When he'd been a boy, this had been almost the edge of the world. Only one building stood here, the Bluebell Shop and Café; it had never seemed to be open then and, true to form, it wasn't open now. A carved plaque set high in the stonework read

Built in the Year 1837
534 Yards from the Sea

and when he looked down the track towards the dunes at his left, he guessed that there had been a significant change in the yardage over the century and a half. It was in that direction that the old wooden beach cottages had stood, the ones where he and Johnny – well, Johnny, mainly – had entered off-season and gazed in wonder at the cast-out ornaments and second-best china with which the summer people had furnished them. Would the houses still be standing, he wondered now? He reckoned that either they'd be gone completely or they'd be totally unchanged. Like soap bubbles, he thought.

What had it been, that strange bond that had formed between the two of them? Nick was beginning to feel that if only he could work out the answer to that one, it would somehow unlock the doors to so many other things in his own life that he couldn't understand. They'd been so unlike, even then. Johnny had been pushy, upfront, loud and vain, without any detectable trace of a conscience. Beatings made him yell, but they didn't make him any better. A break-in was as nothing to him . . . nobody was home, so where was the problem? But he'd also had charm, and he'd had a sense of humour way ahead of his years. Nick had been a wary boy, quiet and self-preoccupied, and so unforthcoming sometimes that he used to dream about his mother losing him in a crowd. While Johnny had been turning out the cupboards, Nick had been watching the horizon and desperately compiling excuses, all of them lame.

Different as they'd been, each had something that the other needed. Being in Johnny's presence again after so many years, Nick had been disturbed to find that he seemed to need it still. He'd as good as shielded Johnny, hadn't he? He felt somehow tainted, like a rescued soul with its secret dreams of darkness.

Perhaps this would fade.

But he suspected that it would take some effort to make it go.

Nick looked in through the smeary window of the café, past the apologetic note that had been taped there. He could make out the old shelving at the back of the shop, stacked with cans of Coke. Perhaps he'd walk over to the beach, see if the landscape had changed at all. He'd mainly come out for a look at the point but, what the hell, he had the rest of the afternoon.

The crossroads was the place at which the headland narrowed down almost to nothing; four miles further out, it did exactly that. With the North Sea to one side and an estuary so wide that it was almost an inland sea to the other, the point was like a long, whip-tailed causeway out to the shore light at its end. Leaving his car – but not intending to leave it for long, because the dunes gave little protection from the sharpness of the North Sea winds – he walked on down the point road to where it ran level with the bay.

Here he left the road, and climbed as high as he could go.

Now he could see both shores at once, but he turned his back to the wind and put up his collar. Below him the land dropped sharply away from the road, petering out into stones before flattening into the sand-tinted shallows of the bay. These were being stirred by the breeze and picked over by gulls that were circling and landing on the offshore mudbanks; a way further out, the sandy colour deepened to that of deep sea water. Beyond this, barely tinted-in on the horizon, stood the far landmass of the rest of the country.

This was how it had always seemed, back in the old days. Magic of a kind but frustrating, too; home had sometimes felt like some forgotten frontier outpost on shifting ground, while the real world was somewhere else and a long way out of reach. Everybody that he'd known, at least in the last couple of years that he'd lived in the area, had talked about the time when they would leave and make their mark elsewhere. They'd talked, but not all of them had done it.

Brian Burton hadn't. Nor had Alice Craig.

And some of those who'd tried, Nick began . . . but he didn't complete the thought.

He walked out along the dunes for a way. Ahead of him, he could see the poles that carried power and telegraph lines marching out along the length of the headland in a curving sweep. Out at the very tip, just about visible over the distance, was the old-fashioned stack of the lighthouse. From somewhere beyond it he could hear the faint sound of a regular offshore siren.

And then he had to stop, because his way was blocked by a new-looking chainlink fence that ran the hundred yards or so from shore to shore. A notice on the fence warned that entry to the nature reserve was restricted, and via the main road only.

Nature reserve? Nick shrugged. Times had changed, all right. He turned into the wind and followed the fence along to the beach, scrambling down at a place where dirt had been bulldozed, weedless and full of stones, to the edge in an attempt at shoreline repair. The sand was firm, when he reached it.

What did he really think he was looking for? And what did he think he'd find? He could no more turn back the clock than he could raise Johnny Mays from the dead. Once he'd run along these beaches and he'd played under these vast, leaden skies, and he'd dreamed of becoming the kind of man that his childhood self might have worshipped. But then he'd grown older and come to realise that, even when it happened, it never happened in quite the way that it should; and that in the end, in getting it all to work, you somehow gave away more than you gained. That was it, that was growing up. And when you got wise enough to see it, you were somehow supposed to be strong enough to accept it.

And that was all?

The way that he felt right now, only an act of faith could tell him otherwise . . . and Nick wasn't up to acts of faith, at least not today.

Instead, here he was.

Down river again, and wondering how it could all have gone so badly wrong.

———

The ruined book held close to his chest, Johnny lay amidst the coats on his borrowed bed and stared at the ceiling. Sleep was bearing down on him hard, like a set of bench weights that he wouldn't be able to hold up for much longer. His mind raced, to no particular purpose. Sometimes Johnny was afraid of sleep.

He didn't dream like other people did. Of this much, he was sure. Could ordinary people's dreams be so vivid, so complex, so crammed full of meaning? He'd always told himself that he ought to start writing them down, but so far he never had. He would, though, someday. They'd make an incredible book. Johnny had always known that he could write the most incredible book, something that would really shake people and make them sit up and realise exactly who it was they were dealing with, here. The movie would be even better, with Johnny playing himself.

Only one thing had stopped him so far, and that was finding the time.

For the moment the only book in his life was the black one, and it lay under his hand as if receiving a blessing. Messy and illegible now, it had never been much to look at anyway; the book's real power lay in its secret soul and that, like Johnny, seemed able to survive any fall. Johnny only had to close his eyes for a moment, and he could see its true form. Black as midnight. Bindings edged and decorated in silver, incorporating the skulls of birds and the bones of small animals and jewelled drops of human bodily fluids. The covers locked by a tiny knucklebone, fitting flush into its socket and opening with a pop. And inside . . .

He opened his eyes. The weariness was seductive.

Some dreams were easy enough to deal with. The one he had at least once every year, for example, usually around September, where some unexplained administrative mistake had him back in school on the first day of term. It had unsettled and depressed him the first few times around, but he'd seen it enough to be able to deal with it now. Or the one from when he'd broken his nose in a pub fight on patrol, where he'd woken up in hospital to find a doctor dragging yard after yard of bloody packing from out of his nostrils. Or the weird one about potatoes that he'd been having since childhood.

Some were easy, some were less so.

But the one that he actually feared was the one where he made it all up with Alice.

The settings varied. Sometimes the boardwalk, sometimes the beach. They'd be walking along and he'd have his arm around her shoulders and he'd be holding her tightly against his side, and he'd know that his life wasn't just a one-way street of mistakes and lost opportunities but that it could suddenly all come good. Everything that he'd thought was leading him away from her, had actually led him here. He was never sure what they said, or how it had happened. There was just the utter, utter bliss of that moment, so perfect that he could almost cry. The hard pressure of her side against him. The pure electricity of her. He'd feel an elation that would beat any cocaine rush; there was nothing of the usual nightmare stuff in it at all.

What scared him was the waking afterwards, and the realisation that none of it had been true.

So he lay, and he stared at the faint patternings of mould on the bedroom ceiling, and he told himself that sleep was nothing, and that there could be rest without it.

He told himself that it was a matter of will power, like sticking your hand in a flame.

He told himself.

He tol

He

14

As Bruno climbed the open-sided stairway to the third floor of the flats, he marked every turn with a mild curse on the name of Nick Frazier.

It's nothing personal, he was thinking. But couldn't you have picked someone else to dump all this onto, you miserable bastard? Nick had now been out of town for four days, and it hadn't been until the third of these that Bruno had finally caved in and taken the envelope from his desk drawer. Bruno wasn't bent; not in any sense; he'd once accepted a discount on some furniture but that hadn't really amounted to anything, and he'd had his car serviced free a couple of times, but where was the harm in any of that? The fact of it was that when somebody had offered him any material advantage, even in the most routine and innocent way, he'd usually felt too awkward to accept it and too embarrassed to go back again afterwards. Bruno had heard of officers so corrupt that they'd take stolen goods in evidence and then sell them back to their owners, but he liked to think that if ever he came across such a scenario he'd have no hesitation in pulling the plugs on it instantly.

The rules were the rules, after all.

But he also understood that an organisation, like any good machine, needed a certain amount of grease to make it run. Which meant that when you were presented with a situation which hung together and made sense and that everybody was happy with, where Johnny Mays came out of it looking good and where even the monitoring committee couldn't get a convincing objection together, then it only seemed reasonable to let everything stand as it was. Things that weren't broke shouldn't ought to be fixed, as Bruno's father had often been heard to say . . . like the time he'd said it about five minutes before a shelf had come crashing down in the garage and splashed creosote in through the open windows of the car.

This, Bruno had felt with a growing unease as he'd taken out the envelope and turned it over in his hands again and again, was perhaps another of those situations. Looking the other way had its limitations, as defensive strategies went. It certainly wouldn't be much help in the face of an oncoming truck.

So he'd opened it.

He paused to get his breath when he came out onto the third-floor walkway. He wasn't anything like as fit as he ought to be. He was alone, and hadn't told anyone where he was going. Now he stood and looked out across the windswept plaza at the heart of the bullring, and wondered who in their right minds could ever have pictured ordinary people wanting to live in a place that looked like a derelict set from an Italian gladiator movie. Architects who lived out in the greenbelt, he supposed, in mock-Tudor residences with ivy on the walls.

Well, wasn't it always the way.

He walked along, counting the doors because so many of them were missing their numbers. Most of them were missing their tenants, as well, the flats gutted and left for kids to break in so they could light fires and piss in the corners. How long before the entire area was due to come down, now? There had been a time when a lone police officer walking around here could feel about as safe as Colonel Sanders' pet rooster, but there had been other times before that when the estate had actually been sought-after by slum families who'd never before known decent plumbing, and who'd kept it semi-respectable for decades. Now it was to become just what the town needed, another derelict site. Someone obviously thought that there weren't enough of them around.

Nick's account hadn't mentioned the cardboard that someone had tacked up to replace the glass that had been broken out of the door, but the detail came as no surprise to Bruno. He waited after knocking, and it was about a minute before the door opened a few cautious inches.

She knew him from the inquest.

"You've got a nerve," she said.

"I'm not here to stir up trouble," he said. "Can't I come in?"

She let him in reluctantly. She wore a blue nylon overall and carpet slippers and although she couldn't have been much older than Frazier and Mays, she looked about thirty-five going on sixty. Bruno had heard that she'd been ill and that she'd had to give up her day job on the old outdoor market because of it; her voice was hoarse enough to have been run through a grater.

The inside of the flat was unexpectedly neat and clean but terrifically overdone, too much furniture crowded into too little space and a huge colour TV dominating everything from one corner of the room. Woolworths' prints hung on palm-tree wallpaper, and over on the sideboard about a dozen ready-made photoframes in different sizes were pushed together with a few pieces of mass-produced china.

One of the frames, Bruno noted, had been hung with black crêpe for mourning.

She didn't invite him to sit, didn't offer him anything. She'd let him in because he was the law, but that was as much as she was prepared to do.

"I'd like to talk to the younger boy," Bruno said. "He was with the others on that night, wasn't he?"

Her eyes were small and dark and bitter, and they burned like tiny coals. There might be many reasons why the police would want to talk to her children, but concern had never been one of them. "Haven't you done enough?" she said.

"Just to talk. Nothing else."

Talk? She had plenty of that and it came out all of a sudden, hoarse as she was. It rapidly became clear to Bruno that she was ready to give as many alibis as her boy might need, many of them self-contradictory and most of them less than credible. Her son was a good boy, a good son to her. Bruno tried to get a question in and she showed him some object of indeterminate purpose from the mantelpiece and explained how the boy had made it for her at school, with his own hands.

Bruno finally managed, "Where is he? Can I see him?" But by now she was too well into her stride to be stopped so easily.

"He's out somewhere right now," she said. "He does good turns for old people. He's probably doing some old lady's shopping or cleaning her windows."

At this, Bruno winced. Shoplifting he might have believed, but shopping? he thought. Do me a favour.

Moving over towards the sideboard, he said, "Perhaps I can wait."

"He goes off for days, sometimes. He goes to stay with his dad."

"Any address?"

But of course there wasn't, because he knew from the inquest that the best information on the father's whereabouts was that he lived in a caravan in North Wales and somewhere close to the beach. Bruno was now pretending a casual interest in the snapshot collection, and looking at a wedding photograph showing a wide-boy teenager alongside an averagely pretty girl whom he could barely connect with the woman alongside him. Next to this, hung with the black crêpe, was a professional studio shot of two boys in clean shirts and with their hair spit-combed and their smiles closed over gappy teeth. The older boy, he'd last seen being lifted like so much laundry. In the picture, his cheeks shone like apples.

Bruno knew a losing streak when he saw one. His best chance would have been to catch the boy at home. He could wait around for a while, but could he face any more of the propaganda? Now she was telling him all about Billy and his good works for the church and Bruno, who'd realised some time ago that he wasn't going to live forever, said resignedly, "Okay . . . thanks for your time."

And just as he was turning to leave, a shadow appeared on the outside of the door, seen through what remained of the frosted glass panelling.

The shadow of somebody not too tall.

The cardboard was punched in and a child's arm reached through, groping for the latch. Bruno was momentarily hypnotised by the sight and it was enough to give the woman a chance to shout, "Go on, Billy! It's the police for ye!"

The arm instantly withdrew, there was a crash as something was dropped outside, and Bruno had to move fast as the woman reached to grab at his jacket. He shook her off and got to the door, and as he emerged he almost fell over an electric kettle that was lying on the walkway outside.

Something connected with Billy's good works for the church, Bruno assumed. Of Billy himself there was no sign, but when Bruno stopped to listen he could hear running footsteps on concrete echoing from somewhere around. But where?

He ran for the nearest stairwell, which wasn't the one that he'd come in by. What he could see was mostly the plain timber of boarded windows with graffiti spilling across the panels and onto the brickwork, and what he could hear was mostly the thin howling of the wind three floors above ground-level. The open-sided gallery ran on ahead of him, five yards wide and empty of all souls until an elderly man stepped out of one of the few occupied flats.

He stood there and stared at Bruno, making no attempt to disguise his interest.

"There was a boy," Bruno said breathlessly. "Which way did he go?"

"Little bastard," the man said promptly, "I'd show him." And Bruno's heart began to sink at the prospect of a conversation about Law and Order and Kids Today and The Way It Used To Be Around Here.

"Just tell me which way," he said.

"Soon as a flat's empty, they're in. I phone the police, and what happens?"

"*Which fucking way?*" Bruno screamed at him, and saw the man flinch back under the blast.

It was just then that he heard a faint *No, mister, no!* carried down to them from somewhere on the deck overhead; and then before Bruno could move, Billy went by in free-fall on the far side of the rail.

He passed within reach, but Bruno could never have hoped to be fast enough to do anything. He got a quick flash-impression of Billy struggling like a sleeper caught up in invisible sheets, and then the boy had gone.

It all happened in silence.

Bruno resisted the impulse to look for the landing, a body run through with an instant shockwave that would pulp him inside his own skin like fruit in a bag, and instead he ran on to the stairwell and up.

The next deck was the uppermost, with nowhere higher to go, and it was empty; solidly boarded the full length of its frontage and knee-deep in trash and broken glass, it looked like wall-to-wall bomb damage. On the ply nearest to Bruno, somebody called Gaz had written his name in dogshit.

Seeing no-one around, Bruno went to the rail and looked down.

He was almost on the spot from which the boy must have fallen; his flattened body was directly below, a scruffy-kid doll beaten all out of shape with a single blow. A couple of stray mongrels had come sniffing around, curious but not daring to get too close. Bruno could hear a car starting up somewhere, a sluggish whining like that of an old clunker with a nearly-flat battery, but when he tried to place its direction he was defeated by the distorting echo of the building itself. It was probably coming from one of the access tunnels, and it could have been coming from any of them.

And let's face it, he was thinking . . . the boy hadn't simply fallen.

The boy looked as if he'd been thrown.

Now the anonymous car was history, and somebody was screaming down below. Bruno saw heads sticking out on other decks, and faces turning up towards him. Jesus, he thought, where were they all coming from? Somebody pointed, and then somebody else, and he could feel their anger rising up like vengeful heat.

It was pretty clear that they were all assuming that he'd done it.

Bruno ran for the stairs.

The elderly man was still outside his flat, goggling over the rail like everybody else.

"I need your phone," Bruno told him, and hoped that he *had* a phone.

"It's in the back," the man said, and he followed Bruno into his dim and lace-curtained parlour with all of its must and stale odours.

Bruno said, "Lock that door and put a chair against it."

"What for?"

"Do it!"

The first of them arrived a couple of minutes later, while Bruno was still talking on the phone to the ops room sergeant. He could see their shadow-shapes against the curtains, and their numbers were steadily growing. They had the definite air of a lynch mob. The old man checked the placing of his best dining chair with shaking hands; unable to understand the dynamics of the situation he'd become as malleable as a child, doing as he was told and wedging the chair firmly under the handle on the inside of the door. He'd found a duster that he'd wanted to slide in to keep the polish from getting scored, but Bruno had cupped the phone and barked for him to leave everything as it was.

Somebody started to rap on the window with a coin.

Others joined in, hammering on the window and on the glass in the door, and then fingers appeared through the letterbox and Bruno realised, too late, that the old man kept a key hanging on a string as a defence against locking himself out. The string was being drawn through the open flap and the key was rising as if being levitated, and Bruno knew, just *knew*, that he could drop the phone and dive across the room and no matter how fast he moved, he wouldn't be there in time to stop them getting it through.

He did. He wasn't.

He knew that there was no other way in or out because he'd checked, and he had no choice but to sit tight and wait for the sirens. Please God, he thought, let the boys find me quick and not go wandering all over the show trying to work out where they are. Put in one beat copper who knows the ground and I swear I'll start going to confession and look at me, I'm not even a Catholic. He held the chair fast as they got the key into the lock, and it took all of his weight to keep it down as the door began to thump inward showing a sliver of light along its edge with every charge.

The old man was whimpering.

Bruno was sure that he must have had worse times, mostly in his nightmares.

But he couldn't offhand remember when.

15

For the first time in as long as he could remember, Nick went to church.

It was the big old stone church at the heart of the village where Johnny's parents now lived, a crumbling gothic on raised ground overlooking the heart of town – if you could call it a town – and the drained lands to the south. It was early in the evening when Nick stepped inside and pulled the heavy door closed behind him, and saw that the nave was all but empty.

Tomorrow morning was the date set for Johnny's memorial service, this church was the venue, and Veronica Mays was setting out the flowers alone.

She hadn't heard him come in. He waited at the back for a while, wondering if he could bring himself to disturb her. She was down beyond the altar rail and absorbed in what she was doing, a stout figure moving slowly. Between them was a world of high vaulted gloom with a chill in the air, white stone shot through with yellow and heavily stained around the walls and column bases by penetrating damp from the graveyard outside. The only hints of warmth came from flowers, velvet, and wood, and from the gilt highlights on the altar screen.

He detached himself from the shadows, and walked down towards her. She picked up the hollow sound of his footsteps and turned, sensing him like a blind thing; but then when she saw and recognised him, she gave him a smile which was pleasant even if it was a little restrained.

She said, "Hello again, Nick."

He stepped up into the carpeted area between the choir stalls. "Mrs Mays," he said with a nod.

"Were you looking for somebody?"

"I only wanted to ask if there's anything else you're going to need."

"You already asked me that," she said, "the last time we met."

"So I did," Nick said, and stopped short of the altar rail steps with his hands in his pockets. Were hands in pockets okay in church? He knew that you couldn't wear a hat, but that was about as far as his knowledge went. He hadn't felt this awkward since . . . well, since the last time he'd talked to Veronica Mays. He studied the woodwork and tried to think what to say next.

Johnny's mother said, "What's troubling you, Nick? Is it something you'd like to tell me? Something about Johnny?"

"More like something I wanted to ask you," he said, scuffing the carpet on the steps with his shoe. "But somehow I get the feeling that it could be a touchy subject."

"Nothing like that could matter now."

Oh, no? he thought. Try this.

He began, "Did Johnny keep in contact with any of his old friends around here?"

Half-turning back to her flowers, she said, "I expect that he did. He never told us much, but he was very well liked. You just wait until the service tomorrow, and you'll see what I mean." She shot him a look. "You *are* coming to the service, aren't you?"

And Nick, who hadn't planned to, said, "Of course."

Veronica Mays nodded. "You'll see how many friends he really had."

"What about Alice Craig? Were she and Johnny ever close, at all?"

Something in her froze.

And something in her eyes set like concrete.

"I really wouldn't know," she said, and the subtext

signalled to Nick was that she didn't want to be pressed any further on the matter. She busied herself, moving away and avoiding Nick's eyes.

Feeling pretty low for doing it, Nick followed her. He said, "I met up with her again. She didn't know about him until I told her. She took it . . . well, she took it kind of strangely."

"I can't imagine why," she said.

"Are you sure? Because he kept a photograph of her from way back."

This caught her by surprise, and for a moment she was too taken aback to keep on pretending. "He did?" she said, and he hurriedly dug in his pocket and brought out the sliver of a snapshot that Johnny had been using as a bookmark. Apart from that one encounter at the fair, he'd had no success in tracing her. An afternoon in the hotel with the phonebook had proved a total waste of time.

But the tougher it became, the more convinced Nick was that he had to find her again. Alice had taken the news strangely, all right; surprised, but not exactly what Nick could have called unhappy. He sensed history, there, and he wondered if persistence might bring it up to the light.

Veronica Mays stared at the innocent-looking picture of the girl on the radiator, and Nick read what he could from her expression; sadness, regret, a hint of pity for her boy and his lifetime's worth of unshown feelings. Up in the clocktower, the quarter-hour bell began to chime.

"I really don't want to talk about it," she said.

"I'm sorry. Do you want this?"

She shook her head, and he returned the picture to his pocket. "He was a sensitive child," she said. "I don't know why, but I'm the only one who ever seems to have seen that in him. Excuse me, Nick."

Nick nodded, and she moved away; over to the far side of the church and into the Lady Chapel where, with her back to Nick, she stepped into a pew and knelt. She bent as if in prayer, but Nick didn't have to be able to see her face to know that silent tears were running.

He hesitated for a moment. He felt low and responsible, but he couldn't see anything that he might do which wouldn't make it worse.

So, as quietly as he could, he left her there.

———

Hell could never be so cold.

But then again, heaven could surely never be so bleak.

The fire had burned itself out while he'd been away, and getting it going again hadn't exactly been easy. Johnny didn't seem to be able to keep his concentration on any one thing for too long. Driving had been no problem, that was automatic, but finding his way back here had been something else. All of the country lanes looked the same and the light had changed on him, and this had to be the reason why the access road had been so difficult to find.

Now he was back, but it didn't feel much like home.

When he'd put the car away he'd taken a look into the adjoining shed, out of curiosity. He had a vague feeling that he'd looked in there before, but he couldn't be sure. He'd found a couple of dead animals under a coat in one of the stalls, looking as if they'd once been sheep or maybe even dogs; they'd been so chopped-about, it was difficult to tell. The instrument that had been used on them, a sickle of some kind, had been hanging on the back wall of the shed. Blood had run down the boards and dried in thin streaks from its clotted and matted edge. Johnny had looked at the blade and then gone back to look at the carcases again, chipped bone showing white here and there and the dark meat blackening around the edges of the cuts. Death fascinated Johnny, always had. Some of his better dreams were of death, as a river dreamed of the sea.

Sometimes it was of death, sometimes horses by moonlight. When you were dreaming, you took what came along.

Now, with the last of the coal and the old man's Bible stoking up into a respectable blaze in the grate, Johnny went through into the kitchen to see what was on the menu. Every time, it was like a discovery; the stock was getting smaller and nothing new was being added, but he never even seemed to be able to recall what his last meal had been, let alone what he'd left behind. Each time he opened the cupboard doors he'd been faced with soup, and beans, and cheap Irish stew, and he'd taken whatever was nearest. He'd carried it through in order to sit with it by the fire, and he'd hacked open the can and eaten the contents cold. It didn't matter to him. It might as well have been dog food. He tasted nothing.

He ate in the same way that an athlete trained, shut off from his senses and his mind on some further goal. Exactly what that goal might be he still couldn't say for certain, but with concentration he knew that he'd get there. It was like watching the sky for aircraft. Most of the time you were staring out into nothing, but you couldn't let your attention slip for a minute.

Like this morning. This morning he'd –

He'd been out, hadn't he?

Hadn't he?

Desperate with panic and the food forgotten, Johnny ran to the stairs. He stumbled on the first couple of steps, flew up the rest with only his speed keeping his balance, and grabbed at the wall as he reached the turning. It was a narrow space and dark because it had no window, but it *did* have the mirror.

Johnny looked into the glass.

I'm Johnny Mays, he whispered, and like a junkie on a heroin rush so pure that it was deadly, he felt the warmth of certainty go rocketing through all of the cold spaces in his heart.

There are three great evils that go beyond forgiveness,

the devil behind the glass reminded him. The first is betrayal, the next is inconsistency, and the third and the last of these is unfinished business. Johnny closed his eyes in relief as he leaned on the wall. The greatest sin of all was betrayal but the other two were its wingmen, tucked in close and not so far behind. He knew where he'd been, now, and what he'd been doing. He could remember the eight-year-old, the one that he'd last seen grinning wildly at him from the back of the stolen BMW. He hadn't been smiling when Johnny had dumped him over the side; he'd been fighting so hard that he'd almost struggled his way out of his shirt, and hauling him out over the rail had been the cleanest and simplest way to deal with him. Go join your brother, Johnny had said to him as he'd shaken him free, and the child had screamed *No, Mister, no!* as he'd danced in the air. Johnny had walked away then, not even staying to watch him fall.

As far as Johnny was concerned, business had been taken care of.

He descended the stairs, slowly.

He didn't know how much longer he'd be able to stay here. He knew that it would have to be a way station only and that there would be nothing permanent for him, not now or ever again. In his life he'd walked a thin line and now, in this period that was something other than his life, he'd clearly crossed it. He was in strange territory and casting a long shadow on unfamiliar ground, but the strength of his purpose would carry him through.

His campaign.

His crusade.

Johnny stepped around the dead man's chair to get to the fire. He'd been sleeping on the rug, curled up and facing the blaze to get the most out of the heat. When it came to betrayal, inconsistency, and unfinished business, there was only one authoritative guide for him to follow. It was the Baedeker of evil, a user's handbook in a world of the fallen.

From the small heap of his possessions that he'd moved through from the kitchen to the hearth, Johnny took his Little Black Book.

He'd managed to open some of the pages with a table knife. They were utterly destroyed and impossible to read, but that was no problem for Johnny. For hours now he'd been studying them, and somewhere between the page and his mind an image would begin to form. Memories of good times might fade away like cheap photographs but a slight, given a little effort, could always be recalled. He settled on the rug and, with a brief shiver at the evening chill that had taken up residence outside this circle of warmth, he threw a couple of old bookclub titles onto the fire.

Wasn't there something about food, he thought? But the thought didn't stay around for long enough to get itself noticed. More important matters were to hand.

With his attention fully on the ruined paper before him, Johnny Mays started to plan his return from the dead.

16

There were no more than a dozen traders on the village main street, most of their premises dusty and closed. Goods on display said that nearly all of them were still in business, but nothing said when. Nick was still in his car across from the menswear shop and beginning to worry when, at four minutes after ten, the blinds were still down. At eight minutes after, he got out of his vehicle and went over and hammered on the door.

Nobody but a small-town operator could hike his prices so high and then make the stuff so hard to get. Nick could remember how his mother had hated them, not as individuals or even as a species, more an entire sub-classification somewhere on a level with the invertebrates. One of his earliest memories was of her telling him how they'd turn the sign in your face on the dot of five o'clock and then stand on the other side of the glass shaking their heads, and of how the local shops always stank of cooking from somewhere in the back. Now most people got what they needed from retail hypermarkets on the edge of town, and the small traders were going to the wall. They complained all the way about the disappearance of their unique service, but nobody seemed to want to hear. The big five o'clock had finally arrived, and the sign had been turned around to face the other way.

After a couple of minutes of making a noise, he got in.

Nick followed the owner back into what could only be described as a fashion museum. Nobody dressed like this outside of a catalogue, he thought as he waited for the window blinds to be raised and the lights to be switched on. Mud-coloured knitwear and folded Y-fronts were stacked under a glass-fronted counter on open shelves; around the walls were racks of trousers and jackets and raincoats that wouldn't have looked out of place on the streets of Moscow in 1953. Nick told the owner what he wanted, and the owner hummed and muttered and dug around and finally came up with a flat box containing a tissue-covered selection.

"See anything here?" he said, and without any deliberation Nick pointed.

"That one," he said.

The owner lifted the dark tie up to the light. "I wouldn't call that a black," he said. "It's more of a dark blue."

"That'll be okay," Nick said. "It isn't quite a funeral."

The morning of the Johnny Mays memorial service had called for some pretty fine timing, and Nick could only hope that this delay hadn't thrown his schedule out. Get there too early, and he'd have to mingle with the crowd on the steps and look solemn. Walk in on the service late, and every head would turn to look at him. Leaving his car on the street and knotting the new tie as he went, he headed for the church as fast as he could without actually breaking into a run.

He was late, and the show had started; but it hardly seemed to matter, because the church was almost empty.

About a dozen people sat in the first couple of rows, and that was it. The choir area had been closed off with an ornamental gate and then a couple of candlesticks and a lectern had been brought forward to make a smaller worship zone alongside the pulpit, but there was no disguising the paucity of the turnout. Not one of those that he could see could have been described as a friend of Johnny's; these were the friends of Frank and Veronica Mays, full stop. As Nick came forward down one of the outer aisles, he could hear the eulogy being relayed through small and incongruous speakers that had been fixed at shoulder height to the stone pillars supporting the roof. *Jonathan pursued a difficult path in difficult times*, the vicar was saying, and Nick could see him over the two rows of greying heads and floral hats, most of them bowed; he was youngish, bearded and bespectacled, and he had the long-haired look of a born-again folk singer. If ever he'd actually met Johnny Mays, it had to have been in some other life and in some other form.

Nick slipped into a pew about five rows back. He'd stand for the hymns and incline his head for the prayers, but he wouldn't pretend to join in; he'd lost religion a long time ago and, perversely, had experienced his few real glimpses of mystery since then. He'd learned nothing of Johnny's views on theology in the time that they'd been together again, although he *had* heard his opinions on the likes of the vicar; Johnny had reckoned that hippies ought to be dug up and gassed, like badgers.

Everybody bent their heads to pray.

Nick couldn't have joined in even if he'd wanted to, because everybody else seemed to have a printed card to follow and he didn't. So he looked around, instead, and wondered how long before it would all be over. The church was pleasant enough as old buildings went, but there seemed to be more of death than of life about it. Carved wall plaques that had been intended as eternal monuments now stood unread, and even the daylight that lay across the pews had been stained yellow by the age of the glass that it had passed through.

A soft footstep sounded on the stone just behind him; a verger bringing one of the crib sheets, he assumed, but when he glanced around he saw that he was wrong.

It was Alice Craig, and she slid into the pew to sit alongside him.

Because of the situation he couldn't look at her, at least not beyond that first nod of recognition as he hitched along to make more space, but his very skin seemed to be aware of her as she sat beside him. He wondered at this. The prayer ended and a man that Nick didn't know, but whom he assumed to be a friend of the family, moved over to the lectern and began to give a stiff but sincere reading from Ecclesiastes about how there was no remembrance of former things, nor would there be any remembrance of things that were to come with those that would come after. Nick's mind started to wander. It wandered to Johnny Mays, ten years old, torturing the ant colony on the railway embankment with a tin of lighter fluid and some matches.

The service ended on a hymn with accompaniment from some unseen organist, one dozen reedy voices raised and lost in the gloom overhead. When the final verse was over and the organ was playing out its last few bars, Nick was able to look at Alice again.

"I'm glad you came," he whispered. She wasn't in black but she was soberly dressed. Her jacket and skirt didn't look cheap but they didn't look quite new, either; he guessed that she'd probably taken time off from her office job to get here.

She was looking at the rest of the congregation, who were now beginning to stir. Her voice as low as Nick's, she said, "How much did I miss?"

"Most of it. Want to grab a sandwich in the pub when it's all over?"

"I've less than an hour. Is this *everybody*?"

"Just you, and me, and the blood relations. And *I* nearly managed to dodge it."

The vicar was moving down to speak to Veronica Mays, and everybody else seemed to be reaching for hats and handbags. Alice said, "I think we ought to leave," and there was a hint of urgency in the way she said it that made the words more than a suggestion.

Nick saw why a moment later, as Veronica Mays turned to look back down the mostly empty church; Alice was moving now and Nick had risen to follow, so he alone saw the darkness in the older woman's expression as she recognised the two of them. The vicar had taken her hand and was telling her something with great earnestness, but she didn't even appear to be listening. She looked on Alice Craig without warmth, without sorrow, without any human emotion at all; she watched her as she moved toward the door, and then she glanced briefly at Nick before turning away.

Nick followed Alice out, and around the side of the church away from the main doors. She was waiting for him, looking over the inscriptions on some of the older stones. This was the quiet side of the building, where a perimeter path ran out between the built-up graveyard and a tall hedge of ferns to a little-used lane. The turf around the headstones had been recently mown, and was crossed with long, drifting trails of dying grass. Some of the stones themselves were leaning danger-ously; others had weathered so badly that their inscrip-tions were illegible.

Nick said, "Why did you come, if you and Johnny were never close?"

"I didn't say we *never* were. You want to know the truth, I came to see you."

"Me?"

"I wanted to apologise. I kind of left you flat, back at the fair the other night."

You did, you did, thought Nick, but he said, "That's okay. I didn't take offence."

"Apology accepted, then?"

"Apology unnecessary. It wasn't the best way to get bad news."

She smiled briefly. Her smile was a little crooked. He remembered it now. "Bad news?" she said. "I suppose you could call it that," and then she moved on to the next stone.

Nick kicked along after. Where the gravel had thinned, it was possible to see the original path of herringboned brick that lay underneath. He said, "I don't want to pry into any big secrets, but . . . what exactly went on?"

"There are no big secrets," Alice said. "Just sad little ones that look big to the people they affect."

"If you'd rather forget it, just say the word."

She seemed to be looking so far inward that the moon and the stars would have appeared less remote.

"That's the word I've been looking for, most of my life," she said.

And then she moved along a stone.

Feeling more certain of the ground with every step that he took, Nick said, "You know, I never realised it until I saw you grown-up. But every woman he ever chased looked a little bit like you."

A mistake.

He knew it as soon as he saw her expression as she turned to him; or rather, the way she turned *on* him. He realised then that his confidence had been misplaced, that he'd been walking on the thinnest of thin ice, and now suddenly he'd fallen through. Eyes wide, the sudden anger was radiating off her like heat. He almost took a step back and he was thinking Oh, shit, how did I manage *this*?

"Is that your sick idea of a joke?" she demanded.

"It wasn't meant that way," Nick said hurriedly, and as an excuse it sounded lame even to him.

"I don't *care* what you meant. I'm going, now. I don't want to hear from you again. Don't even think about trying to get in touch with me."

The metal kissing-gate crashed behind her as she went out into the lane behind the church, leaving Nick standing there and wishing that it was possible to be in two places at once so that he could give himself a good kick up the arse. He knew better than to follow and plead with her; even if it worked, he reckoned, you did yourself too much damage for any of the consequences to be worthwhile. There were cars parked out in the lane, their roofs just visible above the low brick retaining wall, and

Alice stopped by one of these and then moved down and out of sight.

He heard the car door slam.

Nick ran to the wall as she started the engine and pulled out. Her car was a red hatchback, almost new, and as he hopped onto a raised stone for a better look she was out into the lane and angrily stepping on the accelerator. Thirty yards down she braked, turned, and was gone.

But not, Nick reflected as he climbed down from the low monument, so quickly that he hadn't had a chance to memorise her registration number.

Hoping that the mourning party would now have cleared the church, Nick went looking for something that he could use to write the number down.

At least, he thought, Johnny would have approved of his methods.

17

Being one of the less attractive Pennine villages, it had come through the last couple of decades pretty well unscathed. Poets and artists, most of them looking for places that resembled pictures in the storybooks of their childhood, had passed on through without a second look. They'd made instead for the Dales villages, places with whitewash and watermills and pubs with oak beams, and weren't even inclined to slow down for a place whose main features were a pub so spartan that its lounge resembled a Sunday League changing room, and beyond that a roadside croft with about a dozen second-hand Land Rovers permanently on sale. Nobody moved into its empty barns to make pots that nobody wanted, and not one regional TV executive had taken up weekend residence; such people were all somewhere else, buying up the houses and vainly searching for the spirit of Nutwood.

Which pissed off Bob Woolton mightily, since for ten years now he'd been the owner of two inherited properties that he'd given up all hope of being able to sell.

Bob was a dairy farmer, moving his herd around rented acreage that consisted of a number of different fields scattered all about the village. He was short and he was wiry, and even his old mother would have conceded that his resemblance to a rat or a whippet was too striking to ignore. The living was okay even though the hours were long; simply keeping on top of the fencing repairs was a full-time job, because the stone walls between the fields were so decayed in places and the barbed wire so old and rusty. He'd tried chicken wire and it had seemed to do the trick for a while, but walkers prised out the staples so that they could get their dogs underneath.

Because of this, he was used to getting calls about stray cattle; there were weak spots in the boundaries that nothing short of a brick wall could plug, and in some places a reasonably agile beast could scramble up onto an overhanging embankment and then be too nervous to make the leap back to its companions. Strays were no big deal, even if they happened to get out onto the roads – he'd once had a heifer that had been hit by a car and then walked away shaken but unscathed, while the car had been a write-off – but all the same he wished that they could choose some other time than four o'clock in the morning to turn up in somebody's garden.

This time was different. This time he got the call mid-afternoon and it wasn't somebody's garden, it was the main street right in the middle of the village; the missionary's widow who lived around behind the old chapel had been coming out of the Spar grocery store when the animal had thundered out of an alleyway before her like a bolting horse. It had seemed frightened, confused; far more so than she would have expected, and she'd said that it had been in a pretty rough state physically, as well. This last part was a puzzle, because he'd split the herd only a couple of days before and taken a close look at each of the animals then. None was underfed and none of them had been showing any signs of illness, but the widow had been definite about the yellow tag in the beast's ear. That was Bob's marking, sure enough, and so he'd abandoned his quota forms (not without a certain relief) and gone out to the delivery truck that stood in the yard.

He'd always lived here. Until the age of eleven he'd attended the grim-looking village school with its asphalt yard that had torn the skin off his knees more often than he could count, and by the time that each school day started he'd already put in a couple of hours on deliveries. He'd gone out with a student nurse for over a year, but his wife came from another farming family less than ten miles away. He had three daughters, and even the youngest of them could drive a herd with nothing more than a switch and a loud yell. He didn't love the place or the life, exactly. He simply couldn't imagine doing anything else.

Derek, the landlord of the Black Dog, was waiting out by the side of the road to flag him down, and he waved the truck on into the car park around the side of the inn. This was less than a hundred yards away from the widow's sighting, and probably meant that the escapee had gone to ground. The parking area was almost empty at this time of the day, just Derek's new Vauxhall and his son's old Volkswagen, and Bob saw the animal immediately; it was running along the back fence of the car park and looking for a break in the planking, apparently having found its way in and now unable to find its way out.

Bob was shocked. The beast was a mess.

It was a young animal, stumbling and on the point of exhaustion like a fighting bull at the end of its run. Its eyes were glassy and rolling, its mouth trailing foam, ribs like an old tin washboard. Bob got out of his truck and walked over, approaching warily. The bullock was standing still and panting and then making sudden, jerky movements as if its limbs were under some random remote control.

"Get us a bucket of water, can you, Derek?" he said, and Derek backed off to comply.

As he waited for the water, Bob studied the animal from a safe distance. It seemed calmer now, as if it real-ised that someone around here understood it at last. Bob had never seen a worse case of dehydration in an animal. He hoped that it wouldn't turn out to be anything more serious. He needed an epidemic about as much as he needed his dick tattooed.

Derek came out with a gallon of lukewarm water in

the stainless steel slops bucket from under the bar. The bullock's head came around at the scent of it and Bob moved in, talking to calm the animal as he set the bucket down. As it drank, the gurgling sounds from its insides were as deep and remote as castle plumbing. Bob patted and stroked its flank, feeling the poor condition of its hide.

"One of yours?" Derek said.

"You cheeky bugger," Bob said. "Does he look like one of mine?"

"He's got your tag."

"And so have a dozen others that I've sold these last two years."

"Whose, then?"

Whose, indeed.

Bob stroked the desperate animal's side, and wondered.

––––––––

"Bruno?"

"That Nick?"

"The same."

"You're a bastard, Frazier. You've really dumped me in it."

"Dumped you how?"

"I don't think I even want to talk about it. What are you calling me for?"

"Would you believe plain old friendship?"

"I'd rather believe that the Pope was circumcised. Is there a point to this, or are you just ringing to tell me about your trip?"

"The trip's a revelation. They're building a Sainsbury's where the old house used to be, and Johnny Mays' mother still cuts the crusts off the sandwiches."

"The *point*, Frazier."

"What happened to *Nick*?"

"If you knew about the time I've been having because

of you and your fucking envelope, you wouldn't even ask."

"Rough, huh?"

"I went to talk to that other kid. You know the one, the little brother? Well, he took off when he saw me coming. Tried some fancy evasive tactics and took a swan-dive all the way down from the top deck."

"Messy?"

"He was just a bag of pulp when they tried to pick him up. It's a damned good job that I had a witness, or I'd have been hard-pushed to prove that I didn't toss him over."

"I don't know what to say."

"I bet."

"But there's something you could do for me."

"Am I hearing this right? There's something you want *me* to do for *you*?"

"Run me a license number, Bruno. Just the one."

"For what?"

"For old times' sake."

"I mean, for what purpose?"

"I want to track down a woman."

"You randy little git. I'm facing a hurricane full of shit over here, and you want help with your sex life?"

"That's not how it is. I think she's an old girlfriend of Johnny's."

"So what?"

"I think maybe something happened between them. I don't know what, but I wonder if it had something to do with the way that he turned out."

"We're talking about history, here."

"Cause and effect, Bruno. Cause and effect. She turned up at his memorial service."

"To fan an old flame?"

"Actually, I think she may have come along to reassure herself that he really was dead. Are you going to check this number for me, or not?"

"I'm thinking about it."

"Well, don't think all day, will you? I'm paying hotel rates on this phone. Bruno?"

"Bruno?"

"How about it, Bruno?"

———

Bob had sent his eldest daughter into the farm office to check the bullock's tag number against his sales book, although this had been for confirmation only; even as he was hitching the converted horsebox onto the tractor out in the yard, he was wondering exactly what might have happened with Mad Jack.

A terrible nickname for a simple old recluse who threatened nobody, but one that Bob used without even thinking about it. Mad Jack was a part of the landscape, something that he'd grown up with and so never even thought to question. When Bob had been a boy, the biggest dare around had been to go into the hills miles from anywhere and hammer on Mad Jack's door before running away. He'd seemed ancient even then, although he couldn't have been much older than in his fifties. Bob had never tried it himself, although he'd lain in hiding and watched others who had; one time there had been no reply, the other time Mad Jack had come out and looked around his yard and the open country beyond, squinting as if he perhaps needed glasses or the light wasn't good enough for him, and he'd called some name that Bob hadn't quite been able to catch. Then he'd gone back inside, and that was it.

Not exactly the most demented of performances. But still the nickname stuck.

There were rumours and stories, of course, the strongest of these being that Mad Jack's wife had died young and that the son that he'd struggled to bring up alone had been lost at sea. The facts, as Bob knew them, were

scarcely more detailed. Mad Jack rarely came down
into the village, but took one delivery of groceries
every month. These were left in a cardboard box on
a flat stone by the lane at the end of the dale, where
payment was always waiting. He hadn't seen a doctor
in more than twenty years. At nights he either walked
the lanes or drove around in his old Morris Traveller,
which he ran without road tax or insurance. His two main
appearances of the year were at the summer show and
the cattle market twenty miles away; he'd buy a young
heifer or a bullock, raise and fatten it, and then sell it as
a yearling and start over. As far as income went, this was
all he seemed to have; if he was due any state benefits,
he never picked them up.

Bob had done business with him the once, at the last
summer show. It was absurd but he'd felt shaky, almost
overwhelmed, as if he'd come face to face with a legend.
The Mad Jack of a boy's imagination had faded before
this tall, bony, sad-eyed and softly-spoken gentleman
with the worst teeth that Bob had ever seen. His clothes
had been threadbare, but carefully darned and patched,
and he'd taken the payment from a folded envelope that
he'd kept in an inside pocket. It was as he was counting
that Bob had realised that the notes were old money, a
design that hadn't been in circulation for ten years or
more, and he almost pointed the fact out; but he'd said
nothing, and the bank had exchanged them with no
problem. Perhaps there was something in the stories
about insurance money, it was impossible to say.

He'd had his chance to ask a couple of days later when
he'd delivered the bullock to the house at the top of the
dale, but he'd let it pass by. The weird feeling persisted.
This was the same yard that he'd watched so many years
before, unchanged in any detail; and this was Mad Jack,
shyly inviting him inside and offering him a brew. The
house was dark and damp and neglected, but it was tidy.
Back in the old days he and his friends had explored
any abandoned or derelict building that they could find,

and Bob could remember the buzz that he'd get from the discovery of some forgotten domestic detail like a scrap of old wallpaper still in place, or some floor tiles showing through on the bare ground where a house had once stood. Well, here was a mass of such details, a mouldering museum of a house, and here was its tenant doing his best to make some conversation when he'd obviously forgotten how. Bob sat there in the room's one good chair with his tea in an old-fashioned china cup, and he thought about how he couldn't wait to tell somebody about this.

But he didn't. The remarkable thing about the afternoon was that it had been so unremarkable. What kind of a story was that going to make?

No story at all, he thought, so you might as well let it pass.

Now there seemed to be some trouble, and Bob feared the worst. Mad Jack was getting on, after all, and how did that old rhyme go? About how no-one lives forever, and dead men rise up never, and even the longest river winds somewhere safe to sea . . . and if Mad Jack's river had finally wound its way down to its ultimate destination, then the hour ahead was going to be more memorable than pleasant.

His eldest girl climbed into the tractor cab behind him, and with one of the farm dogs running alongside they set out on the bumpy ride that would take them out around the back of the village and up to Dale Head. He'd hesitated about taking Debbie along. She was fifteen and forever being mistaken for a boy in her farm overalls and with her red hair cut short; too young for this kind of thing, perhaps, but with an inner toughness that he could only marvel at sometimes. She'd never knuckle down and be a farmer's wife; it would be more a matter of finding a young man who'd knuckle down to being a farmer's husband.

Not a bad day, he reckoned as he cast a weather eye at the distant hills, and he thought that maybe it wasn't a day for dying after all. Debbie jumped down and ran to open the first of the gates, and the animal in the trailer behind gave a bellow as its box was jarred in passing over the cattle grid. The beast was in a bad way, but it would live.

The journey took about twenty minutes.

"There's still police doing things down at the reservoir," Debbie said as she stood behind the saddle and craned to see down the slope, just before they made the turn which would lose them sight of the dam.

Mad Jack's gate stood open, as ever. Leaving the tractor's engine running, Bob climbed down and went over to knock at the door. When there was no reply he tried the handle, but the door was locked. Frowning, Bob moved along to the window. Jack had told him that he never locked his door, and that the last time he'd done it he'd shut himself out and had to break a window to get back in. Bob had considered the risk that he was running if there *was* insurance money in the house, but he'd said nothing. You couldn't tell old people about that kind of thing. His grandmother had kept her money in the tea caddy for years, convinced that it was a hiding place so original that nobody would ever guess at it, because she'd said that she didn't trust banks.

Debbie came around behind him, looking over his shoulder.

"Can't see anything inside," she said. "Should we break in?"

"Not unless we have to," Bob said. "Go see if there's any feed in the shed."

There had been no smoke visible from the chimney as they'd come up the dale, but from the narrow view of the fireplace that he could get from the window he thought that he could perhaps see a glow of embers. There was a lot of rubbish around the hearth, opened cans and rucked-up blankets, but he couldn't see too much of this because the armchair was in the way. The back of it blocked the view. For all that he could see from here, Mad Jack might even have been sitting in it.

He'd be able to see better from the other window, over on the far side of the house. As he made his way around, he fought down a sense of being watched. He was no teenaged trespasser, at least not any more; and he set down the unease that he felt as no more than an echo of old guilt, still sounding like a distant bell across a gap of years.

He bent and squinted through the grime on the glass, trying to make out the scene on the inside. The armchair was facing him now.

And as he slowly straightened, he could hear Debbie. She was calling to him, and she was calling with some urgency.

She was calling from one of the sheds.

18

Where was the point of it all, Alice sometimes wondered?

She didn't wonder it often, only when she hit a low spot, and this had to be the low spot to end them all. She'd been working in the property business for more than two years now, and reckoned that only the fraud squad could beat it for seeing people at their dissembling worst. Vendors and buyers, they were all as bad as each other. The only ones who were worse were those weird couples who regarded viewings as some kind of free entertainment, an excuse to get a look around the inside of someone else's home without any intention of making an offer. They almost always said they were going to, but then they'd disappear; on to other estate agencies, other appointments, other excuses to view.

Sometimes she wished she was still at her desk job with the employment bureau; at least she could have hunted herself up something better. Anything other than waitressing again. Restaurants were one of the few places where nobodies seemed to feel that they were buying the privilege of behaving like pampered scum. The shipping office hadn't been too bad; she'd even managed to get a couple of trips out on the regular freight runs, but then the line had been taken over and the office had been closed down.

She knew why she felt like this – or, at least, why she was feeling like this today – although she tried not to think about it.

The reason lay with Johnny Mays, for sure.

She'd all but forgotten him, as far as that was possible. But wasn't it just like Johnny? The moment you believed that you'd broken free of him at last, he'd find some way of getting himself back into your thoughts. She hadn't seen him in, what – ten? Fifteen years? But still he hung around in the back of her mind as if he had nowhere better to go.

Maybe now that he was dead, he'd finally stop haunting her. You as good as saw his funeral, now buckle down, she told herself. You've got work to do, here.

Alice worked in a small-town agency, one of a chain with a partner on the premises; sometimes she ran the desk but mostly she typed up the sheets and occasionally took out a client when Hathaway or his junior couldn't make it. The junior was Hathaway's nephew, and he was hopeless. Alice shared the office with Sandra; nineteen and strikingly good-looking, Sandra thought that the Beatles had been an over-rated group and that the Monkees were better. The office itself was a converted shopfront on the end of a row, carpet-tiled and overlit, with hessian panels displaying details of all the properties on the books. Hathaway's nephew had a desk by the window, Alice and Sandra had their wordprocessor screens half-hidden behind a Reception counter, and Hathaway himself had an office at the back where, when business was bad, he sat like some forgotten Santa Claus in an overlooked grotto.

These days, business wasn't so great. Only one skiing holiday in the past six months? Hathaway was really suffering.

Alice was in the midst of amending the commercial list when Hathaway put his head around the door to his office. Sandra was on the phone and the junior was staring out of the window, as usual. "Alice?" he said.

And Alice said, "Yes, Mister Hathaway?"

"Do you have two minutes?"

"Of course, Mister Hathaway."

"I want to run over the details for the Sisterkirke vicarage."

So then Alice went over to the big filing cabinet, and sorted through the area files; Cleton, Dimlington, Monkwell, Old Kilnsea, Out Newton, Sand-le-Mere, Sisterkirke. They read like train stops on a foggy night in some 1930s film comedy. Taking the Sisterkirke folder, she followed Hathaway through the door that he'd left half-open for her. Sandra was still on the phone, but Alice knew that she was watching.

Once inside, she closed the door behind her.

"Is this actually business," she said, "or have you finally thought of some excuse for standing me up?"

Hathaway was over on the other side of his desk, not seated but glancing over the notes of a couple of surveys he'd done that morning; he looked up at her and it was plain that he'd made up his mind that he wasn't going to be furtive or defensive about this, and equally plain that he was onto a loser from the beginning.

"Alice," he said, "I couldn't *help* it! There was a family crisis. I honestly couldn't get away."

"Not impressed, Max," she said.

"What was I supposed to do? You're not even on the phone!"

"So get me one."

"Ruby would love that. She got suspicious enough when I fixed you up with the company car."

"So how about just keeping the appointments that you make? I think I'm at least worth the consideration that you'd give to a client."

Alice laid the Sisterkirke file down, its purpose served. Hathaway was looking out of the window now, avoiding meeting her eyes. He was on a hook, always was when they argued. He had a great-looking wife and two wonderful children, and life might have been storybook-perfect had it not been for the fact that Ruby seemed to find housework more compelling than sex.

Something seemed different, today. He didn't rise to fight, he didn't rush to reassure her.

He said, "You know, when we started this, I felt about fifteen years younger."

"And now?"

"I feel like a middle-aged man in a young man's race, and I'm not staying level any more." He looked at her then. "I'm trying to say that I'm calling it off, Alice."

She folded her arms. "Let's just get something straight, Max. You don't call anything off. I do that."

He shrugged. "Whatever. But it can't go on. I had a great time and it was at everybody's expense but my own."

"And now you want to wind it up to suit yourself, as well," Alice said angrily, and she couldn't believe the gall of the man; after the way that he'd pursued her, persuaded her, bought her stuff she didn't even want . . . and if she'd made him dance around and panic a little every now and again, well, wasn't that just the rules of the game?

"Katie's pregnant," he said, and he looked at her then. "She's fourteen years old, Alice. We only found out about it last week. You'd think Ruby would understand it better than me, but she doesn't. That was why I couldn't meet you at the fair."

And Alice said, "Oh."

Then she said, "You're right, Max. I don't think I can compete with that."

"I'm not trying to beat you down with it. I'm telling you the way it is, that's all."

"Understood," Alice said quickly, and she dug around in the pocket of her blazer. She was feeling more embarrassed than she was angry or upset; mostly, she just wanted to turn around and get out.

She threw her car keys onto Hathaway's desk. "I'll clear the rest of my stuff out later in the week," she said.

Hathaway was looking blank. "What do you mean?"

"I'll bring the car papers in with me when I do. Goodbye, Max."

"Alice," Hathaway began, "this isn't necessary," but Alice was already halfway to the door. She hesitated before opening it, and looked back at him.

"Promise me something, Max," she said.

"What?"

"Look after her. Katie, I mean. And if you're ever going to *keep* a promise, make that the one."

Hathaway nodded. "It *was* a great time," he said. "I meant it."

Sandra said something to her as she crossed the showroom, but it didn't register. She scooped her shoulder bag from where it hung on the back of her chair, and made straight for the door.

The cold air of the street hit her and brought tears to her eyes. She saw a blurry figure move out to meet her, someone who appeared to have been waiting around on the off-chance that she might emerge; she tried to blink the image into clarity, but then she had to give in and wipe the tears away with the back of her hand.

And when she could see who stood before her, she said, "Look who's here. It must be the deaf man."

"Yeah," Nick said brightly. "What a coincidence."

He was standing there with his hands in his pockets and his shoulders hunched against the wind, and he looked as if he'd been hanging around for quite some time. Alice didn't need this. Not anytime, and especially not now. "Don't tell me," she said. "You just happened to be passing."

"Okay, I won't tell you."

"How plain do I have to make this?"

"You made it plain enough. You don't want to talk about Johnny Mays."

"And I don't want to be followed around and pestered about him either."

"Understood," Nick said, following her as she set off down the street.

"So say you're sorry, and say goodbye."

"I bought you a present."

"If it's flowers, you wasted your money. I get hay fever if I look at a gardening calendar."

"It isn't flowers."

Nothing seemed to be working, here. Nick seemed either dim or determined, and she wasn't sure which. They got level with her car, which she'd left at the roadside in front of a pet shop, and here she stopped.

Nick's present lay across the bonnet.

It was a cricket bat, with a huge pink bow on its handle.

She stared at it, blankly.

Nick said, "You can hit me with it, if that would make you feel any better."

Still too taken aback to give any reaction, she picked it up. It was definitely a cricket bat, although the chances of her first impression having been wrong were somewhere around zero.

"Apology accepted?" Nick said hopefully.

She was holding the bat by the handle. She transferred to a two-handed grip, and the weight of it felt just about right; she made as if to take a swing at him, and Nick winced as if he wasn't one hundred per cent certain that she wouldn't do it.

But he didn't back down.

And, damn him, he'd actually broken the mood. She gave him a playful jab in the middle which left the bat in his hands and, shaking her head and half-smiling in spite of herself, she moved around to open the driver's door.

Nick said, "Perhaps next time I'll pick a present that doesn't leave bruises."

"There'd better not *be* a next time," she warned, and as she was saying it she was also belatedly realising that the car wouldn't be going anywhere, at least not with her behind the wheel; she'd only the one set of keys, and she'd thrown these down in Hathaway's office as part of her great dramatic exit. Alice had a hair-trigger temper, sometimes, but she was no fool. If she was going to walk away from this – and she was no longer even certain that she was – then she was going to make sure that she'd be toting along all of the worldly goods to which she had any claim or title.

But this was hardly the time to turn around and go back.

She said, "If it's forgiveness you're after, you'd better start earning it."

"Just say how."

"Well . . . to begin with, you can give me a ride home."

Nick drove and Alice said that she'd call out the turns as they came up, although she kept forgetting until they were almost past the junctions and then he had to find somewhere to turn around and go back. It was obvious that she had something on her mind; the route wasn't even complicated, because the centre of town was so small. Once they were onto the coast road that would take them out past the hotels and the holiday beach toward the fishing-port area, that was more or less it.

He was relieved that she'd come out when she did. He'd been hanging around outside for half an hour, feeling vital bits of himself going dead in the cold as he tried to think of something that he could say to her if he should actually go into the office. He couldn't think of anything that would guarantee him no rebuff and no long walk back to the door with his last chance in ruins. He'd rather have caught up with her at her home, but this was made difficult by the fact that he didn't yet know where she lived; the car had been registered to the agency business, and even though the information had brought him into the general area of this small fishing town about twenty miles up the coast, it still fell some way short of the ideal. The phone book hadn't helped, and he'd never been much good at finding his way around an electoral roll.

And Alice apparently hadn't signed up for it, anyway.

He glanced across at her. She was looking around at the car.

She said, "Is this yours?"

"Rented. Why?"

"It isn't you."

"Cars that are me have a tendency to break down and fall apart. The door handles come off and you have to climb in through the windows. Last car but one, the floor dropped out from under me when I went over a bump in the road."

"What about the last one?"

"Believe me, you don't want to *know* what happened with the last one."

It was working. She wasn't quite laughing. But it was close.

She said, "You don't exactly sound like the luckiest man in town."

"I wouldn't be the luckiest man on the Marie Celeste. What about *your* car?"

"Long story. Let's just say that it came with the job, and right now I'm back on the open market."

"Something serious?"

She sighed. "No. It's not serious. It's happened a couple of times before. It's not the best job I could ever wish for, but it's worth hanging onto. I'll give it a few days and then I'll tell them I'm going back."

"You can do that?"

And at this Alice looked out of the window, her lightening manner undercut by a trace of sadness.

"Get the right kind of leverage," she said, "and you can do anything that you want."

The boardwalk and the fishing-boat wharves lay ahead. Alice told him to get ready to make a turn. This wasn't what Nick had been expecting, but he slowed and took the ramp that led down to the quayside as instructed. He took it slowly; more of a slipway that was partly cobbled and partly concrete, the ramp seemed to be for access to the harbourside buildings only. They came out into a narrow alley which ran between the sea wall and a grey, windowless customs shed.

"This is my place," Alice said, and Nick looked around and wondered where she meant.

She got him to pull in to a spot just beyond the end of the shed and in the shadow of the sea wall, an open area that seemed to be used as a dumping ground for maritime scrap iron; there were lengths of rusty chain laid out more or less straight, a couple of big dredging scoops that had obviously been standing there for quite a long time, stacks of tackle, empty cable drums, acetylene cylinders . . . Nick parked alongside a Peugeot pickup with a *Support the Lifeboats* sticker showing in its rear screen, and the two of them got out.

This didn't exactly look promising.

There was little here other than a couple of low brick buildings which, in the season, would serve as a hot dog stand and a rock and novelty shop. Beyond these, a blue-and-yellow painted shed that housed a chandlery and which had those old urine-coloured sunscreens drawn down across its tiny windows to keep the stock from fading. Otherwise . . . what? Alice was walking back along the alley by the customs warehouse, and Nick moved to follow. He'd had a hard time finding her again, and he wasn't about to let her get out of reach.

"Here?" he said, trying to keep the disbelief out of his voice when he caught up with her.

The customs shed had turned into something else about halfway along, its well-kept boards giving way to corrugated iron cladding that had been painted once and then never again. There were windows of frosted glass protected by framed chickenwire, but the windows had been boarded on the inside and the boards had been painted black with silver stars spray-stencilled all over. Above the doorway where Alice was fumbling with a padlock almost bigger than her hand, a header sign read *Tea, Coffee, Ices, Fresh Popcorn*.

"Yes, here," Alice said. "Home sweet home. It may not be much to look at, but the lease is paid-up. Want to come in for a while?"

"That depends on whether I'm welcome."

"There's only one condition. No talk about Johnny Mays. I don't even want to hear his name, not in my own place. Agreed?"

"Agreed," Nick said.

Her eyes held his own for a moment, to be sure. Something inside him seemed to catch fire, as if he'd just crawled up to the edge to take a peep over into a bottomless canyon and couldn't help imagining, for one brief moment, what it would be like simply to let go and slide forward.

"Come on, then," she said, unhooking the padlock and pushing the heavy door into darkness, and Nick held up the cricket bat to show that he hadn't come along empty-handed.

"Better put this in some water," he said as he followed her inside.

"I hate coming in this place," Wilson said. "I think I hate the music they play more than anything else about it."

"Right," Jennifer said, and she popped a surreptitious Rennie. They were on a moving stairway that was taking them up to the top level of the vast, untidy shopping centre that had taken over several blocks in the middle of town, and Wilson obviously didn't think much of it. Wilson didn't seem to think much of any building that had been raised any time after around 1930.

"It's just an ant farm with Mantovani," he went on. "People shouldn't be expected to live like this, it demeans them. What've you got, an ulcer?"

"I think it's nerves," Jennifer admitted. "If I mess this up, I'm going to kill myself."

"Loosen up. I've never lost a trainee yet."

"Famous last words."

"We're tracking dodgy teddy bears, not the Brighton bombers."

"Right," Jennifer said, and she absently inspected the green light that shone up through the narrow gaps between the escalator steps.

This was her first full day on CID probation. She'd been teamed with Wilson, an older and experienced Detective Sergeant, with the unofficial promise of something more exciting when she'd learned something of the department's procedures. Wilson seemed solid and reliable, but he was hardly likely to set the world on fire. Right now they were going around the various toy shops and bargain stores in the middle of town, trying to get a lead on a lorryload of soft toys that had been hijacked on its way out of the county; the bears in question were known to be dangerous – they were held together with spikes, they burned too easily, and they'd been on their way back to the importer when stolen – but they'd been seen on sale in some respectable outlets, repackaged and selling under counterfeit brand names.

Wilson was right. The shopping centre was the architectural equivalent of a lobotomy.

Jennifer had enough to contend with. She didn't need this. She'd been in the place when it had first been built and it had been too hot, there had been no daylight, it had been drab and depressing . . . the developers had been working it over in the last couple of years and now each level had a new Italian tiled floor and a lot of wrought iron and painted trellises, and it was still too hot and the daylight getting in was still barely worth mentioning. Jennifer felt that it was like walking in a pressure cooker with the lid on. She knew that the indefinable tension that crept into her belly wouldn't leave until she got back outdoors again, and then if it left her completely she'd be lucky. It was a sensation that couldn't fully be overcome by the presence of expensive plantlife or the big aviary that stretched three storeys up through the middle of the escalator well.

They'd checked on seven places already and they hit lucky on the eighth, a medium-sized barn of a toy store that was brightly-lit and based around the principle of stack 'em high and move 'em fast. The deadly bears stared balefully through the cellophane windows on the front of their boxes, and Wilson called the manager down and, when the manager tried to argue that he'd come by the stock legitimately and wasn't obliged to take it off the shelves, Wilson casually beheaded one of them and held up the four-inch fixing spike in front of the man's eyes. They looked over the bogus paperwork, they took statements, they promised they'd be back. As they were leaving, Jennifer saw a teenaged boy in an overall restocking the gap in the display with Cabbage Patch Kids and Pound Puppies. As he took the bears down, he threw them into a cardboard box. Not the brightest-looking of youths, nor the happiest.

Wilson reckoned that they'd earned themselves a break.

They got into one of the mall cafeterias, nothing more than an open square of the main concourse sectioned-off with waist-high barriers and crowded with too many tables around a self-service counter. Half of the stuff featured on the pegboard menu would be permanently unavailable and many of the tables, even though they were newly occupied, stood uncleared. Any chance of peace was destroyed by the coin-operated kiddie rides just outside the enclosure, rotating spaceships and boats and trains with flashing lights.

"So," Wilson said. "What do you think?"

Jennifer debated with herself for a moment, and then decided to tell the truth.

"Something doesn't feel right," she said. "They're reacting to me like I'm just along for the ride. I ask a question, and they turn around and give you the answer."

Wilson scratched his chin, as if he'd just found a patch that he'd missed when shaving. "That's maybe ten per cent true," he said. "The rest of it's your imagination."

"It's because I'm a woman."

"It's because you've been used to the uniform, that's all. Give yourself a chance."

Knowing that there was no way that he could understand, Jennifer sighed and looked out across the concourse. A shabby, wide-eyed man was ambling through the crowds and looking as if he'd been stunned, unable to make the connection between what lay around him and any kind of reality.

She said, "I bet it really pissed you off, being landed with me."

"And give me some credit, as well. I've got daughters." Wilson waved vaguely back in the direction of their last enquiry. "I get real problems. I take them into places like that and they're full of Tonka trucks and train sets and robots that turn into jet planes and motorbikes. We go around into the little-girls' section, and what's the most challenging thing I can find for them? Brush the pony's tail."

"So what are you saying?"

"That my kids have got an interest in someone like you making a success of what you're doing. I don't want them to grow up thinking that working in a beauty shop is like sitting on the roof of the world."

"Would you want them to be policewomen?"

But at this, Wilson half-smiled and pointed a finger at her, the way that a small child might make a pistol out of its hand. "Different argument," he said.

But it had worked, and Jennifer's edgy mood had been

broken. "Okay," she said, and she made an effort to relax.

They watched the world go by for a while, or at least as much of the world as happened to be interested in the jeans shop or the eyecare centre or the compact disc store that accounted for most of the foot traffic in the vicinity, and they talked about the differences between detective work and being in uniform. Wilson seemed all right, now that Jennifer was getting familiar with some of his more obvious hangups.

After a while, he said, "Can I ask you a personal question?"

"You can *ask* it," Jennifer said guardedly.

"Are you still with Nick Frazier?"

She hesitated for a while.

Then she said, "We split up."

And Wilson nodded, as if this was the answer that he'd been hoping to hear. "You did right," he said. "Strictly off the record, you want to hear some of the things that Bruno's been turning up about him and Johnny Mays." He leaned back in his chair. "Mud doesn't just stick, it splashes. But I suppose you realised that."

"Yes," Jennifer said quietly. "I suppose I did."

After a check around the market hall they went back to Wilson's car, which he'd left half-on the pavement in a loading zone of windowless walls and graffiti-sprayed stockroom doors. "Now for the exciting stuff," he said as they bumped down from the pavement and lined up for a U-turn. "The paperwork."

But the paperwork was going to have to wait.

The reason lay in something that Jennifer overheard in the operations room, where she'd been sent to see if she could beg, borrow or otherwise make off with a couple of sheets of carbon; it was even harder to get hold of around the building than soft toilet paper. She'd worked in ops for a while, and knew people here; and although she was anxious not to be seen timewasting on her first day of probation, it was hard to get away in a hurry.

When she got back to the CID squadroom, Wilson said, "Any luck?"

"What's the chance of us getting out to Ashness Close this afternoon?" Jennifer said.

"Why?"

"There's a worried-neighbour call that the uniforms won't be able to follow up until later, maybe even tomorrow."

"So it's a low priority. Ease off, kid, you're CID now. Let the uniforms handle their own calls."

"I think that maybe Ashness Close had some unusual fascination for Johnny Mays, when he was alive."

"You got this from Frazier?"

"It could be nothing. It could be coincidence."

"But you want to chase it."

"I want to chase it."

"Okay, but there's only one thing I need to know."

"What?"

"Where the hell's my carbon paper?"

There was a Porsche out in the Close, just as she remembered it from the day of the drive-past with Nick.

Wilson didn't approve of the flats any more than he'd approved of the shopping centre; he said that gold taps in the bathrooms and a Georgian door on the garage didn't make any difference, he knew cheap-shit building when he saw it. The Close was part of a private development estate that reminded Jennifer of a student residential hall; red-brick apartments, walkways between the blocks, communal parking, shared staircases . . . the only real difference lay in the price tag for a two-bedroomed shoebox with underfloor heating. The place had a superficial kind of class, but she wouldn't have wanted to live here. It would have been too close to the middle of town for her, although that was supposed to be one of its attractions.

The neighbour who'd phoned in met them at the foot of the stairs. A smallish man, sharp-featured and in his fifties, Jennifer could have imagined Doctor Moreau going into the operating theatre with a ferret and coming out with him. He was wearing expensive slacks and one of those sports shirts with a little crocodile on it, and his grey chest hair looked like wire wool in the V of the collar.

As he led them up he said, "It's been a couple of days, now. Their milk keeps on coming and I've been pushing their newspapers through. There's been a light burning in the bathroom, as well."

Wilson said, "Do they always tell you if they go away?"

"Not always. They're away a lot. He has a company selling timeshare apartments all over the continent."

"Timeshare?" Wilson said. "Isn't that the kind of arrangement where you buy a piece of a nice-looking place and then fifty other families come in and kick the shit out of it?"

"I just bought one of the units myself," the neighbour said stiffly, but Wilson's smile didn't waver.

"What do you know," he said amiably.

On the top floor, three flights up, they rang the bell and waited.

"I've tried that," the neighbour said, and as Wilson explained to him why they had to handle it this way Jennifer tried lifting the flap of the mail slot in case there might be any chance of seeing anything through it. Wilson asked if the occupants argued and the neighbour said that he didn't know, they hadn't been together all that long.

Jennifer said, "Do you have a breadknife?"

He looked puzzled, confused, and slightly panicked. "Sorry?"

"I need a breadknife. Do you have one?"

He had to go back into his own place across the landing to fetch it, and when it came Jennifer slid the blade through and used it to lift the privacy flap on the other side of the slot. She studied the view in Cinemascope for a few moments and then called to Wilson to take a look over her shoulder.

He looked. He was looking for a long time.

Straightening, Wilson said, "Is there a master key to these places?"

There wasn't, so they broke the door in.

A middle-aged man lay at an uncomfortable angle against the wall to their right. A one-colour rainbow arced, magic-marker style, down the plaster where his head had wiped as he'd fallen. Jennifer looked at the neighbour and said, "Is that the tenant?"

The neighbour blinked, his face all drained and slack, and said, "That's him."

"We're going to have to ask you to stay outside," Wilson told him, and the neighbour said quickly, "Don't worry."

Stepping carefully and touching nothing, they moved through into the main lounge. There were none of the instant signs of burglary. All of the furniture was new and the pictures on the wall didn't appear to be prints, but originals. European landscapes, mostly, but even they didn't give the place much of a personal touch. There were no photographs, no bric-a-brac. The kind of place that Jennifer could imagine a businessman moving into with his ex-mistress for a doomed second marriage.

Wilson said, "I hear water," and moved on through to take a look around the rest of the apartment as Jennifer tried to guess what might have happened here. Perhaps the doorbell rang, the tenant answered, never even saw the approach of the blow that killed him. It had happened in the early evening, at a guess; the fancy roller-blinds at the windows were pulled most of the way down and there was a fierce red eye burning on the front of the compact disc player in the rack system. Try playing loud music late at night in a place like this, and people too polite to bang on the ceiling would send around an injunction instead.

She heard Wilson say, "Jee-sus!"

The two of them nearly collided in the short corridor which led past the bedrooms to the bathroom, but Wilson was in too much of a hurry to pass her even to notice. What he'd heard was the running of the shower. The water had run cold and there was no steam.

She was lying half-dressed in the bath and with the shower beating down on her body. One leg dangled over the side. The instrument that had been used on her lay on the tiled floor. The deep colour that Nick had described to Jennifer as looking like a solarium tan now proved to be authentic, as was witnessed by the whitened strip across her hips; but by the same observation, Nick had been right about her peroxide job. Jennifer could tell straight away that there had been no robbery motive. The victim still had too much gold around her hands.

Oh, and something else. It looked as if she'd given birth to most of her own insides.

19

The instrument was a short wooden pole with a metal hook screwed into its end, identified as a home-made device for catching the rings on the blinds to draw them down when they were beyond reach. A short time later, when the big murder machine was well in motion and the building was crawling with senior detectives and ancillary services, the device was being carefully picked up and bagged at about the same time that Wilson and Jennifer were being told that they were no longer needed.

They pushed their way out through police and press and cameras and the usual crowd of gawkers waiting to see the bodies emerge. There would be further questions for Jennifer, but these would come later. Right now, it was taking all of her concentration to keep her walk steady.

"You feel sick?" Wilson said, and Jennifer had to nod. "I think there's an old carrier bag in the car," he told her, and with a firm hand on her arm he guided her away from public view.

He drove her about half a mile to some waste land, and there he got out of the car and looked the other way for as long as it took her to do what was necessary. This was high ground, and from here he could see all the way across town to where the hills began. It was getting late now, and the daylight was fading, and the cityscape of roofs and flats and factory chimneys was dotted with intense pinpoints of artificial light almost like some kind of a fairground. Manhattan, it wasn't; and if a town could be said to have a character and a sense of purpose, then here was a place that had lost its identity when the mills and the docks had finally closed and which was reaching uncertainly and in near-darkness to find itself again. More than once, Wilson had promised himself that he'd uproot and find somewhere better for the girls to grow up. But where? They had friends here, they liked the big old house where they lived. And it solved nothing, simply to move one's ground; there were no solutions in the landscape because the vista was exactly that, a view, and the only useful answers lay somewhere on the inside. No matter where you went, it was the inner landscape to which you ultimately had to return.

He told himself that he was feeling jaded. Who wouldn't, after what they'd seen today?

But he also knew that he was right.

He glanced back into the car. Jennifer was a healthier colour, now, and she managed a weak and apologetic smile as she met his eyes through the screen. He moved around to her window and said, "Better?"

She nodded. She'd screwed up the neck of the plastic carrier that she'd been using as a sick bag, almost as if she was afraid that he'd want to lean over and try to take a peek inside.

He said, "I *have* seen worse, but not much. Want to head back into town, or sit for a while?"

"Go back," Jennifer said, and so Wilson went around to the other side of the car and got in behind the wheel.

"You can just toss that out," he said, nodding towards the bag. "It can hardly make any difference, around here."

"I'll hang onto it for a while," she said.

She couldn't have done much. Probably hadn't even eaten breakfast, if her earlier first-night nerves had been anything to go by. He'd seen plenty of probationers come and go – some of his earliest trainees even out-ranked him, now – and she was brighter than most. If she could get over her difficulties of self-confidence, he could see her becoming another of them. A small part of him wanted to resent the fact; but mostly he thought of his girls, and wanted her to succeed.

And then he thought of the woman in the bath, and wondered if *she'd* ever brushed the pony's tail. And for the first time since they'd discovered her, he felt a rush of pity that was greater than his initial disgust.

He looked at Jennifer. "Rest day tomorrow?"

She nodded.

"You'll be okay," he told her, and he started the car; but then, before pulling out, he looked at her again as another thought struck him.

He said, "You didn't know her personally or anything, did you?"

But Jennifer shook her head.

So they drove on.

———

Alice's place was an upstairs flat, and quite livable; the shuttered cafeteria with its dead expresso machine and its sheeted amusements was somewhere that had to be passed through to reach the stairs, but it was altogether separate. Pitch-dark and dusty and about as downmarket as an arcade could get, its gaming machines and pinball tables didn't appear to have been used in at least a couple of years. The rooms above were something else.

Nick wandered around the sitting room while Alice was in the kitchen. There was a personality about the place, and it wasn't hers; she was there in some of the added touches like the dozen or so old photographs of family, friends and remembered good times that she'd stuck in around the frame of the sideboard mirror, dressing-room style, but the framed music-hall handbills and the showman's memorabilia indicated that she was a comparative latecomer to the scene.

Nick called through to her. "What's the story with this place?"

"Does your family have any black-sheep uncles?" she called back.

"More than its share."

"Well, ours ran off with a travelling fair when he was thirteen. Came back to visit six years later in an open-topped car and a check suit so loud that it could drown out conversation. Thirteen years of being told that he was a dead loss and that he'd never land a good job with the council like his older brother, and Uncle Jim comes rolling back in a Javelin while Uncle Phil's still modelling the latest in bicycle clips. Jim had taken over the slot machine concession on the fair and he was doing pretty well. Made everybody really sick. I thought the jealousy part of it was terrible."

"People don't like bad pennies to come good," Nick said, moving over to take a look at the beached yachts and the view of the square harbour out of the window. "It makes them feel insecure." The mud down below had been carved and sculpted by the outgoing tide; its lines seemed almost to have been set in stone, but it was work that would be wiped away and redone within hours.

"They got their own back later on. He could make the money, but he couldn't hold onto it. Not that he cared very much. He'd bought property like this all along the coast and it kept him for a few years, but he had this terrific knack of hiring crooks for managers. By the time I got to know him, this was the only one left and he was living over the shop. Those were the days when my mother used to let me stay here and work through the summers. When he died, he left me the lease and I moved in. I've tried to sublet the downstairs part as business premises, but I've had no takers."

"Does that explain what you were doing at the fair?"

"Just about."

"And this is where you used to disappear to every summer?"

"Don't tell me you used to miss me."

211

"All right, I won't tell you."

He heard her moving from one room to another; *Jennifer*, he found himself thinking briefly, but he turned from the window and pushed the thought out of his mind.

She said, "I don't know what part of it I used to like the best. The stories he'd tell me or the sunsets or the arcade lights in the last hours of the day."

"Or the people?"

"The people were mostly silage. Don't let's get too romantic, here."

Standing by the mirror again, he took Johnny's photograph of her from his pocket to compare it with the others. Most of them seemed to date from much later. He didn't see any way that he could raise the subject and stay true to his promise about not mentioning Johnny's name. Maybe she'd bring him into it, if Nick didn't push.

And if she didn't . . . well, what did it really matter? Because Nick was beginning to realise that he was having quite a pleasant time, everything considered.

It was starting to get dark, and Alice switched on a couple of lights. She brought through coffee on a tray and the two of them sat and talked about their lives over the years since they'd originally known each other, and Alice admitted that she'd made a mistake about the country dancing and that she'd been thinking about some other kid named Norman Lee, who hadn't even *looked* like Nick, and that she'd remembered Nick more clearly because he was the one who'd nearly killed the caretaker's cat with a javelin one school sports day. Nick said that he forgave her for the mixup, and Alice said that she forgave him for the pee stain story, and then they talked about some of the half-heard reports that had reached them about the lives of some of the others.

Some of the others, that was, with one particular exception.

Nick said, "How well have you kept in touch with anybody?"

"Only a little," Alice admitted. "Most people have drifted. Some of the news comes back, but . . ."

"The past isn't a place you'd care to live."

"Right."

"Where would you be if you had the choice?"

"No problem," she said, holding her coffee mug in both hands and looking out over it into a distance that nobody else would be able to see. "Straight through the looking glass and on into Wonderland." And then she gave Nick a wry smile. "What else would you expect from a girl called Alice?"

The problem for Nick was that most of the things that he'd heard about the old days, he'd rather not have known. Like the same Norman Lee, a quiet boy who'd never let himself get dirty; when Nick had encountered him ten years later, he'd been on a gross indecency charge that had brought him a suspended sentence and lost him his job. He told Alice the story, and Alice said, "If we could have seen where we were going . . . I mean, if we could have known then how everything was really going to be, for any of us . . . I wonder how we'd have reacted."

"Disbelief," Nick said with total conviction. "When you're a kid, reality just doesn't make it. You have to grab as much ground as you can before the world gets its hands on you. If you're lucky, you'll store up enough magic to get you through."

Alice stood and moved over to the window, where she looked out into darkness. Nick could see her reflection in the glass, a ghost portrait on still water.

She said, "Are you living with anybody right now?"

"I was," Nick said, "but I'm kind of in transit."

Alice nodded, as if she understood completely. "What was her name?"

"Jennifer. You wouldn't know her. She wasn't . . . she was someone I knew later."

"You mean," Alice said with some perception, "she wasn't one of us."

"That's probably it," Nick admitted.

"It's true what they say, isn't it? You really can't go home again."

"That sounds pretty deep."

Her reflection smiled as she started to turn. "I read it in a Peanuts strip," she said. "That's how deep *I* go."

She found a big old cracked vase in one of the back rooms and they stuck the cricket bat in it for a laugh, its bow making it look like some oversized sunflower. She found crackers and cheese in her understocked larder and made more coffee while Nick browsed through her bookshelves, and he wondered whether they had the start of something going here, or not. He didn't much want to look too far into the future. For one thing, he'd find Bruno and the consequences of his letter waiting there. Deep inside, he knew what was coming. He'd be asked to leave, of that he was certain. Probably what he'd been wanting all along, only he hadn't been able to raise the nerve to do it on his own.

And what he'd do afterwards, he had no idea.

Finally he said, "Well, it feels like I ought to be going."

"Why?"

"Because I've been having a good time and I'll outstay my welcome, and then you'll have to kick me out."

"So you're getting in ahead of me?"

"Exactly that. What are you going to do next?"

"I'll probably give it a couple of days to cool off. Then I'll get back to business as usual."

Nick said, "I'll be around a while longer."

"Good. We'll do this again."

"Fine by me."

And they broke it there. But it wasn't easy.

———

When Nick had gone, Alice moved to clear up after them. There wasn't much to do. She wished that she'd been better set-up for entertaining, but he hadn't seemed to mind. He'd left his mug over by the mirror and when she went to get it, she noticed that one of her photographs had fallen out of the edge of the frame. It was only when she picked it up to put it back that she realised it was one she hadn't seen before.

She looked at herself. She looked awesomely young. She had to have been, what, about fifteen in this? She couldn't remember anything about it being taken but she thought that she could remember the setting, which was the old common room at the side of the school. A year or so earlier, then, from the sixth form. She shook her head slowly and she thought *Nicky Frazier, you dark horse*. She could hear him outside, still trying to get his rental car started, and so she went through to the window which overlooked the alley and opened it to lean out.

He was still by the tackle dump at the far end of the customs shed, and just getting out of the car. The bonnet was up and the engine still wasn't running. She stuck her fingers in and whistled to him, and he looked up at her. It was dark by now, but there was a streetlight on the promenade almost directly above.

He said, "I'm not sure what I'm supposed to do. Can I use your phone to call the rental company?"

"This place doesn't have a phone."

"Where's the nearest box?"

"It's out of office hours by now. You'll never catch anyone."

"Train timetable?"

"They closed the line."

"Buses?"

"No."

"Taxi?"

Alice shook her head.

And so Nick said, "Well, could you throw me down a blanket?"

"You'd better come back in. You can use the sofa-bed for tonight and then get it all sorted in the morning."

215

"Won't the neighbours talk?"

"What neighbours?"

And when he looked around he could hardly argue the point, and so he slammed down the bonnet and locked up the car and walked away from it as if he didn't care if it never ran again. As if it could stay there to rust, along with the old chains and the dredger buckets; as if it could join the rest of the parade of junked autos that had marked out his car-owning life so far.

———

"Tokens," Alice said, and lifted up a canvas pouch from behind the counter.

They were downstairs now, and she'd thrown a breaker switch on the fusebox to bring the arcade into life. The machines flickered and brightened, one by one, waking like cave beasts from prehistory whose rock had just fallen away from the cavemouth for the first time in a couple of millenia. And Jesus, some of these things were *old*. One of those nearest to Nick was a one-armed bandit with *Lucky Stars* lettered across its header, and Nick could see the names of some of those stars on the rolls lined up in its window; Cornel Wilde, Hedy Lamarr, Betty Grable. But the pinball tables didn't look so dated and there were some early video-era arcade games, and at the back there were a couple of rows of fruit machines that were probably worth real money on the collectors' market. As they lit up, some of them started to sing like demented robots.

Nick said, "Paradise. What do I do when the tokens run out?"

"Start using money," Alice said. "It's about time this place started earning its keep again. Have fun."

And then she disappeared upstairs to sort out the sleeping arrangements, leaving Nick to go it alone for a while.

Places like this tended to look seedy enough when

they were in regular use, but disuse sent them running downhill fast. Dust was thick everywhere, even on those machines that had been under sheets. The walls, ceiling, wiring and everything had been painted black, and illumination was from coloured spotlights. It was like a disco for the dead. The flooring was of grey linoleum, wide sheets of it joined with aluminium strips, and the floorboards underneath were delineated in ground-in dirt; the lino stopped at the cafeteria counter, giving way to red and grey vinyl tiles in a checkerboard pattern. Some of these had lifted, showing blackened hardboard underneath. The counter itself was of riveted blue formica, and apart from the chromed towers of the expresso machine it carried a jetspray juice cooler that looked like a piece of redundant medical equipment. The wall beyond was mirror-panelled, the mirrors decayed around their edges and carrying the old, faded circles of milkshake stickers. Nick could see himself in the middle of all the junky glitter, and he wasn't certain that he liked what he saw; the reason being that he looked as if he more or less belonged there.

He worked a couple of the rows, feeding slots and pulling handles, but it was less than the great fun that he might once have expected. He found that he was moving on without waiting to see the result of each play; one of the slots about three machines back began to pay out, but he didn't even go back to look. He'd been part of a regular card school one time on his old division, but he'd only stuck with it for long enough to realise that the mainline kick of gambling lay not in the occasional wins, but in the steady high of losing; and with this realisation he considered his education complete, and quit school for good. The problem here was that the use of house tokens took away even that perverse thrill. This felt about as sporting as nailing rabbits to a table, and then shooting them.

It was a video game called *Motorway Madness* that finally persuaded him that he'd had enough. Cars spun off into bridge pilings and exploded; Nick could feel the reflected light of the screen on his face like so much heat, and he thought *Okay, I give in*. He put the token bag on the counter, bolted the outside door – making a mental note to point out to Alice sometime that a little extra security wouldn't be a bad idea for a woman living on her own – and then, after pulling the plugs on the party sounds, he went upstairs.

He found the sofa-bed opened in the sitting room and Alice in the kitchen again, this time digging around in a big old Electrolux freezer that resembled the back end of a caravan. She glanced up at him and said, "Spend it all?"

"As much as I could manage," Nick said. "What are you doing?"

"Finding us something to eat."

"I thought I might take us out."

"You've been living in the big city for too long. We're out of hours in the back of beyond, now – there isn't anywhere."

He leaned on the doorframe. "I'm a problem, aren't I?"

"But not an unwelcome one." Something sheared free inside the freezer; Nick now saw that she'd been digging into the frost with a table knife, and she'd managed to dislodge a Birds Eye bag of some kind. "Look what I found," she said, bringing it out and wiping thick snow away from the label. "Seafood!"

"Seafood," Nick said hollowly. "My favourite."

At around two in the morning, she came out to see why he was making such a racket in the toilet.

He'd tried to be quiet about it, but found that iron control wasn't exactly easy when in the middle of throwing up. When he stepped out, feeling drained and weak but considerably better, she was waiting for him with a look of concern. She was in cotton pyjamas, he was in an old dressing-gown of her uncle's that made him look like a moth-eaten bandmaster. She steadied him as he walked back to the folding bed, and he held her arm with some gratitude for the support.

"What's the matter?" she said. "Are you ill?"

"No," Nick said, "just too polite for my own good. I should have told you about me and seafood."

"What is it, some kind of allergy?"

"Kind of." He sat down heavily, and Alice sat beside him. "It dates back to when I was a kid and found a dead body on the beach."

"I don't get it."

"He was a fisherman. He'd been lost from a trawler and he'd been in the water for days. I was out on my own and I found him face-down in the surf. He looked like he was trying to crawl ashore, but that was just the tide. It wasn't until you looked closer that you saw how most of him had been eaten away . . . he looked as if he was alive but he was just a mass of shrimps feeding on what was left of the meat."

There was only one light burning in the sitting room, a shaded table lamp that warmed the area around them and lost everything else in shadow; and like any beacon in the night, it seemed to give out a feeling of safety. Alice said, "I'm sure I remember hearing the story. Was that really you? It must have been terrible."

"If you want the truth, it was the best thing that ever happened to me."

"How do you make that out?"

"Suddenly I was somebody. Got my picture in the paper, and everything. People were falling over themselves to do things for me so I wouldn't get permanently warped by what I'd seen . . . the local copper even let me try on his hat and ride around in his car. I think Johnny was nearly sick with jealousy. He was walking the beaches for weeks, looking for a couple of drowned sailors so he could go one better and get a ride in a police car, too. But there are some things that just happen. There's no fixing them.''

Alice was starting to giggle, fighting it but giggling anyway, and Nick started to smile even though he didn't know the reason why. He said, "What's the matter?"

"I'm picturing Johnny, walking along the Bay and hoping for bodies. It's him, exactly."

"So I was a kid who dreamed about growing up and driving around in a police car every day, and then I grew up and did it. Now Johnny's father tells me he followed me into that, as well."

"Not many kids get to do what they always wanted."

"No," Nick said. "But getting what you want isn't always so great, either. I think I'd really like to get out. But I don't know what else I'll be able to do instead."

There was a silence for a while, but not an awkward one. Nick realised now how Alice could so easily bear to live in a place like this; it might be shabby and it might be odd, but it had an atmosphere of ease like some old wooden clubhouse. Nick couldn't help thinking of the freewheeling relative who'd picked it out in the first place, and wondering if anyone had ever felt so welcome in the cold parlours of the family that had disapproved of him.

He said, "I'm sorry."

"Why?"

"We were talking about Johnny, and I promised that I wouldn't."

"It's all right."

And now, at this place and at this hour, Nick could sense that it really was. He said, "You actually remember all that stuff about the body?"

"Something about it. I just didn't connect it with you right away, that's all."

"I don't suppose you ever noticed me much in those days."

"Don't kid yourself. I just wish you'd spoken up more."

"Really?"

"Really. And you're just the same now."

"What do you mean?"

She got up and went over to the mirror, and when she returned to sit beside him again she was carrying the trimmed piece of an old photograph that he'd left behind. She put it in his hand, and he sat looking at it. "I don't even remember when this was taken," she said.

"But you kept it all this time."

He knew that he really ought to tell her the truth.

But "Yes," he said, "I kept it all this time."

She smiled. "You're a funny guy, Nick. Feeling any better?"

"Reckon so," he said.

And then she drew her legs up onto the sofa-bed and leaned with her head against his shoulder; it was the move, not of a vamp or a seductress, but of a child with complete trust.

Out beyond the harbour, the sea beat against cold stone.

"Tell me about the night that Johnny died," Alice said.

And at about three a.m., when there was nobody walking the streets other than late shift workers and postgrad students who'd gone down to the Union building for a drink and lucked into a party, a Pontypridd boy named Henry made his more-or-less steady way towards the big Victorian house in the shadow of the railway. Henry was no late shift worker. He was twenty-three years old, slight and bearded and dressed in dark blue, and he'd have been at the house at around nine if his plans for the evening had gone as he'd intended. Not that his timing mattered too much, because he wasn't going there to meet anyone; he'd promised Elizabeth that he'd stop by and pick up any mail and generally give the place a look over, and that was as far as it went.

Elizabeth's friends were starting to be concerned. They'd always worried for her but now they were starting to worry *about* her, as well. Not that anybody doubted her story, but by its very nature it was almost impossible to verify – the phonecalls and the following on the street and the break-ins where nothing of value had been taken – and the longer it went on, the more tempting it became to wonder whether the pressure of getting her thesis completed and delivered might be bending her judgement just a little out of shape. Everybody had been keen to pitch in and offer their support at first. But come on, they had lives of their own to lead, didn't they? And even Elizabeth's solicitor had told her that unless she was going to come up with some hard evidence of harassment, he couldn't see much point in pushing her case any further along.

So Henry didn't exactly feel guilty about the hour as he stood before the darkened house and scratched around with Elizabeth's key for the unfamiliar lock. Henry didn't get into many parties, and this had been one of the better ones. Pity nobody had told the host that it was going to be taking place. Nearly scored, too . . . which was about as much use to Henry as 'nearly reprieved' to a man on Death Row but still, it was better than no progress at all.

He stood in the hallway and switched on the light. There was nothing on the mat other than a book of coupons and a couple of mailing envelopes from a film processing house, and he scuffed these to one side with his foot. Elizabeth was definitely getting a touch weird, these days. She'd turned up at Karen's place and as good as pleaded for sanctuary. After secret hideaways, Henry wondered what she'd be coming up with next.

He picked up the pay phone, checked that the dialling tone was coming through loud and clear, and set it down again. Was that water that he could hear running, ahead in the kitchen?

He went through to take a look.

It wasn't water.

She'd apparently left her transistor radio playing on the kitchen table, and now its batteries were almost spent and the station had gone off the air. She'd walked out in the middle of a meal, as well, if the state of the rest of the table was anything to go by . . . and here Henry stopped, because since when had Elizabeth eaten soup and beans straight out of the can?

He saw the open doors of the food lockers, wood showing raw where their padlock staples had been prised out. He moved over to the kitchen door and tried it but that had been levered open, too. So then he quickly went back into the middle of the room and lifted the paraffin heater aside to uncover the loose board under which Elizabeth had hidden one of her thesis drafts; she had copies in all kinds of places and Henry had begun to attribute this to her growing paranoia, which he'd thought unhealthy even if it wasn't entirely unfounded, but now he was thinking that perhaps there weren't so many bats in her attic after all.

The draft was still there, nearly three hundred sheets of double-spaced A4 in a taped polythene bag. It hadn't been discovered. Now the question was, should he put it back, or would it be better if he took it away?

"You may as well just put it on the table," a voice said from the doorway, and Henry looked up with a startled expression like a rabbit caught in the beam of a truck's headlights.

"Who are you?" he said.

The man moved into the room, hands deep in the pockets of an overcoat that was a couple of sizes too big for him. He was unshaven, tousled, and although he was smiling he had eyes that burned into Henry like a couple of lasers. Henry had been in London just a few days after the big fire on the Underground, and even though he'd been in a different part of the system he'd been standing on the platform when air had been sucked through from somewhere down the line;

he'd taken an involuntary step back because it had been like an onslaught of gases belched up out of Hell, but even that was nothing compared to the feeling that this stranger brought along.

He nodded toward the thesis and said, pleasantly, "I'm a friend of the young lady who wrote that. And I'd really like to talk to her about it."

20

Nick went out early to find a pay phone, and when he got back Alice was already up and in the shower. He told her through the bathroom door that the rental company would be sending somebody around from a local garage to pick up the car within the hour. She said fine. He said that unless she had plans, it looked as if she'd be stuck with him for the morning at least. She said fine. He said that he could go off somewhere and find himself something to do if he was going to be in the way, and she said, can we *please* continue this conversation when I'm dried-off and dressed and out of here?

And Nick said, fine.

They breakfasted on Digestive biscuits and oranges, because these were the last items out of her cupboard. "My mind's never on it when I shop," she admitted. A mechanic came by in a breakdown wagon to take the rental car away, leaving a card and suggesting a call around lunchtime; they watched him from the upstairs window as he hooked up the towing straps and winched the end of the vehicle into the air. His wagon passed below them slowly, its driver watching the sides of the narrow alley as he filled it with revving and noise. Somebody had written *Wash Me* in the dust on the roof of his cab.

Nick sat around and read some of Alice's old magazines while she wrote out cheques for some overdue bills, and then they went out to drop them in the nearest postbox. On the promenade level, he stood by a yellow pay telescope on a pedestal and looked back along the way they'd walked. He didn't need the telescope to be able to read the word CAFE that had been painted in fading white letters six feet high on one side of Alice's roof. He asked her if she'd ever considered re-opening the business on her own. She said that she'd rather handwash King Kong's underwear.

With about an hour to kill, they walked down by the fishermen's wharf. And when the conversation turned again to Johnny Mays, it was without any forcing from Nick and without resistance from Alice.

She said, "Did you ever hear the saying anywhere about, if you love something then you should set it free? How if it comes back to you then it's yours, but if it doesn't then it never really was?"

"I think so."

"Well, that was me and Johnny. I went out with him for about six months, the winter after you went away. That would make us about what, sixteen?"

"About that."

"It was nothing serious as far as I was concerned. But when the summer came and it was time for me to start my usual holiday job in the arcade, he didn't want me to go. I was already starting to get pretty sick of him looking over my shoulder all of the time; it was like he just wanted to push all my friends and all my other interests to one side and fill the world with wall-to-wall Johnny Mays. It was only insecurity, I can see that now. But at the time, it really pissed me off."

"What did you do?"

"I quoted the old saying. Johnny set me free, and a week later I wrote to say that I wasn't going back to him."

"How'd he take it?"

"You knew him. How do you think?"

"Not well, then."

She gave a wry smile that had little humour in it, more an acknowledgement of old pain that had left her with a few scars. "He came out," she said. "He tried to make a scene in the arcade, but my uncle threw him out. So then he'd hang around outside and wait for me, so I didn't dare go out without asking one of the regulars who hung around the place to go along. They were a rough-looking bunch and Johnny knew better than to mess with them. I only wish that I'd known better, as well. I think I got pregnant that year . . . I didn't know enough about it to be sure. If I did, then I lost it a few weeks later. I couldn't tell anybody, or ask anybody for help. I think Johnny got a pretty good idea of what was going on. And I'm pretty sure that he'd be thinking it was all one big performance for his benefit."

"Did you ever hear from him again?"

She leaned on the wharf rail and looked out over the forest of masts belonging to the private yachts and sailboats out in the main part of the harbour. The tide had come and gone again since the previous night, and the mud channels down below had all been recarved. The details had changed, the pattern was the same. There was a pumping engine turning over on one of the boats across the way, but Nick couldn't have said on which.

Alice said, "No, I never did." She shook her head, sadly. "Poor Johnny. He could never understand how whenever he got his hands on something, it would always somehow end up wrecked."

They'd walked out as far as they could get, and now there was nothing for them to do but turn around and go back.

———

"You're in luck," the mechanic said, leading them through the barn-sized workshop to the office where the keys were held. There were cars up on four of the six hydraulic lifts, and not a damned thing appeared to be happening with any of them. They'd already passed the rental car, which was out on the forecourt with an oil-smudged ticket in its windscreen. He said, "It was a simple job, just a wire pulled loose on the distributor.

Can't see how it happened, unless someone had been messing around."

Alice gave Nick a look of half-suspicion as the man hunted up the papers for him to sign. Nick gave her a face of seamless innocence.

Once they were outside, she said, "Well, I *was* thinking of asking if you'd like to stay for a couple more days."

"Just thinking about it doesn't get us anywhere."

"How would you rate the idea on a scale of one to ten?"

"Are you kidding me? Preying on women of property is the one thing that I do best in the whole wide world."

"Okay," she said. "You go and get your stuff, I'll straighten out my job situation, and we'll meet up again tonight."

"I could be late."

"Why?"

"Most of my stuff's back at Jennifer's."

"Jesus, you're fast. I said a couple of days. I like you, Nick, but let's take it one step at a time, shall we?"

"Don't worry, I'm not planning to be the Man Who Came To Dinner. But I *do* have to go back over there."

"Today? For what?"

"I'm resigning. I've decided I'm going to jump instead of waiting to be pushed. I'll drive straight over, see who I have to see, and come straight back. I'll be here tonight, that's a promise."

"Are you sure about this?"

"I feel like a six-foot bear who's about to be let out of a four-foot cage. I'd rather stick around the bay and turn into a beach bum than go the way that Johnny did. I'm better than sure."

Johnny, meanwhile, was entertaining Henry.

He had him sitting upright in one of the hard kitchen chairs, and every now and again he'd retie the washing line that was holding him there. Henry was trussed like a cheap roast for the oven, and his circulation was suffering. The phone had started to ring around nine, but Johnny had ignored it.

Henry could do nothing other than watch. If he spoke, the stranger told him to be quiet. Henry wasn't about to argue. Johnny was sitting at the kitchen table and he was looking at each page of the thesis manuscript, holding the sheets only inches from his face and frowning hard as if he couldn't even recognise the marks as writing. His concentration was total, his patience apparently endless. He remembered Henry about once every hour, and then he'd get him a glass of water and untie his hands so that he could sip at it, or else he'd loosen the line and then retie it some other way that was just as tight and no less uncomfortable.

And sometimes Henry whimpered, either from the pain or just from plain old fear, and Johnny would raise his eyes from the paper and look at him with a momentary vagueness which told Henry that yes, for a while there he'd been completely forgotten. Henry was terrified of Johnny, and ashamed of his terror. Johnny seemed to radiate dark energy like a dynamo.

Time passed, and Henry waited to find out what was to happen to him.

When the phone rang a second time, around ten, Johnny laid down the manuscript. He was about halfway through, and the discarded pages were all over the table in no particular order. The caller was more persistent this time, but Johnny paid no more attention than he had before; and after about two dozen rings, the hallway was silent again.

Johnny looked at Henry, then at the rope.

"Tell me if it hurts," he said.

"It hurts," Henry said, so Johnny got up and came around behind him. This was the worst of times for Henry, not being able to see what Johnny was doing. He'd had a teacher at school who'd pulled a similar

kind of trick, hovering around behind and then taking
a swipe at the back of a kid's head when he wasn't
expecting it. You knew it was coming, but you didn't
know when. He'd thought that he'd escaped that kind of
tyranny for good, but this was worse. He couldn't turn,
he couldn't stand, he barely even had any opportunity
to flinch.

Johnny loosened a couple of the knots; and this time,
he left them loose.

"Better?" he said, and Henry nodded.

Johnny went back to the table and sat down again. He
seemed rational. There hadn't been one moment when
he'd seemed anything else, and that was probably the
scariest part of any of it. Now he was looking at Henry
with a certain sympathy.

"I'm sorry about this," he said. "You just happened
to be in the wrong place at the wrong time. You aren't
even in the book."

"I haven't got a phone."

"I mean, *this* book." He looked around inside his outsized overcoat in a way that suggested that it was unfamiliar to him, and after a few moments he came out with
a water-damaged notebook so swollen that only a razor
would be able to separate most of its pages. Holding it
up so that Henry could see, he went on, "Not that it's
much use to anyone now, as you can probably tell. I'm
having to work mostly from memory . . ." He smiled,
briefly. "Which isn't the most reliable technical aid I've
ever used."

He dropped the black-covered notebook onto the table
with all the out-of-order thesis pages.

Henry said, "Who are you?"

And the stranger said, "I'm Johnny Mays. Perhaps
you've heard of me."

"Sorry."

Johnny Mays seemed disappointed, but he took it
well. Picking out one of the typescript pages without
even looking at it, he held it up for Henry to see. He

said, "I've been trying to get through this, but it's been heavy going. You've had an education. Perhaps you can help me out."

"How?"

"Just tell me if I'm in it."

"I don't know that I can," Henry said nervously as Johnny Mays gathered the manuscript together and made a very rough job of putting it back into shape.

"I'm warning you. Don't mess me about, Henry," Johnny said, and he laid the stack of pages on the table where Henry could get to them with his limited reach.

"I'm not a sociologist," Henry said desperately. "I'm postgrad archaeology."

"Sounds close enough to me."

"Look, I'm only here to check on the house and pick up the mail. I don't even live here."

"Did she send you?"

Lying wouldn't help, Henry could see that; so he said, "She asked me to call by, yes."

"Why didn't she come herself?"

"I think you know why. She's scared shitless."

To Johnny Mays, this seemed like faintly surprising good news. "Of what?" he said.

"Of something like this."

"But it didn't worry you."

"Only because I never really believed her."

"What exactly did she tell you?"

Henry took a breath, and then launched in nervously. "That from the day she tried to get reaction from the police to some of the source-material in her study, she was subjected to some kind of campaign. She said cars followed her. When she was on her bike, she'd be stopped for no reason. The phone would ring at odd hours and there'd be nobody there. Some papers disappeared from her tutor's office one time."

"Sounds like the rambling of a very sick girl, wouldn't you say?"

"Then there was a break-in right here. Nothing was

taken except for her notes. She complained again. Your people said they'd have her for wasting police time."

Johnny raised an eyebrow. "My people?"

"That's who you are, isn't it?"

"You've got no idea who I am."

"You're Johnny Mays," Henry said, and was immediately sorry.

He sat with the feeling that he'd had one chance to come out of this unscathed, and he'd just blown it. Johnny was looking straight at him now, and he seemed to be making some kind of wry reassessment of Henry as a previously under-rated opponent. Henry was wishing that he could have kept his mouth shut. Even if he did come through in one piece, he knew that nothing in life would ever be the same for him again. A world where you reached for bedrock and found the likes of Johnny Mays . . . well, it held out about as much hope for the future as a walk in a poisoned garden.

Johnny said, "You're supposed to be so bright, tell me this. Did you ever dig up anyone who came back from the dead?"

"No."

"You think it's possible?"

"No."

So then Johnny nudged the stack of papers a half-inch closer to Henry, and when Henry looked up and met his eyes he saw a gleam that he'd never encountered before this morning, but that some primal part of his mind was instantly able to recognise. It was the light from beyond the Edge, and it burned with a terrible glow.

"Then start reading to me, Henry," Johnny Mays said, "or you're going to get the chance of a first-hand confirmation."

21

Nick paid his hotel bill by credit card, which made it a problem for some other day. He felt a mild confusion about what he was doing – was he going home to pick up some of his stuff, or was he picking up his stuff to bring it home? – but it was nothing that he didn't feel he could handle. He'd been in transit for so long that it had begun to feel almost like a way of life; apart from the first couple of years in police dormitories and the time that he'd been billeted in some village that he'd never heard of during the miners' strike, he'd mostly lived in places where someone else's name was taped above the doorbell. There had been Angela, who'd finally returned to South Africa for family reasons, and before that there had been Rebecca, who'd given Nick the push when she'd found out about Angela; it was only in the last three years that he'd lived on-and-off alone in a place that he'd been buying, and that was somewhere that he'd had to let go when his professional difficulties had suggested an urgent change of air. When he'd told Alice that his speciality was that of preying on women of property, it had been with an uncomfortable awareness that this wasn't a million miles away from the truth. Not the truth exactly, but something that could look awfully damned close to it whenever his self-esteem was at a low.

Nick took his bags across the lobby and out to where he'd left the car on the narrow hotel forecourt. He'd felt better about himself than he did now, but he'd also felt considerably worse. At some point during the last

twelve hours with Alice he felt as if he'd turned some
kind of a corner, and he sensed that something similar
had happened for her. It was as if they'd both been
carrying matched halves of a puzzle, and now the two
pieces had clicked together to make something that they
could finally bury and forget.

And if there was ever going to be anything more to it
. . . well, only time could tell them about that.

He came out through the west side of town along
by the fairgrounds. The fair itself had now packed
up and moved on. A few lorries stood on the land,
but mostly it was empty space criss-crossed with lines
where temporary cables had been buried under humps
of tarmac and then ripped out again like a dissected
system of veins. Next year it would happen again,
the same garish atmosphere painted in new strokes of
light, and Nick wondered if he'd still be around to see
it. Maybe they'd need a new geek for the Ghost Train,
so that he could join up and go along with them.

Or maybe he'd have found something better by then.
Who could say?

The drive was an easy one. There wasn't a thing
wrong with the car apart from the wire that he'd pulled
loose to guarantee him a few more hours of Alice's
company. He wasn't looking forward to facing Bruno,
but he knew that he'd have to do it; putting his resig-
nation into the works would at least take away some of
the inevitable heat, and with any luck he'd be able to
walk away more or less clean. The mud could splash,
but let it fall somewhere else. Nick had confessed to
nothing that could be used against him outside of a
disciplinary situation.

By Jennifer's place, he parked the rental car alongside
her own.

Knowing that she was home, he didn't use his key but
rang the chimes instead. Already he felt like a stranger,
standing here in the hallway and listening to the faint
sounds of her coming to the door. When she opened

234

up, she was momentarily blank with the surprise of seeing him.

"Nick!" she said. "I thought you'd be at least a couple of weeks."

Jennifer wasn't as he'd been expecting to see her, not at this hour of the day. She was without makeup, pale and tired-looking, and she was wearing the baggy track-suit that she sometimes wore instead of pyjamas when sleeping alone on winter nights.

Nick said, "This is just a flying visit. Thought I could pick up some more of my gear, if it's okay with you." There was an awkward pause, and he added, "I can come back later if there's somebody here."

"Nobody's here," Jennifer said. "Come in."

She hadn't sounded offended, but nor had she exactly sounded indifferent to the inference. Nick hadn't meant anything by it, and as he followed her into the flat he was even less inclined to read anything into the way she was dressed or the fact that some of the curtains were drawn in the daytime. The place seemed unusually untidy, and he picked up a trace odour of disinfectant in the air. In the lounge there was daytime television playing with the sound turned down almost to nothing, as if only for company.

Nick said, "Is everything all right?"

"If you can call twelve hours of trying to puke up nothing 'all right', then I've never been better."

"Seafood?"

"Murder scene."

"On your first day of probation? That's going some."

She picked up a half-finished glass of what looked like dirty water but was probably Alka-Seltzer gone flat, took a sip, and grimaced. "I'd trade it for just about anything," she said.

"Ever have to attend a post-mortem?"

"Yes, and this was worse. Don't even *ask* me what they did to her, I'll only start again."

"Second thoughts?" Nick said, and he saw Jennifer

make a real effort for total control.

"No second thoughts," she said.

"Good for you. I mean it."

"Thanks." Now she almost managed a smile. "I thought you might still be angry with me."

"Never was. Bags still in the same place?"

"I haven't moved a thing."

He stepped back into the hallway and opened the door to the airing cupboard, where his two big suitcases stood on end in the space underneath the hot water tank. He'd picked them up cheap at a lost property sale and they looked like twin echoes from the days of steam trains and telegrams, but they'd served Nick well in the past and would probably outlast him. As he was heaving them out, he said, "Any more trouble with the heater?"

"No," Jennifer said, "You did a good job on it." And then she said, "We've missed you."

"We?"

"The heater and me." She smiled, nervously, as if she wasn't quite sure of her ground; it was a revelation to Nick, who couldn't ever recall seeing her deeply uncertain about anything before this.

"But as far as the rest of them are concerned," he suggested, "I'm still about as welcome as a case of crabs in a diving suit."

Now she looked down. "More or less."

"I only came back so I could make arrangements to quit the job for good," he said with what sounded almost like a hint of apology. "It sounds like you've been doing pretty well so far, Jenny. Don't wreck your chances now."

Still without looking up to meet his eyes, she smiled ruefully. "Burned some bridges, did I?"

And because it was a question for which he had no ready answer, Nick left his cases by the front door and moved past her into the kitchen. She followed him, but slowly.

He said, "I'm going to leave you a forwarding address

on the board. I don't know how long it'll be good for."

She waited in the doorway as he wrote it out on the noteblock, and then read over his shoulder as he pinned the sheet into a space on the cork board between a dairy calendar and Jennifer's out-of-date library tickets. She said, "What kind of a place is that?"

"One that belongs to an old friend."

"Male or female?"

"Does it matter?"

She immediately sensed his evasion, and seemed a touch put out. "Well, you didn't waste any time," she said, but Nick noted that she wasn't exactly devastated by the news.

"It isn't how it looks," he said, and then, "I'm going to go, now. Look after yourself."

When he'd opened the door and was picking up his bags to walk out of the flat for what would probably be the last time, Jennifer said, "See Bruno before you go anywhere else."

"I was planning to."

"I mean, see him now. He's been trying to get hold of you. And it's not just him, it's most of the people upstairs."

"What do you mean?"

"I didn't want to be the one to tell you this, but it looks like I'd better. They don't think that he's dead, Nick."

He lowered the bags, slowly. He didn't have to ask who she meant, even though he could hardly believe what he was hearing.

"They don't think he's dead, but they're damn sure that he's dangerous."

———

"No doubt that it's him?" Nick asked Bruno, and Bruno shook his head.

"Not unless there's somebody else with his fingerprints. He spent a good few days here, as far as we can tell. The ground search didn't reach this far."

They were up at Mad Jack's ramshackle farm on the moors, to where Bob Woolton had summoned the local man after looking in through the window and seeing Mad Jack's days-old cadaver still sitting with its death-grip on the threadbare arms of his chair. The body had now been taken away, but Nick had looked through the polaroids of the discovered scene. They'd a preliminary diagnosis of heart failure from the police surgeon, and there were no signs of foul play on or around the cadaver at all; the way that it seemed to read was that Mad Jack had pulled a live body out of the reservoir one night, and that the effort of bringing it home had just about killed him. Exactly *who* he thought he'd been bringing home was another matter. They'd heard the old rumours about his boy, and were left to draw their own conclusions. Johnny had stayed here for a number of days, at least, and appeared to have taken Jack's untaxed and uninsured old clunker of a car when he'd gone.

"Gone where?" Nick said.

And Bruno said, "I wish I knew. We've got some ideas, but nothing that'll tell us where he is. Did he ever talk much about wanting to settle old scores?"

"Did he ever? This is the guy who kept a book, remember."

Bruno winced. "That's what I was afraid of. Looks like a lot of people won't be safe if Johnny Mays is back and baying at the moon."

"Maybe he's in no state to do anything about it."

"Tell that to yesterday's bride in the bath."

They were walking across the yard at this point and here Nick stopped, his breath feathering in the cold air.

"You're kidding me," he said. "You think *that* was Johnny?"

"Yeah, I know," Bruno said. "That's everybody's reaction. He was a mad bastard, *but*. Well, it's *but* nothing anymore. He's working off all the old scores and if you're in the book, you've got trouble. Johnny Mays' hate list wasn't exactly hard to get onto."

Nick looked around the yard helplessly, as if there might be answers hidden in the walls or the stones or the wide open land beyond. Bruno waited with patience for Nick to stop floundering and start thinking. They'd seen everything now; the animals in the shed, the littered hearth, the bedroom where Johnny had begun his recovery. There were still about half a dozen technicians in the house, and as Nick had arrived two officers from the video unit had been lugging their U-matic equipment out towards the cars and vans that were jammed in at the top of the narrow lane.

Bruno said, "Any bright ideas?"

"What about the car?"

"Nobody remembers its number. Swansea haven't been able to give us anything on the original registration yet, but they're still looking. There's a call out on the model and Traffic have made a few stops, but nothing's come out of it."

"But you did say the car was untaxed."

"The local man says he used to turn a blind eye. Warned the old guy a number of times, but didn't take it any further. He's now having reason to be sorry. What I want from you, Nick, is some idea of who he might go for next."

So Nick took a guess.

———

They went back to town in the rental car, with Bruno's driver following them down. Nick's mind was racing, bouncing him around like a pinball, although on the outside he stayed pretty well in control. His feelings defied any easy explanation; he felt elated, he felt scared . . . but mostly, he felt like an idiot. He'd even turned up for the memorial service, for Christ's sake.

Nick went straight for the student house by the railway.

Bruno rang the bell and Nick stood back and looked

up at the house. The place was a mausoleum in design, all right, and Nick could only hope that it had stayed empty and now wasn't a mausoleum in fact, as well. The bell rang out unanswered and Bruno said, "Is there another way in?"

"Around the back," Nick said, and led the way.

Nobody appeared to be taking any interest in them in the back alley apart from a cat who watched from a shed roof in an adjacent yard. The alley was crossed by washing lines without washing, and there were weeds growing up through the cobbles. The yard door pushed open unlatched when Nick tried it, and the two of them went through.

The kitchen door stood open. The frame had been cut and pieced-in around the lock plate after Johnny's first visit, but the new work appeared to have been smashed out with a single kick. They stepped into the kitchen and listened, but the house made no sound.

"Smell something?" Nick said.

"Paraffin," Bruno said after a moment.

Nick crouched briefly by the free-standing heater (which, he saw, had been moved from its usual place in the middle of the room), but the heater was cold.

"It isn't coming from this," he said, and so they moved cautiously through into the rest of the house.

Most of the ground floor had been thoroughly ransacked. The bedroom at the front of the house, the one which had drawn Johnny the one time that Nick had followed him in here, had received the most attention of anywhere; the others were a mess, but this one looked as if its contents had been fed through a shredder and then scattered. Bottles had been smashed and there was a heady mixture of perfume and sandalwood oil hanging in the air, but even this couldn't overcome the pervasive kerosene smell that had drifted in behind them like some ghostly manservant trying to keep up an unobtrusive presence. Bruno stepped over a coat that looked as if it had come off worst in a fight with a fistful of razors, shaking his head in disbelief; Nick knew that it wasn't the damage that was impressing him so deeply, but rather what the damage had to say about the perpetrator's state of mind.

Nick glanced upward. There was another floor above this one, and probably a livable attic above that; he listened for a few moments, but no boards creaked. The only sound was that of Bruno as he crouched and turned over what had once been a spiral-bound notebook.

There was green bottle-glass all the way down the stairs, some of the pieces wax-encrusted. They crunched underfoot as Nick ascended. It looked as if a bottle had rolled across the landing and come bouncing down, smashing on its second or third skip. There was no turn in the stairs, just a straight run up with nowhere for anyone to hide; Nick was almost certain that Johnny had been here and then moved on, but he kept himself tense and wary all the same. One thing that he couldn't forget, and it was the last thing that Johnny had told him; by Johnny's own declaration, Nick had earned himself a place in the book along with all the others.

The thought made him feel a little sick. He felt tense, he felt vulnerable.

He went on up the stairs. The smell was stronger here than anywhere. There was a paraffin drum standing to one side on the landing, and another tipped over and rolled against the wall; they looked as if they'd hold enough when full to make lifting them a two-handed job, but these were unstoppered and empty. There was spillage everywhere, soaking into the rough matting that served in place of a carpet, and it seemed to lead in a distinct trail to the bathroom at the end of the landing.

The bathroom was high-ceilinged and narrow, shabby around the edges but still as serviceable as the day it had been built. The windowledge was crowded with toothpaste tubes, brushes and toiletries, the towel rail was piled high with mismatched bath towels that looked as if they were used and re-used and only very occasionally run through the washer, and the bath itself was filled from end to end by a young man tied to a chair.

He'd not only been bound, but also gagged with tape; the paraffin level in the bath was almost up to his chin and he was staring in fascinated terror at a half-inch stub of candle that had been jammed into the wire soap rack only inches in front of his face. The candle had been considerably longer when lit, if the trail of solidified wax that hung down under the rack was any guide; in minutes or less, the wick would drop into the paraffin below and the bath would undergo an instant transformation into a boiling crucible of fire.

So Nick spat on his fingers and pinched out the wick, and the young man gave a long, low groan of relief behind the gag as he let his head drop back stiffly. The paraffin washed up and around his gag and he began to cough and choke; Nick ripped the tape away and called out, "Bruno! Up here!"

Bruno came running, and together they were able to lift the young man out, dripping chair and all. They set him out on the landing and found a knife to cut him free, and then they had to carry him downstairs between them because his legs had no feeling and even his hands were like useless, drawn-in claws.

Nick asked his name. "It's Henry," the young man told him, "and by Christ, I bet this is going to hurt."

Henry wasn't wrong.

Nick walked him around for a while, mostly supporting him as his circulation returned; Bruno was on the pay phone out in the hall, and had to stick a finger in his uncovered ear because Henry was yelling and crying so much. In between circuits, Nick sat him on the sofa (slashed open but otherwise serviceable) and worked on his legs.

The pain had just about become bearable by the time that Bruno had finished on the phone, although Henry still couldn't stand unaided. Bruno joined them, listening from the doorway as Henry was saying, "I didn't tell him anything, but I think I shit myself. How about that?"

"Happens to us all," Nick said.

"Speak for yourself," Bruno said drily.

"Ignore Bruno, he only came along because he likes to ride around in the big cars. Who did this?"

Still shaking a little, Henry looked from one man to the other.

"He said his name was Johnny Mays."

Jennifer checked herself in the mirror. Maybe Nick's unexpected appearance had been what she needed to snap herself out of it; just about the last thing that she'd wanted at this moment had been for him to see her looking like this. No excuses, now. Nobody was going to turn up on her doorstep and tell her everything's all right, and here's exactly what to do; if she wanted to be taken seriously, then she'd have to regain at least a measure of her control and composure.

The problem was that she couldn't help remembering what she'd seen. The sheer vividness of the victim's mortality. Any of us are the same, she thought; touch us, and we may so easily explode. Her eyes in the mirror gazed back steadily, and she knew then that she'd managed to pull herself through the worst of it.

The chimes rang.

Nick, she thought, and hurried out to answer.

But it wasn't Nick, just one of the other plainclothes officers holding up his warrant card for her to see; pocketing it again, he said, "They sent me to get Nick Frazier. Is this where he lives?"

"No," she said. "I mean, not any more. He moved out."

"Do you know where he'll be right now?"

Jennifer frowned. "Why?" she said, and the officer looked down at himself and gave a half-apologetic smile.

"Don't go by appearances," he said. "I've been on the street with the drugs squad for the past three weeks. All this is just protective colouring." He glanced around the empty landing, as if wary of being overheard. "If I can come in for a couple of minutes, I'll explain what's going on."

Jennifer backed off to let him in.

"Better make it quick," she said. "I'm just making myself fit to go out." And, leaving him to close the door, she turned to go back down the hallway.

"This won't take any time at all," the officer said, and she felt his hand grasping the back of her head as if he was getting ready to pitch a basketball no more than a split-second before she was slammed face-first into the wall.

She lay there almost helpless as he quickly checked all of the rooms, and then he came back and hauled her to her feet. She was dazed, and unwittingly compliant.

He said, "Does it hurt? It shouldn't bruise too much." And then, with less concern and considerably more interest, "I want to know where he is."

Jennifer felt as if she'd been jarred completely out of synch. "Why?" she managed.

"I'm Johnny Mays. I've got a lot to do, and I don't know how much time I'll have. I need to know where Nicky's gone. Where's your address book?"

"In the kitchen. By the phone."

"Show me."

He supported and guided her, holding her like a nurse teaching someone to walk again, and when they reached the kitchen he pulled over a chair and sat her close to the wall. Then he tilted her face to the light and studied it for a moment; "I know what you need," he said, and he went over to the sink and turned on the cold water tap. Jennifer raised her hand to her head, touching it gingerly; she'd taken one hell of a thump when her forehead had met the wall, and she could feel the beginnings of a bruise centred around the bony angle above her right eye.

She was angry at herself. How could she have let him take her so easily? On the street it would never have happened but this wasn't the street, this was her own place and her defences had been down. Too busy thinking about her own problems to remember that sometimes, the world outside didn't operate to expectations, didn't keep itself in neat compartments. He was soaking and wringing out her dishtowel now, folding and then refolding it to make some kind of a compress . . .

And Jennifer was sitting right underneath the cork board, where Nick had left her a note of where he'd be staying.

Johnny Mays turned from the sink and came back over to her; he put the damp cloth into her hand and then guided it up to her face, where its cool touch was like bliss. "This'll stop any swelling," he said, helping her to position it.

"You're supposed to be dead."

"I know. Just hold it in place for a while."

He straightened up, and stood looking down at her. Nick's hastily-scribbled memo would be at his eye level and almost directly in front of him now; he only had to look up, and he'd be staring at it.

But he didn't look up. He studied her a while longer.

He said, "You remind me of someone I used to know. But then a lot of women do that, just a little." And then his tone changed, hardened. "I've got business with Nick. Where is he?"

"I don't know," she said.

"You can tell me, or I can find out for myself. That probably means that you'll tell me, anyway. All I can say is that it won't be much fun for either of us. I've hit one dead end today, I really can't handle another."

"Honestly, he never said where he was going."

He was thinking about it; she could almost hear his disc drives running as he weighed the information and

tried to work out what it was worth. Not much, he'd
conclude if he could read her as well as she feared he
might, although it was impossible to tell. She turned the
makeshift compress around and applied its other side;
anything to avoid meeting his eyes and having him see
all the way through her.

"I hope you're not going to be difficult about this," he
said.

"Look in the book," she protested. "See if I'm lying."

He lingered a moment longer and then he did exactly
that, not only riffling through every page in her address
book but also sorting through the jottings and odd notelet pages that lay in a stack alongside the phone.

His back was to her again. Was there anything to
hand that she could grab and use to brain him before
he could sense that it was coming? She didn't think so.
He had an advantage of size and strength – even his
touch had been hot, as if he was burning up energy like
a furnace – and whatever she did, it would have to be
something that she could follow through. If she'd known
that her kitchen would one day become a combat zone,
she'd have planned it differently. There was a cast-iron
casserole somewhere, but she hadn't used it in ages and
wasn't even sure where she'd put it; and her head still
hurt, and her legs still felt shaky . . .

But at least she could hide Nick's address from his
sight.

She reached up, glancing at Johnny Mays as she did;
he was still busy, and so she stretched out her hand without making a sound, and caught the corner of the paper
where it stuck out from the board at an angle. Maybe
she could cough or fake some wincing sound, jerk the
paper away from the pin in one clean motion and then
perhaps quickly fold it into the middle of her damp cloth
to conceal it. And then, having frustrated Johnny Mays'
long-term aim, she could turn her attention wholly to the
matter of immediate self-preservation.

She got ready to pull.

She glanced at him, to see what he was doing now.

He was watching her.

"Leave it where it is," he said quietly.

She let her hand fall, almost in shame at having been caught, and she sat twisting the washcloth nervously as he stood over her reading the memo. He seemed to be taking a long time about it. When she glanced up at him, he seemed drained and in shock.

"This, I don't believe," he said, finally taking the paper from the board.

And then he looked down at Jennifer. "This is where he's gone?" he demanded. "And is *she* still there?"

She snapped the washcloth up into his face. He hadn't been expecting anything and although he raised his hand to protect his eyes, he wasn't fast enough and he screamed as the whipcrack blinded him. He was standing with his guard wide open and she followed through with a two-fisted punch that she rammed into his stomach, and then as he doubled over she had a choice of the bridge of his nose or the back of his neck, but his arms were in the way of an uppercut and so she came down over his head, two-handed again in a bellringer's grip, and she dropped him like a bull in a slaughterhouse.

He was down, but he wasn't out. He was down on one knee and he was howling, but any moment now she was going to lose her advantage as he came surging back up again, twice as mad and three times as dangerous. The only guaranteed way to stop him would be to switch out his lights for good, right there in the middle of the kitchen floor; and while she was mad enough right now to know that she could do it if she had to, she knew better than to kid herself that a few holds and throws learned in evening classes would be enough to make it happen.

What did that leave her? Knives? The window?

(The curtain hook?)

She took a grip on his ear, and didn't release it as she stepped around him; he screamed again as his ear twisted, and when she took hold of the collar of his coat and lifted he came up with the pain as if weightless. Keeping him bent over and off-balance, she ran him out and down the hallway. He'd left the front door open to the landing and she sped him on through it, and as soon as he was clear and tumbling she stepped back and slammed the door and threw the bolt. She could hear the crash as he came up against the safety rail over the stairwell, but by now she'd engaged the deadlock and was putting on the chain that she'd never used once in all the time that she'd lived here. She fumbled it, dropped it twice, finally got it into the channel. She wondered if Johnny Mays had gone through the safety rail and fallen down the centre of the well, and for a moment she fervently wished that he had; by the time he hit ground level, he'd be like a sack of broken biscuits.

But when she listened, she could hear him getting to his feet outside.

Her own injuries forgotten for the moment, Jennifer ran back along the hallway towards her phone.

Johnny got to his feet, blinking. He held onto the rail for support and put a hand to the back of his neck, where it felt as if he'd stuck his head out of a window just in time to be hit by a falling safe from the floor above. His eyes burned and his shoulder hurt from where he'd come to an abrupt halt after skidding across the polished floor of the landing.

There was something in his hand.

He brought it around where he could see it. He was holding a crumpled piece of paper.

Wasn't this supposed to have some kind of significance?

He smoothed the paper out and studied it. An address, in a handwriting that he felt he really ought to know. Now he remembered.

And then he turned and stared at the door to Jennifer's flat; stared for a while, frowning as if he was aware of its significance but somehow couldn't quite grasp it right now. He concentrated hard. The cheap little slit had messed him up somehow, hadn't she?

Then he looked down at the paper again.

The bitch had messed him up, all right.

He folded the paper carefully into four, put it into his pocket, and dusted himself down. He knew who he was. He knew where he was going. He knew what he would have to do. Anything beyond that was just bookkeeping.

And, walking more or less steadily, he made a start by moving towards the stairs.

22

Out on the coast, Alice was wondering if she'd done something that she was going to regret. It didn't feel as if she had . . . but then, it never did. She wouldn't have taken a stranger in like this, and she hadn't seen Nick in so long that she could hardly claim to know him well; he could have turned into a confidence man or a deep-dyed sinner with a convincing line in midnight confession, or he might – in the worst of all possible worlds – turn out to be another Johnny Mays.

But she couldn't believe that.

The truth of it was that there was more to bring them together than to keep them apart; they'd known each other in a time of comparative innocence and now, having recognised each other in a strange and less familiar landscape, they found themselves being drawn together like exiles in the shadow of war. If Nick was going to be bad trouble, she'd have sensed it long ago. She'd sensed it in Johnny, and she'd cut him loose while she was still able; and while it had taken nearly twenty years for that story to reach its conclusion, just look at how right she'd once been.

She'd help Nick out. He'd help her to heal, belatedly. Whether they became lovers or not . . . well, that didn't really matter. Sometimes friendship could be much more important. She'd gone through enough lovers to worry her into taking an HIV test about eight months before, but a list of the friends that she'd kept over the years could be jotted onto the back of a business card. And which did she really miss more?

She took the bus into town. It was the slow service, and ground all around the outlying villages for nearly an hour before dropping her across the road from the office.

She waited for a space in the traffic, and crossed over.

Sandra was dealing with some people at the counter. The junior was gazing at all of the different colours in a box of plastic-headed pins on the desk in front of him, shaking the box to mix them around. Alice went straight on through and into Hathaway's office without even knocking.

He was on the phone, and looked up with a startled expression as she came in and closed the door behind her. "Four-thirty it is, then," he said to whoever was at the other end of the line, and Alice could see that her unexpected arrival had thrown him a little; his smile was awkward as he gestured for her to take a seat and then quickly wrapped up the call.

"Client?" Alice said as he hung up.

"Katie's headmaster," Hathaway said. "So much to consider, you wouldn't believe it."

"I'd believe it," Alice said. "I know you've got trouble enough already, so I'm going to keep this short and simple. I'm staying."

"Oh."

"What's the big surprise? We've done this before."

"I know. Only . . . I thought we understood it would have to be final, this time."

"You and me, that's final. It's the job that I'm keeping, Max. I'm not so much in demand that I can really afford to do anything else."

"Are you serious?"

"Damn right I'm serious. If having me around gives you problems then I'm sorry, but I'm not just going to disappear. You've been playing around outside of the rules, Max. That leaves you open to certain penalties. Look at it from my point of view, I've been wasting my time going nowhere with you. That means I'm due some measure of consideration."

"Like what?"

"Like a modest payrise and two weeks' leave, starting today. And where's my car? I didn't see it outside."

Hathaway was growing paler. "I've given it to Ruby."

"Better give her the disappointing news tonight, then. Unless you'd prefer me to stop by and tell her."

"There's no need for all, this, Alice. No need at all."

Alice got to her feet. "You can walk out on me, Max, but don't think you can walk over me. This is nothing compared to what Ruby would get out of you under the same kind of circumstances. You're the one who wanted to end it, so all I'm doing is telling you the cost of the settlement. Just consider yourself lucky that something good's starting to happen in my life right now, or I might *really* be inclined to put the bite on."

And with that thought, she left his office.

As she stepped out into the street, she glanced back through the window; his door had stayed open and she could see all the way through to where he was still sitting behind his desk. He was looking faintly sick, and hadn't moved. What had he expected her to do, pack up her French underwear and go off to be a nun on an island somewhere? Or did he have some idea that she'd simply hail another married man like a passing taxi, and be conveniently whisked away and out of his life for good?

Perhaps one time, she'd have done exactly that. But not any more.

Hathaway shouldn't complain. For a lesson in living, he was getting it pretty cheap.

Bruno sometimes wondered whether the best way to deal with bystanders at an incident scene wouldn't simply be to turn a fire hose onto them until they got the idea and went away. How long it would take the message to get through, he really didn't know. Bruno was convinced that he was dealing with a special kind of mental defective, here, a species most readily identified when seen hanging around open-mouthed and staring at the camera from the background of a TV news report. And they'd appear anywhere; traffic had regular problems with people who'd hear about an accident on the local radio news and then turn out in their cars to take a look. About fifty such people had materialised in the street outside the big old house, and after first blocking the way for the ambulance they then blocked the way for the fire crew who'd been called in to make the bathroom safe and to check out the drainage system. If too much fuel had leaked down the pipes, then an underground fire could be a real possibility.

"Get them pushed right back to the end of the street," he told one of his sergeants as most of the herd were craning to get a look at Henry being helped into the back of the ambulance, "and put someone down there to make sure they stay."

"I'll use a couple of cadets."

"Use a whip and a chair if you have to, but tell them the show's over."

Bruno walked back toward the house after this. Nick Frazier had been with him until only a couple of minutes ago, when someone had come over with an urgent message for him to phone Jennifer; and now, as Bruno climbed the steps to the wide-open front door, he could see Nick at the pay phone in the hallway. Deeper in the house, other officers were moving around.

Nick beckoned to him.

As Bruno moved in alongside him, Nick turned the receiver so that he'd be able to listen in. *Jennifer*, Nick told him in an almost silent whisper, and Jennifer was saying, "He was here, Nick. He's back and he was here and he's worse than anything you told me."

Nick said, "Did he . . . did he *do* anything?"

"I didn't give him the chance. You've got to watch out for him, Nick. You're the one he was looking for, and he knows where you've been staying."

"How?"

"He looked on the board, how do you think? And he seemed to recognise the address."

"Jesus," Nick breathed, and Bruno could see that this had hit him as a matter of some considerable significance – even more than Bruno might have supposed.

"Don't even think of going back there," Jennifer was warning him, and Nick put a hand to his head as if to help clear it.

He said, "I'm glad you're okay, Jen. I have to go. Bruno's here now, and I want you to give him all the details."

Without waiting to hear Jennifer's reply, Nick handed over the receiver and was out of the door before Bruno could stop him. Bruno shouted his name, but Nick didn't even break his stride as he ran down the short path to the street; so then Bruno turned to the phone and said to Jennifer, "Where exactly are you?"

"I'm at home. What happened to Nick?"

A car door slammed somewhere over beyond the police vans, and an engine raced for a couple of seconds before suddenly taking off. From here, Bruno couldn't even see in which direction.

"He's away up the road and burning rubber. Tell me where he's aiming for and I'll get some local men in ahead of him."

And Jennifer said, "But that's what I was trying to tell him! Johnny Mays took the paper away, and I can't remember exactly what was on it. I don't know where he was going!"

He knew they'd be looking for him. They might even know where he'd be heading by now, and this was why he'd avoided the obvious route and taken one of the old pass roads, those roads that in winter would become snaking ribbons of darkness and which fog and blizzards could so easily close. The ageing Morris made heavy weather of the slow climb, engine clattering like a tin can filled with nuts and bolts, and on a couple of the steeper sections Johnny was beginning to wonder whether its heart would give out as surely as its owner's had; in the lower gears it seemed to be trying to shake itself apart, but then on the level section over the top everything seemed to even out and Johnny began to believe that there was a chance of making it to the end, after all. The road came down through forestry land, winding like a switchback along the way and giving occasional glimpses of the lowlands ahead over dense stands of pine trees, and now the old rustbucket seemed to be cruising so smoothly that Johnny might have sworn that he could hardly hear the engine note over the noise from the road.

Which he couldn't, as he found when he tried to speed up on one of the less tortuous stretches and discovered that he was making no difference to the power output at all. A glance at the dash confirmed it; somewhere in the last couple of miles the fuel gauge needle had settled on zero, and he'd been freewheeling ever since.

For now the road continued to descend, and so Johnny simply put the gear shift into neutral and carried on rolling. He'd almost no money, just the loose change that had been in his pockets when he'd driven over the dam plus a handful of coins that he'd found in a jar in Mad Jack's kitchen. But this didn't worry him too much; he'd planned to dump the Morris anyway as soon as he could, and had been looking for an opportunity from the moment that he'd left the outskirts of town. Only one had presented itself, in the form of a lone driver changing a wheel at the roadside about twenty miles back; Johnny had slowed down to get the measure of the man but had picked up speed again after a closer look at the car.

A *Skoda*?

You've got to draw the line somewhere, he'd thought, and had driven straight on by.

He didn't know how much further he'd be able to travel like this; one good dip in the road and he'd better start thinking about walking. If he could make it all the way down to the flatlands, he'd be into an area of expensive and isolated houses with two-car garages and a good chance of being able to pick up something sleeker and faster that would get him out to the coast in reasonable time. Or he could walk along by the roadside and try for a lift and he might get really lucky, but he doubted it. He'd seen himself in the mirror, face to face with the devil behind the glass, and he knew that he looked like a walking disaster in search of somewhere to strike.

The road came down alongside a fast-flowing river for a half-mile or more, and then swung around to cross it by a stone hump-backed bridge. Johnny didn't brake, took the corner wide, and then came up and over the bridge so fast that all four wheels left the ground for what seemed like forever and was probably a little over a second. It was sheer good luck that there was nothing coming up on the other side as the Morris slammed down again with every bolt and rivet straining to fly apart at once; the vehicle came close to exploding like a clown car in the circus, but somehow it all held together and kept on moving.

But more slowly, now. The road was running almost level, and the Morris was running out of energy. Johnny realised that he'd been holding his breath since the bridge, and now he let it out. For one moment, there, as he'd hit the rise and the car had taken off, he'd looked forward and seen nothing but darkness; it was the middle of a well-lit afternoon and he was looking down a long tunnel of headlight beams shining into a void. But then he blinked and everything came back to normal, and he was left with no more than a lingering uncertainty like a half-remembered dream.

The Morris coasted on for a while longer, long enough to bring it down from the forested lower slopes and out into the lusher territory below, but this was getting ridiculous; Johnny could walk faster, and so he steered over to the side of the road and let the car come to a final halt. He got out and walked away from it without looking back, without even bothering to close the driver's door; the Morris was as good as forgotten already as he headed off down the little-used country road and scanned the horizon for houses.

Nothing yet. He walked on.

This was mostly grazing land, stone-walled and rolling. There had been industry in the valleys around here at one time, small mills and foundries, but now these buildings would mostly be windowless shells reclaimed by the greenery. Johnny's interest was in the kind of residence that would be owned by moneyed people who'd commute the twenty miles or so into the big steelmaking town at the end of this particular yellow-brick road; people who'd dream of dead leaves and log fires and who'd hang their heads in shame at the very thought of being seen on public transport. Jaguar people. Mercedes people. People who, at the very least, would probably keep an MG Metro in the garage for a runabout.

The first place that he saw was a working farm set some way back from the road, its outbuildings patched with different colours of brick and overshadowed by a tall green silo. He passed it by. Too open, too many people, and probably too many dogs as well.

The next one looked better.

This was a one-storey building with a gated drive and its name upon the gate; Johnny couldn't see much of it from the road but what he could see seemed promising, and so he let himself in. When he passed an old KEEP OUT sign nailed to a tree about ten yards on up the gravel, his sense of having discovered a worthwhile prospect increased. A Ferrari, even? He'd never *seen* a Ferrari outside of a motor magazine.

The main part of the bungalow was about thirty or forty years old, but it had been extended at least twice to become a substantial if sprawling property. The exterior was all white, the woodwork and drainpipes were black, and for decoration there was a cartwheel leaning on the wall by the main entrance door. Johnny crossed the wide turning circle in front of the house and made straight for the double garage that had been built onto its end.

The wooden sliding door stood open about a couple of feet, and Johnny widened the opening so that he could step through and take a look inside. He made no attempt at stealth, no pretence at secrecy; he'd never sneaked around like a lowlife before, and he wasn't about to start now. It was gloomy inside, and so he reached over and switched on the lights; and as the overhead fluorescents stuttered into life, he saw that half of the garage was empty. But in the other half, across the bare concrete floor with its oilstains, stood the car that would be taking him to Alice.

A Scimitar. Blue. Not too shabby at all.

"What do you think you're doing?" demanded a voice from the doorway.

Johnny turned, unruffled.

There was a woman outside. That was about all that he could see of her through the small frosted panes in the upper part of the door; she stood ready to slam it shut on him if he should take a step towards her without explaining himself.

"I'm a police officer," he said. "I've been ringing your bell for the last five minutes, but you didn't answer."

It worked, as he'd known that it would. She didn't relax, exactly, but he could sense it as a little of the apprehension went out of her.

"It was working only this morning," she said with some puzzlement. She made no move to come in. "What exactly was it that you wanted?"

"There's a car abandoned just down the lane, we're

looking for the man who was driving it. Have you seen anyone?"

"Nobody at all."

"No strangers? It's important to know."

"It's a quiet area, strangers stand out." Through the glass he saw her blurred image turn and glance behind her nervously, as if she sensed that the world outside had suddenly turned more hostile. "This man . . . would he be dangerous?"

"That could depend."

She moved into the garage then, stepping quickly through the doorway and into the light. She was about Johnny's own age. Hadn't begun to let herself go in the way that some of them seemed to, reading all the stuff in their magazines about dieting and exercise plans and never doing a damned thing about either. Not bad looking at all, if you liked the type.

Dangerous?

"Yes," Johnny said. "He's dangerous." And he walked toward her. "Is your husband home?" he said, and she shook her head.

"No," she said, "he's in town."

"Lucky I came by, then."

And as he was saying this Johnny reached around her, and pushed the door closed.

———

It was beginning to get dark by the time that Alice reached home; she was laden down with bags and swearing to herself that, whatever happened in the future, she'd happily suck on a slug rather than give up her car in a passing mood of annoyance again. The stuff that she'd bought weighed like hundredweight sacks of coal, but at least now they'd have something edible on the premises that wouldn't have to end up in the toilet at two o'clock in the morning. She'd never been one for keeping the kitchen well-stocked; never been one for much of anything around the home, really. She got her mid-day meals from the sandwich shop along from the office, ate very little in the evenings, and only tidied around when it suited her . . . and mostly, it tended to suit her to leave it until some other time. Of her old boyfriends, only Richard had ever complained about this haphazard streak in her nature; and Richard had been a mother's boy whose idea of a good time had been for the two of them to sit watching his dog eat.

She unhooked the padlock on the street door, and pushed her way in. The gaming machines hulked in the gloom like some waiting street gang. How long had Nick been gone, now? He'd left late in the morning, say at least a couple of hours for the journey each way . . . allow an hour for the business at the police building, another hour with this Jennifer. Perhaps even longer. They'd have things to talk about, wouldn't they? Arrangements to make? It didn't have to mean anything.

But then she wondered, what if he didn't come back at all?

It could happen.

And if it did, it wouldn't be anything unique in her life. She tried to tell herself that it wouldn't matter to her one way or the other, as she hung the padlock on the inside handle and slid the security bolt. She was in near-darkness now with only a faint grey twilight showing the lines of the stairway from above, but she knew this place well enough to be able to navigate her way around it in a blackout if she had to. She'd worked over behind the expresso counter for at least six summers without a break, and between cutting bread and pumping steam she'd walked the aisles with a change bag and a bunch of keys for troubleshooting the slots. But that was then, and this was now. There was no way of going back, and she didn't particularly want to. Happy times for Alice had always seemed to lie just ahead, and she chased them like a child might chase a wave down a beach.

At the foot of the stairs, she set down her bags. Nick would return. She ought at least to show a little faith.

So then she went back to the door, and undid the bolt so that he'd be able to get in.

Less than an hour later, as she was halfway into the boiler cupboard at the back of the bathroom and poking around with a needle in an attempt to get the gas jets unblocked, she heard a car stop outside. Nothing so unusual in that, she thought, but when she tried to carry on she found that her concentration was completely blown. So then she thought, Who am I trying to kid? And she stripped off her rubber gloves and threw them down by the bath and went through to take a look out of the quayside window. She didn't even notice that she was running by the time that she reached it.

Just about enough streetlighting got down into the alley from the promenade above. There were more shadows than lit areas but she had a clear view of the open quay beyond the customs shed, dredger buckets and abandoned equipment standing like old stage properties from long-forgotten shows.

Wrong car.

I'm not disappointed, she thought. I'm not. And she turned away from the window and started the slow walk back to the bathroom. There was still time for Nick to get here; just being late didn't mean that he'd changed his mind.

She stopped.

The arcade door almost directly below her was being pushed open.

He hadn't changed his mind. Obviously he'd changed the car, and this was the reason for the delay. Alice was a little embarrassed at her own anxiety, and hoped that Nick wouldn't be able to read it in her when he came up; she stopped briefly before the mirror to check herself for straying hair or unbecoming smudges of soot from the boiler.

And froze, at the sound of the voice that came up to her from the bottom of the stairway.

"Alice?" it said. "Alice, are you there? It's me, Johnny. We have to talk."

Alice stared into her own disbelieving eyes. He was starting to climb the stairs.

"Don't be scared, Alice," he was saying. And then; "All this time, I wondered where you'd be. Never even imagined you might still be here."

Something was dragging on the steps as he ascended.

It sounded like a chain.

23

For Nick the journey was a blur, its length measured by the slow fading of the day. Johnny had a head start on him, but Nick had a better car. The possibility that Johnny might dump the Morris and pick up something faster was one that he didn't care to think about too hard or for too long.

It was dark when he finally reached his destination; he missed seeing the slipway and so, rather than turn around, he abandoned his car up on the promenade and made for the nearest set of steps to the lower quay. There were lights ahead of him in Alice's windows, warm as the lights of home; the empty boardwalk thundered as he ran for them.

He hit the door.

The door was open.

On the threshold he had to stop, and force himself to be cautious.

"Alice?" he called from the doorway, but there was no reply.

So then he eased the door shut behind him, and moved towards the stairs. She might not have heard. She could be sleeping. She could be waiting for him now, planning to spring some kind of a surprise. She might even be out. The stairs creaked a little as he climbed, and he called her name again.

The sitting room was empty. Nothing seemed to have changed in there since he'd last seen it, only a few hours before. There were supermarket carrier bags in the kitchen, the goods half-unpacked by someone who'd apparently lacked the patience to complete the job in one. Nobody in her bedroom, the big double bed still unmade. The same with the bathroom, and with the big dusty stockroom at the back where gumball machines and broken slots and a stripped-down jukebox waited for repairs that they were probably never going to get. He moved back into the skylighted hallway which ran the length of the building's upper storey, stepping around two full-sized carousel horses which leaned against the wall with their paint chipped and their poles broken off a couple of feet above their saddles. He called her name again with about as much effect as before, and then he wondered what the hell he was supposed to do now.

Go back into the sitting room and wait? Yeah, some chance of him being able to settle to that. He could about as easily sit through an entire Shirley Temple movie. He stopped and rubbed at his road-tired eyes, as if trying to shape himself up for some useful ideas.

"I think I might have hurt her, Nick," Johnny said from the shadows at the top of the stairs.

Either he'd come up in silence, or else Nick had been making so much noise in moving from room to room that he hadn't noticed. Nick stayed where he was, hand raised before his face, blinking a little. Johnny stepped forward into the light. He didn't look as if he'd slept off his feet in about a week but he seemed sad, quiet, and rational.

Nick lowered his hand.

He said, "Where is she?"

"I've been walking in one of those dreams," Johnny said, seeming not to hear. "It's been a bad one. I'd have killed you if I'd found you. I'm glad that I didn't."

"Where's Alice, Johnny?"

"But now I know I'm awake," Johnny persisted. "And, you know something? This is a lot worse."

"Johnny . . ." Nick said with a note of warning in his voice, and Johnny Mays nodded, slowly.

"We went out," he said. "I'll show you."

He turned, and began to descend the stairs again.

Nick moved to follow.

Once they were outside Nick let him lead the way along the boardwalk, staying far enough out of reach to be able to watch for any sudden surprises. Johnny didn't even seem to notice. He wasn't so much a man any longer, more a threadbare image of one; he walked along with his hands thrust into his outsized overcoat pockets and his shoulders hunched as if facing into a cold and bitter wind.

"I'm in a mess, Nick," he admitted as they came out by the side of the customs shed. "Nothing's clear any-more."

"It never was, for you," Nick said.

"No, you're wrong. Just for a while, there, I had every-thing balanced up just right. I had it running like a machine. But then I got here and it all seemed to fall apart."

"Yeah, I saw some of the work you'd been putting in. What did you think you were? The exterminating angel?"

And at this Johnny glanced at Nick, and managed a weak smile. For one moment, it was the old Johnny who looked out at him from the grey and driven shell of the new. He said, "I think I missed my chance at anything like that. Wouldn't you say?"

They went on by the low brick building with its Portakabin extension that served as headquarters for the local Fishermen's Selling Company, stepping out and around the tar-stained barrels and stacks of Castrol tins that were only the beginning of a clutter that had turned this part of the long, narrow quay into a hazardous junkyard. From here the harbour wall ran out at right angles to the shore, no more than a car's width separating the sea rail and a long row of lockup cabins. These had the names of different vessels stencilled on each door, *Lola Montez, Miranda, My Darling*

Clementine . . . those further out were lost in deepening shadow, as the boardwalk ran on through darkness to a single light shining over the harbour entrance at its far end.

They appeared to have the entire seafront to themselves. There wasn't another soul in sight.

"Where are we going, Johnny?" Nick said with some suspicion.

"Just a little further," Johnny said, and he made a vague gesture indicating somewhere ahead of them. "This is where I came with Alice. All I wanted to do was talk." Nick was still hanging back a little, wondering if this could be leading him into some kind of a setup, but it was something that Johnny didn't seem to notice. He went on, "This wasn't entirely my fault, you know. The two of you shouldn't have gone behind me like that."

Nick said, "You've killed her, haven't you?"

But Johnny didn't answer him, not directly.

He seemed to be taking Nick the full length of the jetty. Nick was feeling a sick kind of dread. However he tried to read it, this wasn't looking good. When they'd gone as far out as they could go, Johnny stood by the rail and said, "This is where we came. I don't know how she fell."

Nick hesitated, still wary. Johnny was holding onto the rail and looking down; after a moment he sensed Nick's reluctance and moved back, hands raised to show the innocence of his intentions.

Nick moved to the rail, and looked over.

The tide was out, and he was looking down at harbour mud. Shadows from the light above him gave it a slaty and chiselled look, making its water-cut contours sharper and more hard-edged. She lay face-down, half-in and half-out of the jetty's own shadow. She was embedded to a depth of a foot or more, probably by the impact of her twenty-foot fall from the rail. She looked as if she had been dead before she landed. The chain that Johnny had used on her had been thrown down alongside her body, and this also had sunk in deep for a good part of its length.

Nick turned away.

He wasn't shocked, or even surprised. He'd been rehearsing something like this in his mind, over and over for at least the last couple of hours. Johnny had moved back from the rail and was standing almost directly under the harbour lantern, his head bowed and his face mostly in shadow.

"Damn you, Johnny," Nick said quietly.

At this Johnny raised his head, and his face came into the light again. "There's no call for you to talk to me like that, Nick," he said. "I've lost more than you have." And then, sharply, as Nick began to move from the rail; "That's close enough."

Nick stopped. Johnny was dangerous, and Nick was no fool. Another time, some other place, but not here and now. He said, "For a while, there, I was sorry you'd died. Now I just wish you'd stayed that way."

"Wishes are for little kids, Nick. They never brought me one damned thing."

"And what do you want now?"

Johnny sighed, and briefly looked up at the stars. "To turn it all back," he said. "All the way back to the beginning again. Take a second run at it, see if I can't make everything come out better this time. Can you make that happen?"

Nothing from Nick. And again Johnny half-smiled, sadly.

"No," he said, "I didn't think so."

And then he shrugged up his collar, put his hands back into his pockets and, after stepping by Nick in the careful way that one might step around a dog on a long leash, he started to head back along the boardwalk alone.

"I'll be coming after you, Johnny," Nick called to him before he'd gone too far to hear.

And Johnny glanced back, briefly. He seemed more than a touch weary.

"You'll have to find me, first," he said, and he sounded as if he didn't much care exactly how it would go.

He turned again.

He walked on.

PART THREE

The Poisoned Garden

24

The day started early at the Red House Café. Big trucks were already lining up on the forecourt before first light, vans and wagons and continental road trains; some were regular traffic, and many had disembarked from the overnight ferries and were now heading on up the coast. The menu read *All-Day Breakfast* but the fact of it was, there would usually be a post-dawn lull and then a short-lived pickup and then anything after eleven was a bonus. They'd see a few salesmen or even some tourists in the season, but for the rest of the day the Red House was mostly a checker-cloth graveyard. Mickey would walk out and set an *Afternoon Teas* sign by the roadside, but as bait this had to rate somewhere lower than the lugworm.

It was now a little after nine, and the last of the commercial drivers had just handed his plate over the counter and departed. That left Mickey with only a hitch-hiker, and the weirdo sitting over in the corner.

The place had been almost derelict when Mickey had picked up the lease about five years ago. The last owners had blown it completely, people with a young family who'd tried to arrange the business around themselves instead of meeting the market on its own terms. They'd let the filling-station side of it go and they'd all but run the Red House into the ground, and they'd begun to get desperate when Mickey had stepped in with a rock-bottom offer. Mickey had been a haulage driver himself for more than twenty years, many of them spent in runs over this very route until his doctor had advised him to find some other line, and he had a pretty good idea of where the site's potential lay. Now he ran the kitchen while Margaret ran the counter, joked with the punters, and shouted the orders back through the service hatch.

Margaret had taken the van out to the Cash and Carry as soon as the morning's trade had started to slow. She was aiming to be back by eleven, but Mickey wasn't counting on it. Isolation was one of their biggest disadvantages, here, and when business dropped for the day Margaret seemed to feel it the worst. She had tablets, but she wouldn't take them. So now Mickey had been left flying solo, he had the griddles to scrape down, there was an Australian soap coming up that he'd planned to watch on the portable TV as he worked – Des and Daphne's wedding, and he didn't want to miss it – and here he was instead, watchdogging a shabby-looking hippie who'd rolled up in a Scimitar and who'd been nursing the same blue-ringed mug for the best part of an hour.

If it hadn't been for the car, Mickey would have given him marching orders long ago. But a Scimitar owner was hardly likely to start pocketing the cutlery when the owner's back was turned (although Mickey had known stranger things to happen), and there wasn't exactly a heavy demand for the tables, and besides . . .

Besides . . .

Mickey had never been one to worry about a risk of confrontation, but something about the weirdo said *Don't Touch*. He seemed intense and empty, both at the same time. To hell with it, Mickey thought, and decided to leave him alone. For the sake of what was owed the man was hardly worth watching, and Mickey would still be able to keep half an eye on him with the hatch open. Folding his newspaper and dropping it under the counter, he withdrew into the kitchen and switched on the TV with its sound turned low.

The man didn't stir.

So now Mickey looked out of the kitchen window to

see how the hitch-hiker was doing, but he couldn't spot her. When he'd last checked about ten minutes ago, she'd been over across the dirt forecourt by the petrol island. She'd looked a lonely figure with her tote bag and her cut-down winter coat, waiting by the wrecked pumps and the vandalised pay booth that stood open to whatever weather might care to come along. She was – what, sixteen? Seventeen? But a lot of the drivers seemed to know her from some of their other runs, and they treated her like a daughter with what seemed like a genuine concern. Maybe she'd been picked up by the Dutchman who'd just left. This would be a lousy spot to get stranded. Nothing on this side of the road for a couple of miles in either direction other than the Red House itself, and nothing across the way but a wide sweep of grass leading out to far-off dunes and then the cold sea beyond. Little wonder that Margaret found it so difficult, sometimes. But at least they had each other, and daytime TV.

Somebody pushed open the cafeteria door. Mickey's assumption that the weirdo must be leaving was proven to be wrong when he leaned over to look through the hatch and saw that no, it was the hitch-hiker coming in. She closed the door behind her, and made straight for the weirdo's table. The man didn't even seem to be aware of her approaching, just kept on staring into the empty mug that he held in his two hands.

She stood before him, and said with a brightness that sounded natural but which, looking at the man, surely had to be an act, "Hi. Where are you heading?"

The man reacted slowly. He seemed to wake from a dream.

He looked up at her and said, "Excuse me?"

"You wouldn't be going up the coast road, would you?"

He stared without answering, first with uncertainty and then with what seemed like wonder.

The girl began to grow uncomfortable and she said,

smiling unsteadily and starting to back off, "Okay, I just thought I'd ask."

"No, wait," the man said quickly, seeming to make an effort to snap himself out of it. "I mean, yes. Anywhere. Anywhere you want to go," and he pushed back from the table and started to rise.

"What?" she said, glancing behind her to ensure that her way to the door was clear; she was obviously feeling that approaching this stranger had suddenly turned out to be the biggest mistake of her day so far. Mickey laid down his scraper and, picking up a cloth to wipe his hands, he moved around the gas range towards the connecting door.

"Just tell me where you want to be," the weirdo was saying. "I'll drive you anywhere."

"No, forget it," the girl said, about halfway to the exit door now and obviously not wanting to turn her back on him. "I made a mistake."

The man stared at her, still with uncertainty.

"It *is* you, isn't it?" he said.

"Please, just forget it."

She let herself out in a hurry and the weirdo made to follow her, but his oversized coat was caught on the chair and it slowed him. "No, wait," he called out with what sounded like desperation, "I mistook you for someone I knew, that's all. Don't go, not yet. It can happen, can't it?"

But she'd already gone, and as the weirdo made to follow her Mickey stepped out into his way from behind the counter, the drying cloth still held in his big trucker's hands.

He said, pointedly, "Was there anything else?"

The weirdo stopped.

"No," he said falteringly, and after a moment's hesitation he started to go through his pockets. He seemed confused, and was trying to cover it. Mickey watched as the man dug out change to cover his bill, mostly in pennies; these he scattered onto the nearest table in twos and threes until he'd managed to come up with enough.

"Have a nice day," Mickey said stonily as the weirdo finally made his exit.

When Mickey went forward to the bow window by the door, he could see that a big car transporter had pulled in over on the far side of the road. The girl appeared to have flagged it down and she was talking to the driver; she seemed to know him and he to know her, because he leaned across to open his passenger door and girl started around without any hesitation. He wasn't headed the way that she wanted to go, but right now this seemed to be one of her lesser priorities. Most drivers on the run worked under a strict 'no riders' rule, but like many other rules it was frequently bent. As she was crossing in front of the cab, the girl glanced back.

The weirdo sat in his expensive car, not even appearing to watch.

Mickey shook his head, and turned away from the window. Some people were just too fucked up to be allowed to walk around, let alone drive. He stopped to pick up the pennies from the table on his way back to the kitchen.

Outside, the Scimitar was being started . . .

But in all honesty, Mickey was more interested in how Des and Daphne were getting along.

———

In the dream, it's dusk. Nick knows it's a dream and that somehow makes it worse, because he also knows what's coming; he knows that he's going to fail Alice again, and again, and that he'll probably go on reliving his failure forever. After scorching to a halt at the end of the boardwalk, he runs the rest of the way to the arcade. He can see lights on up above; everything looks reassuringly normal. As he enters, he's calling Alice's name.

There's no reply.

His confidence begins to falter . . . and then he sees half a dozen jerrycans stacked at the foot of the stairs. He turns . . .

And Johnny's behind him. Hello, Nicky boy, he says, and then BANG.

When Nick revives he's being hammered by light and sound; all of the video games have been tipped onto their sides and are stacked close around him to make a kind of cell of screens, and they're all working. He's immobilised, roped firmly with a flex to a pinball table that has been turned onto its end. Outside this makeshift box, Johnny has rolled back the linoleum and is tearing up floorboards. By the sound of it, they're rotten enough to be crumbling in his hands.

After a while he comes around to check on Nick, and finds him conscious. He squats down before him, nodding pleasantly. *I congratulate the two of you, he says . . . all this time, and I never even suspected. I suppose you know what she is, don't you?*

Nick doesn't answer.

Johnny says that the boards and the petrol are to make a fire that will finally burn everything clean; if there's enough wood left over he'll make a cross for Nick and nail him to it. He's scarily rational about the whole thing. *You want to see her to say goodbye? he says,* and shifts one of the machines to give Nick a narrow field of view of Alice. She's lying unconscious on her side, one arm thrown protectively before her face. Johnny goes over and splashes her with petrol from one of the cans, at which she stirs slightly; then he comes back and does the same to Nick.

Remember the ants? he says, and then he goes and drags Alice out of Nick's line of sight.

And yes, Nick remembers the ants. They'd swarmed in their thousands around one particular area of the railway embankment where the tracks ran along behind the beach for a way, and they'd been one of the great discoveries of Johnny's young life. He'd returned with matches and cans of lighter fuel to napalm their cities and surround their fleeing refugees with rings of fire. Some he spot-cremated, others ran across soaked earth which exploded beneath them. How it must have seemed from the ants' point of view, Nick could only imagine. Johnny was a jealous god of awesome power, and he grew giddy with it. His eagerness had been such that the fire had spread to the underbrush and pretty soon they'd had to make a withdrawal as the entire embankment began to smoulder like wet hay, and with a smell like burning mattresses; the fire brigade turned out, one of the other kids ratted, and Johnny was dragged home and beaten.

But, sorry? No. Johnny had never been truly sorry about anything in his life.

Nick flexes, and the glass top of the pinball table against his back splits under the pressure and gives him enough leeway to get free. He runs at Johnny, who swings a board at his head. He's faster than Nick, and he's stronger. Nick hits the floor at the edge of the hole, and the remaining boards give way.

He falls.

And hits an iron crawlway about four feet down; directly below is where the rocks meet the sea. He looks up to see a shadow moving over the hole, and scrambles out of the way just as one of the video machines comes crashing down, still working for a part of the descent. It smashes through, taking a section of the crawlway with it, and moments later he hears it bounce into the surf. Nick has no choice but to begin making his way back to the edge of the boardwalk.

Up above, Johnny starts his fire.

The trip is only a matter of yards but it's a hellish one, with fireglow and smoke coming down through the gaps between the boards; and before he reaches the end Nick looks forward to see that Johnny is waiting there for him with a stick of burning wood. One touch, he tells Nick, and you'll go up like a torch . . .

And then, at the sound of approaching sirens, he glances briefly over his shoulder and then lobs the blazing stick.

Nick can't get back fast enough.

Everything around him explodes.

Nick hated to sleep in cars. Waking up in yesterday's clothes with stiff joints and a headache and nowhere to pee had never been his idea of a good time. As he slowly came around, he tried to recall whether he'd been dreaming. He couldn't be certain, although he thought that he probably had.

He cranked the seat fully upright, looked about him, and then checked his watch. Christ, it was after nine. When he'd pulled onto the waste ground behind the station at around three in the morning there hadn't been more than half a dozen cars on the entire rough acre, but now they were bumper-to-bumper. There must have been plenty of noise and activity over the last hour or so, first office workers and then college traffic and finally the shoppers – how could he have slept through it all so easily? It felt almost like an act of betrayal.

There was a ticket under one of the wiper blades. When he got out of the car, he left it in place.

Partly revived by the morning air as he walked around the station building and in through the yard entrance, he completed the job by splashing his face over a basin of cold water in one of the second-floor washrooms. He dried himself on a roller towel, and straightened his hair as well as he could without a comb. Facing himself in the washroom mirror, he decided that this was about as good as he could hope for. He had the look of a man with a bad hangover or a damaging illness, but he'd pass.

First call, the evidence store.

The property room, as it was more accurately named, was at the back of the building in a wing that had been added a few years after the original construction. Nick had always thought that it had the feel of a sculptor's studio, although he couldn't exactly have said why; perhaps it was because of the high roof and the barred skylight windows that ran from end to end and filled the room with a soft grey light that threw no shadows. The floor space was rigidly divided into avenues of Dexion shelving, and on the open shelves lay tagged items of found property and pieces taken in evidence. Everything here had to be logged through the property book, and the policy was to hold onto nothing for longer than was absolutely necessary. Stuff was moving in and out all the time, and what Nick had in mind would seem like nothing special.

The property clerk looked up as Nick stepped through the door of the adjacent office. Nobody else was here, which suited him fine. The clerk was a civilian, one of the building's many unsworn personnel; as recently as a couple of years ago the property room would have been run by a constable under a sergeant's supervision, but the force's civilianisation programme had brought about this and a number of similar changes. The idea of the programme had been to free the sworn personnel to get back out onto the streets; the flipside of the plan, although none of the brass would have been prepared to admit as much in public, had been the creation of an unstated caste system within the building.

Nick said, "Do us an evidence box, will you?"

The clerk reached for the current book of triplicate forms and said, "What's it for?"

"More forensic tests, I think," Nick said, borrowing a ballpoint from the clerk's plastic desk tidy. "I really don't know for sure, I'm just the errand boy today."

The clerk got his keys, and they went along the corridor to the locked storeroom. Nick wondered how the clerk could stand it, office to storeroom, storeroom to office, and in between patiently filling in the same form with more or less the same information every time. An hour for lunch, taken at his desk with the phone off the hook and a library book to read. And at the end of his day, did he go home happy?

He looked as if he probably did.

He switched on the overhead fluorescents for some extra light in the aisles, and Nick followed him down the marked rows that so resembled a left-luggage check-in. Just about everything found its way in here, apart from animals. They had a lost-and-found book of their own, and went out to shelters for safe keeping.

The clerk finally stopped by one of the marked positions, and double-checked the paperwork. On the shelf behind the number stood a plain cardboard box, and next to it something that had been bundled into a polythene sheet.

"One crossbow and bolts, unassembled," he read. "And one thirty-eight calibre Webley revolver without ammunition."

"It's just the Webley I need," Nick said.

He stood out in the corridor as the clerk switched off the lights and relocked the door behind them. He'd have to stick around now until late afternoon, but he had an idea of how he could make some use of the time.

The clerk said, "You were on the cars with that Johnny Mays, weren't you? The one who drowned?"

Nick watched the man as he withdrew the keys and stepped back; yes, he thought, he's on the level, he genuinely doesn't know.

"I was with him, once upon a time," he said.

The clerk nodded, as if in sympathy. "Still no body in sight?"

And Nick said, "Watch this space."

25

"Stay here," Johnny told the tarpaulin-covered shape that now lay in the back of the Scimitar. "Stay right here, because there's somewhere that I really want to see." And the shape, which had been lashed with rope and actually had no choice in the matter at all, lay as unmoving as a sack of stones.

Johnny could hardly believe it. To his eyes, the old Mays' transport yard hadn't altered at all.

Maybe just once, as he walked out across the open area before the big double-fronted garage, where the engine oil stood in pools and about a thousand tyre tracks had ironed out the shale, maybe for a second there his vision faltered and he saw something else; he glimpsed derelict buildings and one crappy old charabanc on blocks that wouldn't be going anywhere ever again, he saw gaps in the fence and blown-down sale boards that nobody had bothered to replace, he saw junkyard heaps of corrugated iron and asbestos board, he saw piles of old engine parts and springs that had once been stacked up for some indefinite future use but which had now rusted beyond salvation. He saw all of this, but his mind said *no*; and then, with a little extra concentration, he was able to push it all down beneath the surface again.

And then the yard re-emerged exactly as it once had been, breaking through like a well-preserved wreck rising up in the surf.

He made for the house. The house and the yard had been pretty much as one, back in the old days; part of the upper storey overlooked it, and Johnny had lost count of the number of times that he'd climbed out of his bedroom window onto the slate roof of the office. From there it had been a short hop, via the coalshed, to ground level.

There was glass underfoot as he walked. When he reached the office door he found it standing open; there was darkness ahead, and a damp smell as if something or someone had crept in and urinated in the corners.

Johnny stepped inside.

The office counter was still there, but chunks of the plasterboard had been ripped from the walls and there was fibrous stuffing hanging out of the holes. A calendar, five years out of date and featuring some of the ugliest-looking nudes that Johnny had ever seen outside of a "Readers' Wives" page, had been ripped apart and its pages scattered about the floor. These lay amongst empty beer cans and the mouldering remains of a supermarket loaf, and over by the window there was a blackened patch to mark where someone had tried to start a campfire.

Was this how it had been? It seemed all wrong.

Didn't it?

Johnny frowned down at Miss September, a short-haired brunette with an operation scar who was looking coy and holding a banana. Wasn't there something just a *little* familiar about her?

But then he looked up, sharply.

He could hear voices.

His faint smile of recognition died as he realised what was being said. They were angry with him. He'd been helping himself to money out of the petty cash drawer and they were treating him like he'd done something really wicked; demanding an explanation and then shouting him down when he tried to give them one, when all that he'd done was exactly what he'd seen them do on so many occasions. They treated the cash drawer as an available resource and so he'd done the same, and now they were threatening him with a policeman if he didn't confess.

Confess? What was there to confess? He couldn't see it then, and he didn't see it now. But he'd learned one important lesson on that day – that guilt was entirely relative, and depended not so much on what you'd done as on where the power resided. Johnny shook his head as if to clear it, and looked around the office again. This was definitely wrong. Whatever he'd managed to grasp, he was losing it.

He went outside. So many details, it was impossible to keep a hold on them all – as he tried to concentrate on one, all of the others would begin to slip away. Life was too much like a moving train, passing by too close and too fast even to count the windows. There were thistles growing up through the stones underfoot, and there were bright shards of silver in amongst the weeds; looking up, he could see that vandals had stoned out the angled spotlights that had once illuminated the yard at night.

So then he looked back at the office; and, there on the outside wall, he saw the yard's old business registration plate. It read

> ### FRANK MAYS
> *Haulage Contracts, Private Hire Coaches*
> *Car and Commercial Vehicle Repairing*
> *Paint Spraying and Coachpainting*

and Johnny stepped forward with his hand outstretched, relieved and grateful because here was something so solid that not even the years could have diminished it; the plate was solid brass and he could remember clearly the day that it had gone up, even though he couldn't have been more than three or four years old. If he couldn't hope to bring everything back, perhaps he could settle for a piece of it . . .

But his fingers met the bare wall, rough and unpainted in the square where the old plate had been levered away.

Still touching the wall, Johnny closed his eyes. It was easier, with his eyes closed. Lost cities could rise from the dust, and the dead could walk and converse.

For a while, he could shape the world exactly as he'd wanted it to be.

That was, until he opened them again.

26

Henry was waiting for Nick on the steps of the Students' Union building when he arrived, and as they went inside he told him that he'd met a lot of resistance in setting up the meeting that Nick had requested in that morning's phonecall.

"But you fixed it?" Nick said.

"I fixed it," Henry told him, and they went over to the Porters' desk so that Nick could be signed in.

It was late in the morning and the Union building was busy, but even in amongst the crowds Nick felt uncomfortably conspicuous. The year's look tended towards shaving-brush haircuts and denim work clothes under dark jackets, so that it felt as if he was making his way through a mass of young Belgian factory workers. The building itself was standard modern Polytechnic, low-ceilinged and cheaply finished, and there were at least three competing sound systems belting out rock music from different quarters. They moved past stalls in the foyer selling radical magazines and imported French and American comic books, and went up a short stairway to the bar.

Nick asked Henry how he was doing.

"Physically okay, although I don't sleep so well," Henry admitted after a moment of hesitation. "And if I get one whiff of paraffin, it's like I just die on the spot."

The doors into the bar were hidden under a mass of posters and notices, most of them handwritten in magic marker. Nick tensed a little as he went through; he knew that his welcome here was going to be a limited one, if it was going to be any welcome at all. Without Henry to speak for him, he doubted that he'd have made it past the desk.

She was sitting at a table alone; the tables were divided off like those in a cafeteria in a rough compromise of purpose between coffee bar and licensed premises. Her name, Henry had told him, was Elizabeth. She was in her mid-twenties, wore glasses, didn't appear to wear makeup, and as Nick slid along opposite her he noticed that she cut her nails short. Johnny would probably have called her a dyke on sight; Nick saw a nervous girl in a woman's shell, probably suppressing all of the usual signals in the hope of being overlooked.

She put a battered Philips cassette machine on the table between them, and set it to record.

"Something has to be understood," she said. "I didn't want to get involved in this, but I'm doing it for Henry. He's the only reason you got past square one."

"I appreciate that," Nick said.

"I won't tell you where I'm staying now. You even ask me, and this is over."

"I'm not out to add to your problems. I'm just hoping you can shed a little light on mine."

She glanced at her machine, to check that the cassette was turning. Anything, it seemed, to avoid meeting his eyes. Nick could sense her anger. Intense and slow-burning, it was like electricity in the air between them. She was scared but she had nerve, he'd have to give her that.

She said, "In return for what?"

"I don't know what I could offer that you could use."

She said, "You could tell me if Johnny Mays is a serving police officer."

Now it was Nick's turn to glance at the machine.

"Either you tell me for the record," she said, "or I'm walking out right now."

"Elizabeth . . ." Henry began from alongside Nick, but Elizabeth silenced him with a glance.

"That's the deal, Henry," she said, and then she looked at Nick again. "Well?"

"Yes," Nick said. "He is."

There was a silence.

"That's all I wanted to know," Elizabeth said then, and she switched off the recorder. It took Nick a moment to realise that she was rising to walk out on him, but then as she was drawing the machine across the table he reached out and put his hand on it to stop her. The response to his move was instantaneous and totally unexpected; suddenly all of the people at the tables around them had risen to their feet and Nick was surrounded by a wall of bodies. He took his hand off the machine, and Elizabeth gathered all of her stuff together.

"What about the deal?" Nick said.

"Make an official complaint," Elizabeth suggested, and withdrew.

Henry said, "Just give me a minute," and went after her.

Nick stayed in his seat. There had to be about fifteen or twenty young people around him, all of them watching him, none of them saying anything; a mute chorus of witnesses, and not a single one of them on his side. He glanced up once, but he was too uncomfortable to try to get on a wavelength with any of them. He could just about see through them to the bar entrance, where Henry had caught up with Elizabeth and was making a couple of strong points. He was obviously mightily pissed off at her behaviour, and seemed to feel that she was forcing him into a position of betrayal.

Whatever he told her, it worked. She returned, although reluctantly. She slid back into her seat and set up the recorder again; Henry sat next to her this time, so that Nick sat alone. Nobody else around them made a move.

"You've got five minutes," Elizabeth told him.

Henry said, "The council's Police Monitoring Unit

were helping Elizabeth with her research. It all started when they came in one morning to find that the office had been broken into and the notes and records all disturbed. After that . . ."

"After that," Elizabeth said, taking up the story, "it was as if I couldn't step out of the house without being followed. Sometimes it was uniformed men in marked cars, other times it was just strangers who didn't even identify themselves. They wanted to know if I was a member of CND and what political party I belonged to. If I knew anyone involved in Irish politics. They'd say, 'Don't fuck us about, what's your interest in the police?' And when I started to object I got called a whore, I got called a dyke, I got called a bolshie troublemaker with a bad case of sexual frustration. I was explicitly threatened with rape on two occasions." Her eyes shot a warning to Nick. "Don't dare try to tell me you understand how that felt."

Nick said, "What did you do?"

"I made an official complaint to your Boys' Club. That went nowhere and suddenly the campaign became more subtle. I was getting anonymous phonecalls at all hours. My tutor's office was burgled and nothing was taken. By then I was pretty sure that it had all narrowed down to one officer, your Johnny Mays. He persisted when all the others let it drop."

"Any idea why?"

"Not until now. Tell him, Henry."

Henry said, "None of us could work out why this one officer should persist when the others had all got bored and let it go. But Johnny Mays as good as told me why when he made me read through the carbon of Elizabeth's thesis."

"It wasn't even about the force, as such," Elizabeth said. "They only came into it as the subject of the verbatim interviews that I was analysing for cues and responses. You know the biggest joke of the entire situation? The police were coming out of it pretty well.

I had a couple of bad-apple stories that the monitoring unit had lined up for me, but that was all."

Henry said, "When I reached the first one of these, that's when Johnny Mays hit the roof."

So then Nick asked if she could give him any details, and after a moment Elizabeth looked up and nodded to somebody in the crowd. There was some fumbling around and a quick whispered argument about who was supposed to have been looking after what, and then a canvas shoulder bag, the kind that people always seemed to bring back from Greek holidays, made its way through from hand to hand. From this Elizabeth drew a red plastic ring-binder which had worn so thin around the edges that the cardboard stiffener was showing at the corners. She opened it out on the table, and started to search through the pages. It was the thinnest, cheapest kind of paper, and densely covered with single-spaced type.

"You want it word for word, or the condensed version?" She said. "I'd better warn you, your time's nearly up."

"Make it quick and simple," he said, "so then we can all go home early."

So she began to summarise, glancing down the page and skipping entire sections as she went. There was a lot to skip, as it was a verbatim transcript of an interview with a prostitute whose beat area had covered the gaming arcades around the centre of town, and the woman's encounters with the plainclothes division (or the 'vice squad', as she insisted on calling them) had been regular and frequent. As far as Nick could gather, most of the events that she was describing had taken place at least two or three years before; some of the officers that she named – and she'd been on first-name terms with a number of them, in the easy manner of the hunter and the hunted who each acknowledged that the other had a job to do – had moved on to other assignments long before Nick had been drafted in.

"He made me read every frigging word of this," Henry

said sadly, as Elizabeth flipped over two pages to get to the good stuff.

The un-named woman's main story concerned not the vice squad, but a uniformed officer who'd seemed to take an excessive interest in her. He'd pull over and tell her to get into the car as if he was making an arrest, but then he'd just drive her around for a while before letting her go. This happened five, six times, and was starting to become like a regular thing; the woman began to realise that the officer wasn't even on duty when these pickups took place, and when she tried to identify him so that she could ask some of the others if they knew what his game was, she saw that he'd covered the last two digits of the service numbers on his uniform with small pieces of insulation tape.

It was a real annoyance. Genuine police pickups were an occupational hazard that she accepted, but all of this pointless riding around was costing her business. She reckoned she knew what he really wanted, and that he was either too shy or too weird to say it straight out; so one night she said it for him, and they drove somewhere dark and climbed into the back seat.

He was useless, she said; all tight and locked-in, and the harder he tried the more difficult it seemed to get. He called her some name that she didn't quite catch, and then a lot more names that she could hardly mistake. She could see how ugly he was turning and so she got out, fast; he tried to follow her in the car and she thought that he might even have tried to run her down, but she cut down between some houses and lost him.

He never picked her up again after that. Sometimes she'd see him watching her, only now he'd be out of uniform and in what she assumed to be his own car. Whenever he was around, she'd make sure that she wasn't walking home alone. It made her nervous enough to quit the game and get a job boxing tubes of toothpaste.

Closing the file, Elizabeth said, "Was this what you wanted? Or has it been a waste of police time?"

"No," Nick said. "It hasn't."

"Because that's what they're charging *me* with," Elizabeth said, and she pulled the cassette machine over towards her and switched it off. "Thanks for the leverage," she said, stacking the recorder on top of the file and putting both of them into the shoulder bag. "It'll make quite a difference."

Nick said nothing as she rose and slid along and out from behind her side of the table, with Henry moving to let her out. She said, "You know, my mother and father always taught me to respect the police, and I did. Ask me now in public, for the record, and I'll probably have enough sense to say the same thing. But in *here* – " she tapped herself on the chest " – I hope you all burn."

She left.

Nick stayed where he was as she departed. He said nothing more, and didn't even watch as she went. Henry hesitated for a moment, and then followed her. Then one of the other students who was standing just behind him leaned forward and said, in a low voice, "Will you leave the building now, please?"

And Nick nodded and, still meeting nobody's eyes, got to his feet to go.

———

It was about twelve-thirty when he returned to the main police building, and this time instead of entering through the main foyer he went down the cobbled slope and around to the back to where there was a flight of steps leading into the basement. There was a firing range down below, and it opened up for the lunch hour on three days of the week; run on a voluntary basis by a small committee of officers, it wasn't an official facility but more a private gun club on police premises where certified weapons owners could go along to get practice. Although he'd spent some time on the authorised list, Nick had never actually owned a handgun. The club had two or three loaners that never left the premises, and he'd mainly used these when polishing up for the last couple of the quarterly requalification tests that he'd taken.

The range was basically a long, windowless cellar room entered through a glassed-in control box. Big fans that had been bought second-hand from an aerospace plant sucked out all of the vapours, and lighting levels could be set in a rough simulation of night-time visibility. There were four shooting positions, all supervised from behind the glass by a retired sergeant; two were occupied when Nick arrived.

The booth had a few low chairs, a coffee machine, and a couple of tables scattered with old copies of *Guns and Ammo*. Nick waited around until the armourer could transfer his attention away from the range. He was around sixty and he walked stiffly, as if arthritis was beginning to take a hold, but he also didn't look like the type who'd appreciate attention being drawn to the fact. One of the older breed, probably with an army background in his days before the police service.

He said, "Nick Frazier? Haven't had you down here in a while."

"Let me have two dozen rounds and a .38," Nick said. "See how long it takes to get my eye back in."

The retired sergeant went over to the gun cupboard and unlocked it, bringing out one of the loaners and a box of shells. He said, "Thinking of getting back onto the register?"

"Don't know if I will or not," Nick said. "Might have to see how well I do here, first."

The sergeant opened the intercom system and called for a break, and after paying for the ammunition Nick picked up some ear protection and went on through into the range. The big fans were pumping but the smell hit him anyway as he stepped through the door, a scent of burned compounds that always reminded him of standing up too close to the fence at a speedway circuit. The other two men were reloading and glanced at him only briefly; he walked past them to the furthest stall, and broke open the borrowed Smith & Wesson that the ex-Sergeant had handed over. The handgrip was worn, but the gun itself was well-serviced and had been recently oiled. There was a big paper tag on its handle.

He waited until the go-ahead came over the intercom. One of the other officers had brought along about five different guns but was now using a Mauser, a real old collector's piece that had been designed to convert into a crude rifle with the addition of a wooden stock and a barrel extension. The nearest man was alternating between a 9mm automatic and a silver-plated Colt in a wooden presentation box. When the three of them levelled and fired together, the resulting noise battered at them like the wind from a fast-moving train.

Ten minutes later, when the next stand-down order came, Nick collected his paper target and went back through into the control booth.

"Well," he said, "there's a question answered, anyway," and he presented the .38 with its cylinder opened for inspection. The ex-sergeant checked the gun and then unlocked the cupboard for its return.

Glancing at Nick's target he said, "Sent a few of them wide, did we?"

"Sent 'em everywhere but where they were supposed to go."

"So, what happened here?" The ex-Sergeant was pointing to the fact that all of the eight hits on the target had punched through the high-scoring inner circle.

"Fluke, I suppose," Nick said, and he screwed up the target and tossed it into the waste bin under the workbench.

"Keep at it," the ex-Sergeant suggested. "Flukes like that should happen to everyone. You could be as good as any of them."

But at this Nick only smiled, briefly.

"They're welcome to it," he said, and walked out.

The range closed about half an hour later, and the ex-Sergeant let the blowers run for a while before he went in to clear up after the marksmen.

Marksmen? The dickhead with the silver Colt certainly didn't merit the name, and he put in more hours on the range than just about anybody. The others called him Buffalo Bill because a buffalo was probably the smallest target that he'd be able to hit. He'd brought the silver Colt back from a trip to Tombstone, had fixed up a special import licence for it and everything; it was one of a limited centenary edition and God only knew what it had cost. He'd a leather belt and holster, owned every record that Marty Robbins had made, and still couldn't understand why the Tactical Support Unit wouldn't put him on its firearms team.

Shaking his head, ex-sergeant Morrison limped along the row picking up the plastic margarine tubs that he'd set out earlier to receive the spent cartridges after each reload. The club had been his life, once; good friends and good times shared, but then the good friends had mostly drifted away to other things and the good times were mostly memories. Sometimes he wondered why he helped to keep it going, for no pay and for precious little thanks, either; most of those who came down here to practise would draw long odds in a shootout with Stevie Wonder.

At the end of the row he stopped, and frowned.

He'd been tipping all of the cartridges into a single tub as he'd gone along. 7.63mm from the old Broomhandle Mauser, .45s from the Colt, and Luger shells from the 9mm Automatic . . . only Nick Frazier had been using the .38 calibre, and he'd taken two dozen rounds for it. Something here wasn't right.

So then Morrison carried the tub through into the control booth where the light was better, and dumped all of the brass cases out onto the workbench. He cursed his stiffening fingers as he spread them out and sorted through them.

He found only eight spent cases of .38 ammunition.

Eight, out of twenty-four.

He sat back, wondering.

Now, what the hell was *that* supposed to signify?

27

You'll have to find me first, Johnny had said.

Nick had a feeling that this wouldn't be too difficult. Johnny's options were running out fast and so, presumably, was his cash. And he was hardly a dangerous mastermind on the run; dangerous yes, but confused and uncertain and with only the shakiest grip on reality. He'd stick to the ground that he knew, and it was on this ground that Nick was convinced that they'd meet up again.

You'll have to . . .

But so much could change, given time. Hadn't he already found as much, since the day of his own return? It was wrong to think of the past as some kind of a museum, a place that could be re-entered if only the secret door could be found and opened with a magical key, where happiness stood like a Polyphon awaiting a coin so that its mechanical music could be heard all over again. The past was more like stage sets and carnival floats; paper-thin and insubstantial, they were abandoned to the wind and the rain when the bright lights had moved on elsewhere.

One example: the Red House Café.

Nick hadn't even realised exactly where he was until he got out of the car. He'd already pulled off the road and onto the forecourt before he'd seen that the pumps out front weren't in use, but he decided to take the brief stop anyway and see if he could pick up a map of the coast. Walking over to the main building, it suddenly came to him; it was on the low wall before the petrol island that he'd once sat with a man whose name he didn't know, waiting for the police to arrive so that they could all troop over the dunes for Nick to show off his drowned fisherman. He stopped. The site was barely recognisable to him, but for a moment he tried to see something of the place as it once had been.

He was pretty sure that it had been a Shell garage back then, but the partly-obliterated names on the pumps read *Avia* and *Imperial*. On the small pay booth behind these, the front door stood open with a busted lock so that he could see all the way through to where the back door flapped open into the daylight beyond. Inside, there was nothing other than open empty shelves and peeling wood-effect paper.

So then he carried on towards the Red House itself, a low 1930s-looking building set about thirty yards back. It had two big bow windows at the front, an entranceway with an awning and brick steps with a pot of flowers to either side, and a short square tower above carrying the name so that it could be seen from the road. The entire restaurant had been painted white, and the paint was peeling away from the outside like a flaking skin. There was a small garden around at the side, with a wooden garage and a big old caravan just visible behind.

There were no cars, other than his own.

There seemed to be nobody inside, either; he could hear a radio or a TV set playing somewhere in the back, but he had to wait at the counter for a minute or more before anyone appeared. The man who eventually came through had the look of a short-order cook, which was to say that he had the brawn of a transport driver under a chef's apron. His sleeves were rolled back and his arms were as hairy as those of Zorba the Greek. Nick explained what he was looking for, and the man moved down to the end of the counter where the sales goods seemed to consist almost exclusively of key rings and copies of *Trucking* magazine.

"I've got this tourist map," he said, producing a dusty

box from somewhere underneath. "Not much in the way of detail, but it's got all the main sights. You know anything at all about the area?"

"Yes, but from a long time ago," Nick said.

"No point trying to dress it up for you, then." From the box he took a glossy brochure; it unfolded on the counter into a three-colour map of the coast and the bay, showing the few main roads and with bright orange symbols for all the churches, fishing spots and nature reserves. "The sea's always in the same place and the shoreline isn't, and that's about all there is to be said about it. You'll get birdwatchers and the odd marine biologist, and almost nobody else. If you talk about sea and sky and rain on the way, you've just about covered everything."

"Doesn't sound too good for business."

"We get by. Can't ask for too much more than that, around here."

Nick picked up the map, and started to refold it. He said, "Ever think of leaving?"

But the man shook his head, smiling as if Nick had just made some kind of a joke. "No," he said. "This is the Bay. Nobody ever really leaves."

"I did," Nick said.

And the man shrugged, as if his point was made.

Well, it was a start. Nick sat back and let the car find its way first to the no-man's-land where the bay met the town, and then on into that area of the part-industrial, part-residential Twilight Zone where the Mays' transport yard had been located.

It was pretty quiet around here, now. He could remember biking over to play in the yard with Johnny; Johnny almost never came over to him, because his own place was so much smaller and they could barely pitch a tent in its tiny back garden. At the yard, there had been the garages and the outbuildings and there had always been vehicles off the road that they could play in. Some were off the road more than others, and seemed mostly to be going rusty around the seams and rivets; but then all of Frank Mays' coaches and lorries took a good hammering, and some had been battered and resprayed and then battered again.

Nick stopped his car on the street.

The big house stood dark, its windows boarded. On the gap-toothed fence outside, he could still read the Frank Mays name through the later and cheaper overpainting of another owner's trademark. He pulled at the slatted gate, expecting it to have been nailed shut; but the gate swung open, and so Nick stepped through.

It fell closed again behind him, drawn by a crude arrangement using a nailed-up length of cable and an old truck wheel for a counterweight. Once inside, it was as if he was looking at a half-acre of Hiroshima. There was broken glass, there was rusty metal; rubbish had been dumped over the fence from outside, including bags and bags of decaying household waste and a couple of weevilly mattresses. Towering out of this, rising like some skeletal Gargantua from the weeds, was the stripped-out shell of an old twenty-four seater coach. It looked as if it had been shot by poachers for its ivory, and then left to rot.

And there, right beside it, was the blue Scimitar that he'd last seen on the quayside by Alice's place the night before.

Nick stopped at the sight, so much taken aback by the immediate success of his search that he'd momentarily forgotten his reason for making it; and as he was standing there by the gate, Johnny Mays came ambling out of the offices and into the open air. He showed no sense of danger, and waved as if nothing had ever been wrong between them.

"Nick!" he called out. "Hey, Nicky, it's me!"

But Nick's blank spot didn't last any longer than the

time that it took for Johnny's words to reach him. From inside his coat he drew out the old Webley .38, cleaned and greased and loaded with six of the rounds that he'd taken out of the police range. He slammed off two shots as Johnny broke into a run and dived for cover, and Johnny went down into the weeds and out of sight. Nick scanned quickly for movement, trying to make out which way Johnny was going now; somewhere in the undergrowth at the far end of the yard were telegraph poles that had been laid end-to-end as wheel-bumpers to prevent vehicles from reversing too far and hitting the walls, and Nick's guess was that Johnny would be using these for protection.

He wasn't wrong. He glimpsed Johnny briefly as he came up a couple of yards from the Scimitar, but by the time that he'd brought the Webley around to bear Johnny had crossed the distance and was back under cover behind the car.

Nick kept the revolver level, waiting for Johnny to show again.

But Johnny stayed down.

"What did you lose, Nick?" Johnny called to him from where he was hiding. "Your aim, or your nerve?" He didn't sound at all fazed, as if being shot at was one of the more common of the elements that made up his day.

"I warned you about this, Johnny," Nick shouted back.

"Yeah, you warned me, but you couldn't actually *do* it, could you? Couldn't just put me down like some dog. How many people did you kill before today? A dozen? Five? One?" Johnny let the question hang for a couple of seconds, and Nick quickly flexed all of his fingers and established a tighter hold on the grip of the Webley.

Johnny went on, "Not quite the same as snuffing a paper target, is it? Not even the same as offing some stranger."

"Try stepping out," Nick called back, "and see what happens."

"Still wouldn't work, Nick. Whatever you've been thinking about me, I know we're still friends. We're still the same old team. See?"

And in order to demonstrate his confidence in this theory, Johnny emerged from hiding.

Do it, Nick thought.

Johnny was standing clear of the car, both arms raised – not in submission, but as if to present a better target. Maybe he'd missed him before, but Nick surely couldn't miss him now.

Do it.

But he already knew that the moment had come and gone.

"Listen," Johnny said. "Don't worry about it. I know what it's like, you're forgiven. I got pretty angry myself for a while, back there – I mean, over you and Alice. But it didn't get me anywhere. I couldn't see her get hurt."

"You're sick, Johnny," Nick said, still with the revolver levelled and wondering if the sting of hearing Alice's name from Johnny would be enough of a goad to get his gun hand to obey.

Remember the chain, he tried to tell himself.

Johnny said, "You mean, you didn't know?"

"Know what?"

"She isn't dead, Nick."

For a moment, there, Nick almost believed him. Mostly because he wanted to, and partly because Johnny so obviously believed it himself. Backing slowly around the Scimitar and keeping himself in full view, Johnny went on, "All this is for nothing, you know. I can prove it to you."

One-handed, he raised the tailgate. Then he bent forward and reached inside, and Nick suddenly thought *It's a stunt, he's going to dive in and scramble over the seats to the wheel and drive off*, but then Johnny was heaving out a long, limp, sacklike bundle that Nick recognised as a human form even before it was halfway out. It had been wrapped in a tarpaulin, and trussed with rope like a crude parody of something found in a sarcophagus. Johnny barely got it clear before he had to let its weight fall to the ground, and it landed heavily.

After landing it stirred a little, a slight movement that was no more than the rope would allow.

It wasn't much. But it was life.

You saw her dead, the voice at the back of Nick's mind warned him, but he barely heard it. He was remembering the dream of the night before that he'd so far been unable to recall.

Johnny was stepping back. "I'm not too clear on exactly what happened," he admitted. "It's all such a weird mess in here, sometimes." He looked straight at Nick, with no deviousness written on him at all; just confusion and concern, and an earnest wish to be doing whatever was for the best.

He said, "I don't want to let her go . . . but I really think she'll be safer with you."

Johnny continued to back off; now he was moving around behind the Scimitar again. Nick did nothing to stop him. The Webley had fallen to his side.

"Look after her for me, Nick," Johnny said, and then quickly got into the car.

Nick was moving as the Scimitar's engine turned over, and running as it pulled away. Johnny swung around and behind him in a wide circle, and it briefly crossed Nick's mind that the entire routine might have been a trick to get him into the open so that Johnny could run him down. But Johnny was bumping on across the rubble towards the gateway, and as Nick reached the trussed form and dropped to his knees beside it he could hear the wooden gates bouncing back as the Scimitar nosed through.

Johnny was gone, his car's sudden acceleration already no more than an echo in the empty street outside as Nick worked at the rope. Maybe someone in the area had heard the shots, it was impossible to say. If they had, and if they'd reported what they'd heard, then Nick didn't want to stay around here for one minute longer than was necessary. He managed to free off the noose around her neck, and as he sat her upright and pulled down the makeshift hangman's hood of stiffened canvas the rest of it fell slack around her body.

Her hair was down over her eyes and, gasping with relief, she threw it back.

She was nobody that Nick had ever seen before.

She managed to walk with him, just about, as he supported her out of the yard. Her tote bag lay by the side of the road where Johnny had thrown it about a minute ago; Nick sat her in his car and went to pick it up. She looked about sixteen years old. The zip on the tote bag had burst as it hit the ground, and Nick quickly stuffed back the pullovers and the underwear that were bulging out of the split. When he threw it onto the back seat and got back in, she was drying her eyes and blowing her nose on what looked like the flimsy of the hire agreement from the glove compartment.

"Sorry," she said. "I reached in, and I thought it was a tissue."

"Feel free," he said, and started up so that he could get them to somewhere else.

She told him her name. She told him how she'd made the biggest mistake of her life by asking Johnny for a lift back at the Red House, and how he'd looked up at her in a way that had scared her beyond belief. Somebody watching from ten feet away probably wouldn't have noticed a thing, she said, but take a Halloween mask and put a candle inside it and the effect would be about the same. She'd thought that she'd managed to lose him, but she hadn't. He'd simply followed her lift in his car, and when she'd been set down on the hard shoulder about five miles down the road he'd hung back until she was alone and then moved in.

This time, he'd been more plausible. He'd explained that he was with the police.

"Even showed me a warrant card," she said. "What was I supposed to believe? He seemed dead level then, said he only looked such a mess because he was undercover. Said there had been a couple of girls hitching who'd been roughed up and that he'd run me out to the nearest big road."

"Then what?"

"Then he started calling me Alice. Telling me how sorry he was. But it was too late by then, he already had me in the car."

"He didn't know you at all?"

"I don't think he even knows what planet he's on. Next time, I'll stick with the first impression I get."

"Well," Nick said, "he's known about. You want to be involved?"

"Not if I can help it. I'd settle for a ride out of town."

"After this?"

"I know some lorry drivers," she said defensively. "I'll be all right."

He did as she wanted. She was almost certainly underage and in any other circumstances he'd have turned her over to the local uniforms, but instead he drove her out to the western side of town where the bulk of the docks traffic would be heading through. It was late in the afternoon now and the daylight was starting to fade into the textures of early evening, but she seemed to think that she'd be okay. At one of the big edge-of-town roundabouts, they passed a police Range Rover that had stopped and was scanning the traffic flow.

"They looking for him?" she said.

"At a guess." Nick was assuming that the manhunt machinery would be up and rolling by now, although he'd picked up no details; he'd made one brief call from a coast road booth after Johnny had taken him out to see

Alice, just to ensure that she'd be found and recovered before the tide could take her, and from then onward he'd made a point of dropping out of the official picture. He knew only too well how it would be – they'd find out how much more he knew, and then they'd shunt him off somewhere to keep him out of the way. Nick's plan was to stick with it, but for that very reason to carry on alone. He'd tried channel-hopping news broadcasts on the car radio as he'd been driving back earlier that afternoon, but they'd carried nothing about Johnny at all.

The girl said, "What if he just switches cars?"

"It won't matter," Nick said. "He's not going to leave the area."

He left her at a truckers' pull-in about fifteen miles out of town, an older, shabbier, busier-looking version of the Red House with the lorries ranged outside like great beasts grown too big for the stable. It was almost fully dark by then and the place had a steamy, bright-lights feel. Nick stayed in his car and watched her as she ran to the door and opened it to go inside; she went in with the look of a long-distance traveller finally reaching home. It was impossible to see much more through the blurry windows, but he thought he could make out shapes rising from their tables at her approach and heard the faint, faraway sounds of greeting before the door swung to and cut them off. Nick couldn't have explained it, but for a moment he felt something that was almost envy.

But then he turned his mind away from her, and turned his car around to head back to where he knew he had to be.

No, Johnny, he thought. You won't be leaving.

And after finding you once, I'll find you again.

Before the rest of them do.

By around nine, Johnny was getting hungry.

It came to him suddenly, like a revelation; he'd been

driving around aimlessly, up and down the coast road and along the narrow back lanes through farms and villages, through woodland parks and around closed-down caravan sites, when his mind seemed to hit one of those lucid patches where he stood outside and saw himself with a momentary clarity, even as the dream began to seduce him back in like a lover who wouldn't let him leave before the dawn.

He stopped the car in a woodland lay-by and hopped over the barrier into one of the sites; it was easy enough to break into a couple of the caravans, but they'd been squared away for the off-season and he didn't get so much as a glass of water out of the expedition. Then somebody came checking the site with a flashlight and a dog – he'd been smashing open doors with a couple of big stones, and supposed that he must have been making some kind of noise – and so he'd had to drop the idea altogether. He kicked the dog and put a big scare into the old fart with the flashlight by stalking into the beam with his coat flapping and his arms raised like something out of a B-movie, and the old fart dropped the light and ran. Johnny went back and got into his car, and set off again to look for some more promising prospect.

The Scimitar was starting to judder one time as he was passing through the outskirts of an inland market town about an hour to the north of the city. By now the ache that he'd taken for hunger had turned into a serious and persistent pain, and car trouble was a less than welcome addition to his problems; but at least he was on a lighted road and somewhere close to a centre of population, so he started to look for somewhere to pull in. The Scimitar was losing power rapidly. He saw the parking sign of a railway station, made the turn, and just about got onto the asphalt before the car died under him like a broken horse.

Could be worse, he thought, could be worse. He got out stiffly, and grabbed at the door as he almost lost his balance. Steady, Johnny, he told himself, and then he took aim and headed for the station concourse.

Nobody was manning the barrier at this hour. Once it had been a steam-age edifice of regional significance, now it was a two-track stopover that carried enough rail traffic to justify a magazine stall (closed) and a platform cafeteria, and which died between trains so that it had an atmosphere like some forgotten old church. Johnny descended a broad wrought-iron stairway to platform level; big old stations had always excited him and did even now, even when he had so many other things crowding up in the back of his mind and awaiting his attention.

Well, they'd have to wait. He'd get to them, in time. The station manager's offices were dark but the buffet was lit, and some way beyond that was a spotlighted area of the platform where parcel trolleys had been lined up ready for loading onto some later service. Everything that wasn't painted iron was either in brick or stone, and facings were streaked with water damage in places where the overhead awning had leaked. Johnny bypassed a couple of platform vending machines and went straight on in through the buffet door.

There was nobody on Johnny's side of the counter; about twenty tables, all of them empty, and the only sound coming from one of those manic fruit machines that was the size of a small piano. Staff presence came in the form of a redheaded teenager with big ears and freckles, standing behind the counter in some kind of uniform with a little paper hat. He flinched a little as Johnny bore down on him, and Johnny said, "Listen, I just hit a problem."

"Really?" the boy said, all polite and nervous.

"Yeah, I just put some money in one of the vending machines and nothing happened."

"Which one?"

"I don't exactly remember, it was one of those outside somewhere."

Both of them knew that he was lying. But the boy didn't care to cross him and Johnny simply didn't care, period. Whatever Johnny said, the kid was going to agree; it was late and he was alone and it wasn't his railway, and Johnny was exuding such an air of restrained danger that anything other than co-operation would be strictly for heroes.

And the boy, who reckoned that he would always be a hero some other time, said, "You want a refund, then."

"I don't want to put you to any trouble," Johnny said. "Why don't I just take stuff to the value and we'll call it even?"

"Fine by me."

Johnny was already helping himself to sandwiches and other goods from the open counter. He said, "I knew you'd see it that way. Slide a couple of those rolls along to me, will you?"

And the boy said, "Sure," and did as he'd been asked.

He watched as Johnny piled the food up in his arms. He seemed to be grabbing at least two of everything. After a while, the boy ventured to say, "That must have been an awful lot of money that you lost."

"Yeah," Johnny said, "it was a twenty-pound note. I'll just wait over here for my train, okay?"

And as Johnny was taking his haul over to a table by a window overlooking the platform, the boy said, "Sure, why not?"

Johnny dumped everything onto the formica and dropped into one of the four contoured plastic seats that were bolted into permanent place around it. He caught his breath for a moment, and then finally allowed himself to relax. Even God had given himself a break after six straight days of knocking the universe together, and Johnny felt as if he'd been working at least as hard. He tore the wrapping off the first of the sandwiches, and waded in.

Less than a minute later, almost with the very first mouthful, his appetite seemed to die on him.

He glanced up to see if the kid was watching, but he seemed to be making himself scarce somewhere at the back of the counter area. Wise move. One false step, and Johnny would have yanked him over and snuffed him; nothing personal, it was simply the cleanest way to proceed. And he'd done it often enough now to wipe out any traces of guilt that might have lingered after the fall; he'd even done it for Alice.

Johnny lowered his head.

For Alice.

He couldn't understand how his hunger could leak away so fast and yet leave him with this ache. Frowning, he unbuttoned his coat and opened it.

It stuck. When he pulled it free, it was like he'd suddenly been speared in the side and the spearhead yanked out.

He'd been bleeding profusely, inside the coat. Mostly it had spread and dried, but down just under his ribcage it still glistened wet. When he held up the side of the overcoat that he'd pulled away, he could see a tiny spot of light through the fabric; a small, neat hole in the material, just about a size that he could push his finger through. He was tempted to try; but instead he carefully rearranged the overcoat and rebuttoned it, patting everything back into place as if to say there now, everything looks all right, so what could possibly be wrong? Then he sat for a moment and rubbed at his eyes, and then abruptly he lurched to his feet.

As he emerged onto the platform, he was barely aware of the fact that a night-train had pulled in; shock was catching up with him fast, and he was walking as if under the constant battering of a storm. His head was full of hammers, and his body was on fire. To the youth behind the buffet counter, he had the look of someone about to throw up and who was trying to make it to the toilet without breaking into a run; but the most important thing to the boy was that he was leaving, with a bonus in that he'd abandoned untouched most of the stuff that he'd lifted. The boy's main thought was to get it all back onto the counter before the night supervisor called by to pick up the till receipts, and so he wasn't even close to the window when Johnny reached the stairway and started to ascend.

Coming out into the night, Johnny could hear the train's departure from back and below. He took a breath of the air, and made for the Scimitar.

The car wouldn't start. The engine turned over but wouldn't fire, and when he belatedly thought to study the readouts on the dash he saw that the fuel gauge needle was pointing straight to *EMPTY*.

Well, that was that. He slowly got out and looked around; there were about half a dozen other vehicles in the car park and he tried some of the doors on the nearest, but all of them were locked. Nothing he couldn't get around – for speed and simplicity, you couldn't beat a quick cut through the rubber of the windscreen seal before ripping it out to lift the glass away whole – but his energy and his concentration were deserting him fast. He considered the possibility of climbing into the back of the Scimitar and going to sleep, but dismissed it.

They were looking for him, after all.

He patted the car on the roof before he walked away. Cars were okay. It was people who made you promises and then really let you down.

Leaving the lights on and the driver's door wide open, Johnny walked off into the darkness.

Around the time that Johnny was stalking along the bypass in search of a car or a ride or a warm place to hide, Nick was realising that in the last twenty-four hours he'd completed some kind of a circle; because it was late in the evening and here he was again, back on the quayside and looking up at Alice's darkened windows. After dropping off the hitch-hiker he'd gone over about a dozen places where he'd thought that Johnny might be, but as fishing expeditions went it had been one of his least successful. Johnny had gone to ground for a while, was his guess. It had occurred to him that Johnny might even come back here, but it seemed unlikely; Nick's main reason for returning was that he had nowhere else to go.

The quayside door was locked, but the bolt was absurdly easy to slip. He stepped into the darkness of the arcade and took a rough guess on the direction of the stairway; after bumping into a couple of the machines and groping his way along them he found a light switch, and was able to ascend.

The sitting room reminded him so much of her that it almost hurt. He couldn't even bring himself to take another look at the old photographs around the mirror. He'd sleep on the sofa, if he could bring himself to sleep at all. She wouldn't need her bed again, but the thought of him using it now seemed all wrong.

Wearily, he sat down.

The Webley was an uncomfortable weight against his side and so he worked it out of his jacket and then sat with it in his hand, wondering if he had the energy to give it a partial strip and clean. There didn't seem to be much point. Years of neglect had probably pitted the inside of the barrel and screwed up the rifling, and it was little wonder that his two shots at Johnny had apparently gone wide. The miracle was that the damned gun hadn't blown up in his face.

He opened it, reloaded, and spun the chambers. That was his only reason for missing, wasn't it? That, and the fact that even the finest marksman – which Nick assuredly wasn't – was limited by the fundamental inaccuracy of any handgun over such a distance. Nick had even known of one officer who'd stood over his target, aimed two point-blank shots at the target's head and, fortunately for the poor sod on the ground, had missed both times. By comparison, Nick's failure seemed forgivable.

And at least, as a failure of marksmanship, it was something that he could handle.

A failure of nerve . . . now, *that* would be something else.

He laid the Webley on the coffee table, and sat back. He felt exhausted. A night in the car and a day on the edge of his nerves had drained him like a battery. At least he'd had somewhere that he could finally head for where he'd be able to keep himself more or less out of sight; he'd seen a few small boarding-houses some way along the seafront, but his one boarding-house experience before he'd moved in with Jennifer had been enough to put him off the idea for good.

He sat for a while, frowning.

The bolt had been on the street door.

Not the padlock, but the bolt. Drawn from the inside.

He wasn't alone.

"Where were you, Nick?" she said from the doorway behind him.

28

At first, he didn't move.

She said, "I had to wait here on my own all night. I didn't know if he'd gone for good, or if he'd be coming back, or what he'd do. Where were you?"

He wasn't hearing things. It was Alice. He stood up slowly and turned around. She was standing in the doorway, and she was holding a big rusty spanner from the workroom down the landing. She looked upset, and she looked scared.

More to the point, she looked real.

"I had things to set up," Nick said slowly.

"I heard him coming," she said. "If I hadn't heard him call out my name, he'd have walked straight in and I wouldn't have had a chance. I had to hide in the cupboard with the boiler. You said you'd come back to me, Nick, and you never did."

"Was he alone?"

"There was some woman outside in the car. I don't know who she was."

"I thought that was you."

"She hardly even looked like me."

"She didn't have to, when he'd finished with her."

It was a moment before she'd taken this in. He saw her glance down at the gun on the table, and all of the anger and the bitterness seemed to rush out of her. She let the big spanner fall.

"Oh, Nick," she said. "I assumed you'd know."

Nick wasn't aware of either of them making a move, but suddenly they were together in the middle of the room and holding onto each other so hard that it almost hurt. Her head was buried in his shoulder and his face was pressed into her hair, which had the scent of seawater and honey. It felt as if neither of them would ever want to be the first to let go. She kept on telling him that she was sorry; while he'd been out looking for Johnny, she'd probably been running him down in her mind as feckless, inconstant, a breaker of promises . . . the biggest of her disappointments in a lifetime of hopes revived against the evidence.

And what had *he* been doing? Stalking Johnny Mays. Not because of what Johnny had done, Nick realised now, but because of who he believed that he'd done it to. But now the ground had shifted.

"I feel like he's dragging me down with him," he said. "I don't know what's real and what isn't. I could wake up right now and you could really be . . ."

She pushed away quickly and laid a finger on his lips, to silence him.

"I'm no more dead than he is," she said. "Feel."

And she transferred her hand to his cheek, and brushed it gently. He closed his eyes at her touch.

"I had it all so clear," he said. "For just a few hours, there, everything fell right into place."

"And now?"

"Now, I don't know."

"What are our choices?"

They parted, a touch selfconsciously. The moment had gone by them like the Night Mail, passing through.

Nick said, "Our choices are the same as they always were, I suppose. Either we sit here waiting for the hammer to fall . . . or we run away, and hope that someone else will handle him . . ."

And at this point, he hesitated; but Alice completed the sequence for him.

"Or else we go out," she said, "and we find him for ourselves."

———

Johnny went to ground around midnight.

Two college students had picked him up on the bypass, and he'd ridden back into the heart of his territory on the back seat of their ageing Cortina. He was lucky they'd happened along, because it was pretty unlikely that anyone else would have stopped for him; even they seemed a little uncertain when they saw him close-to, but by then he'd already opened the car door and was getting inside. He stayed on his best behaviour, made what he reckoned was polite conversation – although he saw them exchanging nervous glances at a couple of points, and wondered exactly what it was that he'd said to disturb them – and generally worked to give the impression of an all-round okay person who was simply a little weird on the outside, and where was the college student who couldn't readily relate to that?

They asked him where he wanted to be set down, and he said the coast road. He said he'd tell them where.

Here? They wanted to know when he finally said, and he told them that this would be fine.

So they dropped him off in darkness, with only a sliver of moon to see by, on a lonely stretch of nowhere about a quarter-mile in from the sea.

But Johnny knew what he was doing.

He picked up a pathway through the gorse, the sand trail showing white in the moonlight. He followed it up and over the line of the old abandoned railway, the same line that had once run all the way out to the tip of the headland and which time and the shifting of the land had twisted and splintered. His side hurt. This was hard work. But some kind of rest lay ahead.

He came over the last of the dunes. The old wooden beach houses were just a couple of hundred yards before him now.

None showed any lights. They'd been there for as long as anybody could remember, five of them in a row, no two the same and each with a little picket-fenced garden that consisted mostly of the same sand and marram grass that lay all around. The cottage at the end had been a railway carriage in some other existence, the others were mostly simple huts that had been extended with porches and sheds and odd-sized windows and crooked stovepipes and sometimes an extra add-on room that might once have been a pigeon loft. Strictly for summer use only, they'd lasted way beyond their time and were now held together mostly by fresh paint and affection.

Johnny went down to the third in line, and broke in without too much problem.

The interior was cheap and homely, gloss-painted boards and bakelite fittings. A few unpolished brasses on the walls, old copies of *The Reader's Digest* between bookends on the mantel, a couple of glass-fronted bookcases with more holiday reading inside. More books in the bedroom, and a big double bed covered by a musty-looking quilt. The kitchen was tiny, the taps didn't match, the cooker was a chipped Baby Belling; but when he opened up the larder, it was to discover a mildewed cereal box and some rust-speckled tins.

He picked out one of the tins. Spaghetti hoops.

Fine.

With this and a spoon, he went back into the main room to settle by the empty fireplace.

———

"How hard do you think he'll be to find?" Alice said.

They'd been talking about almost nothing else for the last three hours. Nick stood at the window looking out into the night through the spectre of his own reflection, and Alice sat on the folded sofa with her knees drawn up and her arms around them.

Nick said, "That depends on what he's thinking right now. Anybody with half an ounce of sense would be over the hills and far away."

"But Johnny?"

"I don't know. First place I walked into today, there

he was. Like we were almost sharing the same kind of thoughts, remembering all the same old places. He was right. Twenty years apart and we're still too damn close, and I don't much like the feeling."

"Lighten up, Nick," Alice said. "At least you got one thing to celebrate."

"Oh?" he said, turning from the window. "What's that?" But then he saw Alice's look hardening, and realised belatedly that he'd drifted completely out of touch with the rhythm of her thinking.

"Hey," he said, "I know, I'm sorry."

"I thought my still being around might mean something to you."

"It did. It does."

"So, try showing it."

He crossed the room and sat down beside her. He said, "Blame the late, great Johnny Mays for that, too. Blame the shadow he's put over everything. Seeing you in one piece was the best present I ever had."

She was watching him, a touch suspiciously.

"You'd better mean that, Nick," she said.

"You can believe it."

She held his eyes for a moment before she looked away. The unspoken understanding between them was clear; that as far as their relationship was concerned, the jury was still out. Too much had happened, and too fast. People needed time, and Johnny had taken theirs. He'd rushed them through and then dumped them together, and they'd become awkward and uncertain in each other's company.

Alice said, "Say we find him before the police do. What then?"

But Nick could only shrug. "I don't know."

"What's the penalty for shooting vermin, these days?"

"I'm not even sure that's an option, any more."

"You don't think he deserves it?"

"I can't say what anyone deserves."

She rose to this, as if to bait; she sat upright with her

eyes shining out a warning and said, "Don't start to pity him, Nick. That's about the most dangerous thing you could do, right now. Don't pity him, don't forgive him, don't let him go one inch further if there's any chance of stopping him. Because this is where he's heading for, Nick, he's heading for *me*." She tapped herself on the chest, for emphasis. "He's cutting his way through to me and he doesn't care who else he hurts because what he's seeing is my face on every one of them. Can you even begin to imagine what that's like for me?"

"I don't think I can judge anybody, that's all."

"Well, if he gets that close again," Alice said with some considerable feeling, "you'd better!"

Nick put his hand on her arm, as if to steady her; she'd worked herself up to an intensity like the glow of a burning field, and it was a red heat of hatred and fear. "It's all right," he said, calming her, "he won't get so close again. I'm sticking with you, this time."

"Even if it means you have to stop him for good?"

"Even that."

It began to work. She looked away, took a deep breath, wiped at her eyes.

"Something's changed between us, hasn't it?" she said, putting into words what Nick had been thinking all along.

But he dodged the question.

"I think I can handle him," he said, "if I can get the chance to try. I think I know what he is."

"What? The Prince of Darkness in an Oxfam overcoat?"

"No. Just a child who couldn't scale down his dreams as he got older."

"You think that?"

"I'm pretty well certain of it."

She seemed less than impressed by his thinking.

"Well," she said, drawing away from him and getting to her feet, "*I've* heard it said that a child would destroy the world, if it only had the power."

She went through into the next room; and, moments later, Nick could hear the sound of the taps as she ran a basinful of water to splash the angry tears from her face.

———

At around the same time, back in the railway station car park, Bruno was watching as the late-shift Scenes of Crime team crawled over and through the abandoned Scimitar like white-overalled snakes through an over-sized skull. They'd set up big lights on stands and screens for some privacy, and they were giving the car an inch-by-inch examination. Anything they found – hair, dirt, blood, rust – was marked and photographed and then sampled and bagged. Most of what they were collecting was the hard data of evidence; a simple check on the plate had told Bruno what he really needed to know, which was that the vehicle had been taken from a house less than a mile away from where Johnny Mays had abandoned Mad Jack's old Morris. That it was Johnny who'd taken the Scimitar was now hardly open to doubt; the woman who'd disappeared along with the car had been found in a coastal harbour after an anonymous call the night before. She'd been flogged, quickly and ruthlessly, with a length of chain from the quayside, and then she'd been thrown into the mud where she'd drowned, too weak to raise herself to draw breath. Bruno had been given less than an hour's notice to put a team together and take them over into the alien territory of another county's police authority, where he'd been received with professional politeness and no deference at all.

He'd been pushing for maximum publicity, Johnny's face on the regional TV news and in all the local papers, pictures of the car, names of the victims, anything that would promote public awareness and bring a fast result; what he'd received had been a veiled reminder that he

was a visiting performer with no more than a minor spot
on the bill. Nobody was even convinced that Johnny
Mays was to blame for the local death, so far; the Chief
Superintendent appointed to the case was more inclined
to assume domestic origins, and had pulled in the shell-
shocked husband for questioning. Of the short time that
Bruno had spent in his room at the Railway Hotel, most
of it had been taken up in phonecalls to his superiors
back home. They'd brought him little success; the locals
were going to do it their way, and Bruno at best was
along for the ride.

Well, perhaps now that would change.

He went down the broad stairway to platform level.
The buffet had been re-opened and there were people
inside; through the windows he could see a couple of
uniformed constables, moodily gazing at the empty
counter. Open it might be, but not open for business.

Bruno had already talked to the night supervisor. Two
of the local detectives were talking to him now, but
Bruno didn't stop to listen. He went straight to the boy
who was sitting three tables down, waiting his turn; a
car had brought him in from his home about ten minutes
before. He looked as if he'd dressed over his pyjamas.
An older, worried-looking shadow of a man, almost certainly his father, was sitting beside him.

Bruno nodded to them both. From inside his jacket he
drew a blowup of Johnny Mays' last service photograph,
a washed-out looking Polaroid, and placed it on the
table.

He said to the boy, "You were working here last
night?"

"Until around nine," the boy said. It seemed that
nobody had told him anything about why he was here; he
had the nervous, wary manner of someone anticipating
a blow out of the dark from a stranger.

"Did you see the man in the picture?"

He studied it for a moment, and then nodded. "He
came in just before I was due to close."

320

"What did he want?"

"All the same stuff everybody wants in a buffet. Rolls and cakes and biscuits and crisps and a tin of cherry Coke. But then he left most of it behind when he ran out for his train."

"No kidding," Bruno said. "Which train would that be?"

"I think it was the eight-twenty, running late."

"So you actually saw him getting aboard?"

"Well," the boy said with a slight hesitation that Bruno attributed to nerves, "yeah, I did."

"Show me where he sat."

The local detectives were watching them now, their own line of questioning forgotten, as the boy led the way down the row to the window table where Johnny Mays had settled with his loot. Bruno was thinking that if Johnny had taken the train, they'd have to run a check on every stop along its route. Step one would be to talk to the guard; Johnny would almost certainly have been travelling without a ticket, and the guard might remember him.

At least they'd established that he'd headed out of the area. At the very least, they'd established that.

"He was hardly here for more than a minute," the boy was saying as they moved. His rumpled father tagged along behind, like a hired funeral mute.

Bruno looked over the table. It was bare formica, faintly patterned in dried-out sweeps where it had earlier been wiped with a damp rag.

He said, "How did he seem to you?"

"In what way?"

"Tired? Nervous? Keyed-up?"

"All of that."

Bruno crouched to take a look underneath the table, but he broke off to look up at the boy for a moment. His tone was friendly, confidential.

"Scared you shitless, didn't he?" Bruno said.

"You'd have to see him to know," the boy admitted.

Bruno returned to his inspection, taking care not to touch the table or anywhere around it.

"Don't worry about your image," he said. "As far as he's concerned, it's the best way to be. Who cleans up around here?"

"Whoever's on."

"Well," Bruno said, straightening, "here's a spot you missed." He looked at one of the local detectives, who'd abandoned his questioning of the night supervisor for something infinitely more interesting.

"Take a scraping for a serology check," Bruno suggested, pointing to something that had streaked on the plastic seat and spotted onto the floor. "It's either blood or burger relish, and I think we'd all like to know which."

29

When Johnny woke to daylight, his first thought was that he was back in Mad Jack's cottage on the moors; that no time had passed and that he really had been dreaming, and that nothing had happened which couldn't be set right. But then he tried to move, and his side hurt, and he knew then that he was in exactly the same mess as he'd been when he'd crawled under the musty covers the night before. There truly was no going back; there was only the prospect of staying on the move, and doing his best to keep one step ahead of trouble.

He sighed. If that was what it would take, then that was what he would do.

What other choices did he have?

He got up stiffly, and straightened himself out. Something in his side seemed to settle, a burning jab followed by a sense of relief that was more or less bearable. Gingerly raising his overcoat, he took a look. The bleeding seemed to have stopped, although it had left his shirt as a crusty mess that he didn't dare to peel away from his skin for fear of starting the process all over again. As he was rebuttoning his coat to hide the damage, he looked out of the salt-stained window into the garden behind the beach cottage; like the one at the front it was untended and buried in sand, and the picket fence around it seemed to have been raided for firewood. Beyond the fence lay the dunes. He could hide in the dunes. He'd once thought that he could hide in the dunes for ever.

He went looking for breakfast.

The cold tap spat a couple of times and the water came out rusty, but then after about half a minute it ran clear. He'd found cereal in the box and dried powdered milk in a tin, and now in the pan cupboard under the larder he found a black and white portable TV behind some old jigsaws and children's annuals. He plugged it in and switched it on – when he'd first arrived he'd thought that there was no power, until he'd found the pulled fuses and replaced them – and then played around with the wire loop of the aerial until he found some cartoons. Then, with *Inch High, Private Eye* for company across the breakfast table, he settled down with a bowl and spoon.

He should have offed the students. They might hear something, and tell where they'd dropped him. But then again, say that he had . . . then he'd have another conspicuous car on his hands and two bodies to dispose of. And let's admit it, Johnny, he told himself, we haven't exactly been diligent about covering our tracks so far, have we?

Snuffing people had become a lot easier than he'd ever have believed possible. It was almost like learning to walk; once you'd taken those first, halting steps alone, there was no looking back. When he thought about it, the signs had all been there when he'd first been sent along on a mortuary detail. Christ, what a day that had been. He could remember hesitating over what to have for lunch, just in case he was running a risk of seeing it all again. His first surprise had been in the layout of the place; he'd been expecting the stiffs to be neatly tucked away in storage drawers like in *Quincy*, but instead they lay shrouded on gurneys in a cold room with their clothes in a bag beside them. He had to walk through the cold room to get to the dissection chamber. The shrouds were badly tied and there was lots of skin on show, but he had no real reaction to any of them until he was passing the last one and saw a few curls of human hair peeping through where the cotton cloth had been wrapped around a dead man's face; suddenly it all became real, like driving over a cardboard box and hearing something cry out from inside it.

They'd had two dissection rooms, and the first had been in use for most of the morning; two of the orderlies were mopping the tiled floor, which looked as if it was awash with beetroot juice. The steel table with its complex arrangement of water nozzles and drains had already been cleaned down, and stood empty. The table in the next room did not.

Here was Johnny's case, a teenaged boy who'd died after being stabbed in the neck. Johnny himself couldn't have been much older at the time. The boy was laid out ready on the table, with the young pathologist setting out his instruments on a suspended dish. The boy's head had been turned aside, exposing the wounds; bloodless and dry, they didn't look like real wounds at all. They looked like neat slashes in stretched rubber, their edges dragged apart to reveal the drained and secret works beneath.

And Johnny had thought, hey, this isn't so bad.

The day's lesson had been a simple and revealing one for him. Put simply, it was that death was no big deal, especially when it happened to somebody else. Corpses were just used-up goods, without even sentimental value; there was probably only one that it would ever trouble him greatly to look upon, and this was the very one that he'd never have to see. The pathologist had commented on the state of the boy's liver and Johnny had said Great, I'll take a couple of pounds for the dog.

But this was looking back. He really ought to be looking ahead. He really ought to be trying to make some sense out of what he was doing and where he was going. Hunched over the bowl, he stared through the screen and attempted to take stock.

1. He'd been hurt by Alice. The deepest kind of rejection hurt, the kind you carry around for a lifetime and maybe even die remembering.

2. Because she'd been out of his reach, he'd turned it onto others. Every name in the little black book had been a stand-in for her, he could see that now; taking the scythe to them had largely been a waste of his anger. She was the one he should have gone looking for, forget the black book and return to the archetype.

3. Now Alice was dead.

4. But Johnny still hurt. And anyway, he'd loved her.

5. So it had all been for nothing.

Maybe he needed a break. He could keep his base in the area – right here, even – but work his way along the coast. There were plenty of other towns with other arcades, some of them with other Alice Craigs, where he might find what he was looking for; he might even find something like the moment where it had all begun to go wrong, the very word at which life had begun to veer away from the bright path that he knew he'd always deserved. Then he could make some different choice, and everything would come out right.

Could that happen?

Johnny looked down at his bowl. Something about his breakfast tasted odd, and it wasn't just the milk. As he watched, the surface of the cereal seemed to ripple. Squinting a little closer, he could see that the bowl was crawling with tiny mites. The stuff had outlived its shelf life even longer than he'd thought.

Unconcerned, he raised his eyes to the cartoons again.

And carried on eating.

Neither Nick nor Alice had been in a mood for breakfast. Alice had gone into the kitchen and opened up the cupboards to look over the cans and boxes that she'd bought in two days before – was it really only as recently as that? – but then she'd abandoned the idea. They'd slept separately, as before. Now Nick was in the sitting room, his bed bundled back up into a sofa with a few stray corners of sheet peeking out at the seams, and he was checking the Webley for about the fifth time in the last half-hour. Alice was in the bathroom; this was something that he didn't want her to see. He didn't even like the look of himself in the mirror while he was doing it.

He opened his jacket. He'd cut the lining so that the revolver could sit more securely inside. A part of his mind told him that he'd have to use it, that whatever his reasons he'd committed himself to seeing this through.

Another part of his mind told him that he was mad.

He glanced up, towards the doorway. Alice was watching him. She gave him a nervous smile.

"My knight in shining armour," she said.

"Don't, Alice," he said. "Please."

Her smile died. "I was joking," she said.

"Right," Nick said, and turned away from her as he buttoned his jacket over the gun.

"Where's Frazier in all of this?" the local Assistant Chief Constable said with a doubtful expression. He wasn't looking at Bruno, but at a bowl of green figs in syrup on the hotel's buffet table. He gave them an experimental poke-around with the serving-spoon and then passed along to something else. Bruno moved along behind.

He said, "Frazier's armed and dangerous, but mostly to himself. He's taken some crappy old gun from the evidence room that hasn't even been fired since Adam was a lad. He doesn't know about Mays taking the train last night, so I reckon it's probably safe to leave him scouting around the sand dunes while we get on with the main business of the day."

"Any luck on the railway?"

"Mays must have dodged into the toilet when the guard was doing his rounds. I reckon we can narrow it down to the two stations with the weakest platform security, no exit checks made at all. I need to talk to you about local publicity."

They carried their trays across to one of the window tables; the tall windows of the breakfast room looked out over the station concourse, which was roofed and seemed to be in permanent twilight. The room itself had been recently renovated in line with the rest of the hotel, and resembled a set-decorator's vision of a ballroom in Tsarist Russia. All this, Bruno thought, and still the marmalade's in those godawful little sachets that only a caterer could love. He let the ACC pick out the table – all but a couple were unoccupied, leaving so many empty place-settings that the effect was a little spooky – and set his own tray opposite. This was a far cry from home, and the station canteen. Bruno hadn't been enjoying it much so far, but he could sense that the tide had turned overnight. The ACC's presence this morning was confirmation of it; Bruno and his small team were no longer outsiders to be tolerated, but suddenly everyone's best chance of coming out of this looking good.

And here was an example. Yesterday, the policy had been for a clampdown on publicity as far as it was possible; now they were talking about handbills and press warnings and Johnny Mays' picture on the six o'clock news.

Bruno said, "Any mention of him being one of us?"

"You've got to be kidding," the ACC said. "That'll come out when we're ready, and not before. And listen, you'd better be right about Frazier. It's bad enough having to admit to the Phantom of the Opera, without having Bronco Billy buckling on the sixguns and going after him."

"It won't come to anything," Bruno said, glancing out across the room; one of his CID team was heading through the tables towards them with what looked like a phone message slip in her hand. Either her bruises had started to fade, or she'd covered them somehow.

"Frazier's sound," he went on. "Just a bit emotional, is all I reckon."

"Well, you know him."

"Not well," Bruno admitted, hitching back his chair in preparation for Jennifer's arrival. "But I've someone on the team who does."

––––––––

Johnny had decided that if this was going to be his base, then he might as well make himself at home. Leaving the TV running in the kitchen – pretty much like at home already – he dug around in the cupboards until he found a half-used packet of Zip firelighters which he tossed, packaging and all, into the open grate in the main room. His side flared up a couple of times in warning; when this happened he had to stop, and wait for it to subside. He couldn't turn too far, or bend too much. On top of the firelighters he added a few old copies of *The Reader's Digest* from the mantel, and then he stopped.

He'd heard a car door slam, somewhere outside.

Johnny went into the kitchen and switched off the TV, and then he came back through and stood beside one of the windows. Now he could hear voices, as well. There was a yellowing net curtain which made it unlikely that he'd be seen, but all the same he took care in leaning out so that he could view a widening slice of the world outside.

There was a big Citroën estate car on the track in front of the next cottage, its tailgate open at the end of the garden path. A man of about Johnny's own age was lifting a big cardboard box into the luggage space; the box was overloaded and straining to give way underneath, but he made it. On the ground beside him stood a fan heater and a couple of plug-in radiators, waiting their turn. As Johnny watched, a dark-haired woman came out of the house with a smaller box topped with a reading lamp. There was a girl of about five at her heels, bringing out a toaster and almost tripping over its flex.

Either they were the world's most respectable house-breakers, or else they were stripping the place out before locking it up for the winter. *"Joanne,"* Johnny heard the woman call over her shoulder to the child, *"we'll be leaving soon, so don't go wandering off. Stay close to the houses. Joanne, do you hear me?"* And from the child, who'd placed the toaster neatly in the middle of the path and then walked out of Johnny's field of view, he heard a faint *"I'm going in the garden."*

Well, at least he'd be guaranteed privacy after they'd gone. As long as he stayed out of sight, they weren't likely to give him any problems. Pausing only to take down a basketwork donkey from one of the shelves and toss it into the grate along with the magazines, he went through into his bedroom to take a look at the cupboards in there.

A certain history was in the fabric of the place, for anyone who cared to read it; not the usual stuff of kings and queens, but of nobodies living their lives and getting over their setbacks and sometimes being happy. Of children growing up, and people getting old. Shells picked up and saved, junk ornaments won at long-ago carnivals, school prize certificates in long-unread storybooks. Johnny's interest in any of it had stopped after he'd flicked through a couple of titles without finding a single raunchy scene; the books joined the stack for the fire, and Johnny moved on to the linen chest under the window.

The old pine linen chest, he found, with its curved lid split and its brasswork tarnished, had been pressed into use as a toybox. Or rather, it was more of a toys' graveyard; toys outgrown, toys unwanted, toys too damaged to be worth keeping at home but okay for the weekend place. The only combustible stuff in here was the colouring books and the annuals at one end, and a couple of board games in cardboard boxes. He tossed them out onto the floor and dug around in the battered Dinky cars to see if there was anything else, but there wasn't.

He started to stand. Stopped. Leaned forward and, with a wince at the sudden reminder from his side, picked up one of the hard-cover annuals from the spilled heap.

It was a *Valiant* annual. More than twenty years old, its corners scuffed away but its colours still bright. Did he remember this, or did he only imagine that he did? So long ago, so difficult to say. He stood with it in his hands like some accidentally-discovered Holy Grail. He'd loved the *Valiant*. Christ, what a comic it was. Trash, his father had called it; this was the Frank Mays whose own reading had consisted entirely of *The Daily Mirror* and *The Sporting Life* and copies of a skin magazine called *Parade* which were kept on top of the wardrobe and out of Johnny's reach. Johnny opened the book, and flicked through its pages. Amazing. Here it all was, preserved like in a time-bubble; Captain Hurricane (he of the *ragin' fury*), Hawk Hunter, Jason Hyde . . . somebody had filled in the crossword in big, childish capitals, but otherwise apart from a yellowing around their edges the pages were unspoiled.

Something caught his eye. He looked up at the window.

The five-year-old girl was watching him from the garden.

She wasn't close to the house, but Johnny was close to the window and from where she was standing she could hardly miss him. And besides, she was staring straight at him – how unambiguous could you get? She must have popped through one of the gaps in the fence.

She didn't look scared, or surprised. Just solemn. She was wearing blue jeans and a TinTin sweatshirt and tiny training shoes. Her blonde hair was already beginning to darken. For one moment, Johnny saw himself through her eyes; unshaven, weakened, haggard, his clothes having been slept in several times over. He felt a stab, and this time it wasn't of pain; it was of shame.

There was a call from the far side of the house.

The girl watched him a few seconds longer. Johnny felt an urge to wave, at least to try to explain himself to her . . . it's not the way it looks, there's really so much more to me than this . . . but where to start? And then it was already too late, because she broke away and ran.

Just a kid. Some kid he didn't even know.

He didn't move. He waited to hear the voices.

"I thought I told you not to wander off," the man said, right at the limit of Johnny's hearing like something echoing in a jar.

"I was only round the back."

"And what were you getting up to around the back?"

"I went next door and saw a monster."

"No monsters around here, kiddo. It's not the monster season."

"This one's on holiday."

"What was he like, then?"

Here it came. Johnny flinched in anticipation.

The girl said, *"He was horrible. He was reading comics."*

"Come on. Say goodbye to the house 'til next year."

"Bye, house."

They didn't come for him. Car doors slammed and, on the second try, the car's engine started. Johnny heard its tyres spin briefly in the dust of the sandy track before it got under way; and as it moved off he heard the girl's voice for one last time as she called back to him through the open car window.

"Bye, monster," she called.

The sound of the car receded to nothing, leaving only the wind and the sea and the few gulls that hung over the shore.

Pretty soon, even the gulls had drifted.

Johnny Mays stood unmoving by the window, the old book clutched tightly to his chest. There was lead in his heart. It was heavy, and it hurt.

Much more, he believed, than the bullet in his side ever could.

30

Nick leaned on the roof of the car as he looked across it, and shook his head. It's amazing what you can achieve, he thought, armed only with corporate greed and a bulldozer.

He said to Alice, "Well, another memory bites the dust. Remember this, at all?"

"No. We're getting well beyond my old stamping grounds, now."

From where he'd pulled in they had an overview of a half-finished estate of what the builders were calling 'executive homes'; brick boxes with their windows newly installed and a mire of mud and clay where their open-plan gardens would eventually be. A small dumpster was chugging around at the far end of the site; at this distance, it resembled a Tonka truck in Legoland.

"This used to be the town dump," Nick said. "Paradise on earth when you're nine years old. Now look at it."

"Price of progress," Alice said. "Seems like nobody gives a damn for a decent eyesore any more."

They got back into the car, and Nick drove away.

He was beginning to run out of ideas. Some places were exactly as they'd been, others were changed beyond recognition; the one thing uniting them was an absence of Johnny Mays. Nick's confidence was beginning to go. Their secret world had seemed limitless, once; it was a little depressing now to find that it could be covered by car in the course of a single morning.

He glanced at Alice. She was watching the flat land-scape roll by, showing no expression at all. Nick wondered if they'd do better by heading into town, perhaps check with the Salvation Army and the other hostels; he had to be sleeping somewhere, didn't he? Or perhaps they should have stayed around the estate and looked into the empty houses, at least into the roofed ones where a dosser could find a dry spot in a corner away from the beam of the watchman's flashlight.

If not there, then where?

Alice was watching him now.

"You've thought of somewhere else," she said.

"Maybe," Nick said. "Maybe not."

He aimed back out toward the coast road.

As they passed through open fields and low meadows that had once been marshes, through one-horse villages with crumbling churches and by farms that had been extended to resemble industrial plant, Nick explained about the old beach cottages. At this time of the year, they'd offer Johnny a perfect place to go to ground.

"We used to mess around there all the time in winter," Nick said. "We'd back off in the summers when the owners were there, but that would only be for a few weeks. It wasn't like we were trespassing. It was more like *they* were."

Alice didn't exactly look doubtful; uncommitted, was more like it. She said, "Will Johnny remember them?"

"I know for a fact that he does. He even talked about them, once. If I was in his place, that's where I'd be heading for."

"You seem pretty sure."

"No. All I know is that it fits and it's right. It's somewhere that feels as if it's a million miles from anywhere else and time doesn't count for anything."

"What if that's changed, too?"

But Nick had already covered this ground, almost as the first act of his own return.

"It hasn't," he said.

They were almost within sight of the sea and a couple of miles short of their target when a white police Metro passed them on the road, heading in the opposite direction. Nick kept his speed level, and watched in his mirror. It was the first traffic they'd seen in some time, apart from a steaming silage wagon that he'd slipped by at the first opportunity.

"Oh, great," he said. "Hold tight, this could get tricky." The Metro was making a fast turn in the first available farm gateway. Nick stepped on the gas and the two of them were slammed back into their seats as the hire car took off.

The Metro was no chase car, but then neither was his own. They'd be looking for him because of the Webley, there couldn't be any other reason; so much for his hopes of returning it to the evidence room and then finding some way to steal back the issue forms from the evidence book. He checked the mirror again; he'd lost the Metro for a moment on a bend, but even as he looked it swung out and into sight on the road behind. Another bend took it away again, but not for long. Whoever was at the wheel, he or she was good. Nick wondered how much coverage they'd thrown into the area, and whether he was going to meet another unit somewhere further down the road. If he did, then he'd have no choice other than to give in gracefully. He could spin into a gateway and strike out cross-country, but he could more or less guarantee that such a course would come to a rapid end with a nosedive into a drainage ditch.

He looked at Alice. One hand was braced against the dash, and her eyes were shut.

"I hate anything like this," she said.

She opened her eyes when he opened his window, sending cold air howling through the car. He was steering one-handed and they were swaying at speed, but he kept it up until they took a dip and the Metro was gone and then he flung out the handful of spare rounds that he'd been carrying in his pocket. The wind snatched them away and he started to reach for the revolver, but then he realised where they were; running parallel to the embankment of the old abandoned railway on the inland side, and so instead he switched hands on the wheel and reached for the handbrake.

Alice was looking back over her shoulder.

"Can they see us?" he said.

"Not yet."

He slammed on the brakes and the handbrake at once, and spun the wheel. The wheels locked, the back end of the car began to slide. Alice just about had time to say *Oh shit* and then they were level with and facing an almost-overgrown opening, and Nick was letting off the brake and the car was heading straight into a narrow tunnel with no more than a couple of feet of space to either side.

With a sliding jerk, they stopped.

Nick killed the engine, and both of them turned to look back.

The Metro sped past the tunnel mouth so fast that it was like one odd page in a child's flicker-book, an eyeblink would have missed it. Nick leaned out of his open window to listen, but could hear only the mournful sea-wind in the tunnel; so then he looked down, and saw that his wheels were up to their rims in drifted sand.

Alice was looking out on her own side. "Can we dig ourselves out?" she said.

"Not worth it," Nick said, opening his door. "We can walk the rest of the way from here."

Both of them had to slide out into the narrow space between the car and the tunnel wall; now largely disused, it had only ever been intended for pedestrians and the car now blocked it almost completely. Striking out for daylight and the beach they left it behind them, lurking like a beast in its cave, wearing its scents of hot oil and exhaust fumes like some bizarre and lingering pheromone.

The wind was cold and fresh and bracing. Alice took

off her shoes and carried them, watching the dry sand before her for any broken glass or dogshit. Just along here there was plenty of both, but as they came up over the first line of dunes the sand appeared to come clean. They scrambled down, the sand breaking up and bearing them down like surfers, and came to a beaten track just wide enough for a single vehicle.

"Over the next rise," Nick promised, and the promise came good.

The beach cottages lay about a quarter of a mile ahead, exactly as he'd described. They seemed to stand at a point of balance between the wide shore and the even wider sky, the long beach before them and the rolling, unstable ground behind. Ramshackle and temporary-looking, they waited for the sea and the sand to work out their differences so that one or the other could finally make a claim.

From the tinplate-patched chimney of the third in line, a thin trail of smoke was rising.

Nick nodded, as if this was what he'd been expecting. "Same place, even," he said.

"As what?"

"We broke in there, one time. On a dare. Johnny told me the place was full of ghosts, and I believed it. Then I told him some story about people who'd gone inside and just vanished, and he believed that."

Alice started forward.

"I'll get him to come out," she said.

Nick called her name, but he couldn't get her to stop. She walked straight on into the open and towards the row, and Nick had no choice but to follow her.

As she came within hailing distance, she started to call Johnny's name. Nick wanted to dive at her and clamp his hand over her mouth – hadn't they already had enough of a warning of what Johnny might do? – but he wasn't close enough to make it and already it was too late to pull her down. She was almost at the gate, now, and Nick belatedly tried to draw out the Webley; it snagged in the cut lining of his jacket, and he was struggling to get it free as the door of the beach cottage opened and Johnny Mays stepped out into the daylight.

He looked terrible.

He was drained and pale, with dark circles under his eyes. He'd slung a blanket around his shoulders and it was trailing as he moved; he seemed slow, intense, inexplicably shambling.

With a degree of concentration that seemed almost painful, he headed for Alice.

Alice stood her ground.

"Now, Nick," she said with urgency. "Do it now."

Nick hesitated, and Alice's nerve broke. She backed off quickly, almost stumbled, and then ran to get behind him.

Johnny kept on coming. Wasted as he was, he seemed unstoppable; like a walking corpse from some horror comic, moved by an obsession that transcended death.

"For Christ's sake, Nick," Alice said, "*do* him!"

Johnny started to fold.

He was already on his knees when Nick moved forward, but Nick caught him by the shoulders before he pitched face-down onto the ground. Alice watched, her face showing something like astonishment as Nick helped Johnny to get back onto his feet.

"Give me a hand," Nick said to her. "He's hurt."

But she would only follow as he guided Johnny back inside.

"You'd have let him reach me," she said.

"To do what? Look at him."

She wouldn't approach any closer than the doorway as Nick guided Johnny through to the bedroom and lowered him onto the bed. The place was a mess; every drawer and every cupboard had been opened, and all of their contents dumped onto the floor.

Johnny eased himself back, with a gasp of relief.

"He ought to be looked at," Nick said.

"I'll arrange it," Alice said coldly. "I don't want to be

in here with him." And she turned around and walked straight out of the house.

She was already heading off down the track when Nick got to the end of the garden path; he cupped his hands and called after her, "There's no phone for miles!" But she didn't turn or look back, or even acknowledge that she'd heard; she just carried on walking, a lone figure in an empty landscape, heading onward and probably out of his life forever. He wanted to run after her, to apologise, somehow to explain. But a hesitation would be fatal . . .

And, thinking of Johnny, Nick hesitated.

Wearily, he went back inside.

And found himself looking into the barrel of his own loaded revolver.

"She doesn't know the old places like we do, eh, Nicky?" Johnny said. He'd half-propped himself up on the bed; he still looked bleak and wasted, but his eyes were burning and alert.

"Put that down, Johnny," Nick said calmly. "This is as far as it goes."

Johnny half-smiled. "Isn't *that* the truth?" he said, and with his free hand he raised himself a little to one side and lifted his coat to show his blood-soaked flank.

Nick couldn't take his eyes away. Not until Johnny let the coat fall over the wound again.

"Nice shooting," Johnny said. "I'm sorry if I insulted you. Thought for a while there I'd learned the trick at last."

"What trick would that be?" Nick said. His own voice sounded far away, as if it was coming from somebody else.

"Simple. You want something hard enough, you'll start to believe that it can't help but happen. Don't tell me you've never tried it."

"Not in the last twenty years. That's not a trick you can learn, Johnny. It's just one you can play on yourself."

Johnny smiled again, although most of the smile was

a wince of pain. "Good old Nick," he said. "Always puts me right. Always gets me back on the rails. Where were you, all the times when I needed you?"

"Otherwise engaged, Johnny."

"But now you're here."

"Yes," Nick said, and he held out his hand for the gun. "Come on."

But Johnny's smile died as he cocked the hammer, and Nick stopped in mid-move.

"It isn't over yet," Johnny said.

31

They were gone when Bruno sent in the Tactical Support Group, barely more than an hour later.

After leaving the beach house, Alice had crossed the abandoned railway line and made her way down to the road; a few minutes after that she'd been flagging down the white police Metro, which was slowly retracing its route in search of the vanished rental car. Its driver, a blonde and stocky WPC, had listened to Alice's story and then reached for her radio. Bruno and his people made it to the spot within thirty minutes; the emergency bandwagon started to arrive almost immediately after. There were cars, there were vans, there were dogs, there was an ambulance; Bruno sent over a couple of scouts to watch the house from the dunes without being seen, but kept everyone else on the inland side of the tracks until he was ready to move. The scouts saw no movement, there was no response when Bruno used the bullhorn; and when two armed teams followed up a covert approach with a simultaneous entry from both sides of the building, the only life that each faced was the other.

"They can't have gone far," the squad sergeant told Bruno. They were standing in the wreck that Johnny had made of the sitting room; up above, squad men were scrambling around on top of the roof as they checked for hiding places. "They didn't come our way, so they must have moved further out onto the headland. You ask me, they're trapped like a couple of bugs in a jar."

"Don't tell me about it," Bruno said, "just get the

headland sealed from beach to beach and start a sweep. Let's have them picked up before nightfall."

The sergeant glanced out of the window, towards the sea. "What about some offshore backup?"

"I don't want to waste time waiting," Bruno said. "And I don't see much chance of either of them walking on water, do you?"

He went outside.

It could have been better, it could have been worse. On the minus side; Mays, Frazier, and an unregistered weapon. On the plus side; a long, narrowing spit of land hooking four miles out into the sea and with nowhere else for the two of them to go. They could be driven all the way down to its tip, if necessary. Air support would have been a help; it had been promised, but so far the force helicopter was still grounded at an airbase fifty miles away for running repairs. This, and the fact that the Tactical squad had been out on a practice range without any of their equipment when the call had come through, had begun to give Bruno the uneasy feeling that nothing was going to be quite as simple as it was probably going to look in next week's newspapers.

For God's sake, he thought; let it be clean.

Jennifer waited by his car, as instructed.

"You all right?" he said, and she nodded. "Get anything else useful out of the woman?"

"Only that I think she'd really like to see a Bonnie and Clyde finale," Jennifer said. "I've got no reason to love Johnny Mays, but next to her I'm Mother Teresa."

"What about Frazier?"

"She reckons Nick could jump either way. I don't know how much we ought to read into that."

Bruno glanced around. Men in body armour were swarming all over the dunes; some carried high-powered rifles with scope sights, others carried sidearms. A couple of big, shaggy German Shepherd dogs were pulling at their handlers and having the best fun they'd had in ages. From what he could hear on the car's radio, one of their vans had already got itself stuck on the approach.

"Get on the horn," he told Jennifer. "Say I want everything moved down to the crossroads. We can set up a base and at least pretend that we're organised."

Jennifer got to it.

The place that he had in mind was one that they'd passed on the way to the scene; the Bluebell Shop and Café, built in the year 1837, 534 yards from the sea. They could rouse the owners and set up a command centre, maybe even get serious about soup and bacon rolls. Frazier and Mays might be sitting in the back of a Land Rover within the half-hour, but Bruno wasn't about to take any bets on it. He'd been on a number of operations, and had observed only one prevailing rule; that the perversity of events in the face of judgement tended towards a maximum. In his own mind, Bruno was already making ready for nightfall.

It never did any harm to prepare for the worst.

And after all, there was still nothing said it *had* to happen.

———

"What the fuck's *this*?" Johnny demanded.

"It's a wire fence, Johnny."

"I can see it's a wire fence, but what's it doing *here*?"

They'd reached the boundary of the peninsula nature reserve, and Johnny was staring at the chainlink as if it was something that had been beamed down from a passing starship. He pressed on it, and the fence pressed back. He shook his head, as if he simply couldn't believe it.

"I've been trying to tell you how nothing's the same," Nick said. "Even stuff that looks like it ought to be, we left it all behind. There's no going back, Johnny. Not in the way that you're thinking."

But Johnny was still shaking his head, as if he was

unwilling to accept what he was hearing. The Webley was in his other hand, hanging down by his side as if it was making his arm tired. Nick couldn't guess where his energy was coming from; considering the state of him, Johnny ought to be flat out on his back with people working to keep him alive. Instead he seemed to be burning himself up from the inside out, shining like a flare; and Nick suspected that, as with a flare, the end of the process would leave nothing at all worth saving.

"Come on," Johnny said, and he threw himself at the fence.

It stood no more than six feet high; the boys they'd once been would have been over in seconds with just a few cuts and scrapes to show for it. Johnny scrambled, and struggled, and hauled himself up; his grip on the Webley didn't make it any easier, but he managed to hold onto it. Nick could only stand back, and watch.

He could have turned and walked away, and Johnny wouldn't have been able to do a thing about it.

But he stayed.

Johnny was over the top of the wire now and trying to get down, but he'd snagged himself somehow. His coat was pulling itself half-off so that the harder he struggled, the harder it got. He stopped for a moment and hung on the wire like some great, tattered moth.

"Nick," he said, still game but breathless. "I'm caught, Nick. I need a hand."

And so Nick scaled the chainlink, and dropped down on the other side, and then reached up to get Johnny unhooked.

Johnny lay in a heap at the foot of the wire. He seemed on a high, but Nick knew that it had to be the deceptive kind of elation that would come to a diver just before the air ran out.

"Listen to that, Nick," Johnny said.

Nick listened. In the distance, he could hear something baying.

Johnny said, "They've got dogs."

"No kidding."

"Shows they really rate us, wouldn't you say?"

"I reckon it's something I could live without."

Johnny managed to prop himself up a little. "It's you and me against the rest of them, Nick, just like it always used to be. You know what I think? I think there *is* a way back, after all. Isn't this the proof?"

Nick said nothing. Johnny looked at him.

"I can feel it, Nick. It's like the answer to everything, and it's only just out of reach. Have a little faith, Nick, *please.*"

Nick glanced back through the fence. "And what if they get to you first?"

Johnny's face was serious. "Then I'm dog meat, Nicky, and you know it."

He clambered to his feet, and beckoned Nick to follow.

Which he did.

———

Four miles long, in some places down to just a couple of hundred yards wide; anybody could take a look at the spit and think that it would be an easy place to run somebody to ground, but they'd be wrong. For one thing, there was the brush; it was dense and in places it was tall, and this meant that you could walk within a few feet of someone and not even see them. If that somebody didn't want to be found, all they needed to do was to find a good place to get down and make no sound for a while, and unless the searcher got lucky it was almost as good as owning a cloak of invisibility. The other problem lay in the shape of the land itself; nothing ran straight, nothing ran flat, and the scenery seemed to change radically at least three or four times in every mile.

Their best bet, Johnny seemed to reckon, would be to grab as much ground as they could before the search really got organised. The first stretch would be the most dangerous – the spit was narrowest here and had been largely cleared back in wartime, when a number of cement bases had been laid down for Nissen huts where the ground was more or less level – and so he headed downslope to the road. This was of tarmac for the first hundred yards or so, but it quickly gave way to a more rough-and-ready track of concrete sections. Nick followed him down, thinking that all they needed now was a couple of men in a single vehicle to come through the gateway and it would all be over; but while a part of him was hoping that this would happen, another part of him was hoping with equal fervour that it wouldn't. It was this second voice which surprised him most; not the fact that it was there, but because it had been unheard in him for so long.

Nick knew that there was no turning back the clock, not in the way that Johnny imagined.

But still he followed.

Within a couple of minutes they'd reached a point where the road split in two; there was new road of neat asphalt and there was disused old track that vanished into a wide puddle and a series of heaps of mud and dirt. The new road went off to the right, the old track went off to the left. Without any hesitation, Johnny splashed through the puddle and scrambled over the dirt heaps. Beyond these, the track had been abandoned to gorse and marram and sea buckthorn; Johnny plunged on in like a bear into a pool, both hands raised high to keep them clear of stinging nettles and the Webley waving around like some kind of totem. When Nick glanced back after a few yards, he could see that the tough under-growth had more or less sprung back into place behind them. Even Tonto would have had a hard time making out where they'd been.

The track brought them down almost to the shore; there were old tank traps on the beach here, jagged blocks of concrete reinforced with stones and rusty wire. They were half-buried in the soft sand like chunks of old pyramids, monuments to long-dead monarchs; and low-rent monarchs, too, if the quality of the concrete was anything to go by. Debris had washed up on the high tide and then been beached around and behind them; empty shampoo bottles, blue plastic jerrycans, aerosols, and a big tin drum so battered and rusted that there was no way of telling what it ever might have contained.

They scrambled down to the beach. Johnny whirled around to face Nick, fast and bright. Too bright. Looking into his face, Nick was deeply scared for him.

"Here's the plan, Nick," he said. "We cover as much ground as we can now, and then we hole up until dark. Wherever we can, we check the beaches."

"For what?"

But Johnny didn't answer. He was already turning and ploughing his way along the shore.

It was heavy going for a while. They saw birds being startled up out of the undergrowth on the edge of the land as they went by. They saw driftwood stripped of its bark and bleached by the sea. They found some seaman's long-lost pullover, they found a fisherman's canvas glove with hide-reinforced fingers; they even saw a complete tractor tyre, with its outside edge half-buried and its centre filled up with fine shale like a prospector's pan.

"Given this collection of the bizarre and the wonderful," Johnny said, "You'd think a fucking rowboat wouldn't be too much to ask for, right?"

Now Nick understood. Once they'd found a blue-painted rowing boat on the landward shore. As they'd approached it had looked complete, but then when they'd walked around they'd seen that most of the other side was gone. It looked as if it had been bitten away, chomped and then spat out by Behemoth the Sea Monster, and its wooden ribs were awash with beach sand.

But that had been a long time ago. Now there was nothing here to bear them away to whatever Avalon awaited lost boys and those in search of past selves. Nick glanced back over his shoulder. He'd just caught an echo from somewhere back towards the mainland; it sounded like a bullhorn although he couldn't get any clear impression of what was being said, and it told him that the search was narrowing in.

Johnny had heard it, too. "Don't you just love technology?" he said, and with the Webley he beckoned Nick onward.

They scrambled back up to the highest part of the spit through a dry gully with bracken underfoot, and at the top they came upon the first evidence of where the old railway had run. Nothing much was left of it other than silvered wooden sleepers that were all but buried and crumbling away. They went at what looked like a mad angle, pointing like an arrow toward the sea; Johnny followed them and then started to descend, obviously aiming for the other shore.

It was low tide in the bay. It was as wide and as flat as an infinite mirror, the far sea shading into the far sky with only the body of distant land to indicate the line of demarcation between the two. They crouched by the road as Johnny checked in both directions, and then they scrambled across and into the gorse like a couple of rabbits. Johnny stumbled as he ran, but he picked himself up and carried on without help.

They stopped to rest for a moment, at the foot of one of the power line poles that marched all the way out to the far lighthouse at the tip like Roman crosses along the Appian Way. Johnny slumped down, breathing hard, with the width of the pole at his back.

Nick crouched by him.

"You're killing yourself, Johnny," he said seriously.

Johnny couldn't speak for a moment, so he shook his head twice as hard to make up for it. "I'm doing all right," he managed at last.

"Yeah, it looks like it."

"I'm doing all right," Johnny insisted.

It took them nearly four hours to cover the next two and a half miles. Johnny's rest stops became more frequent, and lasted for longer. They stayed a while under what remained of a trestle bridge that had carried the vanished railway, and heard Bruno on the bullhorn cruising down the road not twenty yards away and appealing for the two of them to turn themselves in. As well as the steady sweep that would be moving outward from the mainland, there were random searches striking out from the road; one of these actually came close to finding them, but Nick and Johnny had found a collapsed birdwatcher's hide of old planks and corrugated tin, and they'd clambered into this and pulled the sheet roof over themselves as the party had deployed from the road down below. The two of them had held their breath as one of the searchers had stumbled through the brush almost within spitting distance, but the man had seen nothing. Another time they hid inside a concrete lookout point, its small high windows boarded with plywood, that had been so completely absorbed into the sand and vegetation that it had vanished almost in the manner of a Mayan temple in the jungle; here Johnny had sat with his forehead pressed against his knees, and didn't even seem to hear when Nick tried to speak to him. *Enough*, Nick thought, and got to his feet with the idea of getting to the road and waiting for the next patrol; but he was barely in the doorway when he heard the distinctive sound of the Webley's hammer being re-cocked, and without even looking at Johnny he'd turned around and returned to his place against the wall.

Neither of them said a word. Nick tilted back his head and let it rest against the concrete, and wondered at the original purpose of the shell that was giving them cover. It was like everything else that they'd seen so far; the entire peninsula seemed to be a place of lost purposes and shifted ground and hard work undone by time. He looked at Johnny, doubled-up and exhausted, and again wondered exactly what he was expecting to find. Just for a while, there, he was almost carried away; he could almost believe that what he'd mistaken for a world of shadows was really a world of absolutes, that Johnny was dead and had somehow escaped on a short lease from hell, and that even as he was running its agents were abroad and scouting to draw him back in. He could see himself going down to the road, and holding up his hand to stop the passing patrol; and the passing patrol would roll to a halt alongside, and he'd be looking down at a weed-streaked BMW containing four white faces lit by a hellish green light from the dash.

Without opening his eyes, Johnny said, "Talk about killing myself. I'm dead anyway after what I've done, you know."

For a moment, there, Nick believed that Johnny had been reading his mind. But right now the truth of it was that Johnny didn't even look as if he could summon up the strength to read a newspaper.

Nick said, "That isn't true, and you know it."

Johnny opened one eye. "You reckon?"

"I reckon."

"I don't mean they'll take me out. But they'll stick me in a little room with a big lock on the door. They'll probably shoot me full of stuff and I'll get old watching *Fraggle Rock* and eating with a plastic fork. I'll get beaten up by the nurses and maybe see daylight once a month. I'm not saying I deserve a good time, Nick. But I don't think I can handle that."

Then he took a deep breath, and it seemed to fill him out a little; enough, anyway, to enable him to get to his feet and take one step to steady himself as his gyroscopes belatedly ran up to speed.

"Time to move on, Nicky," he said, lurching toward the open doorway and beckoning with the gun, and so again Nick moved to follow.

The light was fading when, about a half-hour later, they finally went to ground.

32

Jennifer didn't know for certain how she felt. To be out on a major incident, far from home and in a key position, that was great; but to be stuck in the Bluebell café just short of the action, with a few jotted ideas from Bruno and virtually nothing else for guidance . . . well, that wasn't so great at all. She was sharing the setup with two uniformed sergeants who'd been so eager to grab jobs away from her that at one point she'd had to explode and tell one of them to back off; it didn't matter that he outranked her, he was at least three years her junior and he'd reddened and then shrugged and walked away. Now the two of them probably talked about her whenever she went out to one of the vans, and it didn't take a genius IQ to guess in what kind of terms.

Well, let them. She had other things on her mind.

Nick's safety, for example. And Alice Craig, for another.

Jennifer knew that it was absurd but she couldn't help thinking of Alice as the Other Woman, the one who'd taken Nick away from her; never mind the fact that it was Jennifer herself who'd shown Nick the door, and that it was only afterwards that the two of them had met up again. Maybe that was the problem. They had history, a place they could go to where Jennifer could never have access. Now Alice sat in the corner of the Bluebell, over by the window. If she was aware of Jennifer's attention, she didn't show it. She simply sat at her empty table, chin in her hands, looking out at the various squads and teams as they assembled and took orders and checked their weaponry. Body armour, helmets, rifles, scope sights, handguns, even heat detectors that could see through the densest brush; from in here, it looked like the tiger shoot to end them all.

The second wave of officers was moving out as Jennifer went to take a spare radio to the holding team, over at the spot where the Nissen huts had once stood. The road was single-track and narrow, and there wasn't space to pass. She touched her horn to let them know that she was there; with helmets buckled and face shields down, they probably hadn't heard her approach. They moved aside to let her car through, but they took their time about it and she heard somebody bang once on the roof as she started to pick up speed again. She glanced in the mirror. The men looked like some dark army of even darker machines as they reclosed ranks across the road.

When she got back to the Bluebell, Alice Craig's table was empty.

"Where did she go?" she said. The woman wasn't exactly Jennifer's designated responsibility, but she was the one who'd handled her so far. The two sergeants looked blank.

"Isn't she outside?" one of them said.

"You tell me. Did she say anything?"

One of them shrugged. The other turned away.

Not their problem.

So then Jennifer went outside and stood at the dusty crossroads and looked around. There were police vans and police personnel and the recently-arrived Land Rover of the coastguard service. There was a temporary barrier on the headland road and two cars parked crossways to back it up, and that was about it.

When she turned to walk back into the café, she saw that one of the two men had followed her out. It was the younger of the two, the one she'd as good as yelled at. He looked slightly embarrassed.

"She did say something," he said.

"Did you hear it?"

"I barely caught it. She watched the squad moving out and then she stood up and said something about, how she'd done what she came back to do. Then she left."

"You didn't stop her?"

"Where could she go?"

With the headland sealed and the beach off-limits, she could only walk away. Jennifer looked down the road. It was long, and straight.

And for as far as Jennifer could see, it was empty.

"That's for us, Nicky-boy," Johnny said.

They'd made it most of the way down to the point; another quarter-mile or so, and they'd have nowhere further to go. Some way back along the headland, the line of beaters would be moving steadily outward. Now the day was beginning to slip away from them, so that they crouched on darkening land under a mother-of-pearl sky; they looked down onto the beach at the spot chosen by Johnny as their short-term hideaway, the place where they could drop out of sight until full darkness came. Then, by Johnny's reasoning, they could come out like a couple of bats and cover the remaining distance along the beach to the point. Try it before, and they were almost certain to be seen; the beach would offer no chance of concealment once they emerged.

"Oh, sure," Nick said. "It looks fine now, but will it keep its value when we want to sell it and move up in the world?"

Immediately below them stood a line of concrete defences, each taller than a man and probably the weight of a small truck. They grew blacker and more moss-covered as they marched out across the beach to the waterline. Just beyond these, right out on the edge of the land, was a squat pillbox set on a raft of concrete.

The raft had been gradually undercut by the tide so that the entire structure had tilted like a great slab of river ice toward the sea.

"Nothing more to wait for, Nicky," Johnny said, and he lurched up and started to stumble toward the pill-box.

He was beginning to remind Nick of a manic scare-crow, something out of a nightmare. He couldn't help feeling that whatever Johnny thought he was chasing, it would always dance just beyond his reach even as he struggled to think of its name.

There was no door on the pillbox. Inside, the steeply-canted floor was awash with sand. The windows were narrow slits with rusted machine-gun mounts beneath them, and on the octagon of walls people had scratched names and dates with keys, or possibly with coins. As far as Nick could see in the poor light, none of the dates seemed to go back more than a year. The marks obviously faded quickly.

Johnny dropped by one of the tiny windows, from where he could look out towards the shore. He stretched himself out, and Nick settled across from him.

"Damn," Johnny said as he peered out into the gathering twilight.

"What's wrong?"

"We should have fixed up a picnic."

Nick could hardly believe what he was hearing. "You're too fucking much," he said.

"I know," Johnny said, "I know." And then, after a moment, he added, "But we still should've fixed up a picnic. Few sandwiches, couple of Wagon Wheels . . ."

"We could just walk out to one of the patrols. Then they'd have to feed us."

"Not an option."

"Well, it was worth a try."

"Yeah, good one, keep 'em coming." Johnny winced a little as he held onto the machine-gun mount and shifted his position, but then when he'd made himself more comfortable he shot a look across to Nick. "I'm glad you're here with me," he said.

"Well, that makes one of us."

"Nobody's forcing you to stay."

"Come on," Nick said, and he indicated the Webley which hadn't been out of Johnny's hand once in the best part of four hours. "What about that?"

Johnny held up the gun, and looked at it as if he'd forgotten that he held it. He said, "This? You could have taken it back whenever you wanted. I lost count of the chances you passed over. Here." And without any sign of concern at all, he lobbed the revolver across the bunker. Nick caught it, awkwardly.

Johnny went on, "I'm sick of carrying it. Put it somewhere safe for me."

Nick hesitated for a moment.

Then he returned the gun to the cut lining of his jacket.

He watched Johnny for a while longer. Johnny seemed to be more or less at ease, now; his hand was still gripping the mount for extra security – the sand carpet and the angle of the floor would make it easy to slide down and end in a heap against the lowermost wall – but he'd let himself relax as far as he was able. The soft evening light took some of the hard lines from his face, and the increasing shadows in the bunker did the rest. For the moment, at least, he was Johnny again.

Nick said, "How's the side?"

"I'm trying not to think about it."

"And that works?"

"It helps."

He looked out for a while longer. And then he began to sing, softly and to himself. It was a moment before Nick recognised the tune. Johnny was still mangling the words, and he knew it; he was simply waiting for Nick to catch on.

Every night, I sit here by my window. Looking out, as lonely as a . . .

Nick managed a faint smile, shaking his head and briefly covering his eyes. When he looked up again, it was to see Johnny giving him a sideways glance and a grin.

"This is as good as it's ever going to get, you know," Johnny said.

"That's what I'm afraid of."

Johnny returned his attention to the landscape outside. "Anybody ever tells you there's such a thing as peace, don't go for it. The best you can ever hope for is to stay one step ahead of the game."

"Is that what this is all about?"

"Unless you can come up with anything better." A brief moment of pain flashed across his face as he altered his position slightly, but as soon as he'd resettled it seemed to pass. "You know I always envied you," he said. "Everything I always wanted, you had it. And I'm not talking about stuff you could buy."

"Now you're making something out of nothing."

"No," Johnny said, "I don't think so. I'll tell you what I'd have settled for, though."

Nick said, "Finding the dead sailor on the beach."

"Yeah." But then, Johnny frowned. "How'd you know I was going to say that?"

"Lucky guess. It was no big deal, Johnny."

"Maybe not now. Not from here. But for a while there back in Smallville you were the absolute Bee's Nuts. I used to *ache* when I thought about it. I'll tell you one thing I never told anyone else, Nicky. I hated being a kid."

"Who didn't?"

"No, I mean, I'm serious. When you're a kid you've got it all, except for power. You can't wait to grow up and just go with all the things you dream about, because without control that's all they are, just dreams. Being a kid's worse than being in prison. Doesn't matter how special you think you are, you're just in there with everybody else for as long as it takes to have it all squeezed out of you. I wasn't going to let any of that happen. I was really going to be somebody. But first there was you and the beach, and then there was Alice. I expect she told you about that."

"She said you broke up, that's all. Happens to everyone." And to some of us more often than others, Nick thought of adding, but he didn't.

"But not to me, Nicky, never to me. I'm Johnny Mays. It was like the earth opened up, and when I looked down at the drop it seemed to go on for ever. I wasn't blessed, Nicky. God hadn't singled me out for anything after all. At least with you and the sailor it had just happened, it wasn't anything that you'd aimed right at me . . . but with Alice, it was different. It was like she'd taken a peek right down into my soul and then looked up at me, shaking her head and saying, no, no good. I loved her, Nick. Still do. Doesn't matter to me that she's dead."

"She isn't."

Johnny didn't take this in straight away, Nick could tell. He could see less and less as the light was fading, but it was impossible to mistake the blank incomprehension in Johnny's stare from the opposite side of the bunker. Nick went on, "You're so stoned on guilt trips and fantasies that you can't remember who you killed and who you didn't."

"I watched her fall."

"Somebody else."

Johnny's stare didn't waver. "Tell me you're just kidding me, Nick. Tell me this is just a wind-up."

"Nobody's kidding you."

It sank in at last. Johnny started to pull himself to his feet, scrambling awkwardly. "You know what this means?" he said.

"It doesn't change anything for you, Johnny."

"But it does! It does! It means it isn't too late to turn it all around."

"And what about the others you trashed along the way?"

"Bystanders, Nick. You know how it is."

Maybe Nick had been thinking that there was something salvageable in Johnny until now; it was hard to be sure exactly what he thought in the tangle of old loyalties and uncertainties that had prevented Nick simply from knocking him over and holding him down until the ambulance could reach them. He'd gone along because he believed that, as long as it hadn't actually ended, then Johnny might still somehow be pulled out of it; but now, at this very moment, he realised that Johnny truly was lost. He still believed that, whatever damage he did, he could go on to reshape the world by the force of desire alone. Tell him that Alice was alive after all, and he took it as proof.

He was a child, and he had power, and in the end he could do no more than destroy.

A weak light flooded the bunker, and was gone. And then again.

"Time to be moving," Johnny said.

He moved across and became a ragged silhouette in the doorway as the next beat of the shore light came around. Nick scrambled up and went out after him, only to see him leaping down from the edge of the concrete to the sand some five or six feet below. Johnny gave a cry of pain as he hit and rolled, but as Nick jumped across and down the bank by a less hazardous route Johnny was already on his feet and half-running, half-staggering in the direction of the beacon.

The lighthouse. Johnny was heading for the lighthouse; there was a method in what he was doing after all.

Whether he knew it or not, he had to be thinking of the time they'd run all the way out to the lighthouse in the belief that they were being chased by some older boys. Nick couldn't even remember why but he could remember that Billy Burton, Brian's older brother, had been one of them. Billy stuck in his memory because he'd cracked his head in a fall on a Lakes holiday a couple of years later, and had seemed to be fully recovered until he threw a spectacular epileptic fit after being hit by the strobe lights at his first school disco. As a life-shaping event, the chase was nothing special; the big boys had never even shown up and had probably quit the pursuit after the first hundred yards, but Nick and Johnny had legged it the rest of the way out to the lighthouse building itself and hammered on the big door at its base. After a few minutes the keeper had opened up and looked down at them with surprise; huge (from their angle) and white-bearded, he was a retired merchant seaman who forever afterwards had lived in Nick's mind as a kind of nautical Santa Claus. This wasn't only because of his appearance, but because legend had it that he hated nothing worse than little boys – a sure sign of their desperation when they'd climbed the steps to his door – and the legend had turned out to be full of crap. He'd led them inside and sat them down and listened to their story, and after taking them up to see the big light he'd started up his old Ford Popular and driven them back along the headland to where they'd left their bicycles hidden under some gorse. Billy and the rest of them had been nowhere around.

The light went on, like a slow heartbeat. Evening was coming in fast; the sky had now turned grey and heavy like beaten lead over a mercury sea, and was cloud-patterned into incandescent scales lying in a thin band along the horizon. Johnny was running, a solid shadow against the heaving tide, whilst high above him the first and brightest of the stars were beginning to needle through. Nick could just about see that Johnny was crouched low and leaning a little to his injured side, his coat flapping around him like a Ripper's cape.

Then he stumbled and fell, heavily as if his wires had been cut. Nick thought that's it, he's finished, but even before the thought was completed Johnny was rising again.

Nick called his name. He knew that others would hear, but it was too late now to make any difference. Johnny was up, and again Johnny was running.

So Nick ran on after, knowing that, whatever happened, Johnny was covering the last hundred yards of his freedom.

Nick caught up with him at the base of the light.

Johnny was just standing there, looking up. The doorway was about fifteen feet above him, and the door stood open; it was barely possible to see inside to other doorways and a hint of the rooms that lay beyond. The stairway leading to it had fallen, and lay half-buried in the mud to one side. Only a part of the stairway's top platform remained, rotted through on the cast-iron braces that had supported it. From one of these hung a length of thick orange rope, decayed and choked with seaweed. The windows higher up on the tower had been filled in, and the lantern housing had been dismantled and removed.

No keeper. No protection. No hope of forgiveness.

Nick said, "I could have told you, Johnny. They closed it and set up a lightship. There's been nothing here in years."

Johnny was slow to react. After gazing up at the dark tower for a few seconds longer, he jerked his attention downwards. He swayed a little, took a step to correct his balance; and, before Nick could catch and hold him, he was moving once again.

Nick almost had him, but there was all kinds of debris from the derelict tower half-buried in the mud around its base and he was slowed by cabling and scaffolding poles that he could hardly see. Johnny was moving like a man running over water. He went out and around the base, and when Nick got him into sight again he was down at the water's edge and wading out. Directly ahead of him, about a mile offshore, was the lightship that had taken over from the abandoned beacon. Its beam swept along and across the waves as Johnny splashed out towards it, not even seeming to be aware of the swell as it rose up around him.

Awareness came as the first big wave hit him on the chest; it raised him and dropped him and almost took him from his feet. Nick saw him stagger, and heard him cry out; he plunged in after, as a second wave hit and took Johnny down.

Christ, it was cold. Nick slammed his way through against the pressure of the tide, raising a spray and drawing on reserves that he didn't really feel he had. Johnny was bobbing and scrambling, spitting brine, and Nick managed to get a hand on his collar and to haul him up into the air.

Johnny's face came level.

"What do you reckon, Nick?" he said eagerly. "I *can* fix everything, can't I? Nobody got hurt. Only by mistake."

Nick looked into the eyes of the best friend he'd ever had.

And he said, gently, "Of course you can, Johnny. Just a little further."

He let him go. Johnny set out again, aiming straight for the unreachable light. The next wave broke his stride, but didn't stop him. Johnny spread out his arms to help him to keep his balance, and ploughed straight on.

The first shot took him in the back of the head, and threw him forward. The second hit him in the body, and drove him under. He came back up and Nick looked for an opening for a third, but already he could see that it wouldn't be needed. The first had done it all.

Nick let the Webley fall to his side. His head ached. He wondered if there would be someone onshore who could let him have an aspirin. When he looked back, he could see headlights up on the road; in fact he could see all the way back along the thin curve of the spit to the mainland from here, and there were more lights moving out at the very furthest part beyond the line of the boundary fence. Someone would have heard the shots, and probably his earlier shout as well. But they wouldn't move in until they'd set up an encirclement and established exactly what was happening inside it.

He turned to the sea again. The tide was bringing Johnny back, face-down and gently borne, dark blood spreading in a widening cloud beneath him. As he hit the shallows, he suddenly regained all of his weight and seemed to fall. It was as if he was trying to rise, and the sodden heaviness of his coat held him down.

He was lifted and dragged back, lifted and dragged back, and his hands clawed at the sand and the sand simply ran through his fingers.

Nick watched him for a while.

Then he turned around, and started to walk up the beach. The loose sand that his footsteps threw back made a sound like someone following.

It was a haunting kind of a sound.

Only, Nick didn't hear it.